Critical Acclaim for Allison Brennan

Silenced

"Brennan throws a lot of story lines into the air and juggles them like a master. The mystery proves to be both compelling and complex. . . . [A] chilling and twisty romantic suspense gem." —Associated Press

"The evolution of Lucy Kincaid from former victim to instinctive and talented agent continues in Brennan's new heart-stopping thriller. . . . From first to last, this story grabs hold and never lets go." —*RT Book Reviews* (Top Pick)

"An excellent addition to the Lucy Kincaid series. Lucy and Sean continue to develop as complex, imperfect characters with a passion for justice. . . . The suspense was can't-put-it-down exciting." —*Fresh Fiction*

If I Should Die

"Brennan's Lucy Kincaid/Sean Rogan books are not only excellent procedural thrillers, but also chart the evolution of an intriguing relationship. The peeks into the mind of this heinous killer are all too chilling, making the threat level palpable and the story riveting. Brennan is on a major roll!" —*RT Book Reviews*

"In bestseller Brennan's roiling third suspense novel . . . rooting out the cancer that infects Spruce Lake reveals a convoluted history of increasingly deadly crime." —*Publishers Weekly*

More . . .

"Allison Brennan pens a chilling tale in *Original Sin*, the first in her Seven Deadly Sins series. [It] will keep you up all night—whether it be from the horror or because it's such a page-turner." —*Sacramento Book Reviews*

Cutting Edge

"Both the nature and nurture sides of the 'what makes a psychopath' argument are on display in Brennan's chiller. . . . Leave it to Brennan to deliver the creepy and deadly. This is definitely the stuff of nightmares."

—*RT Book Reviews*

Fatal Secrets

"In this chilling thriller, Brennan explores the consequences of sliding from fierce commitment into obsession. . . . A master of suspense, Brennan does another outstanding job uniting horrifying action, procedural drama, and the birth of a romance—a prime example of why she's tops in the genre." —*RT Book Reviews* (Top Pick!)

Sudden Death

"Fast, fierce fun. Brennan knows how to deliver." —Lisa Gardner, *New York Times* bestselling author

Playing Dead

"The mystery is tightly plotted with the final reveal not happening until the very end of the book. . . . *Playing Dead* is an adrenaline rush of thrills and chills that is sure to win Brennan several new readers." —*Fresh Fiction*

Also by Allison Brennan

STALKED

Allison Brennan

St. Martin's Paperbacks

This is a work of fiction. All of the characters, organizations, and events portrayed in this novel are either products of the author's imagination or are used fictitiously.

STALKED

Copyright © 2012 by Allison Brennan.

For information address St. Martin's Press, 175 Fifth Avenue, New York, NY 10010.

ISBN: 978-1-62090-517-3

Printed in the United States of America

St. Martin's Paperbacks are published by St. Martin's Press, 175 Fifth Avenue, New York, NY 10010.

You have to learn the rules of the game.
And then you have to play better than anyone else.
—Albert Einstein

CHAPTER ONE

Present Day—New York City

Dark cosmic humor was the only explanation as to why FBI Special Agent Suzanne Madeaux was investigating a murder at Citi Field instead of sitting on the first-base line with a beer. Proof that life wasn't fair.

Suzanne stuffed her thick dark blond hair under her Mets cap and left her cool air-conditioned sedan for the early dawn New York summer. The weather didn't bother her—she was born and raised in Louisiana, and New York had nothing on the South for humidity—but the noise from nearby LaGuardia grated on her nerves.

She looked up at the Citi Field stadium and sighed. She'd had a ticket to last night's game and had to give it away because of work. Late to bed, early to rise, no time for her one vice—baseball and beer. Two vices. Now her team was on the road for nearly two weeks and she'd only be able to watch them on television. Sometimes, she hated her job.

She flashed her badge and was let under the crime scene tape. In addition to dragging her out of bed for a case outside of her jurisdiction, her boss had given her no information about why she had to get her ass out to a

Queens homicide after working until two a.m. Murder didn't usually fall under the purview of the FBI, and she had no active serial killer cases.

She'd thought taking the position of liaison with NYPD for multi-jurisdiction violent crimes would be a career boost, but the nominal pay increase didn't come close to making up for her longer hours or the shit she had to deal with from some of the cops who didn't like feds. She had the authority to take jurisdiction, run a case jointly, or keep it local. Considering she had tickets to the first Mets game when they returned—against the Red Sox—she definitely planned to let NYPD keep this case.

"Mad Dog!" a male voice called out.

Suzanne cringed at her nickname. She'd earned it years ago when she had a verbal battle with the media over a brutal murder, but she hated when cops used it. She turned to find the jerk in the crowd and give him the evil eye. She'd learned it from her Cajun grandmother and it worked wonders.

Instead, she said, "Shit."

"Good to see you, Suzi."

Detective Joe DeLucca. She should have known. Most of the cops didn't dare call her Mad Dog anymore, but DeLucca was one of the few she couldn't intimidate. Probably because not only did he know he was sexy, but also he was one of the best detectives on the force. If she was a mad dog, he was a hunting dog—never gave up the trail until he caught the bad guy.

She stared at him. "You can call me Agent Madeaux, or you can call me Suzanne, but if you call me Suzi again, I'll break your thumb."

He grinned, all Italian, all cop. "Promise?" A lesser woman would have swooned. Suzanne kept the swooning in check. No use stroking his inflated ego.

DeLucca—one of her ex-boyfriends. Damn, her exes were adding up. Why was she surprised? Was she ever going to learn not to date cops?

Probably not. Cops were some of the few who understood her schedule, her drive, and, well, *her*. She never had to explain why she was late, never had to talk about her cases unless she wanted to, and never had to curb her language.

But there were certainly problems dating within her profession. Like running into ex-boyfriends at crime scenes.

"Did you call me out here to apologize for being an asshole or because you need the big guns?"

He winked. "Maybe I just wanted to see you again."

"Good-bye."

"Hold up. Damn, you're touchy today."

"It's seven in the morning and I haven't had enough coffee. I'm at Citi Field, but not watching a game. And I was paged in bed, so I didn't even get to run. No run, not enough coffee, makes me bitchy."

Thing was, she still liked Joe DeLucca. But he was divorced with a psycho ex-wife and a son his ex used to keep Joe close to the nest. Suzanne couldn't blame Joe for picking his kid over his girlfriend. She'd do the same thing, if she had a kid. Which as she was single, thirty-five, and had had no long-term relationship in years was fast becoming unlikely.

An airplane from LaGuardia took off, drowning out whatever Joe was saying. He waited, then repeated, "Tell me how your business card found its way into my victim's pocket."

"Who's the victim?"

"No ID, purse stolen. We ran plates on the nearby cars, and we think the woman is Rosemary Weber."

"You're not sure?"

"You tell me."

He lifted the bright yellow tarp to reveal a body. By the extensive pool of drying blood she was killed right here.

"It's her. What happened?"

He dropped the tarp and stared at Suzanne. "Tell me how you know her."

"Don't interrogate me, Joe." He was just doing his job, but she didn't appreciate his all-cop tone. "I knew her because she's writing a damn book on the psycho killer who suffocated four teenage prostitutes between October of last year and February, when SWAT saved the taxpayers the cost of a trial. I worked the case with Vic Panetta."

"Cinderella Strangler?"

She rolled her eyes. "I hate that name. The killer suffocated the victims, took one of their shoes, and the press's label on the case stuck."

"Did you meet with Weber?"

"Twice, because my boss made me. The first time was brief because I was called out to a scene; the second time was the longest hour of my life, where she shared her focus on the book and how she wanted my help. I told her I needed approval from national headquarters before I said one word about the case; then I pleaded with my boss to deny her request. I have no idea where it is in the process."

Her explanation appeased DeLucca, and he said, "She was stabbed once, below the sternum, bled out fast, according to the coroner's preliminary exam. He's getting ready to transport the body, but I wanted you to see the layout first." He motioned to a uniform near the coroner's van and made a circular motion with his hands to "wrap it up," releasing the body to the coroner. He stepped away and Suzanne followed. "Body was found by two fans leaving the game at eleven thirty p.m. Coroner says she died sometime during the game, between ten and eleven. No witnesses, no physical evidence. The crime scene techs have already been through here and they're on a wider sweep now, I have uniforms canvassing, but what really sucks is that there are no security cameras over here. They have them at entrances and exits, but not covering the lot itself."

Suzanne knew that, from being a longtime patron of baseball games. Probably anyone who'd ever been to a Mets game could find loopholes in security without much effort.

"Robbery?" Suzanne asked.

"No purse, and it's obvious the killer removed jewelry, but . . ." His voice trailed off.

"You don't think it's a robbery."

"I don't know enough yet, but in a robbery turned south I'd expect defensive wounds."

"She had none?"

He shook his head.

"You think she knew her attacker."

"Or he was waiting for her."

"Meaning she was a specific target."

DeLucca made a noncommittal grunt, but Suzanne had nailed it.

"She used to be a crime reporter, before she wrote books. I don't envy you—there's probably a lot of people she pissed off."

He narrowed his eyes. "Me?"

"Yeah, you. This is a straight-up homicide, nothing federal about it."

"Your card was in her pocket. She was writing a book about your investigation. Her murder could have a connection."

"This isn't federal." Though her brain couldn't help but tick off all the players involved in the Cinderella Strangler case. She wondered if any of them had the capacity for murder. "Now, what do you really want me for?"

"Other than naked in my bed?"

She glared at him, discreetly looking around to make sure none of the uniformed cops heard him. "Knock it off, DeLucca."

He grinned. "Your help."

"You don't need my help."

"Admitting I'm better at my job?"

"Admitting I'm swamped and don't need another investigation eating into my free time and costing me tickets to a winning Mets game."

"You were here last night?"

"Supposed to be here. Got stuck on frickin' paperwork on a bust I worked with your brothers in blue in Brooklyn." His dark eyes probed hers, and she said, "Dammit, DeLucca, you don't need me."

"Wallet gone, a ring appears to have been taken off her finger—we'll confirm that with next of kin. But that car she was parked next to? The witnesses said they got here early and tailgated. Went in just before the first pitch. Space next to them was empty because they'd spread out, so she got here after the game started. No ticket stub found on her or in her vehicle."

"And?"

"She's in the damn parking lot."

"Maybe she was going to buy from a scalper. Or at Will Call. Or it's in her missing purse."

"We're looking at everything. But who comes to a game alone?"

Suzanne raised her hand.

"You're not normal."

She rolled her eyes. "Joe, I don't want the case."

"New stadium, family friendly, no real history of trouble. Break-ins, car theft, but nothing like this. Anything about the Cinderella case that was wonky?"

"No. The killer's dead, taken out by FBI-SWAT. Clean kill. Weber wanted to write about the whack job's psycho head." And she was far too interested in the two civilian "consultants" whose names were supposed to be sealed. Damn, *was* Weber's murder connected to her closed case?

"Was Weber working on anything else?"

"Don't know."

DeLucca looked at her again with his damn bedroom eyes.

"Fine. You win. You want to split this?"

"I'd rather work side by side."

"Not going there."

"Oh yes, you will." He grinned.

"I'll take victimology; you take the crime scene. Let me know when the autopsy's done, and an ETA on trace evidence. If you need the FBI lab, let me know and I'll expedite for you."

"Dinner, tonight."

"Not on your life." Suzanne started walking away. A plane flew almost directly overhead and she didn't hear DeLucca.

"Great!" he shouted after her. "See you then!"

She turned around. "I didn't agree to anything."

"Sure you did. Seven p.m., Roberta's."

"*No.*"

But she knew she'd be there. Worse, *he* knew she'd be there. It had been their favorite dinner spot when they were involved. She hadn't been there in over a year, since they'd split.

But first things first. Time to find out what Rosemary

Weber was really doing in the parking lot of Citi Field if she wasn't going to the game. Joe DeLucca was right—this wasn't a robbery. This was personal. The killer wanted Rosemary Weber dead. If Suzanne could figure out the why, it would lead them directly to the who.

CHAPTER TWO

Fifteen Years Ago

The night my sister died, our mother gave us the Game of Life.

Mom bought us guilt presents because, as Rachel said, she knew what she was doing was wrong. She thought if we just played quietly in the attic, we'd ignore what went on downstairs. But sound travels in old houses, and even if Mom said it was "just a party," we knew better.

Dad had sort of finished off the attic two years ago, putting in insulation and a space heater and hooking up cable and Nintendo. It became my sanctuary, for me more than for my sister: I guess I just liked having my own private hideout. Mom bought a couple of beanbag chairs and two long, narrow throw rugs that fit the space when laid out side by side.

We were up there with our new game the night of the last party.

It took me nearly an hour to set everything up because all of the plastic pieces came attached to one frame and I had to break each one off. I didn't ask Rachel to help because she was in a bad mood, pretending to read. I knew she wasn't reading because she never turned a page in her book. The sound of the rain pounding on the pitched roof would have been scary if I was alone, but I wasn't scared with my sister here.

"Ready," I said. "There's no purple car; do you want blue?" Purple was Rachel's favorite color. Blue was mine.

"You can have blue." Rachel sighed and put the unread book down. She picked up the red car.

I began to explain the rules, but Rachel cut me off. "I've played it before, at Jessie's house."

"Is that why you're mad? Because Jessie said you couldn't come over tonight?"

Rachel shrugged. "It's not her fault."

That was it. I had only just turned nine, but I knew my sister better than anyone, even our parents. "I wish Grams was here."

"Yeah."

Grams lived in Florida most of the year. Her arthritis was so bad, she could hardly walk when it was cold. Rachel and I always spent spring break with her, and we never wanted to come home. Grams came back to Newark in May and stayed for the summer. After Grandpa died two years ago, she stayed in the guest room and Mom and Dad didn't have parties. They became almost normal parents.

We played quietly, but as the party got louder Rachel started getting mean. When she had to pay income tax, she leaned back and said, "I can't concentrate."

"It's just the luck of the spinner," I said. "But we can play something else. Mario Kart?"

She closed her eyes. "I hate them."

My stomach hurt. She was talking about Mom and Dad. I didn't like this Rachel. I just wanted everyone to be happy and like each other.

"Remember last time when we snuck out and got ice cream?" I said. "Want to do that again?"

"It's raining too hard. I'm not mad at you, Petey, I just don't want to be here, okay?"

"I know." I bit my lip. "What about poker?"

"You'll beat me at that, too."

"I'll let you win."

She laughed, and my stomach hurt less because Rachel's laugh makes me smile. She jumped up and tickled me. "You're lying, munchkin."

I giggled. "Blackjack? Yahtzee? I'll give you a head start on Mario Kart, a whole lap if you want."

Rachel sighed and rolled over to her back. The rain fell so fast I couldn't separate individual raindrops. "Petey? Would you really want to live with Grams?"

"Live? Like forever?"

"When we visit next month, I'm going to tell Grams everything. She'll let us stay. Maybe she'll never come back to Newark, either. She only visits because of us."

The pain in my stomach hurt more than ever. "Don't do that. It'll make Grams sad."

She put her chin on her hand and looked at me. "I'm much older than you. I'll be twelve next week; I know what's best. Look at it this way: Either Grams tells Mom and Dad to stop with the stupid parties and we stay here without all this weird stuff, or we get to live in Florida. Right? And Grams' friend Larry will take you fishing. Remember last year? We had a lot of fun on his boat."

True. But Dad took me fishing, too. Sometimes. I bit my lip when I remembered I hadn't gone fishing with Dad since before Grandpa died, because Grandpa always went with us.

"Mom and Dad would be sad." I sounded like I was

going to cry, and I didn't want to be a baby, but I didn't want anything to change that much. I just wanted a normal family.

"If they're sad, they can cut out this shit."

My eyes widened. "You said *shit*."

"So did you."

"Only because you said it first."

Rachel smiled at me, but it was a sad face. I wished she didn't think I was a little kid. I was nine, in third grade, and I was smart, too. All my teachers said so. They had wanted me to skip third grade, but my parents said no because I'm shorter than all the other third graders.

"Think about it, Pete, okay? I won't say anything if you're not okay with it."

I didn't believe her. Rachel was lying to me. I knew it deep down and didn't know how I knew. Maybe because she wasn't looking at me? Like when she said she wasn't sneaking out to visit Jessie last month, but she did, anyway.

Maybe she was right and we should talk to Grams.

I didn't want to leave.

"I'm going to my room to call Jessie. Set up Mario Kart, we'll play when I get back, I promise."

I did what she said and played a couple games alone while I waited for her. But she didn't come back. I don't know when I fell to sleep, but I woke up to thunder.

The clock on the VCR flashed 12:00. The power must have gone off and on. But it felt later than midnight. I went downstairs, feeling my way down the narrow staircase to the second-floor landing. The house was very quiet. It smelled like it always did after a party, of stale smoke over stinky food and drink. Rachel's light was off. I opened her door. Her night-light shined on her bed. It was empty. She must have snuck out without me. Went to Jessie's without telling me. I started crying. I didn't want to be alone.

I crawled into my sister's messy bed, missing her and mad at her for leaving me.

It wasn't until six days later that the police found Rachel. She was dead. But in my heart, I think I'd known from the beginning.

CHAPTER THREE

FBI Academy, Quantico

"Kincaid!"

Lucy entered the gym with two minutes to spare. Her conversation with her criminal psychology instructor, Supervisory Special Agent Tony Presidio, had taken longer than she'd thought, but she made it on time.

"Yes, sir," Lucy said, pulling up at the end of the row of new agents from Class 12-14.

"Five pull-ups."

"I'm not late, sir." Lucy spoke automatically but immediately realized she should have kept her mouth shut.

Tom Harden stared at her, his expression unreadable. He wasn't an agent but had been an Army Ranger with extensive experience in physical training. He looked every bit a recently retired drill sergeant, with close-cropped hair and a rock-hard body. He'd run New Agent Physical Training for the last three years. He was only five foot nine, an inch taller than Lucy, and stared without blinking.

"Make it ten, Kincaid," he said. "You were the last one out by more than five minutes. No need to pretty yourself for a workout, sweetheart."

Lucy almost argued with him. She wanted to. But she

understood the psychology behind the FBI's New Agent Training program. One of the primary tests—a test they began the moment they set foot on campus—was a stress test. How well did the new agents handle stress? How well did they perform under fire? Could they both take orders and think independently?

She'd prove she could handle stress as well as anyone. Sometimes, she thought her entire life had been one big stress test.

Lucy walked over to the pull-up bar and grabbed it.

She expected Harden to order her fellow agents to start their warm-up run; instead, he turned and watched her, which meant everyone else also stared.

She broke out in a sweat.

Please, please, please, start the drill. Don't look at me.

Lucy's phobia manifested and her arms began to shake. She hated being watched. It wasn't hate; it was fear. Cold, dark, crushing fear that made her want to run. Fear that made her head ache, fear that made every hair on her body rise as she felt the eyes of her friends on her.

She'd been doing so well these last three weeks. No exercises were solo, most were in groups or she had a partner, and even when her team was watching she managed to talk herself out of the panic born from her kidnapping and rape seven years ago. She had convinced herself that her fellow new agents were observing the drill as a whole, or her partner, but never watching *only* her. When she thought of herself as part of a unit she successfully battled her phobia. It worked during their first PT test on day two at the Academy, and it had worked every day since. It had been nearly two months since her last real panic attack.

Not here.

Harden said, "That was a half-ass pull-up. You're still on two, Kincaid."

Bastard.

Did he know about her fears? Of course he did—it must be in her file. Nothing was secret from the FBI. Her file was probably thicker than anyone else's here.

Stress management. If she couldn't control this phobia, she was going to lose everything she'd worked for.

She closed her eyes, but that made it worse because even though she couldn't see anyone the pricks of their eyes on her skin made her squirm. She felt them, a sixth sense that she'd successfully used as a self-defense skill but that she couldn't control. She hung from the bar, her muscles pulling at her, tense not from the pull-ups but from the panic. Locked up so tight that she wasn't able to pull herself up, she wasn't able to stop shaking.

"Three, Kincaid," Harden counted. "No one is doing anything until you're done."

Lucy opened her eyes and stared at him. There was something in his flat expression—hope? Did he want her to fail? To embarrass her? To remind her that she had been a victim?

She pulled herself up again. *Four.*

I am not a victim.

Her arms burned because she'd hung too long, but she was going to make it if she killed herself. She would not fail, and damn if she was going to let a cocky, authoritative instructor make her feel like a failure—or, worse, a victim. She wasn't a victim, and she wasn't going to let anyone make her feel victimized.

Lucy felt her shields rebuilding as she pulled her chin over the bar. It was almost as if the last eight months hadn't happened, that she hadn't learned to be almost normal. If she was going to survive the FBI Academy, she'd have to regain her distance, her detachment, bury her emotions again. Failure wasn't an option—she was going to survive, she was going to be an agent, and if she had to be cold and unemotional she would be.

Five.

Everyone here had stories. Not hers, but the eleven trainees who'd served in the military had faced life and death. Different, but no less soul-searching than her own past.

Margo had joined the Army right out of high school. She'd been a poor kid from New York with a drunk for a mom and no hope for the future. The Army gave Margo a future.

Six.

"Your nose didn't even top the bar," Harden said. "You may be a decent runner, but are you going to run away from danger, or face it? Let's see a real six."

Bastard.

Six.

The Army had given Margo her college education. She'd wanted to be a cop but she'd been recruited into the FBI when she was a twenty-seven-year-old college senior. Lucy felt closer to her than anyone else—and not just because they shared a bathroom.

She and Margo had fallen into a small, dedicated group of new agents—two other military veterans, a paramedic, a prosecutor, a detective, a linguist, and an accountant. The accountant, Reva Penrose, was a math teacher with a Ph.D. in accounting. Reva was Margo's opposite. Petite, feisty, a bundle of energy. Growing up in rural Texas, Reva had been raised with guns and had aced her first firearms test. But while she was a whiz on the range, she'd gotten the minimum acceptable score on the PT test.

Seven.

Focusing on her friends and thinking about them gave Lucy the ability to handle the eyes on her. She'd never forget they were there, that the other thirty-three agents in Class 12-14, and Harden, and the field counselors were all staring at her.

But she could overcome it.

Eight.

Her shell was growing again. Guilt flooded through her. All the time her boyfriend, Sean, had spent helping her be as normal as possible, after three weeks and one punishment it was gone.

Nine.

A sense of loss filled her. She had almost been one of the group, just another new agent among many. But no one else here had these fears, this overwhelming sense of panic. While everyone had baggage, hers still weighed her down. Without a hard shell, she wasn't going to survive the stress of training.

She only hoped she could find a balance between putting up the barrier and having friends.

Ten.

She dropped down, hoping everyone in the room thought the sweat coating her skin was from her exertion and not the simmering panic attack.

But she'd won. This time, she'd battled and won.

She stared at Harden. His expression was unreadable.

He turned his back to her and looked at the assembled group. "Twenty laps. Go." He didn't look at Lucy but said, "That means you, too, Kincaid."

She caught up with Reva, kept to her slower pace, but felt better being in the middle of the pack instead of leading or trailing. Her sister-in-law Kate, who'd worked as the cybercrimes instructor at Quantico for years, had told her to blend in as much as possible. Do well, but keep her head down, don't stand out. Somehow, no matter how much she wanted to be just like everyone else, she'd never been good at keeping a low profile.

Lucy was on her third lap when the new-agent class supervisor, SSA Paula Kean, stepped into the gym and approached Harden. As Lucy passed Kean and Harden, Harden said, "Kincaid, SSA Kean needs you for the rest of the class. I'll expect you to make up the laps tonight."

"Yes, sir." She grabbed her towel from her gym bag and put it around her sweating neck, then followed Kean out of the gym.

They walked down the hall toward Kean's office. The senior agent was in her forties, tall and thin, with shoulder-length brown hair. She wore little makeup except for shiny lip gloss. "Do you know Special Agent Suzanne Madeaux?" she asked.

"Yes, ma'am. She's out of New York."

"She's on the phone for you about a homicide."

"In New York?"

"She said she had to speak with you immediately, didn't give me any details." Kean sounded irritated, but Lucy couldn't tell if it was because of the interruption or the lack of information.

When Sean's seventeen-year-old cousin Kirsten Benton went missing last February, Lucy had helped him track her to New York, where they landed in the middle of a serial killer investigation led by Suzanne Madeaux. Lucy had talked to Suzanne a couple of times since but always related to the Cinderella Strangler investigation, statements, and paperwork.

Lucy sat in the chair across from Kean's desk. The supervisor sat down and surprised Lucy by putting Suzanne on speaker.

"Agent Madeaux? . . . Paula Kean here. I pulled New Agent Kincaid out of class; she's here in my office."

"Am I on speaker?"

"Yes. I'm Kincaid's class supervisor; unless there's a

reason this needs to remain confidential, I'll be in the loop."

"Understood," Suzanne said. "Lucy?"

"Hi, Suzanne."

"I'll cut to the chase. Have you been contacted by a true crime writer, Rosemary Weber? She's writing a book about the Cinderella Strangler case."

Lucy's chest tightened. She remembered the conversation she'd had with Weber, and it wasn't one of her finer moments. She'd never told anyone to go to Hell before.

"Yes. It was the Friday before I reported here."

"What did she call about?"

"The Cinderella Strangler investigation. She told me you were cooperating."

When Weber said that Suzanne had already talked to her Lucy had been at first stunned, then angry, then deeply sad.

"She said that? No way was I cooperating."

Lucy thought back to the conversation. "She strongly implied it. I assumed that's where she got my name."

"I guarantee, Lucy, I did *not* give her your name. I met with her as directed by my boss and listened to her proposal, but offered no information."

Lucy was both relieved and upset with herself for being manipulated by Weber. "I should have called you. But I didn't tell her anything about the case."

Kean interrupted. "Agent Madeaux, what was so urgent that you couldn't speak with Kincaid later?"

"She's been murdered. Last night, in Queens."

Weber had been killed? Before Lucy could ask any questions, Suzanne continued.

"NYPD thinks there may be a connection between whatever project Weber was working on and her death. I'm creating a time line, and because Kincaid's name was in her notes, I needed to know if and when she spoke to her. Lucy, what was she fishing for?"

"She wanted to interview me about my involvement with the case. I said I had no involvement, and that's when she said she'd been talking to you and NYPD."

"I wish you'd called me."

"I'm sorry I didn't," Lucy said. "She was very pushy. I cut her off, and eventually had to hang up on her. I blocked her calls after that."

"Did Sean talk to her?"

"He didn't tell me if he did." She didn't think so—Lucy had told him about the conversation; he would have said something to her.

Kean said, "Kincaid, as Agent Madeaux knows, special agents are not allowed to speak to reporters of any stripe without prior permission from a superior. You should have reported the conversation to me when you arrived."

Before Lucy could comment Suzanne said, "Weber has published three books, all related to federal investigations, and there are interviews with multiple agents in her files. There's a few at Quantico now, and I'll be contacting them if the investigation seems to be pointing at her work as a motivation for the killer."

Kean reapplied her lip gloss, though she didn't need it. "I suggest then that you speak to Assistant Director Hans Vigo, our liaison with national headquarters."

Suzanne said, "The doc got a promotion? Cool."

Lucy smiled, reminded that Suzanne was both smart and outspoken. After a rocky beginning, Lucy had grown to like the seasoned agent and secretly hoped they could work together in the future. Lucy was relieved that Suzanne hadn't discussed her, professionally or personally, with the reporter.

Kean cleared her throat and gave Lucy a disapproving look.

"Do you need anything else from me?" Lucy asked Suzanne over the speaker.

"I'll let you know if I do. Ciao." She hung up.

Kean said, "Don't let Agent Madeaux's investigation cloud your focus, Kincaid."

"I won't, ma'am. May I go back to PT?"

Kean nodded. Lucy left, confused by why her supervisor had wanted to listen to—and participate in the conversation. But Lucy dismissed the unease, more concerned about what else Rosemary Weber was researching—and if her files on Lucy went further back than February.

CHAPTER FOUR

Lucy sulked in her room after her shower. Between the humiliation of the pull-ups and the call from Suzanne about Lucy's name being part of the Rosemary Weber murder investigation, she thought she was entitled to a bout of self-concern. She'd been so preoccupied with the events of the day that she'd performed poorly on the PT drill after she'd returned from Suzanne's call. It went from bad to worse when Lucy noticed both SSA Kean and field counselor Special Agent Laughlin had observed her failure.

"Agent Kean was watching everyone," she mumbled to herself. That was the class supervisor's job, to assess all new agents from day one through graduation. More than ten percent of new agents at Quantico dropped out or were expelled for a variety of reasons. The odds were with Lucy to make it, but because of the difficulty in getting here in the first place she had to be better than everyone else.

But Laughlin was a different problem. Every new-agent class was assigned two field counselors—mentors—not only to observe but also help the new agents with their studies, questions, and any concerns. From the beginning, Lucy had felt uneasy around Laughlin and suspected he disliked her. Which was silly because they'd never met, he'd never specifically said anything to her, and she couldn't think of a reason he would have an issue with her. That he had been watching her so closely made her doubly nervous.

But she wanted to talk to Sean about Rosemary Weber; unfortunately, he was on a commercial flight from Sacramento and wouldn't be landing until late tonight. Lucy considered calling Hans Vigo but immediately dismissed that idea. Now that Assistant Director Vigo was liaison between Quantico and headquarters, she didn't want to use her connections for information.

She tried Suzanne, wanting to talk to her without the ear of Kean, but she didn't answer her phone. Running out of options of who she could talk to, Lucy wondered if Kate was still on campus. Her sister-in-law was the cyber-crimes instructor at Quantico and one of the few people Lucy trusted.

Lucy called Margo and told her she'd meet up with her and the others at the cafeteria, then went to find Kate. She crossed the campus to the Classroom Building, where Kate's long, narrow office had more computer equipment than airspace. Lucy knocked but didn't wait for an answer before opening the door.

Lucy came face-to-face with the back of a broad-shouldered man, standing right in front of Kate's desk. Kate was facing him, the backs of her thighs against the edge. She was saying through clenched teeth, "I'm not going to forget." Kate's eyes widened when she saw Lucy, and she sidestepped the man in front of her. Her mouth was a tight, thin line. "Lucy."

Lucy processed what she'd walked into. While she hadn't seen them in a compromising position, it was obvious that Kate knew the man standing much *too* close to her—and knew him well.

"Excuse me." Lucy's voice was quiet; she was surprised she could say anything at all.

The man turned. Reva had called Special Agent Rich Laughlin "Mr. Tall, Dark, and Handsome," but Lucy didn't see it. Right now all she saw in his pale eyes was hatred.

"Kincaid." Irritation laced his voice.

Her skin crawled, and she considered that Kate's meeting might not have been friendly. She was actually relieved, because for a brief moment she'd thought the worst—that Kate was cheating on Dillon. Of course that wasn't the case, and that Lucy had even thought it for a second made her feel guilty.

She straightened. "Sorry, sir."

"You should wait for a response before entering a room," Kate snapped. "What is it?"

"It's not important. I'll talk to you later."

She left Kate's office, heart racing, wondering what had just happened. She'd known Kate for seven years, had lived with her and Dillon for most of that time, and was closer to her than she was to her own two sisters. Kate could be sharp and abrasive, but Lucy had never heard that tone directed at her.

Lucy needed to talk to Kate, but not while Agent Laughlin was anywhere around. She was too upset to meet her friends for dinner, so made a detour to Supervisory Special Agent Tony Presidio's office.

The basement was a fully self-contained two-story bomb shelter designed and built in the Hoover years so the FBI could continue operating in the event of a major national disaster. Though the Behavioral Science Unit and most other divisions had moved to off-site facilities or elsewhere on campus, there were still people, including Tony, who worked in the windowless offices and would until renovations and additions were complete.

Tony taught criminal psychology and Lucy had liked him from day one. He hadn't been teaching at Quantico long—Class 12-14 was his third. He'd come from the Hostage Rescue Team and was unusually calm and even tempered. While many of her classmates found Tony intimidating and unapproachable, Lucy had developed a kinship with him over the three weeks she'd been here. Lucy enjoyed listening to his stories and asking questions, and she suspected he appreciated the genuine interest she showed in his experience.

Lucy was about to knock on Tony's partly opened door but noticed him hunched over his desk, head in one hand, reading a thick file. He was one of the older agents, in his early fifties and nearing mandatory retirement, but he was physically fit and Lucy ran with him several days a week.

She turned to leave, not wanting to disturb him with something trivial. In fact, she'd almost forgotten why she'd sought him out in the first place.

He glanced up as she turned away. "Kincaid?"

"Sorry to bother you. I was on my way to the cafeteria—"

His eyebrows arched up and amusement lit his face. "By way of the basement?"

"It's nothing."

He waved her in. "I was going to call you anyway. Sit down."

"What about?" She took the chair across from him.

He closed the file he was reading and put it aside.

"Special Agent Madeaux called me. Told me she'd spoken to you about Rosemary Weber's murder."

"Yes." All thoughts of Laughlin and Kate vanished. "She'd called me about the book she was writing."

"Suzanne said you didn't share anything with the reporter."

"I told her to leave me out of it. My involvement was never supposed to be public."

"Suzanne is tracking down how Weber got your name, but the case wasn't classified. She could have learned of your involvement fairly easily."

Lucy bit her lip. She didn't want *anything* she did to be in the public eye. She needed her anonymity.

"Do you want to talk about it?"

"About what?"

"What's bothering you."

"I don't know." She did, but how did she tell Tony that she was worried her past would haunt her for the rest of her life? She'd believed time would erase her history, but it only made it permanent. "Did you know Weber?"

He nodded. "She wrote her first book while she was a crime reporter in Newark. It was one of my cases. A screwed-up case from the beginning, a true tragedy. Eleven-year-old girl kidnapped from her bedroom, raped and murdered. The parents lied about nearly everything, until we had enough evidence to catch them in their lies."

As he spoke, his voice deepened and he held the edge of his desk, knuckles white, anger about the old case still evident.

Kidnapped from her bedroom.

In a low, emotion-filled voice, Tony said, "It was one of those cases that stay with you because it was senseless and so many lives were ruined."

"Did you catch the killer?"

"Benjamin John Kreig. He's serving life without parole." Tony rolled his shoulders and leaned back in his chair, purposefully relaxing. Lucy had often done the same thing. If she could relax her body, she could relax her mind.

But Lucy was focused on what Tony had said.

Kidnapped from her bedroom and murdered.

"Lucy?" Tony prodded.

"You know my nephew was killed when I was seven."

By Tony's expression, he had known. Lucy didn't expect that her life was private, however much she tried to keep her past to herself. Just one more reminder that she'd never escape.

Lucy continued, "Justin was a few days younger than me, and sometimes I made him call me Aunt Lucy just to tease him. I was closer to him than my brothers and sisters, who were all older than me. My sister, Justin's mom, grieved so long, she couldn't stay in San Diego. She moved to Idaho and became a hermit for more than a decade. She called our mom once a week, but Mom was always so sad afterwards, because Nelia wasn't really living. Justin's murder changed all of us. Dillon, for example, changed his focus from sports medicine to forensic psychiatry. When I asked him why, he said he wanted to understand what happened to Justin."

"Is that what drives you? Answers?"

"Maybe." *No.*

"Justice?"

Maybe. "I can't sit by and let bad things happen."

"If we can save one, we have succeeded."

But there would always be evil in the world, and there would always be victims. "If it was just saving one person, I don't think I would be here," Lucy said truthfully. "Putting killers and rapists in prison saves all their potential victims. It's not so much *justice* I crave as protecting innocents."

Lucy asked, "Did you talk to Weber about your case?"

"No. She wrote most of the articles about the investigation and trial, and I didn't like how she sensationalized the tragedy. The parents deserved to be exposed, but they had lost their daughter, and they realized they were culpable."

Her stomach turned at all the awful possibilities of parental involvement in the girl's death. "How so?"

"The McMahons were swingers. They had a party the night their daughter Rachel was killed. They lied about the nature of the party. The critical hours that Rachel was missing immediately after she was abducted were wasted because they misled first the responding officer, then the FBI. Their nine-year-old son was the one who finally told me about the party."

Lucy frowned. "He knew what was going on?"

"Unfortunately. Once we confronted the parents and interviewed witnesses, we learned that Krieg hadn't been invited to the party but two guests saw him. At first he denied being there, so it was easy to bring him in for questioning. It took sixteen hours to break him, but he eventually led us to her body. Six days after he killed her."

Lucy absorbed the information with both revulsion and interest. "And Weber wrote a book?"

"She focused on the sensational—the swinger parties, the history between Aaron and Pilar McMahon, the guests at the parties—and the worst was that, as far as I was concerned, she kept bringing it back to Rachel being in the wrong place at the wrong time. Which was just asinine considering she was in her own bedroom in the middle of the night."

Tony pounded his fist once on the desk, then looked at his clenched fingers and slowly stretched them. "I refused to help her after reading her articles," he said, "but the FBI assigned a liaison, who worked with her to get her facts straight."

"Do you think her murder has to do with one of her books?"

"More likely, whatever she's researching now."

"You mean the Cinderella Strangler case."

"Maybe. She might have been working on more than one. I'll find out. What specifically did she ask you?"

"She thought the whole case was 'sexy'—her word, not mine. Teenage prostitutes being suffocated at underground raves, all connecting back to an online chat room. She wanted to drag the Barnetts through the dirt again, and they're just reclaiming their life."

"Barnett?"

"A wealthy family in New York. They were the subject of the killer's obsession, and Weber said it made a good story. It wasn't a *story;* these were people's *lives.* Four girls died horrible deaths because of that psychopath. I wasn't about to help Weber with any of it."

"I hear a but."

"No buts, I would never have spoken to her."

Tony looked at her pointedly. "But?"

"She asked me too many questions. I felt—she was digging around, trying to find out why I had been in New York, what my history was. And while much of my file is sealed, there's enough that's public." She bit her lip.

"You were afraid she'd end up writing about you."

Lucy took a deep breath and nodded. She had faced her past and survived, but exposing what had happened seven years ago to the public, in the media, would destroy the life she'd built.

"There are laws to protect you from that kind of disclosure."

"I told her to go to Hell and hung up."

Tony almost smiled, then grew serious. "Suzanne asked if I could come up to New York for a day or two, since I'm familiar with Weber's work. While I'm there, I'll dig around her files, see what I find. I don't think she had anything on your past, because Suzanne would have told you. But I'll make sure."

"I appreciate that."

Tony opened his bottom drawer, rummaged through some folders, and pulled one out. "Read this. It's the Mc-Mahon case, the one Weber wrote about in her first book. It'll give you all the background and information you need. It's my personal file, so it's not complete, but it includes my notes."

"Those are probably enlightening."

"I should have been more careful about what I wrote down. Notes can become part of the official record."

She took the file.

Tony leaned back and looked over her head, contemplative. "I always wondered what happened to the boy, Peter McMahon. Rachel's brother."

"You don't know?"

"The case was fifteen years ago. He's twenty-four now, a grown man. I know he went to live with his grandmother in Florida shortly after the murder. He was a brave kid, telling me what his parents were really doing at the party. Turned the case wide open."

"Maybe I can track him down for you."

"If it's not too much trouble. Find out where he's living, what he's doing with his life. Make sure he's okay."

"Do you think he could be responsible for Rosemary Weber's murder?"

"No," Tony said, too quickly. He backtracked a bit. "I doubt it. The book about his sister came out ten years ago. Why now?"

"Because he was fourteen when the book came out and couldn't do anything about it?"

"There had to be another reason," Tony said. "But maybe if you find him, we'll have the answers."

Lucy wondered why Tony didn't use FBI resources to track down Peter McMahon, but before she could ask he said, "You should read Weber's books. Start with the book about the McMahon investigation and go from there. According to the FBI Media Office, they were vetted for accuracy.

"Now," he continued, "you came down here because you wanted to talk to me about something."

She'd almost forgotten about Laughlin. "It's not important."

Tony didn't say anything, but his expression told her he expected her to talk.

"It really isn't important," she repeated. "Rather junior high."

"Try me."

"I just have this sense that Agent Laughlin doesn't like me." She smiled sheepishly. "See? Junior high."

"If it was someone else, I might think that, but your instincts are usually good. Was it something specific, or a vague feeling?"

Lucy considered how to answer. "I suppose there was an undercurrent of veiled hostility from the beginning—which I dismissed because I was nervous."

"Nervous about what?"

"Where do I start?" She shrugged. "You've read my file, I know all the instructors have, and the hoops I jumped through to get here."

"Some people might wonder why you were willing to jump through the hoops, considering you have many career options. Is that what you're thinking?"

"What if someone thought I wanted this *too* much, and questioned why. I've thought the same thing. But if the last few months have taught me anything, I let my goals define me for too long. Had my application been denied, I'd have been disappointed, but I would have been okay. But people see what's on the surface."

"You suspect he doesn't trust you."

Lucy hadn't said that, but immediately she realized Tony was right. "He's been professional, but there's a different subtext when he's with others. Some of my friends have noticed it, too. I don't have the same feeling about the other field counselors."

"Trust your instincts, Lucy. Continue to perform well and there's nothing he can do. Training is just as much a mind game as it is learning the rules and regs and working as a team. You'll be dealing with agents like Laughlin across all agencies. Consider this a test."

It was the answer she'd expected, though she didn't like it. She was tired of being tested when she couldn't prepare, when she didn't even know *what* she was being tested *on*.

"And," Tony continued, "if he goes too far, let me know." She opened her mouth to object but he raised his hand. "Only if it becomes serious. I think you'll be fine."

CHAPTER FIVE

Lucy made herself a quick salad from the salad bar and grabbed a couple rolls before sitting down with her friends at what had become their table. Everyone was there except Lance Orozco and Alexis Sanchez.

Lucy looked at their empty plates. "Sorry—I got sidetracked."

"The Golden Girl," Carter Nix teased.

"Studying again?" Reva said. "Trying to graduate top of the class, no doubt."

Was her drive that obvious? "Not studying," she said. "Talking."

"Any good gossip?" Reva leaned forward. "Why were you pulled out of PT?"

Lucy didn't want to talk about Rosemary Weber or the call from Suzanne. "I can't talk about it. But it has nothing to do with training," she added quickly. They were all a bit paranoid about being under the microscope while on campus; she didn't want her friends to think she was doing anything behind their backs.

"Stop being so nosy, Penrose," Eddie Acosta said. He and Carter were the only two in the class who had known each other before they joined the Academy. They'd been in Marine basic training together, served ten years in the military in separate divisions, and ended up at the same college through the GI Bill.

"Where'd Oz and Alexis go?" Lucy asked.

"Oz is playing video games in the lounge," Jason Aragon said. Jason was a prosecutor from Los Angeles and the oldest of their group at thirty-five. He was also a reservist in the Coast Guard, which Lucy thought was fascinating, though he didn't talk much about himself. There were some whispers that he'd been in a gang in his youth, and he had a faded tat he didn't talk about, either.

"And Sanchez is talking to her daughter," Carter said. He glanced at his watch. "Speaking of which, I need to call home in fifteen minutes, Shelley likes me to call before dinner to talk to the girls." Carter was from Denver, married with two daughters. He talked to them every night.

As Carter bussed his tray, Eddie said, "Hey, I'll meet you in the computer lab at twenty-one hundred."

Carter gave him a thumbs-up and left.

"Ready for the gun range tomorrow?" Margo asked. They were having a qualification pre-test. It wasn't counted toward their firearms score but was their first assessment since day two. Their instructor expected everyone to have improved their scores between the day two test and now.

"Firearms, no problem," Lucy said between bites. "I'm not looking forward to the driving test Monday."

"Driving?" Reva laughed. "One of the easiest tests, from what I heard."

"I don't like driving," Lucy confessed. She felt sheepish and wished she hadn't said anything.

"You're not tested on the course," Eddie said. "Even if you screw up, as long as you have a driver's license and can steer a vehicle that's all that's required. Monday is simply defensive driving."

Margo said, "Don't psych yourself out, you'll be fine."

"I think it's about time to hit the books," Eddie said. He left with Jason. That left Lucy with Margo and Reva.

Lucy found herself relaxing with her group. There were seven of them who had loosely banded together, and while others in her class of thirty-four sometimes ate with them or hung out after hours, the core seven gave Lucy a much-needed sense of friendship and belonging. It had been something she'd missed out on in college because of the rape.

"You don't have to wait for me to finish; I was late," Lucy said.

"I don't mind," Margo said. She eyed Lucy carefully. "Are you sure you're okay?"

"Yes," Lucy said. And she was. After talking to Tony, she had put Laughlin in one compartment, Weber's murder in another, and her past safely locked away, for now. She looked forward to reading Tony's notes on the Rachel McMahon homicide, and maybe she could track down Rachel's brother and give Tony peace of mind. Lucy had no doubt that going through Rosemary Weber's files would be difficult, and she hoped to have good news for him when he returned in two days.

"What's in the folder?" Reva asked, and started to open it.

Lucy put her hand on the cover. "Reva, I can't share. It's a case file—an old case—that Agent Presidio gave to me. I promised to keep it confidential." She hadn't, he hadn't even asked, but she didn't want to have to explain why she was looking at it.

"Anything to do with Kean pulling you out today?"

"Knock it off, Reva," Margo said.

Lucy sighed and gave them a bit of information, mostly to keep Reva from getting even more nosy. "It involves a case I was involved with a few months ago in New York. An agent I worked with needed some information, said it couldn't wait."

Margo diverted the conversation back to the firearms test tomorrow, and Lucy quickly finished eating. The three of them cleared their trays, and both Lucy and Margo grabbed an apple and granola bar for the morning. They'd gotten in the habit of running together at dawn, and neither liked to run on an empty stomach. They'd tried to get Reva to join them, but she wasn't a morning person.

Their rooms were on the second floor of the Madison Dormitory. When the Academy was at full capacity, there were two new agents to a room with a large bathroom connecting two rooms, so four agents had to share. But because of the budget freeze, instead of more than one thousand recruits passing through annually, it was less than half that now, and they had closed down Washington Dorm. Everyone had their own room and only had to share the adjoining bath with one fellow new agent. Lucy and Margo shared, while Reva was at the end of the hall with Alexis.

"Run at six?" Margo asked as she opened her door.

"Sounds good." Lucy went to her own room. She opened the door and found Kate sitting at her desk. One look at Kate's expression, and hope that she'd come to explain what happened with Laughlin earlier disappeared.

Lucy dropped Tony's file on her nightstand. "Kate— tell me what happened."

Kate stared, as if having an inner battle about what to say.

"What's going on?" Lucy pushed.

"Stay under the radar and away from Laughlin."

She sat down on her bed and leaned forward. "Why?"

"It has nothing to do with you."

She was lying, and Lucy called her on it. "It has everything to do with me. And *you*. Tell me, Kate."

"Trust me, Lucy."

"I always have."

Kate sagged in relief. "Good. Just get through the next couple months and all will be fine."

But Lucy wasn't willing to drop it that easily. "I trust you, Kate; you need to trust me. Tell me what's going on with Laughlin."

Kate stared at her, stunned that Lucy had called her on the carpet. Secrets had burned Lucy in the past, she wasn't going to be kept in the dark.

"I can take it, Kate. My imagination is going to create far worse scenarios. Tell me what was going on in your office. What were you and Laughlin arguing about?"

"Let's just say there are people here who will look for any reason to expel you. Keep your nose clean."

"He wants me out of here?"

"It's complicated. I can't go into detail."

"You mean you *won't* go into it. Don't I deserve the truth?"

Kate stood. "I'm sorry, Lucy."

"Kate—"

Lucy wished she hadn't sat down, because now Kate towered over her. "You wanted to get here on your own merits, but nothing is done in a vacuum. It doesn't matter if you're J. Edgar Hoover's granddaughter or the prodigy of Eliot Ness, people have long memories, and some people want to tear down more than lift up. *Never* forget it. It's politics, Lucy, and if you want to survive you'll blend in.

Being right or intelligent isn't going to save you. Being *smart* might."

"Keeping me in the dark isn't going to help, either!"

Kate walked out, firmly shutting the door behind her.

"Dammit!" Lucy walked over to the door, ready to go after Kate, then rested her forehead on the frame. She needed answers, and Kate wasn't going to give them to her yet.

But she knew the one person who could find them.

She strode over to her bag and grabbed her cell phone.

Sean answered on the second ring. "Lucy, I just walked in and was going to call you. You must be psychic."

"Maybe I am." She sat at her desk and rubbed her forehead with her free hand. "I need a favor."

"It's not a favor when it's for the woman I love. What do you need?"

"I think I may have rubbed one of my instructors the wrong way, and I have no idea how or why. I don't know anything about him, other than his name is Rich Laughlin and he's an SA out of the Detroit field office. I can't risk asking—"

"I know exactly what you need, and I'll get it without tripping any alarms."

Always, she could depend on Sean. "You're amazing."

"Luce, why not talk to Kate?"

She sighed. "Because Kate knows why and she won't tell me."

"She knows this guy is harassing you?"

"I wouldn't say harassing, more . . . closely observing."

"I already hate him."

"Kate doesn't like him, either, which makes why she's being so tight-lipped about him even more strange. I want to keep this quiet for now. When we learn something, I'll talk to her." The tension of the day dissipated. "How was Sacramento?"

"Same old. I'll tell you about the job when I see you this weekend—I *am* seeing you."

It wasn't a question. "As far as I know, I can leave."

"I hear a 'but' in your voice."

"It's about me not making waves."

"Is that what this Laughlin thing is?"

"Something Kate said. But, no matter what, I'll find some way to see you."

"It's been nearly four weeks, Lucy—I miss you."

"I miss you, too." She bit her lip, needing to tell Sean about the dead writer but not quite sure how to explain it. "There's something else that happened. Remember that reporter who called me before I reported to Quantico?"

"Rosemary Weber. Of course I remember her. She upset you."

"She was murdered last night. Suzanne Madeaux called me."

"Why are the feds involved?"

"Because Weber was writing about a federal investigation."

"Did Suzanne tell you why she gave Weber your name?"

"She said she didn't. I believe her, Sean. I should have asked her four weeks ago."

"Does she know who spilled the beans about you? Because Weber never called me."

"Suzanne promised to research the leak. Tony is heading to New York to consult with Suzanne and the NYPD, and I'm sure he'll fill me in when he returns. My supervisor has forbidden me from following up with Suzanne without her permission."

"You focus on getting your badge. I'll call Suzanne and let you know what I learn."

Lucy smiled. "Thanks."

"Thank me in person, this weekend."

CHAPTER SIX

New York City

Suzanne was ten minutes late to the restaurant and Joe DeLucca was already there—with two cold bottles of beer in front of him.

She grabbed the full beer. "Thanks."

"I knew you'd come."

"Maybe I'm a figment of your imagination."

"I ordered our pizza."

"I became a vegetarian."

Joe laughed, thin lines framing his eyes. A familiar flutter spread through her body. Suzanne didn't want any of the old feelings. She didn't want to remember how much she'd once cared.

She stared at him. "How's Stephanie?"

He scowled. "Don't."

"Same old, same old." She drank a long swallow of beer. "Okay, sorry. Ex-wife is off the table. But this"—she gestured between them—"is work only, Joe, nothing more."

"Seeing someone?"

"More or less." Less right now. For the past year, she'd hooked up with her best friend and sometime lover Mac whenever she wanted company. Mac was safe, trustworthy, and wanted nothing more from their relationship than she did. But as time passed they'd become better friends and less lovers. Which was also fine with Suzanne. She was too busy to stress over the whole *he loves me, he loves me not* thing. She got over it a long time ago.

Joe didn't blink. "You're lying."

"Any news from the M.E.?" *Keep it business, Suz.*

"Autopsy's in the morning. One visible stab wound, narrow weapon—like an ice pick."

"*Like* an ice pick or actually an ice pick?"

"Impatient, as always. We'll know more in the morning. You can observe if you want."

"Nope." She had no time to hang around the morgue, and depending on who was running the case, it could take hours. "Security cams?"

"The only useful tape showed Weber in her car, alone, entering the parking lot."

"Killer was on foot?"

"Possibly. We have the tape of everyone driving in, but it'll take days to go through all the faces, and unless we get some info to narrow the parameters that's not my focus. However, I have a couple rookies going through everyone who left the stadium thirty minutes prior to time of death. Because the game was close, not many people left early."

"Good idea." She paused. "I don't think the killer was at the game."

"Based on?"

"If you're right and she was killed by someone she knew, someone she planned on meeting at the stadium, why would he buy a ticket?"

"Maybe it's someone who was there with others and slipped out to kill her, goes back in, and sits with friends. Alibi."

"I hadn't thought of that."

"I must be more devious than you."

"Sometimes." She sipped her beer. "Did you print the car?"

He stared at her.

"Of course you did. Sorry."

"So far, nothing. Just Weber, her sister, and Weber's research assistant. Crime techs are looking for trace in the vehicle. Talked to the sister—they lived in a town house on the Upper East Side, inherited from their deceased parents. Bridget Weber, forty-three, divorced. Ex-husband some schmuck who works for the governor in Albany. Sister is an interior designer. Seemed upset, but she does get half of her sister's estate."

"Sizable?"

"The town house has right of survivorship, so that's free and clear. My techs are going through financials; she's probably looking at a quarter mil when all's said and done."

"Life insurance?"

"Small policy—both sisters had a hundred thou, sister said to cover any expenses related to their demise."

"Other half of the estate?"

"Donation to her alma mater, Columbia University. Which brings me to the assistant, a grad student at Columbia who's worked for the deceased only a few months. Seems she gets a new grad student for every project, becomes part of their thesis or some such thing. I talked to the faculty advisor and he's hooking me up with her new assistant tomorrow." Joe grinned. "Want to join me?"

"I have another two dozen calls to make, and I hate the phone."

"It'll be fun. Old times."

They'd met on a case five years ago when Suzanne was first assigned to the Violent Crimes and Major Offenders squad in New York City. They worked well together. Played well together, too.

She didn't smile. "Not old times."

The pizza arrived, authentic Italian according to Joe. Suzanne didn't care—it was simply the best pizza in Brooklyn. They ordered two more beers.

"So was I the only one working today?" Joe said between bites.

"I spoke to half the people from the files you sent over—focusing on those she's interviewing for the Cinderella Strangler case. So far she seems to be in research mode—I have the file with me so I can go through it tonight and try to figure out what her strategy was. She called our civilian consultant from the case, but Lucy said she told Weber she had no comment on the case."

"Lucy who?"

"Kincaid. She's a recruit going through the Academy. Her involvement wasn't made public, but someone told Weber, someone who had enough information to make me think it's one of mine, or one of yours."

"Is she a suspect?"

"Kincaid?" Suzanne snorted. "No. And she wouldn't talk without clearing it through proper channels, just like I would have had to do. But she doesn't want the book written, wouldn't talk to any reporter."

"She doesn't want the book written, but she's not a suspect? What am I missing?"

"I told you, she's at Quantico. And I know her. She didn't do it, but to make you happy I'll verify her alibi."

"Appreciate it." Joe finished off his first slice and grabbed a second.

"I dug deeper into Weber's files and went back to her first book about the Rachel McMahon kidnapping and murder, out of Newark. Fifteen-year-old case."

"That was before my time—I was still at SUNY."

"And I was still in Louisiana. But I knew one of the agents assigned to the case, so thought I'd start at the beginning. SSA Presidio, out of Quantico. He's a profiler and is coming up to help."

"Profiler?" Joe shook his head. He'd never been one to listen to shrinks. "I forgot to mention, the ring the victim wore is worth over fifteen thou. It's looking more and more like a robbery."

"You said it didn't feel like a robbery." Suzanne grabbed her second slice before Joe ate the whole pie.

"You're right—but with a ring worth that much, I have to follow the angle. Besides, I don't like profilers. Good detective work solves more cases than shrinks."

Suzanne used to agree with Joe, but after working with Lucy Kincaid she'd somewhat changed her opinion. She saw value in understanding the psychology of criminals.

"I'll let you know what he says. You might even get to meet him."

"You think maybe someone Weber wrote about was pissed off enough to whack her?"

"Anything's possible at this point. Any threats?"

"Nothing the sister or faculty advisor knew about. I'll ask the assistant tomorrow."

"*We'll* ask the assistant."

Joe grinned. "It's good to work with you again, Suzi."

She glared at him. "That's 'Agent Madeaux' to you, bud." She glanced at her vibrating phone.

Rogan.

"Boyfriend?" Joe asked.

She rolled her eyes and answered. "I thought you might call. How've you been?"

"No complaints. Lucy told me about Weber. I just did a little checking on her. Crime reporter for ten years, then switched gears to write true crime books and special features for magazines. *People, Time, US News,* others. What happened?"

"It's an ongoing investigation, Rogan. I can't talk about it."

"You called Lucy."

"She's one of us now."

"Her supervisor isn't letting her get involved. We need to know how her name landed in the reporter's file. I don't have to explain to you why."

He didn't. Suzanne knew about Lucy's background, and she understood why Lucy would be concerned if she thought Rosemary Weber had information about her past.

"Fair enough. I'll let you know when I find out."

"Why was she killed?"

"That's the million-dollar question."

"I just finished a case, if you need my help—"

Suzanne laughed. "The FBI is working with NYPD on this; why would we need you?"

In mock insult, he said, "Because I'm the best."

She snickered. "Later." She hung up.

"That was interesting," Joe said.

"I'm sure you'll be meeting him in the next few days."

"Who was it?"

"Sean Rogan, P.I. out of D.C."

"And he's in New York?"

"He will be."

CHAPTER SEVEN

FBI Academy

After two hours, Lucy put her books aside.

Tony's file on the Rachel McMahon homicide beckoned her. Not just because it was connected to the murdered writer, but also because there were basic similarities between Rachel's abduction and that of Lucy's nephew Justin. Kidnapped from their home in the middle of the night and murdered before dawn. But that's where the similarities ended.

Rachel McMahon had been a week shy of her twelfth birthday when she was killed. The killer had raped her in her own bed. According to the autopsy report, she'd suffered two cracked ribs and had likely been unconscious or unresponsive when Kreig kidnapped her. Though Kreig never once spoke about the rape and murder, Tony's theory was that the murder wasn't premeditated. Kreig had planned to rape her, but he thought she was dead or dying. In an effort to cover up his crime, he removed her from her room alive. She died of internal injuries within hours. Had she received immediate medical attention, she might have survived.

Though there was an extensive grid search and numerous volunteers and police looking for her, she wasn't found until Kreig led authorities to her body six days later. However, the coroner's report indicated that she'd been dead nearly as long.

MISSING GIRL FOUND DEAD
Rosemary Weber, Senior Crime Reporter

NEWARK, NJ—Six days after Rachel McMahon was abducted from her second-story bedroom, her body was found in the woods less than five miles from her home.

Though police refuse to confirm or deny the circumstances surrounding her death and discovery, sources close to the investigation say that her body was located by cadaver dogs in a shallow grave.

The search for Rachel McMahon began last Sunday morning. Her nine-year-old brother awoke during a storm and went to his sister's room at three a.m., but she wasn't in her bed. The police contacted friends and neighbors, but no one had seen Rachel.

The investigation was stymied by the missing girl's own parents, who had a wild party the night she went missing, later identified by this paper as a "swingers' party" where married couples swap sex partners for an evening of drugs, drinking, and sex. Because of the delay in obtaining a guest list, incomplete statements by both Mr. and Mrs. McMahon, and the two-day storm that destroyed physical evidence, the investigation was delayed.

No one has been arrested for the crime, but sources close to the investigation indicate a search warrant has been issued for one of the McMahons' guests who has been in police custody for two days.

The Newark office of the Federal Bureau of Investigation, working in close conjunction with the Newark Police Department, devoted all available agents to interview witnesses, process evidence, and search for Rachel. Media Information Officer Special Agent Dominic Theissen stated, "We are deeply saddened at the discovery of Rachel McMahon's body late this afternoon. An autopsy and thorough investigation will be completed to ensure that justice will be swift."

The McMahons were unavailable for comment.

The FBI confirmed that there is no connection between Rachel McMahon's disappearance and that of Camille Todd, a twelve-year-old girl who went missing from Newark the previous week.

On the surface, the case appeared straightforward—an eleven-year-old girl had been kidnapped from her bedroom late on a Saturday night. The time of her disappearance was a bit sketchy. No one had seen her between 10:00 p.m. and 3:00 a.m. Her brother told police they'd been playing games in their playroom until 10:00 p.m. when she went to her room to call her best friend. He fell asleep and woke up at 3:00 a.m. The house was quiet, he went to her room, and she wasn't in her bed. Her friend told police, and phone records confirmed, that they'd spoken for nearly an hour, hanging up at 11:03 p.m. Rachel wanted to go over to her friend's house that night, but the mother had forbidden it. For the first day of the investigation, local police falsely believed that Rachel had either run away or left to visit her friend. The search focused on the four blocks between the McMahon home and the Miller home.

Because of the age of the missing girl, the FBI was called more as a formality in case there was foul play. In his personal notes, Tony had written:

The local PD covered their ass by calling us, but they didn't seriously consider her disappearance a kidnapping until they interviewed the neighbors and learned about the party the night before.

An attached newspaper article printed the day before Rachel's body was found illustrated that this wasn't a typical neighborhood get-together.

A neighbor, who spoke on the condition of anonymity, said he was at the McMahons' party Saturday night.
"We're swingers. It's all safe; we have rules; nothing bad has ever happened." The neighbor, who is also married, said he'd never seen the McMahon children at the parties and assumed they were staying with relatives. "We're consenting adults."

The closing of one of the earlier articles, before Rachel's body was found, seemed important to Lucy, so she wrote it down in her notebook.

Search parties have been looking for eleven-year-old Rachel for the past twenty-four hours. Notably missing from the search is her father, Aaron McMahon, who has been interviewed by both local police and the FBI regarding his daughter's kidnapping.

What made that interesting was that the next day the newspaper reported that the mother, Pilar McMahon, was a person of interest. Both McMahons had lied to police about the nature of the party on Saturday night and whether any of their guests knew the children were home. Other inconsistencies in the McMahons' statements had been highlighted by Tony in his own notes. He wrote:

Their daughter is missing yet they both lied about the orgy. Neither admitted, until confronted with evidence and witness statements, that they hosted a sex party for ten invited guests, but a total of fifteen people had access to the home that evening. Originally, Mr. McMahon said that it was a neighborhood BBQ, stating as much to both responding officers, the local media, and in his initial statement to the FBI. Mrs. McMahon said she thought her daughter was trying to get back at her because of an earlier argument, but the longer Rachel was missing, the more distraught she became.

The press had gone after the parents after it was leaked that they were swingers. A new article penned by Rosemary Weber appeared every morning, each one putting a more unsavory and sensational twist on their lives. Nothing was held back. How much was true and how much exaggeration Lucy couldn't tell, but Tony's notes showed deep contempt because of the delay in information coming from the parents. Ultimately, however, their obstructions couldn't have saved Rachel from her fate, because evidence proved she'd been dead within hours after her abduction.

Hard physical evidence had led police to Benjamin John Kreig. Kreig had been stalking Mrs. McMahon after he'd attended one of their sex parties a year before. Two weeks before Rachel's disappearance, he'd confronted

Mrs. McMahon about hooking up again, and she said it disturbed her. She told her husband, but neither McMahon had seen him at the party. Two witnesses said he'd been there—they both saw him in the family room, which was adjacent to the staircase that led to Rachel's bedroom—but no one else saw him.

Police rightfully questioned why it took evidence of his guilt to prompt Mrs. McMahon's memory of the conversation.

But what was the most heartbreaking for Lucy to read was the statement of Peter McMahon, the nine-year-old brother of the victim. Tony, who had a degree in child psychology, interviewed him. The first part of the interview was Peter recounting what he and Rachel did until she left the attic playroom just before ten the evening she was kidnapped. Tony noted that Peter Mc-Mahon's statement was consistent in all the key facts.

Supervisory Special Agent Tony Presidio, Federal Bureau of Investigation, Newark Field Office
    Annette K. Frederick, Washington Department of Social and Health Services
    Peter James McMahon, brother of Rachel Mc-Mahon, 9

TP: You told the police officer who came to your house that you went to your sister's room in the middle of the night. Why?
PETER: Whenever I wake up in the middle of the night I go to Rachel's room.
TP: Not your mom and dad?
PETER: (unresponsive)
AF: Nothing you say here is going to get you into any trouble. I promise you, Peter, you did nothing wrong.

PETER: Rachel always lets me sleep on her floor if I have a nightmare.

TP: Do you have a lot of nightmares?

PETER: Sometimes. Sometimes I just wake up because I have to pee, but I don't like my room because the branches from the tree next door scratch my window in the wind. Rachel's room doesn't have any trees outside.

TP: You fell asleep in the attic?

PETER: Dad made it a real room, and we have a TV and video games and beanbag chairs.

TP: Sounds like a great place to hang out.

PETER: I guess. The rain was really loud, though. That's what woke me up.

TP: And you went to Rachel's room?

PETER: She wasn't there. I thought she went to Jessie's house and didn't tell me.

TP: Why did you think that?

PETER: Because Rachel wanted to spend the night there, but Jessie was grounded.

TP: Does Rachel sneak out of the house a lot?

PETER: (unresponsive)

TP: Rachel isn't in any trouble. I promise you, cross my heart, I won't get Rachel in trouble. It's important we have all the facts so we can find her.

PETER: She did it a couple times. But she always came back before Mom and Dad woke up. So I went to her bed to wait for her.

TP: When you walked into the room, what did you feel?

PETER: I don't know.

TP: Was the room warm? Cold? Was her bed warm?

PETER: Oh. She left her window open a little. I closed it because her room was freezing.

TP: Is that how she sneaks out? Through the window?
PETER: No—she uses the back door.
TP: You thought she was at her friend Jessie's house. You didn't go to your mom and dad?
PETER: (unresponsive)
TP: Peter, why didn't you go to your parents?
PETER: I did, in the morning, when she didn't come back.
TP: But not to their room.
PETER: I didn't want to bother them. In case they had someone spend the night.
TP: Has that happened before?
PETER: Yeah.

Lucy's heart went out to the boy Peter McMahon had been, but her instincts told her this boy was now twenty-four and had had a tragedy heaped onto his dysfunctional upbringing. There had been no signs of physical abuse, but emotional abuse and neglect could be just as powerful a negative force in a child's life.

Tony had a lot of private notes on the McMahon case. It wasn't unusual for agents to keep a second set of private files. They often only contained copies of the official records, but many of the investigators wrote down their personal observations. Technically, anything written down while investigating a crime should be part of the record, but Lucy knew that wasn't always the case.

Lucy now understood why Tony had been melancholy thinking about the boy. He had no one to protect him while all this was going on, no one to shield him from the evil in his life. Violence was part of society, but society tried to protect the young and innocent from the results. And when that failed, hope seemed to be lost.

Lucy sat at her computer and quickly input all the pertinent information about Peter McMahon. Tony had included everything in the file except Peter's Social Security number, but Lucy didn't need that. She had his parents—Aaron and Pilar McMahon—his date of birth, and where he was born. Logically, Tony would have either contacted friends of his involved in the case or used the FBI database, and maybe that's how he found out that the father was in Seattle and the mother had remarried and was living in Texas. Both far away from New Jersey.

Tony had scribbled a note that Margaret Gray had died ten years ago at the age of seventy-nine, and Tony had said that he thought Peter had gone to live with the grandmother in Florida. What had happened to him after? Lucy quickly learned that Pilar's maiden name was Gray, so Margaret was Peter McMahon's maternal grandmother. Further checking confirmed the information.

There was nothing on Peter McMahon that she could find in New Jersey or Florida.

Seven years ago, after Lucy's all-too-public ordeal, she'd considered changing her name. But more than exposure, she feared losing her sense of identity. She could have easily slipped into a made-up life in an effort to forget who she was and what had happened. But changing her name would have been a Band-Aid, and she would never forget what had happened.

Over the years, she'd encountered many victims who had opted to clean the slate with a new identity. Sometimes it was merely changing their first name or going back to their maiden name after an abusive relationship. What if the parents or grandmother wanted to give Peter a clean slate? To help him forget what had happened?

She shivered and didn't know why. Except—a child

of nine would always remember. She would never forget her nephew Justin. They'd been together nearly every day for years, because her mother babysat him while his mother worked. He and Lucy were more like twins than nephew and aunt. If Peter's family wanted to suppress memories of his sister, in their effort to help or purge their own demons and grief, they may have changed his name. Maybe that's why Tony could find nothing on him today.

Lucy put all the notes aside and downloaded a copy of Rosemary Weber's *Sex, Lies, and Family Secrets,* the book about the McMahon family and the tragedy that befell them. While Tony's notes were good, Lucy needed more info about the case. She didn't know if she could trust Weber's writing on the matter, but if she doubted something, she could ask Tony.

All this was a mere Band-Aid, Lucy thought as she picked up her cell phone and called Sean. A book, published when Peter was fourteen and living in Florida with his grandmother, wouldn't tell Lucy where he was or what he was doing today.

Sean answered, panic in his voice. "What's wrong?"

"Why would you think something's wrong?"

"Calls in the middle of the night are never good news."

Lucy glanced at her clock. One forty-five. "I am so sorry, Sean. I didn't realize it was so late."

"So you weren't dreaming of me and just had to call and hear my voice?" he said with mock offense.

She smiled. "It's always nice to hear your voice."

"It would be better in person."

"I'm calling for another favor."

"You know, I'm going to start keeping a tally. All these favors are going to add up, and I'm going to cash them in for a real vacation."

"Real vacation? Maybe it would be safer for us to vacation at home." They'd tried to go away together several times, and each one had ended in murder.

"Superstitious?"

"Of course not."

"Just leave it to me. Tell me what you need."

She quickly explained why she was looking for Peter McMahon, and the loose connection to the Rosemary Weber homicide. "Can you find out—legally—if Peter McMahon changed his name?"

"As an adult, easy. As a child? Possibly. Depends on the circumstances. If I can cut a couple corners, I can definitely get you the information."

"Let's try this legally, okay?"

"You're the boss."

"Can I quote you on that?"

Sean laughed, and Lucy shut down her computer. It *was* late and she had to be up in four hours.

"I'm going to bed," Lucy said.

Sean sighed. "Wish I were there, princess."

CHAPTER EIGHT

Ten Years Ago

Two weeks after my fourteenth birthday, Grams went into the hospital after coughing up blood. The doctor said she had pneumonia and needed to stay, and asked if I had any family. I told them my parents were dead and Grams was all I had. I think the nurses felt sorry for me, because they let me stay with her.

I think *I* felt sorry for me, because I blamed Grams for getting sick. "I need you," I told her. "You shouldn't have been gardening in the rain."

Grams loved her garden. I helped her, sometimes, but I think she liked to be alone to pull weeds and turn the soil and plant her flowers. I helped carry pallets of flowers, mowed the lawn, and trimmed the bushes because the shears were too heavy for her. But Grams spent hours every day outside.

It didn't rain a lot in Florida, but whenever it did Grams got sick. Like now. Except now was worse because she was seventy-nine and had been slowly dying ever since Grandpa died when I was five.

I knew she wouldn't live until September, when she'd be eighty. The doctors wouldn't say it, but they didn't tell me she was coming home, either. They said things like "We're doing everything we can" and "She's strong," and "Give it time." Never that she was going to die, but never that she'd get better.

It wasn't fair! I needed her.

"Read to me, Peter." Grams had been in the hospital for three days. I thought she might come home today, but the doctors said no. She looked sick. She'd never *looked* sick until three days ago. Tired, maybe, but not sick.

I picked up book 6 in the *Chronicles of Narnia* series. She'd bought me the books the first Christmas I lived with her, before my sister's killer was put on trial. I read them because there was nothing else I could do—I couldn't sleep more than a couple hours a night, I couldn't go to school without someone talking about Rachel or my parents. Even in Florida, people knew. Especially after that reporter published a book about it. Why would somebody do that? Write a book about Rachel's murder and the bizarre life my parents lived. People whispered when they didn't think I could hear, even the teachers. Grams got rid of her television, so at home I didn't have to remember if I didn't want to.

But I'd never forget Rachel.

Grams's eyesight was poor, and a few months ago she asked me to read my favorite book to her. I don't know if the Narnia stories were my favorites, but I knew Grams would like them. There was one more book after *The Silver Chair,* and I wanted to finish the series for her. Maybe if I read slowly enough, she'd get better.

I read until she slept, and then I cried. I hated her for being sick, and I hated me for being mad at an old woman. I hated God for killing everyone I loved. My insides were black like an unswept chimney. Dark and full of ash. I didn't want to be here or anywhere. I wanted to die when Grams did.

I was too big to curl up with Grams anymore, but I put the side railing down and put my head next to her thin arm. She smelled old and sweet—the sweet from the apricot shampoo she liked.

Rachel walked into Grams's room. I stared at her, because I didn't believe she was there.

I must have fallen asleep, because ghosts aren't real.

"You can't come back," I told her.

"I know," she said. She looked at Grams. "She's going to die, Peter."

"No, she's not." I sounded nine again.

"What are you going to do?" she asked.

I didn't answer. She wasn't real. She wasn't here. She was dead, and I'd never see her again. When Grams died, I would be alone.

"Are you going home?"

"They moved."

"That's not what I meant."

"I know."

Grams, don't die. Please don't die.

I woke up and of course Rachel wasn't there. But Grams was, and she was petting my hair like I was her puppy. I cried again.

"Shh," she whispered. "You're stronger than you think. Believe in yourself, Peter, like I believe in you."

"I don't want you to die." My voice cracked and broke like my heart.

"We don't have a choice when our Father calls us home. Go get the last book. Read it to me, Peter."

Five days later, an hour after I finished reading *The Last Battle,* Grams died.

CHAPTER NINE

Georgetown, Washington, D.C.

Sean Rogan woke up early Thursday morning and walked eight blocks to the gym with his partner at RCK East, Patrick Kincaid.

"Did you find anything on Laughlin?" Patrick asked.

"So far, he appears clean and I haven't found any connections between him and Lucy or with anyone in your family. But it's taking forever to get what I need."

Patrick laughed. "You get pissy when you can't break the rules."

"I don't break the rules." *Much.* "I bend them."

Sean usually sent the grunt work for background checks to RCK headquarters in Sacramento—they had more staff than the two-man office he and Patrick ran in D.C. In the digital age, information and how it was obtained changed rapidly. It took time to legally and quietly research anyone, and running a background on a federal agent had to be handled with special care.

In addition, Sean didn't want his brother looking over his shoulder. Duke wouldn't have a problem with a pro bono request from Lucy, but Sean preferred to keep his personal projects personal.

"So what *do* you know?" Patrick asked.

"Laughlin's thirty-nine, from Missouri, been an agent for fourteen years, master's from Northwestern in accounting—who gets a master's in accounting?"

Patrick rolled his eyes. He opened the gym door for Sean and they both swiped their membership cards at the kiosk.

"He's worked on the White Collar Squad in Detroit for the past five years, part of the joint gang task force, where his specialty is money laundering. He's SWAT certified, but not part of the Detroit mobilization team."

"Sounds like a good guy."

"On paper." He was harassing Lucy, and that made him an asshole in Sean's book.

"What does Lucy think she's going to get from this information?"

"I'm not done." They dropped their bags against the wall and picked up free weights. "She just wants information to help her figure out why he dislikes her."

"Slight exaggeration?"

"If you'd talked to Lucy, you'd think the same thing. If this guy's harassing her—"

"You'll stay out of it," Patrick said. "Don't make waves, not now."

It irritated Sean that Patrick thought he'd jeopardize Lucy's career. "I'm doing what she asked. She can use the information as she sees fit."

Patrick hadn't been happy when Sean first started dating his sister, but Sean supposed if he had a younger sister he'd be protective as well. Patrick seemed to have adjusted over the last few months, which was a relief, since they'd been friends long before Sean fell in love with Lucy.

Sean continued, "I think she talked to Kate, and whatever happened, Lucy is now more concerned. She didn't give me the details, but there's something weird going on. I trust her instincts."

"So if Lucy knows his history, she can profile him and adjust the way she interacts."

Sean nodded. "That's how Lucy would handle it."

"Maybe it's you he has the problem with," Patrick teased. "From your old days."

Any other time, Sean would have laughed—it was common knowledge that he'd been a gifted hacker and now was hired to test Internet security for companies and governments. But he was worried about one crime no one was supposed to know about—yet at least one person did. Five more months and the statute of limitations would be up, and then Sean could breathe easier.

"Didn't know you were so touchy," Patrick said.

"You might be right, but it might not be me, specifically. Remember how Noah Armstrong hated me because of RCK?"

Patrick glanced at him with mock surprise. "You mean he likes you now?"

Sean glared at Patrick. Special Agent Noah Armstrong wasn't Sean's favorite person. Whether Noah admitted it or not, it was obvious he was infatuated with Lucy, and that irritated Sean. But they had called a truce, and Sean respected Noah. "Regarding Laughlin," Sean continued, "he could very well have a problem with Lucy because of another Kincaid. No military service, but I can go a little deeper. The sooner I find the connection the better for Lucy. Information is power."

"Good thing, it keeps our bills paid. If you need my help, let me know." Patrick waved at an attractive tall and lanky blonde who smiled as she approached them. "I'll see you in a couple of hours."

"Who's that?"

"Brandy. We're playing racquetball."

"Brandy *Dale*?"

"Yep." Patrick had been seeing the daughter of one of their former clients, but Sean hadn't met Brandy yet.

"We should go out this weekend, the four of us."

Patrick shook his head. "It's not going to last."

"You know that?"

"Yeah, unfortunately I do. I'll tell you later." Patrick smiled and met Brandy halfway. He kissed her warmly; then they walked toward the racquetball courts.

Very strange. And it threw a wrench in Sean's life—he'd been counting on Patrick disappearing this weekend so he and Lucy could have some much-needed alone time. But Sean couldn't worry about his partner's love life or this weekend.

Sean finished his basic workout, then ran three miles on the treadmill and considered what Patrick had said about why Laughlin might have an issue with Lucy. By the time he got home an hour later, he had an idea based on the fact that Lucy didn't want to talk to Kate. There must be history between Laughlin and Kate, and it would have to go back to Kate's rookie years in the FBI, long before she'd met the Kincaid family. It was a good place to start.

After his shower, Sean pulled Laughlin's credit reports for the last fifteen years so he could piece together his life in the Bureau. The records provided enough of a skeleton of Rich Laughlin's financial history to give Sean more paths to follow.

After graduating from Northwestern, Laughlin worked fifteen months at the Chicago accounting firm of Glade and Marsh. They specialized in corporate audits. No surprise that the FBI would recruit from there. How did Laughlin come across their radar? Work on a case that turned criminal? Testify in court? Sean made a note.

Laughlin did his time at the Academy but maintained a Chicago residence for several years, even though he never moved back to the Windy City. Why? Had he planned to return? Have a roommate? A lover? There was no record of any marriage in Illinois, Missouri, or Michigan. He finally sold the condo four years after he left.

After he graduated from the Academy, he'd been assigned to the L.A. field office and took up residence in the San Fernando Valley. Two years later his credit profile shifted east, first D.C. for a short time, then Alexandria, Virginia. Sean did a quick property search and learned Richard Douglas Laughlin had owned a town house in Alexandria and still owned it.

That's when Sean's instincts began to twitch.

Sean would bet the bank that Laughlin had worked out of the D.C. regional office before Detroit. There was a slight chance he may have been assigned to national headquarters, but since he only had a few years with the Bureau at the time, Sean gave odds to the field office. Which meant that Laughlin could have worked with Kate.

Sean quickly mapped out a time line. Kate had been in the Washington, D.C., field office twelve years ago—if they overlapped, it would have been only for a few months.

Laughlin had transferred to Detroit five years ago but still owned his town house. Sean did a reverse search and learned that Laughlin leased it to a married couple. A few clicks later, Sean found the current resident: Clark Mitchell, a doctor at GWU, and his wife, Lydia, an analyst for the FBI.

Maybe it wasn't about Lucy but all about Kate.

Sean needed to dig a little deeper, but he couldn't call Kate or Hans Vigo. Noah hadn't been in the D.C. office five years ago. The only thing Sean could do was find out exactly when Laughlin moved to D.C. and determine if

Kate was there at the same time. And if she was, Sean would give the information to Lucy and she could decide how to use it.

It was nearly noon when his computer e-mailed him a report. It wasn't about Rich Laughlin but Peter McMahon. Sean almost forgot he'd started a deep background when Lucy woke him up at almost two in the morning.

Every McMahon it spat out at him wasn't the Peter McMahon Lucy was looking for. Sean did find a Peter Gray who had attended college in New Jersey, but there was no record of graduation or transfer.

Dropout? The name was common enough that tracking the right one, with no address or Social Security number, would be difficult.

But Sean loved a challenge.

CHAPTER TEN

New York City

Suzanne hadn't met SSA Tony Presidio before, but she certainly knew him by reputation. Though he was no longer with the Behavioral Science Unit, he was greatly respected within the Bureau and often consulted on cases outside of his field office. He wasn't a large man, an inch shorter than her five foot nine and trim.

"I appreciate you taking the time to come to New York." She led him through the maze of cubicles and hallways of the New York regional FBI office.

"I'm hoping I can help."

Suzanne opened the door to a small conference room. She tossed her stack of papers on the table and motioned for Tony to sit. "We have a mutual friend, I heard. Lucy Kincaid."

He smiled. "One of my students. She's one of the reasons I'm here. She's concerned about her name being in the victim's files."

Suzanne slid over a thin folder. "This is all Weber had on Lucy, but as you can see, she planned on digging around."

Tony opened the file and skimmed it. "Weber wanted

to play up the FBI's use of civilian consultants. I found out last night from national headquarters that she filed an FOIA for Lucy's FBI file."

"They wouldn't have given it."

"No. She's an agent; basic information would have been released—hometown, college, training—nothing else. But the information is out there; it's just a matter of who talks."

Suzanne eyed him suspiciously. "You're not suggesting that Lucy had anything to do with the murder?"

"You ran her when you learned her name was in the file."

Suzanne nodded. "I ran everybody, but I didn't believe she had anything to do with it."

"You ran her boyfriend as well."

"Doesn't mean I think he did it, either. Just covering all bases."

Tony raised an eyebrow. "I assumed they passed."

"Rogan was in Sacramento; Lucy was at Quantico. I wouldn't say it was impossible that one or both of them *could* have come here, killed her, and covered their tracks, but that's a lot of travel, hacking, falsifying documents, and convincing more than one person to lie."

Tony laughed. "Good to know they're cleared."

"I made you copies of all Weber's files on the Cinderella Strangler case—who she talked to, who she met with, her ideas—but the research for her previous books is stored at Columbia University. Their manuscript preservation program, something like that. Detective DeLucca is tracking down the research assistant now."

"Good. I'll take everything back with me to Quantico—if that's all right with you."

"Less paperwork for me? You can have it."

"I went to the scene last night when I arrived, and concur with the detective's report. Staged to look like a robbery. Do you have her phone records?"

"Just calls—we're getting a warrant for her text messages; it's going to take a day or two. We also have e-mails. Nothing that indicates who she was meeting at Citi Field or why. Except"—Suzanne flipped through papers—"this note on her desk."

She gave him a copy of a sticky note that had a time written down.

" 'Nine thirty—RB.' "

"I don't think it's a coincidence. It was the last thing she wrote on that pad of paper, but she didn't take it with her. Maybe wrote it down when she was on the phone with someone, or got an e-mail, or as a reminder to herself. But she was killed close to nine thirty on Tuesday night."

" 'RB'—initials?"

"Probably. We're running the initials through her address book, e-mails, phone lists. We have eight possible IDs so far, but half of those are outside of the greater New York area. NYPD is interviewing the others."

"Can I see the list?"

Suzanne pulled it up on her cell phone. "DeLucca e-mailed it to me this morning."

Tony looked. "Just names?"

"For now."

"If she was meeting with someone, at night, even at a place she felt safe, it would be someone she'd worked with before or met before. Probably someone with information she wanted on the Cinderella Strangler."

Suzanne nodded. "That was our thought. You said you knew her?"

"I was lead agent on the Rachel McMahon kidnapping

in Newark. Weber was a reporter. We didn't get along, but I didn't have to deal with her directly—that's why we have a media information officer."

"Don't I know it," Suzanne mumbled. She would never live down the one time she spoke to the press and earned her "Mad Dog" moniker. And, by Tony's expression, he knew all about it.

He said, "She was tenacious and liked scandal, always went for the most salacious details of any investigation she covered, but I never knew her to fabricate her stories, or lie about key facts."

"Did you read the book she wrote about your case?"

"No. It came out five years after Rachel McMahon was murdered, and I didn't want to relive that tragedy. Public Relations reviewed it and said there were no factual errors."

"You looked at the reports, you knew the victim, are you thinking any differently than DeLucca and me?"

Tony took a moment to ponder, and Suzanne both appreciated his concentration and worried that she had missed something.

"The killer wanted the police to think robbery, but because we know that Weber had a meeting scheduled with 'RB' I think it's clear it wasn't a random robbery. But I don't think this 'RB' knew anything about it. It was a trap."

"There were no defensive wounds on the victim. Nothing to indicate a struggle or that she fought."

"Because either she knew her attacker, or he acted quickly. No discussion, no hesitation."

"Which holds with the preliminary coroner's report."

"I saw that." Tony flipped through his notes and read, " 'One six-inch thrust into the lungs and heart.' "

"Some knowledge of anatomy."

"Perhaps. Or self-educated. The lack of hesitation tells me he planned on killing her, there was no other purpose of the meeting."

"He."

"Most likely a male. During my flight I went through the Cinderella Strangler case and Weber's previous books and numerous newspaper articles. There are many potential suspects, but I can narrow it somewhat."

"I wasn't a fan of psychology in investigations until I worked with Lucy six months ago."

Tony smiled, but it didn't reach his eyes, which looked sad and reflective. "You use psychology all the time. Most good cops do. Interviewing suspects, using what they say, what they don't say, their body language, all as cues in how you question them. How hard you need to push. Assessing how reliable a witness might be. Knowing whether someone is lying. Most cops will say it's experience, or their gut. It's really psychology they learned simply by doing their job."

"So you can narrow it down?"

"It is definitely someone who feels they or a loved one was damaged by what Rosemary Weber wrote."

"Wrote. Past tense."

"Yes. I don't think her killer has anything to do with the Cinderella Strangler book she was writing."

Suzanne wasn't certain she believed that. "You're going to have to do better."

"When we spoke yesterday, you said she'd just started researching the case. She was gathering files, hadn't interviewed anyone, hadn't spoken to the victim's families. No one knew what angle she was taking, or how she planned on writing the book."

"I can guess. Others may have, too, and not liked it."

"But there's nothing tangible." Tony paused again,

looked at his papers, but Suzanne didn't think he was seeing anything. "I did a cursory assessment of the victims' families and nothing popped up to indicate that any would resort to violence, especially *before* the book was written. If anything, they'd want to use Weber to immortalize their daughters, to show the world their girls are loved and greatly missed. But," he continued, "after the fact, it could be a survivor or a family member who was upset with what was said, and wants to take it back. Or perhaps upset with how they were portrayed. Lucy is reading Weber's three published books now to assess exactly that—anyone who was portrayed in an embarrassing manner."

"But not just her books. It could be an article or something else she wrote."

Tony nodded. "The problem with this theory is that I'd expect to see some sort of verbal or written threat to Weber before she was killed."

"Except that the killer was extremely careful—so far, we have no physical evidence linking the killer to the crime. No hair or fibers, no blood, no security footage."

"Well planned and premeditated. The killer doesn't want to be caught."

"Most don't."

"I wonder. . . ." His voice trailed off.

"What?" she prompted.

"Was Weber his first victim, or were there more?"

"But if it's personal, would there be more?"

"Possibly. I keep going back to the manner of death. The killer did not hesitate with the stiletto. Even the choice of weapon is interesting—why a stiletto knife and not a gun? A wider blade? It's not as intimate as strangulation, but it's far more intimate than a gun."

Suzanne's phone vibrated. "It's Detective DeLucca." She answered. "What do you have?"

"Just met with the faculty advisor for Weber's research assistant. Up to interviewing the kid and grabbing all her research?"

"When and where?"

"Butler Library, twenty minutes."

"Thirty." She hung up and turned to Tony. "Why don't you join me?"

It was just past noon when Suzanne and Tony met up with DeLucca outside of Butler Library at Columbia University. Suzanne introduced the two men.

DeLucca said, "Weber brings on a research assistant for each project through the university's grad program. Prof Duncan Cleveland is the faculty advisor for the program. It's a win-win for the student—they get a stipend and college credit. Weber's current assistant is Kip Todd, and Cleveland says he'll be here. He has a small office on the sixth floor."

"What do we know about him?" she asked as they walked up the wide steps to the main entrance.

"Grad student, got his undergrad in Buffalo in English Lit with a minor in communications. The victim picked him from nineteen applicants to be her assistant—according to Cleveland, she was demanding but fair, and liked to mentor."

"We should talk to her former assistants," Tony said.

DeLucca opened the heavy door and Suzanne stepped into the air-conditioned foyer. The cool air raised bumps on her skin. "I have the list. One is in the city; one has relocated. Kip Todd is her third."

"I thought she was working on her fourth book?" Suzanne asked.

"She wrote the first book while she was working as a reporter in Newark. *Sex, Lies, and Family Secrets.*" DeLucca rolled his eyes.

Tony said, "Unfortunately, I'm very familiar with that case."

"Suzi said you were one of the investigators."

Suzanne punched DeLucca in the arm. She hated when he called her Suzi in public.

Tony stopped them and said quietly, "Have you identified the 'RB' Weber wrote she was meeting the night she was killed?"

"I have uniforms checking them out right now."

Suzanne said, "Tony thinks it was a setup, that the killer used the meeting to get her alone."

"Seems too dumb," DeLucca said. "Too easy to trace."

"Meaning," Tony said, "that the killer isn't the RB she was supposed to meet."

DeLucca considered his theory. "I can see that. But how would the meet be set up? Wouldn't she recognize the voice? There were no e-mails on her hard drive, though I have techs going through deleted messages now."

"Any of the RBs on your list affiliated with the Cinderella Strangler investigation?"

"Yes," DeLucca said, pulling out his notepad. "Rob Banker. He was the lead reporter covering the investigation for the *Times* and according to Detective Panetta, he seemed to have inside information."

"A leak from NYPD," Suzanne said.

DeLucca shot her a nasty glance, but she didn't care. He *had* called her "Suzi."

"Wherever the information came from, he had it," DeLucca said. "The other three don't appear to have any direct involvement with that case."

"A fellow reporter—I can see Weber meeting him in a parking lot," Tony said.

"He lives in Queens—not far from Citi Field. But why would he set her up?"

"I don't think he did—I think the killer used his name."

"Too many what-ifs," DeLucca said. He pulled out his phone. "I'll check him out myself, as soon as we're done here."

He sent a message, then pocketed his phone. "We can't find Weber's phone, but she uses a digital planner that she backed up on her computer. The last back-up was two nights before she was murdered, and there was no scheduled meeting."

"What was her last appointment?" Tony asked.

"The morgue," DeLucca said. "She made a notation to pick up files. We checked with the staff, and she'd filed an FOIA for the official autopsy reports of all Cinderella Strangler victims."

"I talked to Panetta this morning," DeLucca continued, "and she's been hounding him. He keeps sending her to you, Suz, since it became an FBI case when your SWAT team took out the suspect. She'd pulled the initial police reports of each Cinderella Strangler victim from the responding precinct."

Tony said, "I'm going to talk to the librarian and ask them to pull the archived manuscripts and catch up with you."

Suzanne and Joe went up to the sixth floor and asked for directions at the information desk to Cleveland's grad student office. They found Kip Todd sitting at a table with several books open in front of him. He was twenty-six, attractive, blond. By the way his legs were folded under the table, he was at least six feet tall and rail thin. He glanced up when they entered, surprise in his eyes.

"Mr. Todd? Detective DeLucca, NYPD, and Special Agent Madeaux, FBI. We have a few questions about your employer."

He blinked rapidly, then sighed. "I'm still in shock." He closed his books after marking his place. "Professor Cleveland said you'd probably want to talk to me."

Suzanne sat across from Kip while Joe stood. "You spent a lot of time with her. Whatever you know may be helpful in finding out who killed her," Suzanne said.

"I really liked Rosemary. She was tough, but I learned so much."

"You were her assistant for the book she was currently researching?"

"The Cinderella Strangler—" His eyes widened. "You're *Suzanne Madeaux*. Oh, wow. Rosemary really wanted to talk to you. She said without you her book wouldn't happen."

"Then it wouldn't have happened."

Kip looked at her quizzically.

Suzanne said, "It's up to my boss's boss, and they usually assign a media rep to work on these things."

Joe said, "Did you know who she was supposed to meet at Citi Field last night?"

Kip shook his head. "I didn't know anything about the meeting, but that's not strange. She assigned me specific projects."

"Like?"

"She had me pulling records. Do you realize that four different morgues handled the victims and the suspect, depending on where they were killed?"

"I'm aware," Suzanne said.

"That's a lot of groundwork. Then verifying all the information—Rosemary was a stickler for details. Everything had to be verified and reverified."

"Where were you Tuesday?"

"Tuesday I went to the Jacobi Medical Center, in the Bronx. Yesterday, before I knew she was killed, I was taking pictures outside of the suspect's art gallery."

Joe asked, "What about Rob Banker?"

"The *Times* reporter? They were friends."

"Was he consulting on this particular book?"

"She talked to him about it. I wasn't part of those conversations."

Suzanne asked, "Did you or Ms. Weber contact anyone involved in the Cinderella Strangler case who seemed agitated or angry about the prospect of their lives being dragged through the mud?"

"Rosemary handles these situations carefully. She's very fair. Have you read her books?"

"No," Suzanne said. And she didn't want to, though she thought she might have to now. Lucy was reading them; maybe Suzanne could rely on her analysis.

Joe asked, "Did you go with Ms. Weber on the interviews?"

"She hasn't even gotten that far. She sent preliminary communications to the key people in the case—like you," he said to Suzanne, "and Detective Panetta, the reporters who documented the investigation. The guy Barnett."

Barnett, who'd been a key suspect in the Cinderella Strangler case, would not want to be the subject of any true crime book, not when it would drag his younger brother through this mess again. Barnett had a temper as well. But Suzanne didn't see him stabbing Rosemary Weber and stealing her ring and phone to make it look like a robbery. And why would she meet with him in the parking lot of a baseball stadium? Still, Suzanne would talk to him. If he thought that Weber was a threat to his younger brother, he might hire someone to kill her. It didn't feel right to Suzanne, but she'd have to confirm it one way or the other.

"How did the meeting go with Barnett?" she asked.

"She talked to him on the phone; that's all I know. She didn't give me any notes to transcribe."

"Notes?"

"She records everything; I transcribe them. But she hasn't done any interviews yet. The only things I've transcribed were her notes to herself."

"Does she use a tape recorder? Her phone?"

"A small tape recorder. She has several."

No tape recorder had been found on Weber's body.

Suzanne asked, "Did Ms. Weber ask you to research a consultant on the case, Lucy Kincaid?"

Kip shook his head and Suzanne was relieved; then Kip said, "She mentioned her, but didn't ask me to do anything. Why?"

"Kincaid's involvement wasn't part of the public file."

Kip said, "Rosemary knew everyone. And I mean *everyone*. She knew things she probably shouldn't know. You should read her books—you'll know what I mean."

Joe said, "I'll need all your notes and files."

"Why?"

"Part of the investigation." Joe slid over his card. "To my attention, please."

Suzanne asked, "Did Rosemary receive any threatening letters or e-mails?"

"Not that I know of. But she had a P.O. box and she handled her own mail. There was this one guy, though, up at Rikers, who kept sending her letters. Every week. He wanted her to write a book about his crimes and prove he was innocent. She laughed over them and threw them away. Said she got hundreds of letters from prisoners claiming they were framed, but this guy was the most persistent."

"Do you remember his name?"

Kip shook his head. "Sorry."

"If you remember anything else that may be important to the case, please let us know." Suzanne gave Kip her card to go with Joe's. "No matter how small."

Leaving, Joe said, "What do you think?"

"I think I need to talk to Barnett and you need to check out her P.O. box and this guy from Rikers."

"Motive?"

"I don't see Barnett killing her, but he's very protective of his brother, and leave no stone unturned, right?"

"If this prisoner wrote her every week, someone at the prison knows who he is. What about the assistant?"

Suzanne raised an eyebrow. "Motive?"

"Maybe she was going to fire him, or she pissed him off. His professor said he had no complaints about his job with Weber, but you never know. I'll run him, but he seems to be what he is. In the meantime, I'm going to head over to the morgue. Want to come?"

"No. I'll talk to Barnett and let you know what I learn."

"Dinner?"

"No."

"I'll see you at seven. Same place."

"I said *no,* Joe—and this time I mean it."

I hope.

"Where's your FBI buddy?"

Suzanne had almost forgotten about Tony Presidio. She glanced at her watch, then looked at the map of the library. "Manuscript archives." She and Joe found the reference desk and asked about Tony.

The clerk looked nervous. "He's with the head librarian in the storage basement."

"Please take us down there," Suzanne said, and showed her badge.

It was a maze to finally locate Tony. He was talking in a low, angry voice to a middle-aged female librarian.

"You have protocols, but you're saying they weren't followed?"

The librarian said, "I don't know what happened, sir. I've called the director. I'm sure they were misfiled."

"But according to your records, they've never been viewed since Ms. Weber donated her archives to the library."

Suzanne approached. "What happened?"

Tony gestured to two boxes on the floor next to him. "They can't find one of Weber's boxes, but according to their computer, no one has looked at it since it was donated three years ago."

"Which box?"

"The Rachel McMahon murder."

"Security cameras?"

"We have live cameras that are monitored by campus security, but don't keep internal backup tapes," the librarian said.

"And we don't know when it went missing. Anytime in the last three years," Tony said.

He seemed unusually angry about the misplaced file box, but Suzanne didn't know him well enough to know if that was par for the course. She gave the librarian her card and said, "If it turns up, call me immediately."

"I'm assigning two of my best archivists to search for it," she said, eager to please.

"Thank you."

Suzanne walked out with Joe and Tony.

"It's about that case," Tony said.

"We don't know that," Joe said. "Why would the killer wait so many years to go after her?"

"I don't know, but she made a lot of enemies after she wrote that book, particularly in law enforcement."

"Are you saying a cop killed her?"

"No. But she highlighted the flaws in the investigation, which all stemmed from erroneous information that the victim's family provided. By the time we sorted through the truth and lies, Rachel was dead. In fact, she was dead before anyone knew she was missing."

"Maybe the research assistant knows where it is," Suzanne said.

Joe glanced at his watch. "I have to talk to the M.E. Call me if you find anything." He left, and Suzanne turned to Tony.

"Do you have any other information about why you think it's connected to McMahon?"

He shook his head. "It's odd that all three manuscript files were submitted three years ago, shortly after her third book came out, and only that one is missing."

Suzanne led the way back to the sixth floor. Kip Todd was still sitting where she'd left him, but he wasn't working. He was staring at the wall in front of him.

He seemed startled to see her again so soon.

"More questions?"

Suzanne introduced Tony. "We just came from Manuscript Archives. One of Ms. Weber's boxes is missing."

"Missing?" Kip's brows pulled together in confusion. "How?"

She didn't answer. "Did you check out any of them?"

He shook his head. "No."

"Did anyone ask you for the files? Or tell you they were looking at them?"

Again, Kip shook his head. "I'm sorry. I can help look for them; I'm familiar with manuscript archives."

"The librarian is handling it."

"Which box is missing?" Kip asked.

"The first—Rachel McMahon."

Tony said to Suzanne, "I still have my notes. I'll go through them when I get back and contact the other investigators if we need more information."

Suzanne thanked Kip again, and they walked out. "Are you coming back to headquarters with me?"

"I'd like to speak with Rob Banker."

"Right after I verify that Wade Barnett had nothing to do with this."

CHAPTER ELEVEN

FBI Academy

Glock in hand, Lucy Kincaid aimed and fired all fifteen rounds into the target. When her magazine was empty, she ejected it, popped in the second magazine, and fired fifteen more rounds.

She quickly hid her smile. If this were her official qualification test, she'd have passed with flying colors. She didn't even need to see the sheets to know that she'd scored the requisite minimum 85 of 100 points. She may have topped 95.

She glanced at Reva as the petite blonde put her own gun down, grinning. She gave Lucy a thumbs-up.

Lucy glanced in the other direction to where Alexis Sanchez was still shooting at her target. She hesitated before each shot and Lucy cringed when she realized that most of the rounds hadn't even hit the black portion of the target. Alex was book smart, focused, and brilliant with numbers—unfortunately, she had no firearm skills. They'd already lost two recruits opening week who failed the physical test; no one wanted to see anyone else leave.

"Cease fire. Guns down on the table. Step back from your station and await your score."

There was no privacy here at the gun range. All thirty-four recruits in New-Agent Class 12-14 would know who passed, who failed, and what score they got.

Carter and Eddie were standing at the two stations to the right of Lucy, between her and Reva. They had a friendly competition about who would score higher, but Lucy suspected they both had perfect scores. The eleven recruits who had military experience had an upper hand at the gun range.

Special Agent Joel Kosako went down the row to announce their scores. Lucy had heard from her sister-in-law Kate that over 70 was acceptable at this stage, because they would be practicing rigorously before the actual qualification round.

"Jackson, seventy-five. Caruthers, thirty-three."

Ouch.

"Penrose, seventy-two."

Lucy looked at Reva and smiled, but Reva frowned. She'd expected a higher score.

"Acosta, ninety-eight. Nix, ninety-eight."

"Tied?" Carter exclaimed. "Rematch!"

The instructor frowned at him and moved to Lucy. "Kincaid, ninety-three."

"You sure you weren't a soldier?" Carter asked her.

"My brother was Army," she said. "He trained me. He's going to expect me to get a perfect score before I leave." But Lucy was very happy with her score. It was her personal best on this range.

"Not that there's pressure in *perfect*," Eddie teased.

"Fields, sixty-eight. Dorfman, forty-one. Sanchez, twelve."

Carter whispered, "I'm surprised she hit the target at all."

Lucy winced. "We need to help her," she said quietly. "She'll never pass at this rate."

There was one perfect score for the first round, a former Marine. Lucy was the top female scorer, beating out Margo. Lucy was surprised, since Margo had been in the Army for three years. Had this been the real qualification round, only thirteen new agents would have passed. They had two weeks to get the others up to speed.

Kosako, a former drill sergeant, called everyone to gather in a circle.

"This is one of the worst group of shooters I've had in years," Kosako said. "Only a third of you would have passed if this was the real test. We'll be spending extra time on the range for the next two weeks, all of you. Now, we're doing it again. Reset the targets."

As Lucy jogged toward the far end of the range, a familiar shiver ran down her spine. Someone was watching her.

She shook it off—Kosako was watching all of them. She'd done well in the drill; she shouldn't worry.

She reset her target and turned to jog back to her station. She was tense as she scanned the crowd, trying to figure out who had eyes on her.

She spotted Class Supervisor SSA Paula Kean standing with Agent Laughlin right behind Lucy's station. They hadn't been there during the first round.

Laughlin caught her eye, then said something to Kean, who nodded, and glanced at Lucy.

She swallowed and turned her back on them. Put on her ear and eye protection, checked her weapon, reloaded. Focus on the routine. Focus on what she knew.

When Kosako cleared them to shoot, Lucy's muscles froze. She couldn't shoot if she was this rigid. Her first shot missed the target completely, hitting the dirt hill behind. She mentally ran through her inner procedures to calm herself, but she was now behind everyone else, and that made her more tense. Her neck ached the more she tried to force calm.

What did Laughlin want from her? What was going on between him and Kate? It was obvious Kate didn't like him, but she had refused to explain exactly what was going on. Had he threatened Lucy and Kate was trying to protect her? That would only make it worse. Kate should know that.

Yet all this speculation was only making Lucy more worried. She couldn't focus and was the last to finish. She knew she'd done poorly.

Carter leaned over and asked, "What happened?" He looked at her hands. "You're shaking."

She didn't want to talk about it. She glanced over her shoulder and saw Laughlin watching her, neither smiling nor frowning. Just staring.

"I choked," she said.

"If I hadn't seen it, I wouldn't have believed it. I didn't think anything fazed you." Carter sounded worried, and while she appreciated his concern, she didn't want anyone to worry about her. He glanced to where she'd been looking and said, "Is there a problem between you and Laughlin?"

She sighed and tried to keep the hitch out of her voice. "I don't know."

Kosako finished going through the scores and shook his head. "Saturday morning, everyone will be here at the range for extra practice."

He looked directly at Lucy. "I'm surprised, Kincaid, I had high hopes for you after day two. It's about consistency. And from what I'm seeing, Sanchez is better than you because she's consistently a bad shot. When your partner is depending on you, are you going to hit or miss? When it's not fun and games, are you going to choke?"

Lucy's chest felt like it would explode with shame and embarrassment. She'd let the pressure of being watched interfere with her performance.

She stood ramrod straight and said, "I won't choke again, sir."

Kosako said, "Let's hope you find your comfort zone, because if you shoot like you did today you won't be around for graduation."

She turned to gather her equipment. Usually, cleaning guns with her friends was both fun and social—but when she saw Agent Laughlin staring at her, her stomach sank, and she finished as quickly as possible.

Lucy focused intently on her classes that afternoon in a futile effort to block out her failure at the gun range. The deep concentration left her with a throbbing head-ache.

Thirty-two. I got a damn thirty-two!

That it wasn't the real qualification test didn't matter; it was that she'd failed because someone had been watching her. She hadn't been able to focus on the target, only on why Rich Laughlin disliked her and what it had to do with Kate.

Four weeks ago when Lucy first walked onto campus, she hadn't seen anything to make her think that either of the Class 12–14 mentors had an issue with her. Seward was from Denver, Laughlin from Detroit. Laughlin hadn't been particularly friendly, but he hadn't been critical, either—not until after she walked in on him and Kate yesterday.

But did it really matter? She'd allowed his presence to affect her performance and by doing so had jeopardized everything she'd been working so hard for. Who could she blame but herself?

Because it was still too hot to run, Lucy asked Margo if she wanted to swim, but Margo had plans with Reva for their online course work. Lucy went to the gym and stretched, then worked on free weights, then the punching bag. She was surprised no one was around. Normally at the end of the day a dozen agents from the three classes currently in rotation would be working out, including staff.

She wanted to swim. In the locker room she changed into her blue one-piece Speedo, then redressed in her shorts and gray T-shirt with her last name stenciled on the back. It was against the rules to swim without a partner, and she hoped to find someone when she got to the pool.

She opened the door—empty.

"Dammit."

"You weren't planning on swimming alone, I hope." Harden's voice behind her made her jump.

"No, sir." She closed the door. "I'd hoped someone was already inside."

"You want to swim that badly?"

She didn't know what to say. If she said yes, he'd think she was reckless and would have gone in alone until she saw him. If she said no, he'd think she was wishy-washy or lying.

Instead, she said, "Swimming is a stress reliever."

From the small twitch at the corner of his lips, he hadn't expected the answer. Sean would call that his "tell," a physical sign of either lying or surprise.

"I have some time."

"Thank you, sir."

The humidity in the room hit Lucy like it always did, warm and thick, but she'd gotten used to it since being here.

"I won't be long," she said.

"Take your time. Want me to time you?"

She raised an eyebrow. "I planned to relax, not compete, sir."

He seemed mildly disappointed but nodded and walked over to the mats and free weights in the corner, checking for wear and damage.

Lucy removed her outer clothes and dove into the water, the temperature a few degrees warmer than she preferred. Soon her body adjusted and she swam perfectly centered in the middle row. The pool was half Olympic length at eighty-two meters, a good practice size. She'd been on the swim team in high school and college, had been good enough to try out for the Olympics, but her heart hadn't been in it after everything that had happened when she graduated from high school. Still, water was the one constant in her life, from her time before Adam Scott and his cronies raped and nearly killed her to now. She was certified in water search and rescue and had recertified earlier this year.

She had to find a way to ignore Agent Laughlin, but the more she thought about him the more she realized that something was up with Kate. Kate had said Bureau politics, and Lucy wanted nothing to do with jockeying for power. She just wanted her badge and a position. She'd earned it, and she couldn't let someone else's game stop her.

And then there was Harden, who had forced her into the center of attention yesterday. But Harden had to be tough on them because it was his job to make sure they were all fit when they left. It wasn't personal with him.

As she realized the difference between what Harden did yesterday and how Laughlin made her feel today, she realized that it *was* personal with Laughlin. That she'd solved one problem but now faced another, bigger issue irritated her. She swam harder, focusing on the fluidity of the water, her breathing, and her strokes.

And she realized that in the back of her mind was the murder of Rosemary Weber.

What if she was digging into my past? What if she planned to write a book about what happened to me?

No one Lucy cared about would have talked to the woman and so much about what had happened to Lucy was still sealed, but that didn't mean Weber couldn't have made Lucy's life a living hell trying to dig up the facts. And because Lucy's rape had been shown on the Internet, there were still digital files out there. She'd never truly be free of her past.

That Weber had been murdered left Lucy feeling guilty, with relief that was short-lived. Rosemary Weber wasn't the only true crime writer out there. What if she had a partner? What if her notes were passed on to another writer?

There was nothing Lucy could do to change what might happen, and that, coupled with the watchful eyes of Rich Laughlin, had combined to throw Lucy off her game today.

She couldn't let it happen again.

Her 32 on the range was her own damn fault, not Laughlin's or Kate's or Rosemary Weber's. Lucy had allowed Laughlin to get into her head. Ninety-three was her best, but she would work her ass off to get a perfect score. She'd match the soldiers in her class as if she'd been trained in the military herself. When the real test came up, she was going to ace it, because she knew she could do it. She had to.

If she allowed stress to affect her shooting or her ability to handle physical challenges like the pull-ups, she didn't deserve to be an agent.

After twenty laps of regular strokes, she flipped and did ten laps of backstrokes. Her muscles burned and she realized she'd slacked off on her swimming regimen. She used to be able to do the backstroke with ease, but it used different muscles, muscles she hadn't used in a long while. She finished her workout with two easy laps and climbed out of the pool. Her heart raced; she felt invigorated and alive.

That's when Lucy felt Harden looking at her.

"What?" she asked.

"You're good."

"I know," she said, then added modestly, "I was on the swim team in college."

He nodded. "Could have gone to the Olympics, had you wanted."

"If you knew, why'd you ask?"

"Why didn't you?"

She shrugged. "Not sure I would have made it. I never tried to qualify."

"You don't seem like a quitter to me."

She didn't like that he was trying to analyze her or her motivations.

She grabbed her towel and dried off. "Can I speak freely, sir?"

He nodded.

"The pull-ups yesterday were unfair and unwarranted. Were they a test? To see how I handle stress?" Maybe that was Laughlin's game as well—to see how she handled the pressure. But then what were he and Kate arguing about?

Harden shrugged, looked like he was going to walk out without saying anything, then changed his mind. "You're smart enough to get through these nineteen weeks. You're physically fit, and I have no doubt you'll pass the PT test with one of the top scores. But the Academy is not just about written or physical tests. Neither is this chosen career. Don't ever forget it."

That was a long-winded *yes*.

"Thank you, sir."

He smiled, the first genuine smile she'd seen from Harden since she'd been here. "If you need a partner to swim in the future, let me know. It's obviously good for you."

After her shower, she found a message on her cell phone from Tony Presidio.

"Lucy, call me. It's important."

He'd left the message nearly an hour ago, at three thirty. She quickly dressed and called him back.

"I just got your message."

"Have you read the file I gave you?"

"Most of it. Is something wrong?"

"I need to see my notes. Something's nagging me and I can't remember what. I'm flying back tonight instead of tomorrow morning. I'll be at Quantico about nine thirty. I'll call you when I get there."

"Did you learn something about Rosemary Weber?"

"All her research and notes from the Rachel McMahon investigation are gone. She'd archived them at the Columbia University library, but the file box has disappeared. They believe it was just misplaced, but I'm certain it was stolen."

"Why?"

"I have no idea, but there's something at the edge of my memory that I'm hoping my notes will jar loose."

"Do you think Weber's murder has something to do with a fifteen-year-old crime, and not her research into the Cinderella Strangler?"

"I thought she was killed because of something she had already written, not what she was researching; and with the McMahon files gone, all fingers point to that case as being important. If you can finish reading her books tonight and put together the list of people who may have a reason to kill her, send it to both Madeaux and me, but the McMahon case is the priority."

"I will." She'd eat in her room and finish the material before he returned tonight.

"For the time being, keep this between you and me. I'll clear it with your supervisor when I get back."

CHAPTER TWELVE

New York City

Rob Banker was seventy and, aside from wrinkles around his mouth and eyes, looked surprisingly fit for being a smoker. He agreed to meet with Tony and Suzanne provided they talk outside where he could light up.

Suzanne hated cigarette smoke. She'd smoked through high school and college, quitting only when she entered the FBI Academy. Being around cigarettes, even after ten years, always made her crave just one. But one would quickly turn into a pack and she'd be back to her old habits.

"Rosie was a good egg," Rob said. "If I was twenty years younger." He took a long drag on his Marlboro.

"This conversation is off-the-record, Banker," Suzanne said.

"Why?"

"Because you're writing articles for the damn paper and I don't want my questions getting in print."

He grinned. "And I don't want to be decked."

Suzanne glared at the reporter. "I'll bring you to the Bureau and you'll miss your deadline."

"Fine, off-the-record." He exhaled, and let out the smoke in a long, angled puff.

"She had a meeting scheduled with you the night she died," Suzanne said. She didn't know for certain that it was Banker, but he'd either confirm or deny.

"She canceled on me. We were supposed to meet at nine thirty at Gilly's, the bar where we usually meet."

"Any specific reason for the meeting?"

He shrugged. "To talk. Rosemary doesn't trust a lot of people, but she and I go way back, and she bounced ideas off me. She called Monday morning and said she wanted to talk about the book—"

"The book she's writing about the Cinderella Strangler," Tony said to confirm.

Rob grinned. "I coined the phrase."

Suzanne glared at him. "The victims were suffocated."

He shrugged, puffed on his cigarette a couple times, took his time to answer. "I said as much in every article. It's what sticks. And it gave the story legs, helped get the word out to potential victims to watch out."

Suzanne wanted to argue with him, but Tony asked, "Did she tell you why she was canceling?"

"Not really. I wish I'd asked her." He seemed sincere.

"What did she say?"

"Only that she was checking out a lead on an informant."

"Informant? Like a criminal informant?"

"No—she meant someone in law enforcement who was willing to talk off the record."

"Don't you call those people sources?"

"Usually, but Rosie had a sense of humor. She liked to call cops informants."

"So she was meeting with a cop?"

"Not necessarily—could have been a secretary, a dispatcher, even a janitor, anyone who worked for NYPD, really. Or maybe, because the case was federal, someone in your own house."

Suzanne doubted that, but Tony looked like he believed it. "Anything else?" Tony asked. "Did she have any sense that she was being followed, that she could be in danger?"

"Not that she told me. But I only talked to her a couple times a month. Her sister would probably know more."

They'd already asked Bridget Weber the same question. Suzanne said, "What about threatening letters?"

"Nothing she shared with me," he said. "I assume you've talked to her new assistant."

Suzanne nodded but didn't give the reporter any other details. She gave Rob her card. "Let me know if anything comes up."

"I'd like to run a quote from you for the article I'm writing on the investigation."

"I suppose 'no comment' isn't good enough."

"Nope." He put out the stub of his cigarette in a can that was just for the smokers.

"I don't have authorization to talk to you."

"Can you confirm a couple things?"

She growled, "Depends."

"I'll make it easy. 'A source at the Bureau confirmed . . .' "

"Still depends."

"DeLucca has the case."

"Yes."

"She was robbed."

"Yes."

"But you don't think it was a robbery. You think it was related to the book she's writing."

"No comment."

"Come on, Suzanne; give me something."

"I'm not playing Clue with you."

Tony said, "I'll give you something, but you need to word it the way I tell you."

Suzanne didn't like Tony stepping in without consulting her, even though he did have seniority.

"Sure," Rob said. He took out his notepad.

"Write: 'A source high up in the Bureau said Weber's killer took her jewelry and purse in an effort to mislead police as to the motive for the murder. According to an FBI profiler, the murder was personal and the victim knew her killer. The jewelry is probably at the bottom of Flushing Bay, the source said.'"

"Okay, okay," Rob said, writing frantically. "And is it related to the Cinderella Strangler case? A relative of one of the victims?"

"Where the hell did you get that stupid idea?" Suzanne said, her temper exploding. *Where do reporters come up with this shit?*

Tony said, "Rob, listen to me—don't say anything else. Just that the police know it was staged to look like a robbery."

"Okay, off-the-record, was it someone related to this book she was writing?"

"No," Tony said. "It wasn't."

That threw Rob for a loop. "Then who?"

"If your story tomorrow leads to us identifying the killer," Tony said, "I'll make sure our media officer talks to you first."

Rob was skeptical but seemed to trust Tony.

"I'll hold you to that, Agent Presidio."

Suzanne and Tony left and she said, "Why'd you play his game?"

"I wasn't playing his game. The killer wants us to think it was a robbery. If he knows *we* know it wasn't, he'll get rid of the ring in an attempt to prove it *was*. Tomorrow, after the paper comes out."

Suzanne snapped her fingers. "And because we have a description of the ring out to all the jewelers and pawn-shops, we may get a call."

"Hopefully a call while the guy we want is still in the building, or at least caught on tape."

"Okay, you win that round. But I still don't like re-porters."

Suzanne drove Tony back to Rosemary Weber's house. Her sister was home, and after introductions she allowed Tony to go through Rosemary's office again, even though the police had been over it yesterday.

"What do you hope to find?" Suzanne asked. She still wasn't sure why Tony had wanted to come here.

"I can't imagine that Weber put *all* her notes in the manuscript archives."

"Isn't that the purpose? To archive all stages of the book, from notes to rough draft to final draft and every copy in between?" At least that's what Suzanne had al-ways thought.

"Yes, but she was a reporter first. She would have note-pads and thoughts that wouldn't make it into the file."

"If they're old, wouldn't she throw them away?"

Tony closed the last file cabinet. "They're definitely not here." He went back to the kitchen where Bridget was making coffee. "Ms. Weber, where did your sister store her old reporter notebooks?"

"The attic. A firetrap, I always told her." She sighed heavily. "Do you need them?"

"If you don't mind."

"If it'll help, please. Though I doubt you'll be able to read her odd shorthand." She pointed to the staircase. "Turn right at the top; the door leads to the attic. The light switch is on the left."

Suzanne followed Tony up two flights of narrow stairs. She looked around the attic, which was piled high with clear plastic forty-gallon bins holding hundreds of long, narrow reporter steno pads.

"Holy shit," Suzanne said. "Please tell me I don't have to read all these." She opened a box and flipped through one of the pads. "It's in a foreign language."

Tony took the pad from her and laughed. "Shorthand. There are people at the Bureau who can decipher these." He scanned the boxes. "All labeled, which is a plus."

"I assume you want the year when her first book came out, the notes from the file that was missing at the library."

"The year before the book came out would most likely have the notes from her research," Tony said. "That, and the year Rachel McMahon disappeared, up through Kreig's trial."

"Why wait years to kill her?" Suzanne asked as she looked at the dates on the bins. Each box covered six months of notes from Weber's reporter days.

"Opportunity, a stressor, a change in the killer's status—for example, if he recently got out of prison. But one thing is clear to me, above all else."

"What's that?"

"Her killer stalked her for weeks, if not months or even years. He knew her routines; he knew her friends; he knew what was important to her and under what circumstances she would meet someone alone. She was a risk taker by nature—just look at the types of crimes she reported and who she spoke with. She didn't feel threatened because she always felt that she was on the side of truth. Here—I found the years we're looking for. Help me with these."

Suzanne moved some of the boxes and Tony pulled out four. "We'll start here."

"This is going to take a shitload of time," she said.

"You sound skeptical."

She was. "It seems like a long shot."

"Maybe we'll get lucky and the information Rob Banker is going to leak for us will yield a suspect. But we can't count on it. The fact that the McMahon files are gone from the archives tells me that the killer doesn't want those found, because something inside points to him."

"Or he's misleading us," Suzanne said. "Sending us in a completely different direction."

"I never used to be a fan of joint task forces," Tony admitted. "But they have one key benefit. It's much easier to run investigations in different directions when you have multiple agencies focusing on what they do best. Let your friend Joe DeLucca handle that investigation, and I'll work on the background. And you do what you do best."

At this point, Suzanne didn't think she was needed.

"What is it?" Tony asked.

"You've taken over my case." That sounded ridiculous. "I mean, you're probably right, you have the experience, but you're leading."

He shook his head. "I'll do this part. This will help me come up with a profile that you can work with. You are tenacious, Suzanne. You know who's lying and you get answers. I have no doubt that you'll find who did this through smart police work. And the best way to do it is gain the advantage by understanding the psychology of the killer."

"And do you have anything yet?"

"If I'm right, the killer is patient, meticulous, and driven by a higher purpose. Rosemary Weber was not his first victim, nor will she be his last." Tony picked up two of the boxes and motioned for Suzanne to pick up the others. "I want to brief the analyst who will be going through these about what to look for; then I have a flight to catch. Something has been bugging me, and I'm hoping after Lucy and I go through my notes I'll figure it out."

CHAPTER THIRTEEN

FBI Academy

Lucy wanted to shower after she finished reading *Sex, Lies, and Family Secrets.* Tony had said that the facts were accurate, but it disgusted her how Weber sensationalized every aspect of the investigation, from digging into the investigators' private lives to vilifying the parents and martyring young Peter McMahon. A collection of color pictures in the center of the book showed family portraits, pictures from the orgies taken by guests, investigators, and the trial. One particularly gut-wrenching picture showed the young Peter McMahon at his sister's grave site, tears on his face, holding a stuffed dog.

Peter would have been fourteen when this book came out, a difficult age for anyone, but that year he'd also lost his grandmother. Even if he'd changed his name to Peter Gray and didn't live in the same state, he might not have been able to escape his past. And even if no one knew who he was, he did. In his heart, he knew that he was that crying child, that his family had been deeply flawed, and that his sister had been raped and murdered.

There was no way of knowing if Peter had gotten help

as a child, if he grew up with any semblance of normality, or if he had become twisted and vengeful over the years. She sent Sean an e-mail, hoping he had some news for her about Peter. Sean responded immediately.

> I confirmed what you already knew or suspected. And it appears that while he never legally changed his name to Peter Gray, he used that name when he registered as a freshman at a Newark high school. He moved back in with his mother when his grandmother died, but ran away a year later. Pilar McMahon remarried and relocated to Houston, Texas. Aaron McMahon has lived in Seattle from one month after Kreig was convicted. That's all I have now—still working on it.

Lucy had a list of every person mentioned in the book and how they were portrayed. The parents, Aaron and Pilar McMahon, would likely be the most upset by what Weber had written. It would be easy enough for the authorities to find out if one or both of them were in New York when Weber was murdered.

Still, why now, ten years after the book was published? Lucy had checked the publisher's Web site and while the book was still in print, there was no new version or reissue.

Weber had both condemned and commended the police investigation by being critical of how the local police first responded to the missing-person call, and because they did not immediately question the parents' story when they found evidence of a party at the house, but she also highlighted the methodical police work that went into disproving the McMahons' statements and gathering physical evidence from Rachel's bedroom. Fifteen years ago, forensics had seen a surge in importance, and the FBI used all their available resources to help local police figure out what had happened. A rookie cop, Bob Stokes, had been the first to the scene after the 911 call, and Weber had written that his concerns about the McMahons had been "dismissed" by his superiors until the FBI arrived.

Tony had been mentioned throughout the book because he was the lead agent, but he was never directly quoted. All FBI quotes were attributed to the media information officer, Dominic Theissen.

It was obvious to Lucy, after reading Tony's notes, the reports, and the book, that any delay in finding Rachel's murderer was directly related to the misinformation the McMahons had given police in the first critical twenty-four hours. However, evidence later proved that none of that mattered—Rachel had been killed hours after she was taken from her bedroom, likely before anyone in the house woke up.

Except Peter McMahon.

If Peter knew the facts of the case, he knew that his sister was alive when he didn't find her in her bedroom at three in the morning. But every way Lucy thought about how the investigation could have gone even if the police were notified at 3:00 a.m., she didn't see how they would have figured out Benjamin Kreig had kidnapped her or where he was holding her until after he'd taken her to the woods and killed her.

But did Peter know that? Did he harbor guilt because he didn't wake up his parents when he couldn't find his sister? She hoped not; that kind of psychological self-torment could severely damage anyone, especially a kid who had grown up as Peter McMahon had.

There were other people who might have reason to

hate Rosemary Weber. She'd named several of the people who had been at the McMahon house that night and exposed their sex lives for their friends and family to read. Benjamin Kreig was still in prison, and he had family who claimed to have distanced themselves from him, but what if they had been ostracized in their towns because of how Weber portrayed them? She'd written that Kreig's mother was "demanding and critical of everything Kreig did" and his father was an "alcoholic, known to pick up prostitutes." In fact, Weber revealed that Kreig's father had hired a prostitute for his son's eighteenth birthday when he learned his son was still a virgin.

One dysfunctional family after another.

Lucy thanked God that she'd had two parents who loved her and her brothers and sisters. The Kincaids weren't perfect, but they were family in the truest sense. Her oldest brother, Jack, had been the closest to their dad, both Army, until something happened and the two didn't speak for twenty years. Their relationship was still strained, but at least now they were talking. And after Justin was killed when he and Lucy were seven, Lucy's sister Nelia had stopped speaking to her. Though she'd come back to the family, Nelia still avoided Lucy for reasons Lucy didn't understand. While her psychologist mind told her Nelia grieved for Justin and unconsciously wished Lucy had died instead of her own son, Lucy didn't understand why even now Nelia couldn't overcome the pain. Guilt for her feelings? Pain when she saw Lucy?

What if that was how Peter had been treated? What if his parents looked at him and he thought they'd rather have had him die than their daughter? If his parents blamed him in some way, verbally or not, a young boy would pick up on unspoken accusations born from grief and guilt.

It was hard to assess the parents based on what she'd read, instead of watching them at each point in the investigation, but it was clear that they'd stymied the investigation and then come clean. What if they turned that self-loathing against their son? Blaming him for not speaking out at three in the morning? Had he harbored that pain all these years? What was he like today?

Lucy had always had the nagging feeling that if only she'd done something different, Justin would still be alive. She'd often spent the night with her nephew, or when his parents worked late he came over to her house. But that week, she'd been sick. She didn't remember why, but she hadn't gone to school for three days. She wanted Justin to come and play with her because she was bored, but Nelia said no, she didn't want Justin getting sick.

Lucy's cell phone rang and she grabbed it. It was Tony. "I'm in my office," he said. "Are you done?"

"Yes. I'll be right there."

She grabbed the McMahon file and left.

Several new agents were in the downstairs lounge watching different baseball games on the two televisions— one showed a game with the San Diego Padres, Lucy's home team.

Carter and Eddie were studying in the corner, one eye on the game. Carter whistled. "Kincaid! I thought you were a diehard fan."

"I had work to do."

"So do we." Carter held up his book.

"It's only the bottom of the fourth; I'll be back before the seventh inning."

"You say that now."

She looked at the screen. Tied at 1. "Okay, I'll *try*." Lucy liked baseball, but mostly because her family were die-hard Padres fans, particularly Patrick and Carina. They could talk baseball with the best of them. Patrick had played baseball in college and could have had a shot at the majors if he'd stuck with it. But then Justin was killed and Patrick ended up becoming a cop.

Tragedy changes everyone it touches.

Lucy waved to Carter and Eddie and went down the hall to the staircase that led to the basement. She waved her ID in front of the security panel and it clicked open.

No one was working this late, and the offices were quiet. She knocked on Tony's door. He didn't respond. She looked at her cell phone—no bars, so she couldn't call him to see where he was. He'd said he was in his office, he could be on the phone.

She stepped in. As soon as the door opened, she saw Tony slumped in his chair, his face pasty, eyes closed, and mouth open.

"Oh, God." She dropped the file on the table by the door and rushed to his side to check his pulse, shouting, "Medics! I need a medic, stat!" Then she realized that no one else was in the basement; it was nearly ten at night. She put Tony's desk phone on speaker and pressed "0."

"Security."

"It's Lucy Kincaid. I need a medic and gurney in Agent Presidio's office stat. He's unconscious."

At first she thought he was dead, but she finally felt his pulse—slow and weak.

"Dispatched," Security said. "Stay on the phone."

In times of crisis, relying on training kept Lucy sane. "I'm checking for external injuries—I don't see any."

"Did you check his vitals?"

"He had a pulse when I came in, but now I can't feel anything."

"Do you know CPR?"

"Yes."

She pulled Tony out of his chair. His bottle of Glenlivit Scotch teetered but didn't fall over. She laid him as carefully as she could on the floor.

"Kincaid, you there?" Security said over the speaker.

"Administering CPR."

"Is he breathing?"

She checked. "His pulse is thready. Skin pasty. He's unresponsive. Starting second set of chest compressions."

Tony, please, don't die.

The staff doctor and a medic rushed in. "We'll take over. Security, you there?"

"Yes."

"Call the Quantico Medical Center and have them dispatch a helicopter to fly Agent Presidio direct to Prince William Hospital. He appears to be in cardiac arrest."

Why hadn't he called someone? A heart attack could be sudden, but he was in his chair; at some point he would have known it was serious enough to call for help, wouldn't he? She'd spoken to him less than twenty minutes ago.

The medic hooked Tony up to an automatic compression machine and put an oxygen mask over his face. Lucy stood out of the way. The seriousness of Tony's situation hit her now that she had nothing to do but watch. He could very well die.

The medic checked Tony's pulse. "Nothing." He and the doctor slipped Tony onto a board, which they then lifted up and secured to the gurney.

Security said over the phone, "Medical transport helio, ETA three minutes."

"Let's get him upstairs," the medic said. "Kincaid, call the elevator."

Lucy ran ahead and held the elevator open so the doctor

and medic could wheel Tony inside. She held his clammy hand on the ride up.

Please, God, don't take him.

They pushed Tony down the hall and out the front doors. Lucy heard the helicopter nearby and watched as the spotlights filled the parking lot, the pilot searching for a place to land. She stayed with Tony up until he was loaded inside. Thirty seconds after landing, the chopper took off with Tony.

"We did everything we could," the medic said as they watched the chopper leave with Tony and the doctor.

"Why didn't he call for help?" Lucy whispered.

"Maybe he didn't realize what was happening until it was too late."

"So he sat back until he lost consciousness?" It didn't make sense to Lucy, but nothing made sense to her right now. "Can I go to the hospital?"

"You'll have to talk to the chief," the medic said. He watched the helicopter disappear from sight. "I'll call and see if I can find out what's going on."

"Thank you." But Lucy had watched and listened to the doctor and medic, and by the time they put Tony on the helicopter, they couldn't find his pulse.

CHAPTER FOURTEEN

New York City

"You didn't show." Joe DeLucca filled Suzanne's doorway, all six feet, two inches of solid Italian muscle.

"I told you I wouldn't."

He made a move to enter, but she blocked him, her hand on the doorjamb.

Don't let him inside.

He raised an eyebrow, giving Suzanne his sexy half-smile that used to melt her, but she held firm. She was crabby and tired from too little sleep and too many questions. "I didn't want to be dragged into this case, De-Lucca."

"I didn't want to hear that your agent buddy leaked information to Banker at the *Times* without consulting with me first."

"I called and told you."

"Left a message." He made another move to enter, and she didn't budge.

"I wasn't going to chase you all over town."

"Do you think he's right?"

Suzanne had waffled on Tony Presidio's theory all evening, but in the end she admitted it was a smart play. "Let's just hope the place our guy pawns the ring has security cameras."

"I sent out another notice about the ring, just to keep it fresh. Told the brokers to handle it as they normally would, write down everything, call me immediately."

"Good." She nodded curtly. "Good-bye."

"I also brought you a copy of the final autopsy report." He held it out, a carrot that she couldn't resist. She let go of the doorjamb to grab the file and Joe weaseled his way inside.

She rolled her eyes. "Come on in."

She closed the door and tried to ignore Joe's smug grin of victory. She crossed her small, fifth-floor loft apartment and stood by the window, putting distance between herself and Joe. Stand firm, she told herself. She could withstand his charm and sex appeal.

You have to. Remember what happened last year.

With new resolve to focus only on the case, she read the coroner's findings.

Weber was stabbed with a narrow metal stiletto six inches long. The killer had at least some knowledge of anatomy, because the blade went in below the sternum, through the lung, and pierced her heart. Death was nearly instantaneous. No hesitation marks, no second stabbing. Marks on the victim's right biceps indicated that the killer was facing her, grabbed her with his left hand, stabbed her with his right. He withdrew the weapon, let her fall to the ground after she was already dead. Confirmed everything the prelim had said, with some added details about the possible weapon. Tox reports showed Weber had a BAC of .03, well under the legal limit, and confirmed her sister's report that she'd had wine before leaving for Citi Field.

"So we're looking for a medic of sorts, someone with

training—EMT, paramedic, pre-med maybe. Nothing we didn't already know. You didn't need to bring me this."

Joe walked over to her kitchen table and spread out the crime scene photos.

"Make yourself at home," she said sarcastically. She look at the photos.

"Thanks." He opened her refrigerator and grabbed two beers, handing her one. "See anything?"

"Other than an annoying ex-boyfriend?"

Joe looked over his shoulder. "Where?"

She hit him in the arm and stared at the crime scene photos. She used the findings in the autopsy report to re-create the scene in her head. The victim was found between her car and the vehicle next to her—owned by the people who found her body.

"She was dragged from here"—Suzanne pointed to the blood pool in front of Weber's car—"approximately four feet to here."

"Correct, we knew that—but what does that tell you?"

"That she'd just left her car and was meeting someone."

"That's what I thought as well, but her prints were on the hood of her car, so—"

"—so you think she was leaning against her car while she was waiting for someone."

"Bingo."

"She knew her killer. We've been over this, Joe."

"Or thought she did. What else?"

"No trail."

"And no weapon found at the scene. The M.E. said the killer's hand would have been drenched in blood, up to his wrist. He wore gloves—powder common in latex gloves was found on the victim."

"He came prepared." Good detail. She glanced down at the autopsy report again. She'd missed it the first time because Joe was making her nervous. She could just see what was going to happen. She'd get involved again, his ex-wife would threaten to take him to court for full custody, and she'd be waiting and waiting and *waiting*. She didn't want to go through that again.

"Could have bundled up the blade, the gloves, maybe even external clothing, and dumped it anywhere."

"Did you canvass?"

He glared at her. "I've been on the job five years longer than you, babe."

"Don't call me that."

"I'm going with you on the bundling, but I don't think he dumped it at Citi Field. Too much chance of us finding it. More likely he took it with him, or he dumped it in the Bay."

They looked at each other. "Bay," they said together.

"Except the stiletto," Suzanne said.

"Why?"

"Because it can be traced. At least, in theory. He planned this—gloves, location, the element of surprise, no defensive wounds, no blood trail. He isn't going to be stupid and dump anything that could lead back to him. I'll bet if we recover the clothing it'll be generic from a major store. Salt water would destroy any forensic evidence."

"I have uniforms looking along the shoreline, going with the tide, to see if anything washed up. But he could have weighted it down and tossed it anywhere."

"That's what I would do," Suzanne said.

"Remind me not to get on your bad side."

"You're already there."

Joe stared at her. "Why can't you forgive me?"

"Who says I haven't?"

He looked into his beer bottle. "I'm not seeing anyone else."

"Of course not. Stephanie won't allow it."

"Why do you always have to bring her up?"

"Because your ex-wife is part of any relationship you have. It's a threesome, and not the fun kind."

"Fuck." Joe ran a hand through his brown hair, leaving it messy and sexy, just the way she liked to see him. She turned away. She couldn't give in to temptation, because it would only lead to where it led before: heartbreak.

"Joe—look, I don't want to fight with you. I don't blame you. Hell, there's no one to blame. Tyler is your son. He's eight years old and he needs his dad. I get that. I like the kid; he's going to grow up and be just like you. But the games that Stephanie plays to keep you from being happy, I can't do that. And I can't stand between you and Tyler. *I won't.*" Her chest heaved and she wished they hadn't had this conversation. Damn, she cared about Joe and she liked his son. But she wanted something that wasn't possible.

Joe put his empty beer bottle down and stared at her. His dark Italian eyes read her, and she forced herself to withstand the visual assault. She stared back, kept her expression blank, kept her mouth closed.

Do not give in. Do not give in.

He leaned forward and kissed her. She should have turned her head. She'd planned to.

But she didn't.

As soon as his lips touched her, the slow boil that had been simmering since she'd seen Joe yesterday morning bubbled over. She grabbed him and held on as he pushed her against the counter, his mouth open on hers, one hand tangled in her hair, the other on her back, under her shirt, clutching her. Flashes of hot, fast, hard sex ripped through her thoughts and she gasped as his mouth moved down her neck and his hands moved everywhere. Joe's thigh pressed between her legs, and she returned the favor, rubbing his dick as it pushed to escape.

She pulled his shirt from his slacks and kneaded his hard chest. Joe was all man, all cop, lean and ripped.

He unholstered his gun and dropped it on the counter, then pushed her onto the kitchen table, her copy of the crime photos flying. Her shirt flew in another direction, and when his mouth found her breasts she moaned. He nibbled at her, hard enough for her to feel his teeth but not hard enough to hurt. He pushed his hand down the front of her jeans and found her wet spot. He grinned at her as he slipped in one finger, then another, a promise for what would come as soon as she stripped. She kneaded her fingers over the heavy bulge in his pants and his cat-ate-canary smile disappeared. He fought with her jeans. "God, Suzi."

She pulled his head to hers and bit his ear, then licked it, his muscles tensing under her moving hands. He unzipped her jeans.

Her phone rang.

"Don't you dare," he growled in her ear, pinning her to the table.

She closed her eyes and reached for the button of his pants.

Her phone kept singing to her. AFI's "Miss Murder." Headquarters.

She pushed Joe off and grabbed her phone.

"Madeaux."

"This is Ray Jordan from the night desk. I have Assistant Director Hans Vigo from national headquarters on the line for you."

"I'll take it."

Joe walked across the room and stared out the window, all sweaty and sexy. She turned her back to him.

Two clicks later and Dr. Hans Vigo said, "I'm sorry to bother you this late at night, but it's important."

"What can I do for you Assistant Director?"

"You worked with SSA Tony Presidio today, correct?"

"Yes." Suzanne knew immediately something was up. Not just because of a call from an assistant director but also because of his tone. "The murder of Rosemary Weber, which I'm working with NYPD."

"I need all your reports and a detailed list of every place Tony went while he was in New York. Anything you can remember about what he said and did."

"Of course; may I ask why?" She picked her shirt off the floor and slipped it on. She held her phone with her shoulder and began to button it up.

"He died of a heart attack thirty minutes after arriving back at Quantico."

Suzanne sat down, forgetting about her shirt.

"He went back early to go through his notes. I had no idea he was ill."

"He left a message for me before he boarded the plane in LaGuardia, concerned about FBI exposure on this case. Do you know what he was talking about?"

"No, sir. We discovered some of Weber's files were missing, and Tony's having an analyst re-create them off shorthand notes. Unless—he did leak specific information to the press about how we know the killer staged Weber's murder to look like a robbery. He's hoping the killer will try to pawn the ring to prove us wrong."

"Thereby proving us right," Hans said. "Sounds like Tony. Stay on it, and keep me in the loop. I'm heading down to Quantico in the morning to take care of Tony's affairs."

Joe smiled but didn't look at her. He walked back toward the kitchen and grabbed his gun off the counter.

"I'll send you everything first thing in the morning." She hung up. "Joe—"

He shook his head, leaned over, and kissed her. "Next time, I'll flush your phone."

"There won't—"

He put his hand over her mouth. "There's always a next time."

CHAPTER FIFTEEN

Ten Years Ago

No one was happy with me that I'd lied about my parents being dead, especially not my parents. But in my defense, they were dead to me. Grams had been my legal guardian for five years, but I was fourteen when she died and the idiot judge thought that I had to live with someone. He picked my mom.

Mom and Dad had divorced after the trial and Mom tried to force me to live with her. Grams had been stronger then and stood up to my mom. Mom cried, but I just kept my thoughts focused on all the lies she'd told. Grams had been as hurt as I was, because Mom was her daughter. I might have only been nine during the trial, but I understood a lot more than people thought. I told Grams not to blame herself, that Mom made me live with the consequences of my bad choices, like when I thought the Jacuzzi would make a good bubble bath or when I went over to Jared's house to play his war games after Mom said I couldn't play any games rated M. I was grounded for a month.

Mom and Dad made bad choices—it was like that FBI agent said; some bad choices have unforeseen consequences. That doesn't make it okay to lie.

Grams and I had a tacit agreement that day. We could talk about Mom or Dad or what happened to Rachel, but we'd remember only the fun things, like when Grandpa taught Rachel and me to fish or when Grams taught us to bake.

And then Grams was gone, just like Grandpa and just like Rachel, who I remembered more than I wanted.

It was my second week back living with my mom, the day I started high school, and Mom drove me to the campus. As if being a freshman who was shorter than everyone else as well as notorious wasn't bad enough, Mom had to pick a fight.

"You need to forgive me."

"For what?"

"For what happened to Rachel."

"You didn't kill her."

"Don't talk about it."

"You started it."

I'd never have talked to Grams like I spoke to my mom, but I loved and respected Grams.

I looked at my mom. Pilar McMahon. Forty-five. Dyed her hair and wore too much makeup.

"Do you know how sorry I am? Do you know how much I have suffered these five years? Knowing what happened to Rachel, knowing that you never wanted to see me again."

And if Grams was still alive, I wouldn't be having this conversation now.

"Peter, please."

Mom didn't know what I knew. That in the last week I'd heard the front door close in the middle of the night. That even when she thought she was being quiet her bed hit the wall. I might not have known had I not been raised to the same sounds.

"Are you still a slut?"

She slapped me. I got out of the car and didn't look back.

The first day of high school wasn't the worst day of my life, but it was in the top ten.

It was the end of the day, when I went to my locker to get my things, that bad went to worse. I found a note.

I'M WATCHING YOU.

CHAPTER SIXTEEN

FBI Academy

During her first week on campus, Lucy had discovered the secluded, parklike area behind Hogan's Alley while exploring the campus with Margo and Reva. She'd come here many times when she needed to be alone. Because of the trees and overhanging branches, the circle was ten degrees cooler in the heat of the day and, better, it afforded privacy.

She sat heavily on a fallen log early Friday morning, after running five miles on the track trying to work out the grief of Tony's death. The run had left her drained instead of invigorated, her emotions on overdrive.

The sun was still low on the horizon, the air crisp and clean in the clear summer dawn. It would be a beautiful morning before the heat became unbearable. But she wouldn't enjoy it. Too many feelings, too many questions.

A breaking twig caught her attention, and then a voice: "Lucy, it's me."

"Sean?" She jumped up, stunned. "What are you doing here?"

"I know you were close to Tony. I asked Kate to get me in." He walked over and hugged her. "Your friend Margo told me you'd probably be here."

"I needed to get away from everyone."

He sat down and she leaned against him. It was good to have Sean here, even if it was just for a few minutes. "Thank you," she said. "It's a long drive."

"Kate said I could stay for breakfast." He smiled, then looked at her, worry in his eyes. "You okay?"

Tears blurred her vision and she buried her face in Sean's shoulder and cried for the first time since she'd heard Tony had died. Sean held her, stroked her hair, didn't say anything. There was nothing to say, and Lucy was grateful that he had come to her. She hadn't even thought to ask him to, but it made all the difference.

Several minutes later she sat up. She touched his damp shoulder. "Sorry," she mumbled.

"Better?"

She nodded.

Sean kissed her lightly. "I was spoiled seeing you every day. I miss you. Talking on the phone just doesn't cut it."

"I know."

"Are you all right?"

"I will be. I've known Tony for less than a month, but I'm still stunned."

"I'm sorry I didn't get to meet him."

"I think I'm going to miss his stories more than anything," Lucy said. "Tony put a personal twist on all the cases he worked. Listening to him recount his process and the different paths he explored was interesting and insightful. He was dedicated. He cared."

"So do you. That's why he brought you into his world." Sean kissed her forehead. "You should have asked for today off."

She shook her head.

"I didn't think you would have, just that you *should* have."

"We should head to the cafeteria. I have class at eight."

"We have a few minutes."

Sean was the type of guy who liked to fix problems, and death wasn't something he could fix. But having him here, at her side, gave her peace and comfort she didn't realize she needed.

"I spoke to Suzanne Madeaux." Sean put his fingers under her chin and looked at her. "I don't want you hurt."

"Suzanne assured me that there was nothing personal about me in her files. Just my name in connection with the Cinderella Strangler investigation." Lucy took his hands. "You can't always protect me."

"When I can, I will."

"Tony knew Weber as far back as the Rachel McMahon kidnapping. He went to New York to help Suzanne with the profile. He thinks Weber's murder has to do with the McMahon case. Her manuscript notes and interviews are missing."

"I skimmed the book she wrote after you asked me to find Peter McMahon."

"I read it as well. Tony wanted me to make a list of everyone she mentioned and rank them in the order of most likely to hold a grudge. But it's been ten years since the book came out. Why wait so long?"

Lucy's stomach flipped. Crime scenes, autopsies, police reports she could handle. They were matter-of-fact and to the point. Books sensationalizing the pain and suffering of others disturbed her. She supposed that was good for a writer, that Weber had a way of getting so deep into the investigation that she could make the reader think she was right there, but Lucy had enough tragedy and pain in her real life; she didn't need to share in the pain of others.

But wasn't that what she did now? Wasn't that why she wanted to be a cop? To give peace to the survivors and obtain justice for the dead?

"Luce?" Sean pushed her hair back and held her cheek.

"I'm okay."

"No, you're not."

"I will be. I was just thinking about Weber and how she approached her stories. I can handle it but the way she wrote—"

"She sensationalized tragedy. Seemed to relish it."

"It was full of melodrama. Tony said it was accurate, but it's how she told the story that made it dramatic. I should turn over the file to Suzanne."

"What file?"

"Tony's personal notes. Did you learn anything more about Peter McMahon?"

"I haven't found him yet, which is unusual."

"Because you're so good?"

"Exactly." He kissed her. "Since I last talked to you, I learned that after his grandmother died he registered for school in Newark and lived with his mother for a year, then ran away. There's a sealed juvenile record on him. I found him again in Seattle, where his father lives, and a record that he received a GED under the name Peter Mc-Mahon Gray."

"Social Services sent him back to his mother?" Lucy frowned.

"What don't I know?"

"I read Tony's case notes. His parents were swingers. That means—"

"I know what a swinger is. And I read the book. Peter filed for emancipation when he was sixteen and got it. Moved back to Jersey, where he went to a community college and got his GED. He was accepted into Syracuse for the second semester, right before he turned seventeen."

"Driven. Determined to do something with his life." Lucy took a deep breath. "His childhood ended when he was nine. Did he graduate college?"

"No. Disappeared two years later. I might be able to find out more, but not quickly—unless I hack into the Syracuse files. I promised I wouldn't."

"Did you check obituaries?"

"In New York and New Jersey. No Peter McMahon, no Peter Gray, and no John Doe of his description reported deceased the year he went off the grid."

"Maybe he just wanted to start over," she said quietly.

"Or to seek revenge."

"Tony didn't make any indication that he thought the McMahon boy was responsible for what happened to Rosemary Weber."

"You're the psychologist, Luce. What would that kind of upbringing do to a kid?"

Anything. But that didn't mean he'd grown into a killer. But it didn't mean he hadn't.

"I wish Tony were here."

"What about Hans? Kate said he was coming here to clear out Tony's files and work with Suzanne."

"I didn't know."

"It's seven in the morning. I'm sure you'll hear about it." He paused, then asked, "Did you ever want to change your name and start over?"

"No."

"Why?"

"Because changing my name wouldn't have erased the memories." She stood and said, "We'd better get to the cafeteria. I don't want to be late for class."

* * *

Lucy walked Sean to his car forty minutes later, after they'd eaten breakfast with her friends. "They're a good group," Sean said.

"I think so."

"I feel better about you being here."

"Sean, you're not going to go all over-protective on me, are you?"

He wrapped his arms around her, dipped her, and gave her a deep kiss. She laughed. "Sean!"

He put her on her feet but held her against him as he leaned on his Mustang. "I'm glad you made some friends, that this isn't all work all the time." He tucked loose strands of hair behind her ear. "You take everything so seriously, but you fell in with a group of people who have fun."

"They take it seriously, but they turn it off better than I do. In fact, they're more like you than me. Maybe that's why I like hanging out with them."

"I found out something about Laughlin. I'll dig deeper if you want."

Lucy's breakfast sandwich felt like a lead ball deep in the pit of her stomach. "What?"

"He and Kate have known each other for a long time."

"I thought they might have had a past." Why hadn't Kate told her?

"He overlapped with Kate in the D.C. field office for six months—the six months before her partner was killed and she disappeared to Mexico."

"The D.C. field office is one of the largest. Just because they were in the same office doesn't mean they would have known each other." But that would explain the animosity. Laughlin was here only for New Agent Class 12-14. It was a temporary assignment, so it may have been the first time he'd seen Kate in more than a decade. "Were they on the same squad?"

"No—he's always been in white-collar crimes. Kate's always been in violent crimes, until taking the cyber-crimes slot here, right?"

Lucy nodded. "But Kate's boyfriend back then was an SSA in the public corruption squad." Lucy bit her lip, a sign that she was nervous or thinking.

"Do you think it's a coincidence?" Sean asked in a tone that told her he didn't believe it was.

Lucy hedged as she processed the information. "Did you see anything in Laughlin's past about Evan Standler?"

He shook his head. "Kate's boyfriend?"

"Adam Scott set up an ambush and killed him." It was clear Sean hadn't known. "It's not something Kate and I talk about. She told me once, right after I moved to D.C., but never mentioned it again."

"Why would Laughlin have an issue with you? Or Kate?"

"A lot of people blamed Kate for what happened, until she was able to clear her name. But by that time, it might be hard to forgive, and maybe he didn't believe her. It's one reason she was assigned here." Lucy was going to have to talk to her sister-in-law; she saw no way around it. "When did Laughlin leave D.C.?"

"Five years ago, when he transferred to Detroit. As much as I hate to ask him for a favor, maybe we should talk to Noah," Sean said.

Lucy kissed his hand. Sean didn't like Special Agent Noah Armstrong, they'd butted heads more times than she could count, and she appreciated that he was willing to put that aside to get her the answers she wanted.

"I don't know that we have to go that far. Laughlin wants me to screw up. If I do, it's my fault, not his."

"Unless he cheats. Does more than just give you the evil eye."

Lucy kissed him again. "Thank you."

"Aw, shucks, ma'am," Sean teased.

She rested her head on his chest and for a moment, just a moment, considered asking for the day off. Her emotions were still in turmoil. But she was already being closely observed; she didn't want to make any more waves.

"I'll see you tomorrow," she said.

"I'm holding you to that."

CHAPTER SEVENTEEN

Georgetown, Washington, D.C.

Patrick walked into Sean's office Friday morning. "Where's Lucy?"

Sean glanced at him oddly. "Quantico. Is she supposed to be someplace else?"

"I thought you'd convince her to come back with you."

"I didn't ask, and she wouldn't have taken the day off, anyway. I'm picking her up tomorrow at noon and teaching her how to drive."

"She knows how to drive."

Sean laughed and put his e-reader down. He was nearly done with Weber's books—he'd been reading half the night and since he'd gotten back home this morning, highlighting important information to discuss with Lucy or verify. The writer certainly hadn't made any friends with the way she portrayed cops, victims, and predators. Essentially, everyone was guilty of something.

"Lucy has a license, but when was the last time you drove with her?"

Patrick hesitated. "Point taken. You know why she doesn't like to drive, right?"

"There's a specific reason?"

"She's never talked about it, but when she was five we were in a serious car accident."

"You were driving?"

Patrick sat down and sipped his coffee. "Dad was. I was fifteen, Carina sixteen. It was a severe storm one Sunday—clear when we left for church, total downpour within the hour. The car in front of us slammed on its brakes. Dad's a good driver. He maneuvered out of the way, but the car on the right slammed on their brakes and hydroplaned right into us and we rolled. We were all knocked out, a couple of broken bones, but we were okay. Three people died in the collision—a twelve-car pileup. Anyway, that's my guess why Lucy hates to drive."

Sean hadn't known, and he realized that even though he knew all the important things about his girlfriend, he didn't know everything. He wanted her to tell him about the accident, because even though Patrick's explanation made sense, it didn't sound like Lucy. She'd always faced her fears head-on—why not this one?

"Working on anything interesting?" Patrick asked. "It's already blistering hot out there."

"Reading Rosemary Weber's books. The woman was a bitch. She pulled no punches. I have a list of three dozen people who might want her dead, just because of what she wrote. Lucy put it together last night, before Tony's heart attack."

Patrick said with fake shock, "I didn't know you were working for the FBI."

Sean gave him a dead-pan expression. "Ha, ha."

"Then why are you doing this?"

"Because Tony Presidio asked Lucy to make this list and she's grieving right now. I'm just doing what she would have done."

Sean went back to the book. He highlighted a name he'd seen multiple times.

Detective Bob Stokes.

Patrick said, "Aren't you supposed to be preparing for an assignment?"

"I have a week before Duke sends me to God knows where."

"Madison."

"Right. Wisconsin." Sean smiled. "At least the weather will be tolerable."

"Believe me, I'd take it if I could."

"You could."

Patrick snorted. "As much as I hate stroking your inflated ego, no way could I crack their on-site security."

"The goal is for me *not* to crack it. Then Duke did his job right. Did I tell you Duke's working on getting us a Homeland Security contract? Last time I flew commercial I sent him a memo—as a joke—about a half-dozen ways I could waltz into secured areas."

"You don't sound interested."

"I'm not. I avoid government contracts." Sean left those to Duke and his other partners. Unfortunately, if they had an airport security contract, it would be up to Sean and Lucy's brother Jack, since they were both pilots and had in-depth knowledge of both private and commercial facilities. He regretted sending the memo to Duke and hoped Homeland Security ignored it.

Sean glanced at his watch. "Want to do me a favor?"

"No."

"Please?"

"You must want it bad."

"It's either take notes on Weber's books or find out about this cop she acknowledged in her first book. He's the only cop she didn't slam."

"He must have talked to her."

"That's what I thought. He might know a lot more."

Patrick didn't move. Sean looked up. "What?"

"The FBI is investigating her murder."

"So?"

"Turn it over to them."

"I will."

"When?"

"When I have something."

Patrick still didn't move.

Sean sighed. "What now?"

"Why are you doing this?"

"I'm bored."

Patrick glanced at his watch and leaned back in the chair.

"You learned that trick from me."

"Is it working?"

Sean put the e-reader down again. "Lucy's name was in Weber's files. I want to know what she has on Lucy and my cousin Kirsten. The only way I'm going to *legally* see those files is if Suzanne shows them to me. The only way she'll show them is if I give her something useful. She and NYPD are running down leads as to who killed Weber, and there's no doubt she'll find the guy, but I don't want *all* her files being part of the evidence."

"It already is."

"For now."

"I hope you know what you're doing, Rogan."

"I always do."

"What's the cop's name?"

"Bob Stokes, Newark. He was the responding officer, and according to Weber, he'd pegged the parents as liars from the beginning, but his superiors didn't believe him, until the FBI came in and cracked open the case."

"And what do you think he's going to do for you?"

"He talked to her. He probably knows what was taken from the files at the library archives. If I can deliver him to Suzanne, I'm one step closer to answers."

"Maybe you should just ask her."

"I will. When I get this."

CHAPTER EIGHTEEN

FBI Academy

During lunch, Lucy found Kate eating in her office. Kate was the senior cybercrimes instructor at Quantico and was part of a joint task force on tracing online child pornography. It was a particularly difficult job for anyone, even a seasoned agent like Kate.

"What do you want?" Kate asked Lucy without looking at her. Her eyes were focused on her computer.

"We need to talk."

Kate stared at her computer for a long minute, then leaned back in her chair. She nodded and Lucy sat down.

"You worked with Rich Laughlin before—before everything." Lucy still had a hard time talking about Adam Scott. "Before you left D.C. twelve years ago."

"I'm not talking about Laughlin." Kate's face was set tight; she was trying hard not to react to anything Lucy said. Why was she being so controlled?

"But—"

"I thought you wanted to talk about Tony Presidio."

"I'm okay. Thank you for signing Sean in; it helped, talking to him."

"And?"

"And what?"

"You and Tony were the subject of a staff meeting this morning. You've involved yourself in the middle of an investigation. I don't have to tell you that being the subject of a staff meeting isn't good."

Lucy shifted in her seat. "I don't understand."

Kate tilted her head and raised her eyebrows. "You didn't know."

"Know what? What's wrong?" Had she missed something? Done something wrong? With all the pressure from Laughlin and her firearms test and Tony's death and Weber's book, had she missed something important?

"Hans is here to put Tony's office in order, and work on the profile Tony began on the murder of that writer. No one knew you were working with Tony until Hans told us."

Lucy said carefully, "There was nothing wrong with me doing extra work. I did it on my own time."

"Not when it impacts your overall performance."

Laughlin. It all came back to him.

"I've done well in all my classes."

"Lucy, I'm not trying to ride you; I'm trying to help." But her tone said just the opposite.

"Then tell me what's going on between you and Agent Laughlin."

Kate reddened and leaned forward. "How dare you," she said through clenched teeth. "There's *nothing* going on between me and *anyone,* and you damn well know that."

Lucy didn't break eye contact, though her heart was pounding. She said as calmly as she could, "I didn't mean you were having an affair."

Kate stared at her, but Lucy held her ground. She'd lived with Kate for the last seven years. She knew her better than she knew her family. If Kate saw any chip in Lucy's armor, she'd find a way to defuse the situation and not tell Lucy what she needed to know. Lucy didn't understand why Kate didn't come clean now, why she didn't just explain what had happened between her and Laughlin. Did she think Lucy wouldn't approve? Or that she'd be upset?

"What are we doing here?" Kate asked quietly. "We're family."

"Yes, we are. That's why you need to tell me the truth. You promised me you would always be honest."

Kate shook her head. "Are you really pushing that button?"

"You know I'm not."

"From my side of the desk, seems you are."

Lucy had learned how to play hardball from the best. "Then I'll find out what I need to know on my own."

"Don't think I don't know you have Sean getting into my business." There was disgust in her voice.

"Sean is trying to figure out why Rich Laughlin is determined to undermine me." Lucy hoped that her honesty would prompt Kate to open up.

"What part of 'keep your head down' did you not understand? There's a half-dozen people who would love to kick you out of here, and you keep pushing."

"I'm not pushing anything!" Was Kate exaggerating? "Laughlin surprised me at the gun range. He knows my fears and is exploiting them."

"Do you think maybe that's part of your test?" Kate said sarcastically.

"That's what I thought at first, but this is more than just testing me." Lucy hesitated, then said, "When he looks at me, I know he hates me. And after I walked in on your argument the other day, I think it's more about you than me."

Kate slowly stood up. Again, she was angry, but Lucy saw fear in her eyes, and fear wasn't something she equated with Kate.

"Haven't you been listening to me? To stand out is a bad thing. Getting perfect scores doesn't make you stand out. Involving yourself in *anything* outside of your daily work does. Stay out of it. The thing with Laughlin has nothing to do with you—not everything is about *you*. You involved yourself in an ongoing federal investigation, and that isn't smart."

Lucy realized that Kate was turning everything around to make it *her* fault. As if helping Tony, her instructor, had been a mistake.

Lucy said, "Is Agent Laughlin harassing you?"

"No one is harassing me. You think I would put up with that shit?"

But her eyes told Lucy she was on to something. Kate was in-your-face angry, but her eyes were scared.

Rich Laughlin was tormenting her, and Kate couldn't stop it. What was it that scared her so much?

"Kate—"

"It's all a damn test, Lucy!" Kate was losing her temper, her voice getting louder.

"This isn't about a test," Lucy said without raising her voice. "Tom Harden tests me. Laughlin wants me to fail."

"You're paranoid."

That stung, but the well-aimed verbal attack meant she was close to the truth.

"It's you I'm concerned about, Kate."

Kate laughed. "You think I'm so weak that I'd let some asshole push me around?"

"No, I don't. Except—" Lucy waited for Kate to look at her. "*Except* if he threatened me. Don't fight my battles, Kate."

"No one has threatened me, or you." Kate stared at Lucy while she spoke, but on the last word her eyes darted to the right before refocusing.

Lucy's suspicions were right. She stood up. "I know Laughlin was on the same squad as your former boyfriend, Evan Standler. I know you were all in the D.C. office together. What I don't know is what Laughlin said to make you scared."

"I don't scare," Kate said. Again, her eyes moved to the right. It wasn't a tell. It was a direction.

Lucy looked where Kate kept glancing. It was a picture of Dillon and Kate, the day they got married, nearly three years ago. But they'd been together much longer.

Lucy picked up the picture. "Dillon loves you. There's nothing you did in your past that could ever change that." She put the picture down. "I think I understand."

"You don't." Kate's anger had lost steam. She wasn't going to tell Lucy what had happened, but Lucy understood. Whatever problem Laughlin had with Lucy was small compared to what he had with Kate. He couldn't get to Kate except through those she loved, because Kate wasn't easily bullied. That meant Lucy and Dillon, the two people Kate loved more than anyone.

Lucy smiled while Kate remained stone-faced. "You may have kept your maiden name," Lucy said, "but you're a Kincaid now."

"What does that mean?"

"You're not alone."

Lucy had thirty minutes before physical training, so went to her room to unwind after her confrontation with Kate.

Someone had been here.

Lucy stood in her doorway, one hand still on the knob, as the skin rose from her arms. What was different?

Nothing appeared out of place. She hadn't made her bed, because she'd gotten up late; her desk was cluttered but relatively tidy. Her bookshelf was packed with her notebooks, textbooks, paper, her own research books—

It wasn't that something was out of place. It was the air. A faint scent that wasn't hers.

Had Margo come in to borrow something? Lucy wouldn't be upset, though she preferred to be asked. Except—it wasn't Margo. She cherished her privacy as much as Lucy. Margo would have at least left a note but most likely would have called Lucy first. Reva? Usually one knock, then walk right in. But she always wore flowery perfume, and this wasn't perfume. It was something . . . else. Sweat, maybe, but not Lucy's sweat.

She searched her room again, looking for even the smallest hint of something off; then she opened her desk drawers and went through her things.

In the bottom drawer, where she had kept the file Tony had given her, she noticed that something was clearly out of place.

Her handwritten notes were gone.

CHAPTER NINETEEN

Lucy found it hard to focus on her physical training, and she didn't know who she should go to about her missing notes. She mentally replayed what she'd done with them last night, before finding Tony unconscious in his office. She'd brought down his file, plus her list of people from Weber's book, but she'd left her personal notes—questions to herself, facts from the book, comments about Tony's notes—in her desk. She was certain of it. Almost.

Paula Kean entered the gym near the end of training and spoke with Harden. A few seconds later, Harden called Lucy over.

"You're free to go with Agent Kean," he told her.

Lucy glanced at the class supervisor, trying to assess why she was being pulled out. Kean's face was impassive, as usual.

Lucy followed her out and down the hall. Kean stopped just outside her office door. "Assistant Director Hans Vigo needs to speak with you." She lifted her chin. "I see his visit is not a surprise to you."

"Kate told me he was here."

"I'll clear your absence in Warrants with your instructor,

but you'll have to make up the work. You can get the assignment and notes from New Agent Aragon—he's a friend of yours, right?"

"Yes." Jason would not only have good notes, but he also had the most experience with warrants and would be able to answer any questions. "Thank you."

"We haven't spoken since you found Agent Presidio. If you need to talk, please let me know. Tony was a good man, and he obviously saw something special in you."

For the first time since she'd arrived, Lucy felt comfortable with Kean. Though her tone was formal, it had an edge of sincerity that Lucy appreciated.

"Thank you. He was a terrific teacher. We'll all miss him."

Kean smiled, a rare warmth in her pale eyes. "He had a reputation for being tough on the new agents, but you seemed to hold up well." She stepped into her office, then stopped and said, "I know you're a personal friend of Dr. Vigo's, but if you'd like me to join you, I'm available."

"I appreciate the offer, but I'm okay." Kean didn't say anything about the meeting Kate had alluded to at lunch, and Lucy didn't ask.

She crossed the courtyard and Agent Trevor Seward was talking to two new agents in the lounge. "Hold up," he told her.

She waited for him in the hall, though she was antsy to see Hans.

"Don't you have Warrants this afternoon?"

"Yes, but Dr. Vigo called me into Tony's office."

"I'll walk you down." He touched her arm. "Are you okay?"

"Everyone is asking me if I'm okay. I am." She glanced at him with a half smile. "But thank you."

"It's my job to help you and the rest of your class get

through the remaining weeks. I was here only five years ago; it can be hell."

"I can handle it. Growing pains, that's it."

Seward stopped at the secure staircase that led to the basement. He swiped his card over the security panel, and the door unlocked. He opened it for her. "Just remember, Agent Laughlin and I are here to help if you need to talk to someone about what happened with Agent Presidio, or anything."

Why did everyone think she needed to talk to someone? She'd been around death and dying enough to know the process. But she simply said, "I appreciate it."

She went down to Tony's office alone. Hans was sitting at Tony's desk going through stacks of files.

"Dr. Vigo."

Hans smiled and stood to greet Lucy. "Sit down." He returned to his seat but moved files to one side so they could talk.

Lucy had known Hans for seven years. Though they'd met after tragedy, Hans and her brother Dillon had worked together often and she'd seen Hans across the dinner table dozens of times over the years because of his friendship with her brother. Hans had helped reinstate Kate to the FBI after she'd gone rogue, had worked with Lucy's other sister-in-law years ago, and had given Lucy a glowing recommendation into the FBI. The Kincaids considered Hans part of the family.

Hans wasn't one for chitchat; he came straight to the point. "Tell me what you were working on for Agent Presidio."

Lucy said, "I'm truly sorry about his death. You were friends."

Hans stared over her shoulder, his eyes unfocused. "Yes," he said quietly. Then he shook his head and looked directly at her. "I'm clearing up Tony's files and taking over his classes, until we find someone to replace him. I've taught here before, so there shouldn't be any disruption. Any help you can give smoothing things over with your class would help."

"Anything you need."

"I talked to Agent Madeaux last night about Tony's work on the Weber case. I don't know that I'll be getting involved, but Tony left a message for me yesterday before he boarded the plane. I didn't get it until after he died."

Hans continued, "Agent Madeaux said you were helping Tony. How so?"

"Before he went to New York, he gave me his file on the McMahon case because we'd been talking about it and Rosemary Weber and whether her death could have had something to do with the Cinderella Strangler investigation."

"You lost me."

"I'll backtrack." Lucy relayed the information as if she were giving a report. She explained to Hans about Suzanne contacting her Wednesday morning, discussing Weber's murder with Tony, and the work she'd been doing reviewing the McMahon file and the analysis of Weber's books while Tony was in New York. "Tony thought it was suspicious that Weber's notes from her first book were missing from the library archives."

"He suspected her murder had something to do with the McMahon case, and not the book she was currently researching?"

"Yes, I'm certain of it, though he didn't explicitly say that. He said something was bugging him and he wanted to look as his notes again. So I agreed to meet him in his office. When I got here, he was unconscious."

"Where is his file? Did you bring it?"

"I had it with me last night." She glanced around the office, but it was much messier than yesterday. She gestured to the table just inside the door. "When I saw him, I dropped the file on that table but it's not there now. It's a file folder about an inch thick."

"I'll find it."

Lucy frowned and looked around the office. "It should be here."

"Lucy, it's okay."

"I need to find it, sir."

Hans smiled. "You can call me Hans when we're alone. No need to be formal."

"It's important. I think someone was in my dorm room today."

"Someone broke in?" Hans raised his eyebrows.

"I don't know. But I made some personal notes about the McMahon case, and I kept them in my desk. I'm almost certain that's where I put them, but maybe I grabbed them when I picked up Tony's file."

He eyed her closely. "But you don't think so."

She shook her head. "I remember everything clearly from the minute I found him, but I can't remember if I picked up my notes. He'd asked for something specific—he wanted a list of every person Weber wrote about, and what she said about them."

"Because he thought someone might have a motive, even ten years later."

"Yes. So I typed up my notes. I included those in his folder, not my handwritten notes." The more Lucy thought about the series of events, the more certain she was that she'd left her written notes in her desk.

"Tony over-involved himself on too many of his cases,

particularly cases involving young children, sometimes to the point of obsession. It's one reason he was here—he's brilliant, but . . ." His voice trailed off.

"I didn't think he acted obsessed, just contemplative. Curious."

"You didn't know him like I did," Hans said, his voice switching from friendly to authoritarian.

Lucy wondered if she should mention Tony's interest in Peter McMahon, decided yes. "Tony asked me to find Peter McMahon, Rachel's younger brother. I don't think he believed that Peter was responsible for Weber's murder, but . . ." She hesitated.

Hans wrote something down. "He thought it might have been a possibility?"

"I got the sense that he was simply concerned about Peter himself. With the media reports on Weber's death, it might drag up old feelings about his past."

"That's stretching. More likely, Tony thought the boy may have grown up with deep resentment. He was a child when his sister was killed, a teenager when Weber's book came out. Now he's an adult. He could have been planning revenge for a long time."

It was definitely possible. She said, "I asked Sean to look for him, find out where he lived and what he was doing. We knew he had been living in Florida with his grandmother, and may have taken her surname. Sean was able to trace him to Syracuse University, but lost him there. He seems to have disappeared."

"No one disappears."

"That's pretty much what Sean said."

Hans leaned back and looked at the ceiling. "Tony's instincts are sharp, but like a lot of psychologists, sometimes he knows or senses things that he can't quite articulate. Gut instinct. Do you think McMahon was involved in Weber's murder?"

Lucy hesitated, then said, "Sean brought it up as a possibility. But I couldn't possibly make that determination without knowing more about Peter McMahon."

"Can you re-create your notes?"

"Yes."

"E-mail me the file when you're done." He smiled sadly. "Get some sleep, Lucy. It's been a long twenty-four hours."

"How did Tony die? Heart attack?"

"That's the preliminary diagnosis. He'd had elevated blood pressure for years, but was controlling it primarily through diet and exercise and a very mild drug, according to his doctor."

"Please let me know. If I did anything wrong when I found him—"

"You did everything you could. Go; have dinner; rest. I'll talk to you tomorrow."

After Lucy left, Hans considered what she'd said and, knowing Tony, what he might have been thinking or working on before he died. Hans had told her about Tony's instincts, but his own were humming right along. He immediately began looking around the office for the McMahon file Lucy had left here yesterday.

"Tony, what were you thinking?" Tony was brilliant, but he rarely brainstormed with his colleagues. He mulled thoughts and ideas in his head until they came together; then when he spoke he was almost always right. Knowing what he might be thinking was nearly impossible.

But Hans had known Tony for twenty-five years. Hans knew how he reasoned out a case. His notes would help, but Hans searched everywhere and didn't find the McMahon file.

Lucy thought someone had stolen her notes from her room. And it appeared someone had taken Tony's files from his office.

Hans stared at Tony's personal effects, which he'd already boxed up to bring to Tony's widow, Shannon. The box included a Glenlivit bottle that was only a quarter filled. Tony wasn't a heavy drinker, but he liked his shot of Scotch at night. When they worked together two decades ago, they'd often shared a Scotch after hours.

The bottle had been on his desk, an empty glass nearby.

Hans didn't think that there was any foul play in Tony's death.

But.

He opened the bottle, and all he could smell was Scotch. He closed it and called the FBI Laboratory. The head of toxicology, Dr. Trisha Morrison, was a longtime colleague and friend.

"Hans, it's been a while."

"A lot of travel, but mostly just excuses on my part."

"How can I help you?"

"I need you to come to Quantico tomorrow and gather evidence from Agent Presidio's office."

"The instructor who had a heart attack?"

"Yes. I want to make sure that there's nothing in here that might have caused him to go into cardiac arrest."

Trisha didn't say anything for a moment. Then, "Are you saying he could have been murdered?"

"No." Then he stated carefully, "I'm saying I want to make sure there's nothing in his office that might have caused him to go into cardiac arrest." If Tony was murdered, that put the murderer at Quantico. As soon as Hans put this in a report, it would be part of the system. Even if they classified it, if someone *had* killed Tony, they would wonder why his file was classified. "I need someone who can be discreet."

Trisha said, "I'll be out tonight."

"I appreciate it."

Hans hung up and then dialed Sean Rogan.

"Hello, Dr. Vigo," Sean said. "I suppose I don't need to guess why you're calling."

"You're a smart boy," Hans said. He liked Sean quite a bit but worried about some of his activities. It was no secret that Sean had had trouble in his youth, but Hans suspected it went a lot deeper than even he knew. Hans felt oddly protective of him, maybe because he'd captured Lucy's heart and Hans wanted to make sure Sean didn't make an illegal detour that would break it.

Still, Hans wanted answers and Sean could get them. "I know you're digging around in this and that."

"You may have to define what you mean by *this* and *that.*"

"Peter McMahon."

"I'm trying to find him."

"Call me if you do."

"Why?"

Hans became irritated. He was an assistant director in the FBI and no one challenged his authority. He had to remind himself that not only was Sean not his employee, but also Sean challenged everyone.

"It's relevant to the Rosemary Weber murder. Lucy filled you in?"

"She did. Do you think he's guilty?"

"I think he needs to be found."

"All right. I'll let you know. Now I have a question for you. Do you know a cop named Bob Stokes? He was a rookie during the McMahon case, became a detective pretty quick. Weber dedicated her first book to him."

"I remember the name."

"I thought he'd be a good place to start, but Patrick found out he died. Six weeks ago."

"What happened?"

"Heart attack."

Hans frowned. "How old was he?"

"Forty-one."

"Was there anything suspicious about his death?"

"No, but they might not have been looking for anything suspicious."

"And you are."

"I'm curious. Just want to answer these nagging questions."

Hans didn't believe in coincidences, yet causing someone to go into cardiac arrest wasn't easy. The killer would need both knowledge of poisons and access to the victim. And there was no guarantee that the victim would die. Such a premeditated murder would need planning and foresight. And there wasn't any connection between Detective Stokes and Tony except a fifteen-year-old case.

"Doc, you there?"

"Let me know what you learn as soon as you learn it, especially if you locate McMahon."

He hung up and pinched the bridge of his nose.

Tony, you knew something. What was it? Did it get you killed? Did it have anything to do with Rosemary Weber?

CHAPTER TWENTY

Nine Years Ago

I kept to myself my freshman year of high school.

I was smart, but that didn't make me popular. I wasn't an athlete because I was too short and, when I was younger, Grams didn't have the energy to take me to practices or games. I had told her I didn't care about playing soccer or football or lacrosse, even though I kind of did. But she needed me and I wasn't going to let Grams down. And then she died and I was back where it all began, and hiding behind Grams's last name no longer helped.

Being smart has its advantages, and I kept telling myself if I could just get through four years of high school I could go to any college I wanted, far away. I didn't make many friends. Maybe because I didn't try and use Rachel as an excuse. I was, after all, the kid whose sister had been murdered by a pervert who went to his parents' sex parties. It didn't matter that my parents divorced, my father moved across the country, or I hated my mother. I was the freak. People either felt sorry for me or thought my misfortunes would rub off on them. I don't know. Maybe it was just because of me.

It didn't help that everyone knew about the book. The

book that reminded me that I was nobody except Rachel McMahon's little brother.

Most of the kids left me alone. They probably thought I was going to blow up the school. I guess I looked like the type of kid who would do that—short; shaggy hair; dressed in black; friendless; and a geek. Sometimes, I thought about doing something big. Not blowing up the school, I didn't want to hurt anyone, except one person. My mom. Or maybe something bigger, like blowing up the prison where Rachel's killer sat filing appeal after appeal in his attempt at gaming the system.

Someone, though, had it out for me. All that year, watching me.

It started with the note in my locker, but it got worse. I never knew when—sometimes weeks would pass, sometimes only a day or two. A picture of my sister. Copies of the articles from the murder investigation. And on the anniversary of Rachel's death, the creep filled my locker with worms.

But on the last day of school, I think my latent instincts kicked into high gear, and I believed for the first time that someone wanted to kill me.

I hadn't planned on going to school. It was a half day, everyone was signing yearbooks, and there wasn't anyone I cared to sign mine. But Mr. Doherty had graded our English essays, and he said he wanted to talk to me about mine. So I rode my bike to school, kept my head down so no one would feel like they had to ask me to sign their yearbook, and went upstairs to Mr. Doherty's class. I waited until he was done talking to some students; then when they left I stepped inside and cleared my throat.

"Hey." Mr. Doherty was my favorite teacher. His was the only class I really liked. He loved to read and loaned me books. I never talked to anyone about what happened to Rachel, but I told him about Grams. Having him listen helped, and every time I thought about running away I remembered I had a book I needed to return or an essay I wanted to finish. He always wore a blazer with leather patches on the elbows, either a tweed coat or a dark blue coat, and the familiarity was comforting, like the smell of my grams's soap.

He smiled. "Peter, come in, please."

I stood in front of his desk, still and silent, my backpack slung over my shoulder. I slid back my hoodie as a sign of respect, the most I'd do for a teacher I liked.

"Sit down."

I didn't want to, but I pulled one of the desks up and sat on the edge of the attached chair. "Do you have my essay?" I had my grades already. The school mailed them to my mother, but since my teachers liked me I just asked them. All A's except a B in P.E. and a B+ in honors physics. I could live with that.

Mr. Doherty smiled. "You have a lot of talent, Peter."

I shrugged. I liked writing. I was good at it. But that didn't make me talented.

He slid the essay over, upside down. I took it, looked at the cover page. A+. I smiled. I knew I'd nailed the assignment, but the validation felt good.

"I'm a little concerned about the pessimism in your story."

I shrugged.

"A couple other teachers have come to me and asked if they need to be concerned about you."

Why'd anyone talk to Mr. Doherty about me? I was quiet and maybe antisocial, but I wasn't a troublemaker. Didn't these people have anything more important to worry about? Like the kid who brought a knife to school last month or the group who smoked pot on the roof nearly every Friday?

"I'm fine," I said. *Fine.* I suppose I'd never be *fine,* but really, what else could I say? I showed up, I got good grades, and I didn't bother anyone. What more did these people want?

"I know this year has been hard on you—"

"No shit," I said. Then I thought of Grams and how much she hated swearing. "Sorry."

"I told them not to be concerned; then I read your story. I could see you in your character Thomas. I was completely hooked by the story, the depth of character, your keen sense of description, the emotions you evoke in just a few words. Then Thomas kills himself. And the comments from your teachers made me concerned that I'm missing signs. I like you, Peter. You have a lot to offer."

I thought a lot about death and dying. And maybe sometimes I thought about *being dead.* I wondered if Rachel could see me, wondered if there was a heaven and if she was happy. Or if there was nothing. That death was final; there was no more.

"It's fiction, Mr. Doherty."

He stared at me. I didn't know what he saw, but he was worried. "I think I should talk to your mother."

My heart skipped a beat, but it was only anger I felt. My mother had no right to know anything of how I felt.

I stood. "No."

"If not your mother, maybe I can find someone for you to talk to."

"I'm not going to kill myself. It's a *story.* That was the assignment, right? A work of fiction?"

Mr. Doherty looked away, then changed the subject. "What are your plans this summer?"

Stay out of the house as much as I could. "My dad's making me visit him for a month."

"Maybe that would be good for you."

I shrugged.

"People change, Peter. You should forgive them."

I walked out.

I could forgive Benjamin John Kreig easier than I could forgive my parents. I thought Kreig should have gotten the death penalty for killing my sister. I think my parents should get worse.

But I couldn't do anything about it. And I wouldn't. I just wanted my mom and dad to disappear. I didn't want to talk to them; I didn't want to see them; I didn't want to be reminded of what happened in our house.

I went to my locker to get the last of my things. I opened it and a vile smell assaulted me. I stared at the bloody mess in front of me, not knowing at first what it was. Then I saw. A dead cat. Flattened, like roadkill. Flies buzzed; bugs burrowed in its wounds. Tears came fast, for the poor animal, for me, for Rachel—I had never felt so alone. Not even when Grams died. Not even when I found Rachel's empty bed.

I slammed my locker shut and ran to the bike cage, ignoring the stares of my peers. *Go to Hell!* I wanted to scream at all of them. Instead, I got on my bike and rode away fast. I didn't want to go home, so biked south, through one old Newark neighborhood after another. I didn't have a destination; I just wanted to get away.

But maybe my heart knew best, because two hours later I ended up at the cemetery where Rachel was buried.

I found her grave. There were no flowers on it. I walked back to the office and bought her a white rose. Not because she liked them—I don't know that she had a favorite flower—but I only had three dollars in my pocket and the rose was $2.49.

I went back to her grave and put the flower in a little cup in the ground. It looked small against the large headstone. I sat on the grass and talked to her. I told her everything that had happened at school, told her about Mr. Doherty, told her I missed her and I was sorry I hadn't visited her since she was buried.

I think she understood. At least, I felt better. Like maybe I would get through this whole thing, that there was hope. A future.

I didn't know how long I'd been there, but it was after six when I looked at my watch. I traced her name with my finger. "I love you, Sis."

Three more years until I turned eighteen and could get out of my mom's house. Then I'd never have to see her again.

It took me an hour to ride my bike home, faster than it took to get to the cemetery, but I'd taken the long way there, probably because I hadn't planned on it.

I glided up the driveway and frowned. My mom had a visitor. I didn't want to talk to any of her friends. Or worse, what if it was a date? She went out every weekend, so I wouldn't be surprised if some jerk had come to pick her up.

I dropped my bike in the side yard and went in through the kitchen door. Saw a meal on the table. Two plates, both empty. A bottle of wine, also empty.

I walked through the kitchen to the living room and stared at the familiar jacket draped across the couch. A tweed jacket, with leather patches at the elbows.

A copy of my essay was on the coffee table.

Someone laughed upstairs. Then came the all-too-familiar sounds of sex.

If I'd had a gun, I might have shot them both. Right then, at that moment, I would have done it. I could see my hand with a pistol aimed at my mother, aimed at the traitor, pulling the trigger over and over and killing them.

But the murderous rage passed as quickly as it crept over me, and I broke.

Broken and free.

I went upstairs, passed her room, and quietly entered mine. I packed a backpack with everything I could carry, and stuffed in a small, framed picture of Rachel, Grams, Grandpa, and me. My family, my only family, and they were all dead.

I took all the money out of my mother's purse—a hundred dollars—and her ATM card because I knew her code. I went into Mr. Doherty's jacket and found his wallet—he had only forty-nine dollars. I took it, too. I packed cheese, crackers, granola bars, and water to get me through a couple of days. Then I went to the garage, got a sleeping bag from the rafters, and tied it to the back of my bike.

Then I left. It was three days before Mom canceled her ATM card, and by that time I had fifteen hundred dollars.

I never would have gone home, except the cops arrested me six months later.

And this time I was unlucky enough to be sent to live with my dad.

CHAPTER TWENTY-ONE

FBI Academy

This was supposed to be Class 12-14's first weekend with forty-eight hours of freedom—they could leave, visit home, go away for R & R, or hang around campus without obligations. But because of the extra weapons training their forty-eight hours of freedom had been nearly halved.

For two hours Saturday morning, Lucy's group learned more than most wanted to know about firearms. Even those who enjoyed the history of weapons left the classroom sleepy and frustrated.

"That was an effective punishment," Carter Nix groaned.

They'd been granted a forty-five-minute early lunch break, then would be required to fieldstrip and reassemble the FBI standard-issue Glock. Everyone would be required to perform the task in less than two minutes. For former military, two minutes was a joke; for most of the class, two minutes made them sweat.

Eddie said to the group, "Want to bet who'll win?"

"It's not a competition," Margo said.

"It's more fun if it is."

"Gordon Ellis wins, hands down," Carter said. "He was an Army sniper, he hasn't scored less than perfect on the range, and he's the only one who wasn't half-asleep this morning."

They went through the line in the cafeteria. Gordon was behind them and said, "I was a Ranger. I learned to sleep with my eyes open."

They laughed and Carter invited Gordon to sit with them. Lucy said, "Maybe you can help Sanchez with her shooting. I offered, but she turned me down."

"Ditto here," Gordon said. They glanced over to where Alexis Sanchez sat alone.

"What else can we do?" Reva asked. "We've all invited her to hang out, and she dismisses us."

"What do we know about her?" Eddie asked. "She doesn't talk to anyone."

"She does fine in class," Lucy said.

"How do you know?" Reva said. "She never talks."

Oz picked up his tray. "If Mohammed doesn't go to the mountain—" He looked around at the group.

Lucy stood up with her tray. "If we all go over, we'll overwhelm her. I think she has social anxiety, and the crowd will make her more nervous."

"Good luck," Reva said without confidence.

Oz led the way to where Alexis sat alone. She looked up at him and Lucy, and Lucy wondered if it was anger or fear that crossed her face. "Mind if we sit?" Oz sat before Alexis could answer. He downed his milk.

"We wanted you to know you're always welcome to eat with us," Lucy said.

"Thanks," Alexis said quietly, focused on her food.

Oz said, "Gordon, our resident gun expert, said he can train anyone to shoot."

"And I need it?" she said defensively.

"Yes," Lucy said, "and you know it. Why won't you take the offer?"

"I'm not like everyone else. I never touched a gun before I came here."

"But you knew you'd have to, right?"

"I didn't think about it," she admitted. "I don't fit in."

"Obviously the FBI recruiters thought you did, otherwise you wouldn't have made it this far," Oz said.

Alexis didn't meet their eyes. "I appreciate the effort, but it's not a good time for me."

"Did something happen?" Lucy asked. When Alexis didn't say anything, Lucy added, "Something at home? You're married, right?"

Her eyes watered. "How'd you know?"

"Good guess." It made sense. If there were stresses at home, maybe Alexis's way of dealing with it was to shut down.

"I missed my daughter's fourth birthday last week. And I started wondering why I'm here. It seemed like a good idea at the time, but now?"

"You'll get through this," Lucy said. "We want to help."

Now that Alexis had opened up, she let it all pour out. "There's only four other new agents who have kids, and all are guys," Alexis said. "It's different being a mother. My husband wanted me to wait until Missy was in school, but I'm thirty-two. The physical training is hard enough now."

"Where do you live?" Oz asked.

"Colorado. Not easy to go home for the weekend. I have a ticket in October, but I can't stop thinking about Missy and Carl. And Carl has a full-time job, so Missy is spending more time with his mom, which is just great because she hates me enough already. What if my daughter hates me when I return?"

"She won't," Oz said.

"Do you have Skype?" Lucy asked.

She shook her head. "I've heard of it."

"Right after we're done today, if you want, I can download it to your computer and show you how to use it. Maybe if you see Missy instead of just talking to her it'll make separation easier. I can walk your husband through it as well."

"He's much more technically savvy than I am." Alexis smiled for the first time that Lucy had known her. "Thank you. I'm sorry I've been such a pill."

Lucy laughed. "It's been an adjustment for everyone. You know, Carter Nix has two girls and it's hard on him as well. You're not alone."

Oz said, "Now, will you please take Gordon up on his offer to work with you? I promise, you won't regret it."

The last two hours of weapons training were almost as difficult as the first two, but in the end Agent Kosako said, "Good work." Praise was sparse at Quantico, and it meant something coming from him.

Lucy walked with Alexis to her room and set up Skype on her computer. She wasn't certain it was the solution to the problem, but at least she felt that she'd done something to help the new agent get through these difficult months.

"You ready to see your daughter?" Lucy asked.

"Do it," Alexis said. "Wait—give me a minute."

"You call when you're ready. Just click here, then here. The computer on the other end will show that there's an incoming Skype call."

"Thank you—I really mean it. Thank you."

She was glad she'd taken the time to help Alexis. No one wanted anyone in their class to be booted, and Lucy hoped this temporary solution would help Alexis and her family.

Lucy packed her overnight bag and called Sean, letting him know she was free until 6:00 p.m. on Sunday. He was already on his way. She needed the night off, to get away and clear her head.

She left her room and crossed the courtyard to the main building, but before she reached the security wing she found Rich Laughlin standing, as if waiting for her.

Of course that had to be her imagination.

"Kincaid," he said with a nod. "Finding Agent Presidio like that must have been difficult for you."

Kindness? From Laughlin?

"He was a terrific teacher. I'm going to miss—"

Laughlin cut her off. "He took a special interest in you. Why do you think that was?"

Lucy didn't know the purpose of Laughlin's question but she replied, "Maybe a kinship, since I'm the only new agent here with a master's in criminal psychology."

"That's right—I forgot you were a psychologist."

Lucy doubted that was the case.

"I figured because he and Chief Vigo were such good friends that Presidio was assessing you."

"You said yourself opening day that all staff were constantly assessing new agents; never let our guard down, right?" She tried to speak lightly, but she intently monitored manner. There was something odd in his demeanor, an intensity that seemed unwarranted.

"Yes, I did. Keeps you all on your toes. But I think you know what I meant."

Lucy didn't, and she called him on it. "Agent Laughlin, I don't know what you mean. I don't understand what I did to irritate you. If you clue me in, I'll fix it."

"Maybe you want this too much. I just have to ask myself why."

"Why I want to be an FBI agent?"

"Why you want it so badly."

His pale eyes didn't leave hers, and if this was a test, he was the perfect person to throw her off-kilter. But she stood her ground. Laughlin was essentially a bully, and bullies wanted their victims to cower. Lucy refused to let him make her a victim.

"Maybe I did before," she said, looking him straight in the eye, "but not now. If something happens and I'm forced to leave, I have other options." She wanted this because she'd been working toward becoming an FBI agent for the last seven years. Though the *why* was different now from when she first made the decision, it was no less important to her. And no way was she discussing her reasons with a man who disliked her.

"Leave? You're a shoo-in."

He scowled, and Lucy realized he knew something she didn't, something that he wanted her to know. Every instinct in her body told her to smile and walk away, but she couldn't.

She needed the truth.

"Shoo-in? Hardly. Though there is a ninety percent graduation rate, so I think the odds are in my favor."

"The odds *are* stacked in your favor. But you know that."

The truth suddenly shone through, and Lucy was almost relieved. It explained why Kate and Laughlin were arguing the other day. If Laughlin and Kate had a past during the first Adam Scott investigation, he would hate that Kate might have the power to get people privileges in the Bureau.

"I think you misunderstood. My sister-in-law didn't pull strings for me. I told her I wanted to be here on my own merits, and she honored my request. I earned this slot. You can ask her."

He tilted his head, a half smile on his face, but it wasn't friendly. She was the canary; he was the cat.

"You can't honestly tell me you didn't know that both hiring panels rejected your application. Assistant Director Vigo himself stepped in and overruled them. Most of the new agents here are relatively anonymous; you already had a history when you arrived. Don't be surprised if other people know exactly what I do." He stepped toward her, only inches from her. It was almost impossible not to step back, but she forced herself to hold her ground.

Laughlin continued. "You got here because the powers that be want you here, not because you earned it."

All Lucy had wanted was to do this on her own. To prove to her family, but mostly to herself, that she'd earned this spot in the Bureau. That the FBI would want her because not only was she a good investigator but also she had suffered and now was whole.

She walked to the tree-lined clearing on the far side of Hogan's Alley, hoping to clear her head and think about what she should do, but she couldn't focus through an overwhelming feeling of betrayal, of being lied to by the people she trusted most.

She sat on the fallen log and looked up through the center of the trees to the sky, wishing for answers but not even knowing what questions to ask.

Was this why Kate hadn't told her the truth about her confrontation with Laughlin the other day? Did Kate know what Hans had done and didn't want Laughlin to tell her?

In the past, secrets had nearly torn apart the Kincaids because her family wanted to protect her from some hard truths. And while Lucy had understood and loved her family for wanting to spare her, she also knew that secrets were dangerous and they could just as easily destroy as protect. Kate had promised to be honest with her, to not keep things hidden under the auspice of protecting her feelings. Lucy was strong enough—she was a survivor.

Lucy didn't understand what Laughlin's endgame was. He didn't hate Lucy just because Hans got her into the Academy; it had to go deeper than that. Something bad in Laughlin's background that she personified. She was a lightning rod for a wrong he hadn't been able to fix. And she had no doubt that between the two of them she and Sean would figure out why Laughlin had put Lucy in his sights.

But that didn't change the facts.

She suspected that the first panel that had denied her application had done so because she'd helped put a former FBI agent in prison for life for spearheading a vigilante group who targeted sex offenders. The actions that led up to the imprisonment of her mentor and former friend had shaken her, so she let herself believe that it was her own psychology and doubts that had screwed up the first panel.

In the middle of the hiring process, she'd learned to trust herself and trust her instincts. It was still hard sometimes to rely on her intuition and experience because of her youth and her past, but maybe it was because of the same fresh outlook and tragedy that she'd developed a unique skill set. When she'd appealed the decision and was granted a second panel interview, she'd gone in knowing that if the FBI rejected her again she would be okay.

For the first time in years she could see a future without her long-held dream of being in the FBI. She believed that change in attitude had given her the edge with the second panel, which had approved her application. Getting past that panel had been the last in a long line of hurdles.

Maybe she'd been wrong and her involvement in taking down the vigilante group hadn't been the primary reason for being denied. Did they distrust her sanity? For a long time, Lucy had questioned her pathologies. Whether her lack of remorse for killing her rapist showed a disconnect from humanity. She had told both panels, when asked, that today she would have done the same thing in the same situation.

And they didn't even know everything. People close to her had buried the truth—that Adam Scott hadn't been armed when she shot him at point-blank range. That she'd known her brother was safe when she pulled the trigger six times, each .357 bullet hitting Scott in the chest. She killed Adam Scott because he was an evil murderer who raped and tortured women for his sick pleasure. And while she'd convinced most people that she didn't remember most of what happened that fateful day seven years ago, she remembered every second. Everything: the smell of fear, the feel of the revolver, the shock on Scott's face when she shot him.

The second time she'd killed a man was to save Sean's life, as well as her own. She didn't regret that decision, either. Any hesitation and Sean would have been dead. She realized then, though she hadn't articulated it, that when threatened she went into a different mode, a different mind-set. She became both survivor and predator. She didn't like it, but at the same time she counted on self-preservation to protect her. It was like the flip of a switch, and she would do anything to save herself and those she loved.

Whether because they didn't trust her psychological makeup or because she'd killed two men to save her life, it didn't truly matter. What mattered was someone stepped in and gave her what she wanted when she hadn't earned it.

She kicked the log. Dammit, she *had* earned it!

What more did anyone want from her? She'd proven she was physically capable, emotionally stable, and intelligent. She *should* be here. She *deserved* to be here. So why did she feel like her heart had been ripped out of her chest? Why did she want to walk away and never look back?

Laughlin told you what Hans did because he wanted to hurt you.

Intellectually, she knew that. She wanted to think logically, to put aside her emotions and move forward. She could dismiss Laughlin's motives much more easily than she could dismiss Hans Vigo manipulating her life. If anyone had the authority to overturn the decision of a hiring panel, it was Hans. For the last several years he'd worked out of national headquarters with Assistant Director Rick Stockton, arguably the most powerful man in the FBI other than the director. Possibly the most powerful man behind the scenes.

That meant something. That someone of Hans's stature and position thought she deserved to be here meant she *should* be here.

Then why couldn't she shake the feeling that it was bordering on nepotism? That no one she worked with would truly trust her and that she'd be constantly trying to prove herself to her colleagues. She grew weary just thinking about constantly being assessed and analyzed and doubted.

And in the end, she wanted to be here without favors, without special privileges.

Lucy's phone rang. "Hi, Sean."

"I'm at the desk."

"Give me five minutes. I have to do something."

"What's wrong?"

"I'll tell you when I see you." She hung up and walked back to the main building, then down to the basement.

Hans was still in Tony's office.

"I thought you'd left," he said.

"Sean's waiting for me."

How she managed to keep her voice calm she didn't know. She didn't even know why she'd come down here to confront Hans.

Except she had to know the truth; she wasn't going to take Laughlin's word as gospel.

"Did you overrule my hiring panel?"

"Who told you that?"

"Am I here illegitimately?"

Hans didn't say anything, and Lucy knew it meant that Laughlin hadn't lied. Her chest tightened with a vise of pain, regret, and betrayal. And anger.

"How could you?"

"You're supposed to be here, Lucy."

"You're the only one who thinks so."

"You never understood what you were up against with the panels."

"I never wanted you, or anyone, to pull strings."

"The odds were stacked against you. All I did was level the field."

"You overruled the panel!"

"No one knows that."

She laughed bitterly. "Someone does."

He didn't say anything.

"I thought you were my friend, Hans."

Hans rose from behind the desk. He leaned forward, palms up. "I am your friend."

"A true friend would let me succeed or fail on my own merits. I don't want be an FBI agent if cheating is the only way I can be here. Yes, I earned this. Yes, I deserve to be here, but if no one else thinks so, I don't want it."

She reached into her purse and took out her wallet. She didn't have a badge or gun to turn in, but she had her new-agent ID.

Hans grabbed her wrist when she held the ID out to him. "Don't be rash."

"Let go."

He didn't. "When you helped put Fran in prison, you made enemies. You knew that would happen. Getting a fair panel at that time would have been next to impossible."

"I don't want this anymore."

"Yes, you do!"

"Don't tell me what I want or don't want." Lucy's chest heaved. She would *not* cry. The tears that were threatening weren't sadness but anger, a rage she'd never quite felt before. Not like this. She'd felt fear, and panic, and regret, but not this fury of being manipulated and used, made worse because it was someone she had respected. "Who knew? Kate? Dillon?"

Hans shook his head. "Assistant Director Stockton agreed with me, and we were the only two who knew, other than the panels. Who told you? We may have a security problem."

"It's not my problem." She jerked her hand free and dropped her ID on the desk.

"I'm not accepting this. Think about it over the weekend."

She shook her head. "I trusted you."

Lucy walked out. She didn't know if she'd return.

CHAPTER TWENTY-TWO

Sean knew something was very wrong as soon as Lucy slid into the passenger seat of his Mustang. But she didn't talk about it. With Lucy, it had to be on her terms. He tried to engage her in conversation, but she was only half-listening.

"We're going to New York," Sean finally said.

"Sure," Lucy said.

"And we won't be back for a week, but I'm sure that'll be fine with your superiors." He glanced at her. She was still looking out the window, oblivious to his joke.

"Sure," she said. Then she looked at him. "What are you doing?"

"You're lost in a world that doesn't look very fun."

"Hans pulled strings to get me into Quantico."

Sean froze. How had she found out? Had Hans told her?

Lucy continued. "They didn't deem me fit for the FBI, and when Hans found out he overruled their decision. *Both* hiring panels rejected my application. I should never have been admitted."

Shit. No wonder she was in so much pain. "He told you that?"

"No. But does it matter?"

"Yes. It matters. I don't care what a panel of bureaucrats thinks, you worked your ass off to get to Quantico, more than anyone else."

"I gave him my ID. Not as dramatic as handing over my gun and badge, but it was all I had."

"You can't."

Sean crossed over three lanes of traffic and pulled over into the breakdown lane. Lucy clutched the dashboard and stared at him as if he'd jumped from an airplane without a parachute. "What are you doing?"

He slammed the car into park and turned to face her. "You can't just quit."

"I did."

"You're not a quitter."

"I'm fine."

"No, you're not."

"Don't tell me how I'm feeling!"

Sean wanted to go back to Quantico, but forcing Lucy to confront Hans now wasn't going to help. No one could force Lucy to do something she didn't want to do. He had to convince her to go back on her own.

"Hans did not accept your resignation."

"That doesn't mean I'm going back." She sighed and took his hand. "Sean, this is my decision to make. Yes, I earned my spot. I absolutely *should* be an FBI agent. But people *know*. They know someone pulled strings to get me this spot, and *that* bothers me more than anything. Remember a few months back when I told you if I didn't make it, I'd be okay?"

"Of course."

"I'm going to be okay now, too. I'll get through this."

Sean didn't doubt it, but that didn't mean she should quit. "Don't do anything rash."

"I won't. But you understand, right?" She squeezed his hand, imploring him with her eyes.

He kissed her. "I understand. Whatever decision you make, I'm behind you." Sean took a deep breath. "But this conversation is not over."

"It's over for now."

Sean reluctantly agreed and pulled the car back in with the traffic. "We're going to New York to retrace Tony Presidio's steps."

"Why?"

"Hans asked me to."

"Great." She closed her eyes.

"I'll have you back by six p.m. tomorrow. I promise."

"I don't care."

"Yes, you do."

He should tell her that he'd known. Right now—except he couldn't. She was angry and upset and he didn't want to compound the situation by telling her that Senator Jonathon Paxton had told him two months ago that Hans had pulled strings. What would it have helped? She already didn't speak to Paxton anymore, and then Sean would have had to explain why Paxton told him, and that was opening a big fat can of worms Sean didn't want to open.

So he remained silent. If Lucy wanted to be an FBI agent, she should be—there was no one here more qualified or capable.

Sean changed the subject and told her the plan. "Patrick is joining us at the airport. We're flying into Newark. Bob Stokes, the cop you flagged for me from Weber's first book, died of a heart attack last month. Patrick's going to pull the report and talk to his partner and widow."

"You think there's something suspicious about his death?"

"He was in his early forties and close to Rosemary

Weber. He'd been the responding officer at the scene, and had gone on record as believing the parents were holding back. Patrick's going to snoop around there, while we go to New York City and retrace Tony's steps. Hans thinks we may be able to find out why he was so hot to look at his notes. You're the last person to have seen them; they're fresh in your head."

"But he was intimately familiar with the case." Lucy paused, then said, "It's hard to kill someone by heart attack."

"What are you thinking?"

"Tony died of a heart attack. He had twice the legal limit of alcohol in his system, which may have been a contributing factor. Or coincidence." Lucy took out her cell phone.

"Who are you calling?" Sean asked.

"I'm sending Hans an e-mail. I don't want to talk to him right now, but when I found Tony on Thursday there was a bottle of Scotch on his desk. They should have it tested. Just in case."

Sean waited while she sent the e-mail. "Lucy, who told you that Hans pulled strings?"

"Laughlin."

Sean wanted to deck the guy. "You don't think there's something suspicious about that?"

"Yes, I do. It tells me that Kate knew and didn't want me to find out. It's what they had to have been arguing about when I walked in. And it would explain why Kate wouldn't tell me the truth when I confronted her about it."

She glanced back down at her phone and said, "Well, I guess I'm not the only one with a suspicious mind. Hans had a forensic team come in from the FBI lab last night. They took the Scotch bottle and glass and collected trace evidence. They're testing everything at the lab, and running an expanded tox screen on Tony's blood work."

"If someone poisoned his bottle, that means—"

Lucy finished his sentence. "There's a killer at Quantico."

CHAPTER TWENTY-THREE

New York City

Patrick met them at the small private airport in northern Virginia where Sean kept his Cessna. "I have a meeting with Stokes's partner, and with the coroner's office, but we need to get going—it's Saturday, and I convinced the coroner to come in on his day off. I don't want to keep him waiting."

Lucy psyched herself up for the flight. She'd flown since the crash landing three months ago when she and Noah Armstrong, who'd been an Air Force pilot, had been shot down in the Adirondack Mountains. But each time she boarded a plane, her heart raced and she had to force herself to remain calm.

While Sean ran through the pre-flight check, Patrick came over to her. "You okay, Sis?"

She nodded. To change the subject she asked, "What happened with Brandy?"

"What did Sean tell you?"

"Nothing—just that *you* said it wasn't going to last."

Patrick shrugged. "Sean has a big mouth."

"He wanted to know what I knew, which is less than he does. I thought you liked her."

Patrick sighed. "She's beautiful and smart, but I just don't feel it, you know? I'm going through the motions and it shouldn't be like that. She called me on it last night, and I let her walk away."

"Is Mom getting on your case because you're next up to get married?"

Patrick paled. "Don't even say it. I'm not ready."

"You're going to be thirty-six next month."

"I'm young at heart."

Lucy laughed and hugged him. "It is Mom. Don't let her push you."

"She has a long arm, even three thousand miles away." In a low voice he said, "She's planning on setting me up with Gabrielle Santana when I go home for Christmas."

Lucy stared wide-eyed. "What? You can't."

Lucy knew Gabrielle, even though the woman was three years older than her. Like the Kincaids, the Santana family was large and Catholic. In high school, Lucy had dated Gabrielle's brother for two weeks, and even in two weeks the stories she'd heard from him about all five of his sisters, and in particular Gabrielle, had Lucy both envious and terrified. Gabrielle had a wild reputation.

"Apparently, Gabrielle is the first Santana ever to get divorced. Mom and Mrs. Santana think I would be good for her. Why do I feel like I'm being set up to tame a shrew?"

"So this means we have four months to find you a girl-friend."

Patrick stared at her as if she'd suggested he become a monk. "No. This means we have four months to find me a job that will keep me out of San Diego at Christmas."

Sean approached. "Christmas?"

"Nothing," Patrick said.

Lucy smiled and whispered, "I'll tell you later."

"You mean this is about the girl your mom is trying to set Patrick up with."

"Shut up, Rogan," Patrick mumbled.

Sean grinned. "Plane's ready; let's go."

At least the conversation with Patrick went a long way in alleviating Lucy's apprehension about the plane ride, and the hour passed quickly while Sean ran through a list of women he could set Patrick up with just for the three days he would be in San Diego. Patrick mostly pretended to sleep and ignored him.

Sean landed them in Newark just after three that afternoon. Both he and Patrick rented cars, because they were on a tight schedule if Sean was truly going to get Lucy back by 6:00 p.m. tomorrow. He didn't believe for a minute that she would follow through on her threat to quit, and he wasn't going to make her late.

Sean turned onto the Jersey Turnpike heading toward Manhattan. "So that's what this whole dating kick he's been on has been about. Finding a girl to bring home to your mom?"

"I guess so. But honestly, I'm glad that's all it is, because I was worried about him. He's not usually like this. Anyway, what's our plan for tonight?"

"Suzanne is meeting us at a bar near the Bureau along with the NYPD detective working the case."

"Vic Panetta?"

"Some guy named DeLucca, out of Queens. Weber was stabbed in the parking lot of Citi Field in the middle of a baseball game. Money and jewelry stolen."

"She was wearing expensive jewelry at a baseball game?"

"According to her insurance records, she always wore her mother's wedding ring on her right ring finger. It was valued at over fifteen thousand dollars. Her friends said she never took it off."

"So her attacker may have asked her to hand it over and she refused?"

"Could be. We'll know more when we read the reports. Suzanne didn't tell me much of anything over the phone. Except she wasn't there for the game—didn't have a ticket—but apparently planned to meet someone."

"No witnesses?"

"None came forward. No security cameras in the area—only on the entrances and exits."

"And Weber herself?"

"I know what you know."

"I thought we were retracing Tony's steps."

"We are. Suzanne will give us the rundown, but he made at least one stop after he left her and that's what we're going to follow up on."

"And Suzanne is fine with us helping?"

"Hans called her already. He wanted this off-the-books because he didn't know what Tony was up to and he didn't want anything in the press." Sean glanced at Lucy. "And I want to know what's in her files."

"Why did we have to come here? Couldn't we have gotten the files e-mailed or faxed? Talked to Suzanne on the phone?"

"We could have, but I wanted to get you away. Last time we were in New York you said you wanted to come back, and this is our chance to have a night off, just you and me." He glanced at her. "You're okay with that, right?"

"Of course I'm okay with it."

"Good. Because I missed you and I only have twenty-four hours having you all to myself. In between this investigation."

"Tonight, Sean, will be ours."

She smiled, and Sean was relieved. While he knew Lucy loved him, he was the more romantic one. He relished these moments when they could get away. And every vacation they'd had to date had ended in disaster. So he wasn't calling this a vacation, but he was going to treat tonight as such.

The time away would help Lucy regroup and think clearly before she decided what to do about Hans, as well as how to deal with the possibility that Tony's death might not have been of natural causes. Sean wasn't convinced it was murder—could a killer get away with two murders, in different states, at different times, staged as heart attacks? That would be pushing it. However, if it worked once, why not again? They needed to find out if there was any connection between Stokes and Presidio other than the McMahon case.

Sean drove straight to the Park Central Hotel where he and Lucy had stayed in February when he was searching for his missing cousin. He grinned at the smile on Lucy's face. "Surprise."

"You're sneaky." She leaned up and kissed him. "I love it."

He glanced at his watch. "We're going to have to hustle to meet Suzanne by six."

They dropped their bags in their room—which had a view of Central Park—and left the hotel. Sean hailed a taxi. "We're not driving?" she said.

Sean always preferred to drive, but he didn't like traffic. "Don't want to deal with parking," he said.

It was less than a ten-minute cab ride and Lucy and Sean walked into the bar and grill. Lucy spotted Suzanne sitting at a table, facing the door. A plainclothes cop sat next to her. Lucy watched as the cop handed Suzanne a twenty.

"What was that for?" Sean asked.

"I was right. I said you'd be here within forty-eight hours. DeLucca doubted me. Good to see you both."

After introductions, Suzanne got down to business.

"I'll let you look at the files, but you're not taking a copy." She stared at Sean. "I'll be watching you."

He smiled. "I don't want a copy."

"You want to talk to the sister. Why?"

"See if she's lying."

"About?"

"Anything."

Suzanne shrugged. "My gut says she's clean, but that's fine with me. And Kip Todd, Weber's assistant?"

"Ditto."

"So you're checking up on me? Didn't you learn last time that I know how to do my job?"

Lucy said, "We trust you, Suzanne. It's my story I don't want getting out. And Kirsten has finally started to get her life back. She's in Los Angeles, going back to school; what happened here is buried. I want to make sure Rosemary Weber's assistant isn't planning on writing the book."

"And that's the only reason you came to New York?"

Sean nodded. "And to find out where Tony Presidio went. Off-the-record."

Suzanne nodded. "Dr. Vigo called me. I told him exactly what happened, sent him my report. I also told him that Tony had some ideas he didn't share with me. But his strategy paid off."

"Strategy?"

"Tony leaked to the press that we didn't think robbery was the motive, and bam, this afternoon we get a call from one of the pawnshops DeLucca briefed. A junkie walks in and pawns the ring. We got his prints."

DeLucca said, "A street thief from Queens, Jimmy

Bartz, I have patrols out looking for him at all his haunts. We'll have him before midnight."

"And that's it?"

"Maybe; we'll know when we interrogate him."

"And why would a street thief kill Weber?"

"Could be that he robbed her after she was killed," DeLucca said.

Sean assessed the cop. "You don't think he killed her."

He shrugged. "I don't know Bartz, but my buddies in Property Crimes laughed their asses off when I said we were looking at him for murder. Stealing purses, rolling a drunk, smashing a window to grab shopping bags—that's Bartz. Not a stiletto in the heart."

"But he *could* have grabbed the ring if he found her in the parking lot," Suzanne said. It was obvious that they had discussed this theory.

DeLucca nodded, but Sean sensed he thought something was fishy about the whole deal.

"Do you know Bob Stokes, a cop down in Newark?" Sean asked.

"Should I?" Suzanne said.

"Weber's first book was dedicated to him. Presidio's phone records show he tried to call Stokes Thursday evening driving from the airport to Quantico. He died of a heart attack."

"Stokes or Presidio?"

"Both," Lucy said. "Bob Stokes died last month. Did his name pop up in any of Weber's files?"

Suzanne looked through her notes. "He was in her address book, that's it. Why was Tony trying to call him?"

Lucy said, "He was very upset about the missing McMahon files, and he called me about his own personal file— he wanted to see it as soon as he got back."

"Did you bring it?"

Lucy hesitated, then said, "It disappeared."

"You lost it?"

"No," Lucy said, "it disappeared from his office be-tween the time of his heart attack and when Hans arrived the next day."

"This is starting to smell like a conspiracy," DeLucca said. "Maybe your federal colleagues are trying to cover something up."

Suzanne hit him on the arm, hard. "Shut up, Joe."

Sean said, "Lucy's the only one who's recently read Tony's file, so we hope if she goes everywhere Tony did, she'll figure out what Tony was thinking."

"It's a long shot," Lucy admitted.

"After watching you analyze that psycho nut job back in February, I'll put my money on you," Suzanne said.

Lucy said, "So essentially, from what you've said and the reports show, the victim was most likely meeting someone at Citi Field, a baseball stadium, in the middle of a baseball game, was killed, and either the killer took the jewelry to make it look like a robbery, or this Bartz guy stole the ring himself after the fact."

"Bingo."

"But," Suzanne said, "what's making me crazy is why did he pawn the ring today, four days after her murder, but only hours after the newspaper came out with the de-liberate leak to the press?"

"It's like he wants you to think it's a robbery," Sean said. "Not very smart."

"Not smart fits Bartz," DeLucca said.

"Why meet someone at a baseball stadium in the first place?" Lucy asked.

"Citi Field is very family friendly," DeLucca said. "We don't get a lot of real trouble out there. It's public; she might have thought it was safe."

"I take it no security cameras," Sean said.

"Nothing on the section of the parking lot where she was killed." DeLucca looked from Lucy to Sean. "Is there anything you know that I should?" he asked. "I don't like surprises, I don't really like P.I.'s doing police work, and I'm not a fan of the feds." He glanced at Suzanne. "Except blondie here."

"Screw you, DeLucca."

Lucy caught the smile between the two. They had been friends—or more—for a long time.

Lucy said, "If we learn anything that will aid in your investigation, you have my word that we'll give it to you. Right, Suzanne?"

"I'm still not one hundred percent sure about this," DeLucca said. He took out a folder and handed it to Sean. Sean turned it so both he and Lucy could see. DeLucca walked them through the photo evidence.

Nothing jumped out. There was extensive blood at the scene—the victim had been killed in front of her vehicle, then dragged approximately five feet to hide her body between two cars. All the cars in the area had been printed and cleared. The knife had never been recovered. No blood trail.

Lucy asked, "Was there anything about the murder that was never released to the media?"

"Only one thing—there was an inscription on the inside of the ring. We gave pawnshops and a few CIs a photo of the ring and the information that there *was* an inscription, but not what the inscription said. 'Love is patient, love is kind.' That's how we IDed the ring and Bartz."

"From Corinthians," Lucy muttered.

Sean's phone vibrated. He ignored the text message but hoped it was info he was waiting for. He turned to

Suzanne. "What's going on with the library archives? Are there computer logs?"

"Yes and no," Suzanne said. "Everyone signs in. Borrowed material is logged in the computer, but if they're simply looking, they have free run of the place."

"So either the documents are still there—hidden or misplaced—or someone with knowledge of the system took them."

"It's a large box."

Sean leaned forward. "I'll bet I can find a half-dozen ways to grab anything I want from the library and disappear with it."

"Not everyone is you, Rogan," Suzanne said.

"But," he continued as if she hadn't spoken, "if I wanted the information to disappear, I'd cloak it. Put it in a different box. Do you know the last person who pulled the box?"

"That's one of the problems," Suzanne said. "The box has been there for three years. No one has ever checked it out. And don't even think about asking for a list of everyone who has checked out boxes from the archives—you're talking about thousands of people."

Lucy said, "If someone at Quantico stole Tony's file from his office, they may have also taken the files from the archives."

Sean glanced at her. "You're brilliant. At my college library, I had to have a card to access much of the building, and definitely to view most of the research material."

Suzanne nodded. "I see what you're thinking. If there's anyone with access to Quantico who also has a Columbia library card. It's a place to start."

"Still a long shot, but not quite as long," Sean said.

Lucy frowned. "It's easy to check the travel of federal staff, and anyone at Quantico would know that."

"We don't know when the box was removed from the library," Suzanne said. "It could have been months or years ago."

"And," Sean said, "it might be someone who had a friend who was a student, or a visitor who found a flaw in the security system."

Suzanne made a note. "Dr. Vigo asked for a report tonight. I'll let him know your theory and let him run interference with Quantico. Thanks."

They exchanged contact information and parted ways.

"Back to the hotel?" Lucy asked.

Sean glanced at his watch. "Let's go meet your brother for dinner."

"In Newark?"

"At the hotel. Patrick is good. He got exactly what we needed, took the train into the city." Sean hailed a taxi. "We make a great team. And there's nothing I'd like more than to have you working for RCK. You're name's already on the door."

Sean opened the taxi door and Lucy slid in first.

"Maybe I should," she said quietly.

He gave the driver the name of their hotel, then leaned over and kissed Lucy lightly. "I know you should. But on your terms, Luce. Because you want to, not because you think it's your only option."

CHAPTER TWENTY-FOUR

Georgetown, Washington, D.C.

Hans stopped by Kate Donovan's house Saturday on his way home.

"I've left you two messages," Kate snapped when she opened the door.

"May I come in?"

She opened the door wider and he stepped in. "I spent all afternoon in a meeting with Chief O'Neal, then went to visit Shannon Presidio."

Kate softened a bit. She would never be a soft woman. But before meeting Dillon Kincaid she was on the fast track to an early death through recklessness. Now she was everything Hans had always believed she could be: smart, focused, dedicated. She still had a reckless streak, but it was tempered by experience.

"Is Dillon here?"

"Sleeping."

It was just past nine. "This early?"

"He has to be up at three to take a military transport to talk to one of those damn serial killers you want him to profile. It's not as easy on him as you think it is."

"I never thought it was easy."

"I'm not sleeping." Dillon came downstairs in sweat-pants and a T-shirt. He shook Hans's hand. "What brings you here?"

Hans glanced at Kate. She scowled and said to Dillon, "I didn't want to worry you."

Dillon put his arm around her and steered her toward the family room.

"Did you come to see Kate or me?"

"Both," Hans said.

"Don't drag Dillon into this," Kate said.

They sat at the kitchen table where Hans had often found himself enjoying a meal with the Kincaids and nearly as often talking to Dillon about work. Though Dillon was a civilian consultant, he spent the bulk of his time on FBI cases. He'd been offered a permanent position when he first moved to D.C. but had declined.

"Hans." Dillon didn't have to say anything else. He took Kate's hand but focused on Hans.

"Did Lucy tell you?"

"That she went to New York?" Kate snapped. "I'm fu-rious with her. I told her to keep her head low and focus on her studies. I suppose I should blame Sean, but Lucy is responsible for her own actions."

"That's not what I was talking about," Hans said. "I asked Sean to go to New York. I assumed Lucy would join him."

Dillon eyed him closely. "What happened?"

"Six months ago, I knew the second hiring panel was going to reject Lucy's application. A friend told me confi-dentially that Fran Buckley still had a lot of friends who thought either she was innocent or she shouldn't be in prison even if she was guilty. I went to Stockton and told him I wanted to overrule their decision."

"That's not done," Kate said.

Hans smiled sadly. "Not often, but it wasn't the first time. Stockton agreed. We sealed it, but the three panelists all knew. They were told it was confidential and no one was to be told. But now Lucy knows."

"Shit," Kate said.

"I want to know who told her."

"I didn't know," Kate said. "Dillon?"

He didn't say anything.

"You *knew*?"

"Not for a fact. I suspected." He caught Hans's eye. "Why would someone tell her?"

"To force her to quit. Which of course she did. I simply didn't accept it. She gave me her Quantico ID. I left it at the security desk and told them she dropped it in Tony's office. But I don't know if she's going to come back."

"Is that why she went to New York?"

"Lucy went with Sean. I had asked him to retrace Tony's steps and try to figure out what he was thinking. I couldn't ask Lucy to go officially, but she's the only one who read Tony's missing file. With her there, she might notice something."

"What missing file?" Kate asked.

"There's a file missing from Tony's office that may have relevance in the Rosemary Weber homicide."

"Is Lucy in danger?" Dillon asked.

"She's well aware that she's the only one, outside of Tony, who knows what is in the missing file."

Kate stared at him. "The autopsy showed Tony died of a heart attack."

"It did. But nonetheless, Stockton is discreetly requesting a more detailed probe. I already had the lab process his office on the q.t."

"Tony had heart trouble, among other things," Kate

said. "You know that, Hans. And you said he'd been drinking right before he died."

Hans knew all too well that Tony had problems he buried deeply. And Hans had been inclined to believe Tony was as responsible for his death as his weak heart.

"Though Tony may have been battling depression again, and his BAC was well above the legal limit, but I don't think he was suicidal. He was too focused on locating Peter McMahon and the missing file to want to kill himself without answers. And I found something on his computer that's of interest."

Dillon leaned forward. "Why would you even think Tony might have killed himself?"

"It wouldn't be the first time he tried." Hans glanced at Kate, then said, "When we worked the Rachel McMahon kidnapping, Tony took the events personally. He knew from the beginning that the parents were keeping something back, and he felt helpless."

"We all feel that way sometimes," Kate said.

"After her body was found, Tony got completely wasted. He came to my apartment and started talking about how nothing we do matters if we can't save the innocents. We argued, and he left, disappeared for two days. When Tony left for New York the other day, he canceled all his appointments. I thought he'd gone on a bender."

"Did he?" Kate asked.

"Maybe—he had been drinking—and after Lucy told me he was digging into the McMahon file again and wanting to find Peter, the victim's brother, I thought he was obsessed. But when we learned the files were missing in New York, and the file in his office, I think he really was on to something. Then I found a letter of resignation on his computer, dated a month ago, but I learned from Chief

O'Neal that he turned in something different. I found the original on his computer."

He reached into his pocket and pulled out a sheet of paper. He slid it across the table. Dillon and Kate read it together.

Kate said, "He was resigning?"

"The original letter was dated two months ago, but I spoke with Chief O'Neal and she said she never received that version. This letter was written three weeks ago, and she agreed to allow him to stay until the end of the year."

"Why December 21?" Kate asked, "That seems arbitrary."

Dillon gave Hans the note back. "It's the day Lucy will graduate."

Hans nodded. "He's been working with Lucy on a variety of things, nothing active, but he asked her to look for Peter McMahon. Not in so many words, but Lucy ran with it, contacted Sean, and Sean and Patrick have been working on it. Now that file is missing, all of Rosemary Weber's files on the case are missing, and someone took Lucy's notes from her bedroom. And not only was Weber killed, but two cops are dead—Bob Stokes, the responding officer, and Tony."

"Did the autopsy show anything suspicious?" Dillon asked.

"Not yet, but we're running a full and detailed toxicology screen, and I sent his Scotch bottle and glass to the lab to be analyzed. They're rushing the tests; I'll have something by Monday morning, if not sooner."

Kate stared at him, her blue eyes wide with shock. "You think there's a traitor at Quantico."

The blunt statement weighed heavily on Hans's heart. He expected danger from the outside; danger from within tested his faith in the Bureau. Their hiring system had attempted to keep Lucy Kincaid out, yet right now she was one of the few whom Hans trusted with his life.

"I'm thinking we need to dig deeper," he said solemnly. "And it needs to be off-the-books."

He continued, "Patrick called me before I came here. He talked to Bob Stokes's partner and learned that Stokes had been looking into the death of a retired FBI agent, Dominic Theissen, who died a week before Stokes's heart attack."

"Theissen was the media officer in Newark fifteen years ago," Kate said. "The only one authorized to speak to the press."

"I knew him well. He tried to rein in Weber, but once the McMahons' lifestyle became public, there was no going back. He vetted the facts that were in her book. Apparently, they kept in touch over the years."

"The facts were correct?" Dillon asked.

"Yes. But that doesn't mean she didn't focus on the scandal."

"How did Theissen die?" Kate asked.

"Subway accident. Almost two months ago. A fight broke out at a subway station in Queens, and in the scuffle he slipped and fell on the tracks. No one was arrested, the police ruled it an accident, but Bob Stokes had asked for the security footage."

"Did he find anything?"

"Not that anyone knows," Hans said.

"Why was a New Jersey city detective investigating a possible crime in New York? Did he have information he didn't share with NYPD?"

"According to Stokes's partner, he'd received an e-mail from Theissen two days before Theissen died. That's all we know. Though he requested the tapes, we don't know that he viewed them. Patrick talked to his widow and received permission to borrow Stokes's personal computer. Something in that e-mail from Theissen had Stokes concerned, but he didn't share what it was with his partner or his wife."

Dillon said, "His death may not be connected at all."

Hans shrugged. "Maybe, but Stokes was in New York the day before he died. Just like Tony."

"And they both died of heart attacks?" Dillon asked.

Hans nodded, and Kate said, "You don't think Tony's death was natural."

"I don't know," he admitted. He had no proof. "I have to look into it. There are too many unanswered questions, and I would rather investigate this as a suspicious death then make any assumptions."

Dillon said, "I can cancel my trip. If you need me, I'll be here."

Hans shook his head. "I appreciate it, but your work is important, and I don't think you staying will make a difference either way." He looked from Dillon to Kate. "This is completely need-to-know. I've briefed Rick Stockton. Other than him, and whichever agent he pulls into the investigation, you're the only person in the Bureau who knows about this investigation."

"Do Lucy and Sean know?" she asked.

"Patrick is filling them in now." He leaned back in his chair but didn't feel at all relaxed. "There's another connection between the deaths. Theissen had retired from the FBI two years ago and was working as chief of security at Citi Field. That's where Rosemary Weber was murdered."

CHAPTER TWENTY-FIVE

New York City

Lucy and Sean left Patrick in his own room, where he'd set up Bob Stokes's computer to find the e-mail that had sent the cop to New York two days before he died.

"We should help Patrick," Lucy said in the elevator.

"It's one computer, one operator. Are you forgetting your brother used to run the cybercrimes unit for the San Diego Police Department? He knows what he's doing."

Sean slid the card key into their door. "And," he continued, "you're so tired you're about to fall asleep standing up."

Lucy fell down on the bed. "True."

"Patrick is taking care of Stokes; we're following Tony's trail. If there's any overlap, we'll find it."

Sean lay on the bed next to her. He kissed her cheek and gently pulled out her hair band. "Sleep."

Lucy would have gladly surrendered except she couldn't stop thinking about the possibility that Tony was murdered.

"If someone poisoned Tony, when was it? If Stokes died after coming back from New York, they both could have been poisoned here."

"What drugs could cause a heart attack?"

Lucy frowned. "Several, but they all have other symptoms. And some are virtually undetectable after they've passed through the system."

"Hans is already suspicious. He's having the FBI lab run additional tests." He kissed her. "You're too tired to think straight. I promise, a good night's sleep and we'll both be better focused."

"It connects to Rosemary Weber. Somehow." Lucy sighed and put her head down again. "But it's not my job. Not anymore."

"You haven't quit yet."

"I'm not quitting. I was never supposed to be there in the first place. I'm righting a wrong."

"No. I'm not justifying what Hans did, but he did it because he knows you're good. He wants you as part of his team, just like everyone at RCK would be thrilled if you worked for us. You're a valuable commodity." He leaned over and kissed her again.

"Thank you."

"For telling the truth?"

"If I don't go back I won't have to worry about the driving test on Monday. And we don't have time for you to teach me."

"You know how to drive. I was supposed to teach you how to drive well enough to ace the FBI track. Is it the test Monday or a practice?"

"Defensive driving. No test, but I have to be able to complete the course."

"You will."

If she was there. "I hate driving," she mumbled. She didn't want to tell him, or anyone, how nervous she got when behind a wheel.

"You're tense." Sean nuzzled her neck. "Patrick told me about the accident."

She frowned. "He shouldn't have done that."

"You're right. You should have."

"Am I supposed to recount everything that has ever happened to me?"

"I've asked why you hate driving."

"It was never the right time."

"Accidents are traumatic. But you've faced far worse than a non-fatal car crash. Which means, Patrick doesn't know everything."

"I was five. It left a lasting impression on me."

She rolled away from Sean, but he pulled her back toward him, spooning his body around hers.

He was trying to make her comfortable, trying to make her relax and share. But it wasn't working. He always wanted to know everything, and he usually just guessed. Most of the time he was right.

"What do you think happened?" she snapped. "You usually know what I'm thinking."

He refused to take the bait. "Not this time. I only know that Patrick has no idea what happened during the crash, and that's what I don't understand."

"I barely remember the accident."

She'd been in the back between Patrick and Carina, who were bickering about something, but in the good-natured way they always had. They were only eleven months apart, and as Lucy grew up she'd been jealous that her older brothers and sisters were all friends and she was the mistake, the seventh child who came a decade late.

She didn't remember much about the accident, only flashes. Like she knew it had been raining, rare for San Diego. Her father had muttered something about drivers being stupid in the rain. Her mother had a rosary in her hands. They may have been coming home from church, or that memory might be because her dad told her later. Patrick had taken something from Carina and had given it to Lucy to hide behind her back. Their dad told them to settle down, and Lucy was giggling. She loved when her big brother included her in his jokes.

Then suddenly everything was moving fast. Loud sounds, Carina screamed, and they were upside down.

Lucy went to sleep, or so she thought at the time. She awakened fast, to a loud noise as their van was hit again. She looked around and no one was moving.

She thought her family was dead.

An involuntary moan escaped her throat.

"Hey, Lucy?" Sean sat up, pulling her up with him and holding her close. "What's wrong?"

"Nothing."

"Don't do that. Tell me, princess. What happened?"

"My family thinks I'm scared of driving because I was in the car accident. I don't remember anything about it, really, just the noise. And everyone was fine, though Carina had a broken rib, I think. Or maybe it was Patrick." She glanced away. "Maybe there was more to it, but I really don't remember. That shouldn't stop me from driving. It's silly."

"Early childhood trauma impacts us far greater than anything else," Sean said.

"Now you sound like a shrink."

"We'll get you through it, okay? Let me help you."

Sean needed to help people. Especially her. He wanted to be the one to fix everyone's problem, and that was endearing and noble, even when he was frustrating.

"I don't remember anything."

"Look me in the eye and say that."

"Stop."

"Why don't you trust me?"

"You know I trust you." She trusted Sean more than anyone, but that didn't mean she could just talk about this.

Sean didn't say anything. But he didn't move, either. He was waiting.

Lucy closed her eyes. Sean wasn't going to budge. He wanted to know. She considered making something up, but he would know. She wished she was a better liar.

"I don't know how to put it in words," she finally said.

"Patrick said you didn't want to get your license when you were sixteen."

"But I did."

"Of course you did; you've never let fear hold you back."

"And it's not now. I'll get through this, Sean."

"What happened?"

"I thought everyone was dead, okay?" Tears clouded her vision. "Damn you, I don't want to cry."

He kissed her lightly. "When I found my plane upside down in the field last May, I thought you and Noah were still in it."

Maybe he did know. "It's not logical," she said. "I was a little kid. But every time I drive, I get tense. Just a flash of memory, me wedged between Carina and Patrick, the blood, the rain hitting our car, and they weren't moving. No one was moving. It seemed like hours that I was there, crying, staring at my dad, who was so big and strong, but blood covered his head.

"It wasn't hours, of course. I learned later less than five minutes passed before someone, an off-duty policeman, came over to our van. Everyone woke up after that, but those minutes were forever to me."

Lucy was grateful that Sean didn't probe her for more

details or offer his sympathy. His even breathing, his chin on her head, was all she wanted—or needed. Comfort.

"Every time I drive, especially on the freeway, I get a flash of my family. When I interned with the Sheriff's department, I never went to traffic fatalities. I found excuses not to go. Not consciously, but I see it now."

"And when you and Detective Reid were run off the road last month, you were thinking about it."

She nodded.

"I knew you were keeping something from me that day." She looked up at him. "Thank you for not pushing."

"I knew you'd tell me eventually." He kissed her, and her muscles began to relax.

"I promised you a romantic night," Lucy said. "And all we've talked about was work."

"And you." He kissed her again. "Lay down. On your stomach. You're still tense."

Lucy complied and Sean pressed his fingers and thumb on her sore shoulder muscles.

"Umm," she said.

"You're really tense. Take off your shirt."

"This sounds like a ploy to get me into bed with you."

"How well you know me." He kissed the back of her neck.

Lucy smiled and took off her shirt. Sean rummaged through her overnight bag and found her favorite lotion. He poured some into his hands and rubbed them together, then straddled her without putting any weight on her. Slowly, he spread the lotion over her back, kneading her muscles from her neck to her hips.

"You're going to smell like roses," Lucy mumbled.

"I'll be reminded of you."

Sean's strong, talented hands smoothed out her stress.

He didn't rush. With each passing minute, Lucy's mind slowed down, pushing aside the case, her grief, her childhood trauma. The world disappeared and all that was left was her and Sean.

Sean reached around and unbuttoned Lucy's jeans and pulled them down her well-formed legs. He rubbed more lotion between his hands and took the massage from her lower back to her thighs and down to her calves.

"Oh, God, Sean," she whispered, and he smiled.

"I wish I could do this for you every night," he said, and began rubbing the balls of her feet.

"I could fall asleep so easily."

"Don't you dare." He wished she didn't get this tense. Tomorrow, she'd be back working on the case, focused on everyone except herself. He would do this for her nightly, and enjoy it.

Lucy rolled over and smiled at him. "Take off your clothes."

"Aren't you bossy."

"I don't like to be naked alone."

Sean stripped, then ran his hands up her legs, across her stomach, kissing her body as he went. He kissed the faded scars across her breasts, then entwined his hands with hers. He stared at her, her dark eyes craving him as much as he craved her. Her lips parted and she tilted her face up to meet his.

"I love you, Luce."

She smiled and kissed him. "Make love to me."

"I've missed you so much." He kissed her lips, her jaw, her neck. He loved her neck, so smooth and soft and sensitive. His tongue explored the sweet trail under her jaw up to her ear and she gasped, clutching his shoulders, when he lightly bit her earlobe.

She breathed his name, a whisper of desire, then wrapped her legs around him.

His penis reached for her as if it had a mind of its own. He thrust into her quickly and she gasped, meeting him halfway. He held himself still, wanting to savor this moment, his hands still clasped in hers, sweat coating their bodies. In tacit agreement they tried to hold off the urgency. Sean moved slowly, needing to relish this moment, to remember every sweet spot of Lucy's body. The way she moved. The way she moaned. The way she whispered, *I love you.*

Lucy shifted beneath him and the friction made him groan. It was always like this with them, he wanted slow and prolonged, but the sexual combustibility always burned hot when they were alone and naked. Lucy had learned that her touch, her scent, her body, her voice, just made him crave her even more; she enjoyed his needs, she enjoyed him. They'd built up trust and love over these months, and Sean would never forget this moment, like he never forgot any of the moments they were together.

He'd never get enough of her, never wanted to get enough. "Lucy," he breathed into her neck; then he leaned up and stared at her glowing face, and her eyes opened. She smiled and surprised him. She flipped him onto his back and sank deeper onto him. Her back arched and her eyes partly closed. Droplets of sweat ran between her breasts, glistening in the faint light, and he grabbed her hips, his orgasm hitting him with a power he didn't want to control. He held her body down on his and she froze, then let out a quiet cry as every one of her muscles tightened then relaxed simultaneously. She collapsed on top of him.

Lucy smiled into Sean's chest, her skin slick with sweat and lotion. She listened to his rapidly beating heart, loved the way his arms tightened around her, holding her close.

"I need a shower," she said.

"Me, too."

"We should conserve water."

"Yes, we should."

Lucy rose from the bed, took Sean's hand, and pulled him up.

"Thank you," she said.

He shook his head. "Never thank me for loving you."

"I meant, thank you for doing all this. Flying me here, searching for answers when we don't even know all the questions."

"Huge hardship. Traveling to my favorite city with my favorite woman and making love in the same hotel where I first told the woman I love that I loved her. Yeah, I'm suffering big-time."

"You know what I meant."

He kissed her. "I do. What's important to you is important to me. I thought you knew that by now."

She touched his face with her fingertips. "I'm very lucky."

He smiled. "Yes, you are."

She laughed and pulled him toward the bathroom. She turned on the shower.

"I'm the lucky one," Sean whispered.

CHAPTER TWENTY-SIX

FBI Academy

For the duration of the investigation, Hans Vigo was staying at a small house on the perimeter of the FBI Academy. It was late when he returned to campus after talking to Kate and Dillon, but he was in no mood to retire.

Something had been bothering him all day. Ever since Lucy told him her notes had disappeared.

What was in the McMahon file that someone didn't want Hans to see? Was it connected to Tony's death or completely unrelated? A crime of opportunity?

The halls were quiet at midnight. Two guards patrolled the grounds, the security desk was manned, but everyone else was asleep. The campus wasn't even half-full—many of the new agents took advantage of Saturday night to get out, visit family, go see a movie. And since it was the first weekend Class 12-14 was allowed recreation, most of them were gone.

Staff was minimal, and only a handful lived on campus—no instructors, only the class supervisor and field counselors. Because of budget cutbacks, only one class supervisor was here now. In the past, there were up to four supervisors supervising up to eight new-agent classes.

Now, there were only three new-agent classes working their way through, and one supervisor.

Times were changing. They could train to cover attrition, not to add to their ranks. There was more crime, smarter crimes, but they couldn't bring on enough people to handle the current workload. Around the country, every law enforcement agency was cutting back, and while the different agencies worked better together than when Hans first started, they were all understaffed.

No sign of that changing in the near future.

Hans turned on the lights. He was the only one down in the basement this late, but he liked working in solitude.

He had already boxed up the new-agent class files for whoever would replace Tony. Hans wished he'd remained close to his old friend. Death was permanent.

Tony had been emotionally tortured, but Hans didn't believe he had been tortured enough to kill himself. Not deliberately. But he'd always had a problem with drinking, and the fact that he was keeping a bottle in his desk had upset Hans. Alcohol was a serious problem in law enforcement, particularly with someone who dealt with the darkest of human beings. Hans had had his fair share of battling personal demons and frustrations, but he hadn't turned to the bottle or drugs.

Hans remembered all too well the Rachel McMahon murder investigation. The jurisdictional fights. The media circus. The lies that the parents told, the friends, the family—until Rachel was found dead and the truth washed ashore from a sea of guilt.

Tony had known from the beginning that the McMahons were lying, but he'd been tossed from the case after he and the chief of police nearly came to blows over the father's interrogation. That was one of many missteps that impacted Tony's career—why he'd never risen through the ranks the way he should have. It didn't matter that Tony had been right on every count; he didn't know when to keep his mouth shut. He broke rules under the philosophy it's better to ask forgiveness than permission.

Unfortunately, he rarely sought forgiveness.

It didn't surprise Hans that Tony had bonded with Lucy Kincaid. Lucy had outstanding raw instincts that couldn't be taught but could be honed. Field experience would turn her into one of the best agents they could train.

Except she also had the same weaknesses as Tony. She tried to be a rule follower; she tried to be who she thought she needed to be to reach her goals. But in her heart she was just like Tony Presidio: gut driven, tenacious, stubborn, empathetic. She would break every rule if she thought she was doing the right thing, and that would leave her where Tony had been: unfulfilled in his career and marginalized because he was unpredictable.

Maybe leaving the Academy was the best thing for her. She could get a job in almost any law enforcement agency in the country. Her skills would be in high demand. And if her past proved a barrier, RCK would bring her on board without hesitation, and not just because Sean and Patrick were partners. The organization had been slowly growing more powerful and in demand over the last few years, and while that worried some people in power, it didn't worry Hans.

Every new agent was thoroughly vetted. Each one went through extensive psychological and background screenings. It was this vetting process that had affected Lucy's placement, because while she passed all the psychological tests, the panels felt she was too calculated in her responses and that her master's in criminal psychology may have given her the leverage to cheat the tests. She had been cold in her interviews, didn't have any outside interests, and they feared she had a vendetta.

But ultimately, Hans was selfish and he wanted to train Lucy to be the agent he knew she could be. He'd been watching her these last four weeks through the one person he trusted to keep his interest confidential. She'd been doing fine, and she'd passed the tests he'd set up for her, confirming that he'd been right to ask Rick Stockton to overrule the hiring panel.

Tony had been drinking prior to going into cardiac arrest. He had his heart pills on his desk, telling Hans that he'd been experiencing chest pains but chose self-medication over the doctor.

A murder at Quantico would be bold, brazen, and extremely difficult. Poison to induce cardiac arrest would take medical knowledge and opportunity.

Why would someone kill Tony? He wasn't involved in the politics of the Bureau, had never aspired to be anything but a field agent. He could be grumpy and he rode his students hard, but he was always fair.

It all came back to the Rachel McMahon investigation and the missing file. Tony had figured something out about the case, and either the file was stolen after he died as a crime of opportunity or he was murdered because of his knowledge of the file.

Hans had read over all the official records this afternoon, but there was nothing that jumped out at him. Nothing that would warrant anyone wanting Tony, Stokes, Theissen, and the reporter all dead.

But while Hans had been involved in the original investigation, he hadn't been as involved as Tony.

Hans pulled the security log from Thursday afternoon to see which card keys accessed the basement. There were no unauthorized accesses, but that didn't mean someone hadn't. Yet circumstantial evidence indicated that if Tony had been murdered, someone he worked with had killed him.

If Tony was murdered.

Hans called his friend from the lab, Trisha Morrison.

"Hans, it's nearly midnight," Trisha said.

"I'm sorry. And you're not going to like what I'm calling about."

"You want results."

"Yes. I know it's early, but—"

"They're being run, Hans. That's the best I can do. I'll be at the lab tomorrow and will check on the tests personally. But it's going to take at least another day, and if we don't find anything, I'll need to run a broader test."

"I appreciate it."

Hans hung up. There was nothing more he could do tonight. He locked up, checked out at the desk, and walked the quarter mile to the small bungalow he was living in for the duration.

The cool, fresh air cleared his head, and he realized how exhausted he was. It had been a long forty-eight hours.

He followed the trail around a fenced construction area, where the new hostage rescue facility was being built. The security lighting was weak and flickered. A scaffolding to his right seemed out of place. He sidestepped it, then tripped over a toolbox and fell hard on his knees.

Pain shot up to his pelvis and he feared he'd broken his leg. He rolled over to catch his breath when a crashing sound startled him.

He couldn't get away from the scaffolding before it came falling down and pinned him to the ground. The weight of the wood and pipe and equipment was stifling. Blood dripped into his eye from a deep cut on his forehead.

He sensed more than saw movement to his left. He tried to turn his head but couldn't. A sharp pain exploded his temple, then he felt nothing.

CHAPTER TWENTY-SEVEN

Six Years Ago

Soon after I became an emancipated minor on my sixteenth birthday, I got my GED and was accepted into SU. It was far enough from my crazy mom and dad that I didn't think about them much. The first year I kept to myself. I was younger than everyone, the classes weren't as easy as I'd thought, and I focused on studying. I just wanted to blend in while I figured out what to do with my life.

The doctor had been wrong—I wasn't going to be six feet like my dad. By the time I was seventeen, I was six foot one with more to grow. I think I always thought of myself as short because my height felt funny on me. I didn't really know what to do with it. I tried to disappear in crowds like I used to, but I couldn't. Too tall, too skinny, and I think people were kind of scared of me because I was so quiet.

Even though I was free, I felt oddly trapped. Like I was waiting. Waiting for someone to tell me my life had purpose. Waiting for someone to tell me what I should be doing. Waiting for answers to all the questions I'd had as a kid—answers that would never come.

Then I met Cami.

Cami was a year older than me. Beautiful. Sweet and shy, maybe a little skittish. We met in the library the beginning of my second year at SU and I think, for me at least, it was love at first sight. Even though we didn't have any classes together and she lived with her aunt in town, we studied together nearly every afternoon. I looked forward to seeing her, and on the days I couldn't or she didn't make it I was sad.

Cami left for the summer, and when she returned in the fall I wanted to marry her. She was everything bright in my life. My past was finally buried; my mother had remarried and moved to Texas, my father was still in Seattle, but I hadn't spoken to either of them in over two years, not since the day I became an emancipated minor. The time, and college, and Cami all healed me.

For the first time since Rachel died, I was at peace.

The peace didn't last.

The sensation that someone was watching me again started at the beginning of my third year. I started to feel the pricks in the back of my neck, just like in high school. The mysterious and cryptic notes began again, only instead of being put in my locker they were left in my dorm room. Or in my car. Or as a bookmark in whatever I was reading.

I became jittery and nervous and all I wanted to do was disappear again. I kept it all from Cami because I wanted to protect her. I filed police report after police report, but after the third time, they just stopped caring. I'd become an annoyance, and one of the cops clearly thought I was lying for the attention.

He certainly didn't know me. I would gladly be invisible if I could.

But I should have realized that whoever hated me,

whoever had followed me from Newark to New York, would try to hurt someone I loved.

My junior year, I moved off campus and gave Cami a key to my apartment. I wanted her to move in with me, because she was having problems with her family. But she was a bit old-fashioned, and I liked that about her. She'd often stay until late but always left in the middle of the night. I wished she would take me to visit her aunt, but she said it was "complicated."

I knew all about complicated families.

It was the morning before Halloween when I had coffee with Cami and asked if she wanted to see a movie that night. She said she'd meet me at my apartment. And she sounded happy for the first time in weeks, and that made *me* happy. I'd been afraid she wanted to break it off because of my questions about her aunt, and my moodiness.

I got hung up after my last class because the professor wanted to talk to me about a story I'd written. He wanted me to submit it to the campus magazine. I said sure, whatever, but he wanted to *talk*. Talking wasn't my strength. So I listened to him, about how talented I was, about how I should be majoring in communication or journalism or the creative arts instead of early childhood education. I listened until he wanted me to give him answers; then I told him I was late for a date.

I had a beat-up old car, but I rarely drove since my apartment was only a half mile from campus. But it was days like this, when I was late, that I wished I had it. I called Cami to tell her I was late, but my call went to her voice mail.

I walked briskly, then jogged, and by the time I got to my apartment I was running. I felt it in my stomach that something was wrong, just like I did the night of the storm when I woke up and went to Rachel's room and she wasn't there.

I ran up the two flights of stairs to my apartment and heard Cami crying from my bedroom.

"Cami? Cami? It's Peter."

The cries stopped, and I ran down the short hall to where she stood in the doorway. I looked over her head and saw everything.

Arcs of blood on the walls. The smell of death. The butchered pig in my bed.

Cami turned to face me, her face white and wet with tears. "I can't be here," she said. "I'm sorry. Oh, God!" She ran out and I let her go. I stared at the gross violence and knew that next time it would be me.

I called the police, and this time a new cop came to my apartment.

His name was Charlie Mead. He looked at my room, then looked at me and said, "Tell me about it."

I told him everything. I told him about being followed in high school, about the roadkill left in my locker, about my bike being sabotaged. I told him why I ran away, how I was sent to live with my father, and why I filed for emancipation. It all came out in a rush; I don't think I'd ever said as much at one time in my life.

Charlie said, "Let's make sure your girlfriend is okay."

I nodded, and he drove me to her aunt's house. I'd never been inside, but I'd dropped her off several times over the year I'd known her.

Charlie walked with me to the door. I stood behind him, mostly because I didn't want Cami to be scared. Charlie could convince her that she'd be safe, and he had some smart questions I hadn't even thought about. Like had she seen anyone, had she touched anything, had she ever seen someone following us.

Charlie was the first cop I'd met since I filed my first report who I thought might find the person who was doing this to me.

An elderly woman answered the door.

"Ma'am, I'm Officer Charles Mead. Is Cami here?"

"There's no one by that name here."

"Cami Jones," I said. "She goes to SU. This is where her aunt lives; I'm her boyfriend, Peter Gray."

The woman scowled. "I don't know any Cami Jones. My name is Edith Jones, Jones is a very common name."

"You're her aunt!"

Charlie put his hand on my arm, but I shook him off. "She calls you Aunt Edie."

Mrs. Jones glared at me. "I don't have any brothers or sisters; I have no nieces or nephews. I'm a widow, and my only son is married and lives in Montreal with his wife. I've lived in this house for fifty-two years!"

I didn't believe anything she said, but Charlie walked me back to his squad car and made some calls. I sat in the back and stared at the house. This was it. *Jones* was on the mailbox. I'd driven Cami here a dozen times.

I looked at the houses nearby, and I wasn't mistaken. Was her home life so bad that she didn't want me to know where she lived?

Charlie said, "Let's get some coffee, Peter."

I didn't say yes or no, because I was still trying to figure out what I had missed with Cami. I understood pain and knew she was a kindred spirit. She'd suffered but never talked about it.

Charlie drove to a nearby Starbucks and we went inside. He paid for me and we went to a table in the back.

"Thank you," I said, and sipped the black coffee. I didn't like coffee much, but I needed something to do with my hands.

"You need to listen to me, Peter. This is important."

I nodded.

"Edith Jones was telling the truth. She has no nieces. There is no Cami Jones registered at SU."

"*Cami* must be short for something. It's a big school."

"I had them run every C. Jones registered. There are four. Three are men. One is a senior from Albany, lives with her boyfriend in town. Christina Jones."

I heard what Charlie said but didn't understand.

"Maybe—"

Charlie interrupted. "The crime scene unit dusted your apartment for fingerprints. There were none."

I frowned. That made no sense.

"Someone cleaned your entire apartment," Charlie said. "Your fingerprints were on the door and the door-frame of your bedroom. That's all we found."

My stomach clenched. I looked at Charlie but didn't see him. I saw Cami put her hands to her mouth.

She'd been wearing gloves.

I ran to the bathroom and threw up. There had to be an explanation. There *was* an explanation.

Why? I didn't know her. I'd never met her until last fall. Who would do that to me? How could I not see it?

A knock on the door startled me.

"Peter, come on out."

I washed my face with cold water and came back to the table.

"Do you have a picture of Cami?"

I slid over my cell phone. "The only pictures I have are on my phone."

Charlie started scrolling through my phone. He frowned and said, "Your SIM card is missing."

I took the phone and looked. The card was gone.

Cami had used my phone earlier, before I went to class.

"She planned it."

"We'll find a picture of her. On Facebook maybe?"

I shook my head. "I don't have any social media. I hate the Internet. I don't even have a television. I had an e-mail account once, and a reporter found me and wanted to interview me. So I deleted the account. I have an e-mail account through the university because I had to get something for my classes."

"You shouldn't go back to your apartment. Do you have someplace to stay?"

I shook my head. "I need to disappear."

"You don't want to do that."

"Yes, I do."

I'd never thought about killing myself. Maybe in passing, but then I'd think of Grams and knew she'd be heartbroken. She was dead, but sometimes I felt her. I lived for those moments.

"Don't run, Peter. Someone had been stalking you since high school. They're escalating. Only you know who it is."

"But I don't! It was all a lie. Cami was a lie. But I swear, she was not at my high school."

"Let me do a little research on her. Maybe something will come up. You can work with a sketch artist; we'll get a good picture of her."

Charlie Mead really wanted to help me.

"I'll try."

"Stay with me tonight," Charlie said. "I'll find a safe place for you tomorrow."

One night turned into two years. I lost a sister when I was nine, but I found a brother when I was nineteen.

CHAPTER TWENTY-EIGHT

New York City

Jimmy Bartz was picked up late Saturday night by uniformed officers in Queens. Suzanne and Joe decided to let him stew the rest of the night, and Suzanne arrived at DeLucca's precinct at eight Sunday morning.

"We could have come in together," Joe said.

"No, we couldn't," Suzanne said. Joe had wanted to go home with her last night, but she had put her foot down and after one beer had left alone. The worst thing was that she had wanted to give in, but reason vetoed her heart. Heart? Who was she fooling? It was her body that craved Joe. She didn't want to fall back into bed with him because then her heart would be at risk and it would only end badly. Just like last time. Because she would not give him any ultimatum that affected his relationship with his son, nor did she want to play the role of mistress with a man who was hiding her from his ex-wife.

"Has he talked?" Suzanne switched the subject back to the case at hand.

"No." Joe checked in with the desk sergeant. "Can you bring Bartz to interview?"

"Room one," the sergeant said. He got on the phone.

Joe led Suzanne through the bullpen to his desk. It was a quiet Sunday morning. Joe sat down at his tidy desk. Suzanne glanced around at the stacks of paper on everyone else's desk. "You have the cleanest crib in town."

"Just in this neighborhood," Joe said. He quickly checked his e-mail, then brought up Bartz's rap sheet. Joe turned his monitor so both he and Suzanne could read it.

"Worst thing is assault—no weapons charges."

"The guys who know him said he never carries a weapon, and it's served him well. Three arrests, all bumped down to misdemeanors, one time-served, and a three-month, then six-month stint in county. No hard-jail time."

"And he then kills a woman for a ring?"

"Could have been hired."

They both shook their heads at the same time.

"Let's play with him a bit. He's a two-bit thief. Money drives him."

The on-call detective said, "Hey, DeLucca, you need to pressure Bartz? Drop his buddy's name—Franks. His stats are in the rap sheet. They're friendly rivals."

"Thanks, Parker."

He turned to Suzanne. "Let's see what this guy has to say."

Jimmy Bartz was a scrappy forty-year-old who didn't look strong enough to snap a toothpick. Suzanne could see why he was an effective thief—he looked harmless, skittish, and had quiet gray eyes. But his eyes became fearful when he saw Joe's stern expression.

"You're not Detective Kramer."

"I'm Detective Joe DeLucca. This is Special Agent Suzanne Madeaux with the FBI."

Bartz looked at Suzanne. "FBI? Why's the FBI here?

Detective Kramer handles property crimes in this jurisdiction."

Joe smiled slyly. "You know our system well. Kramer
is off today. I'm in Homicide."

"Homicide? Why is Homicide handling property
crimes? Why is the FBI here?"

This guy was either a great actor or truly clueless.

Joe said, "You tell us the truth and you'll be able to
walk out the door today. You lie to us and you'll be in Rikers before lunch."

"I told the officers exactly what happened. I found that
ring, just wanted to know how much it was worth."

"You pawned it for two thousand dollars."

"It was worth a lot more than I thought. I thought it
was fake, thought I'd get two bills, maybe three."

"Where did you find the ring?"

"At Citi Field."

"In the stadium?"

"No, in the parking lot."

"Inside someone's car?"

"No, just lying on the ground."

Suzanne said, "Was it on the finger of a dead woman?"

Bartz's eyes darted back and forth between the two of
them. "Dead woman? There was no dead woman. It was
just lying on one of the white lines. I saw it sparkle, picked
it up. I swear to God, I didn't take it off any dead chick. I
didn't even steal it, I swear I *found* it."

Joe leaned back. "I don't believe you."

"Kramer would believe me. Call him; he'll tell you if
I'm lying. He always knows."

"I'm telling you, you're lying." Joe stared at Bartz. The
thief fidgeted.

Joe glanced at Suzanne and gave her a subtle signal.

She stood up. "Well, you can have him, DeLucca. He doesn't know anything, I'll talk to the other guy about the reward—what was his name?"

"Carmine Franks."

"Franks. That's right. Is he next door?"

"Yes, just tell the desk sergeant you're ready."

"Reward?" Bartz said. "What kind of reward?"

"For information leading to the murderer of Rosemary Weber," Suzanne said. "You found her ring, we thought you might have seen something. I didn't want to deal with this Franks guy—he's a jerk—but I need to get information any way I can."

"I don't know anything about a murder, but neither does Franks!"

"How do you know what Franks knows?" Joe asked.

"He's been in Jersey with his daughter all week. Just came back yesterday. His oldest had a baby boy. First grandson and all that. Ask him, because he saw nothing."

"And you did?"

Bartz hesitated, trying to think up something to tell them to get him closer to the fictitious reward. Joe nodded at Suzanne, and she left the room, watching through the one-way mirror.

"Look," Joe said conversationally to the suspect, "you have a ring that was last seen on a dead woman. You hocked it. Now you're telling me you found it at Citi Field."

"Right. Because I did."

"I believe you."

Bartz looked relieved.

"What day?"

Bartz thought about it.

"It's not a hard question, Jimmy."

"Tuesday?"

"Morning or night."

"Night?"

"Why are you asking me? Either you found it Tuesday night or you didn't."

"I did."

Then Joe hit him with the facts. "The woman was killed at Citi Field. In the parking lot. On Tuesday night. And I'm going to book you for murder."

"You can't!"

"I'm a homicide detective. It's what I do."

"But—but—"

Suzanne came in and handed Joe a file. It was blank, but Joe smiled. He didn't say anything.

"Special circumstances," Suzanne said. "We'll take the prosecution, since we can try him for the death penalty."

"You got it," Joe said. "I love this new task force, Agent Madeaux. Especially since New York no longer has a death sentence."

Bartz was shaking.

"I didn't kill anyone. I didn't. I swear to the Almighty God, I swear on my grandmother's grave, I didn't kill anyone, ever in my life."

Joe stared at him. "How did you get this ring?" He slapped the ring, in an evidence bag, on the table.

Bartz stared at it. He seemed to weigh what he should say.

"You just told me you found it Tuesday night in the parking lot at Citi Field. The victim was murdered at Citi Field on Tuesday night. Every jury will agree you just confessed."

Suzanne nodded. "I already ran it up to the U.S. Attorney's Office. They say we have enough."

"No!" Bartz looked trapped. "I—I didn't find it."

"You didn't find the ring." Joe's flat voice told Bartz he didn't believe him.

"I—I—I got it from a guy."

"Does this guy have a name?"

Bartz shook his head. "Just a guy. Said he broke up with his girlfriend and was going to toss the ring. He gave it to me instead."

"Don't fuck with me, Jimmy," Joe said. "This ring"—he held it up—"is worth over fifteen *thousand* dollars. No one just handed it to you!"

Suzanne didn't think Bartz could have grown even more pale. He was downright ghostly. "Fi-fi-fifteen?"

"And a guy gave it to *you*."

"I—I was hustling on my corner, selling pictures, ask Kramer, I sell pictures outside the subway across from Citi Field."

"When?" Joe asked.

"Yesterday morning."

Suzanne said, "The Mets are on the road."

"But there was an event. A charity game, retired players or something. I was there at eleven; game started at noon. I swear to God."

There was a ring of truth, but Suzanne was withholding judgment. This guy was a piece of work.

"An-and it was slow, this guy comes up and asks if I want to buy this ring. Said his girlfriend broke up with him at the game on Tuesday, and he was going to toss the ring, but decided to sell it. See, I sometimes buy things—"

"You knew him?"

"No, I swear, never seen him before."

"What did he look like?" Suzanne asked.

"Baseball cap. White guy."

"A white guy in a baseball cap. That's the best you can do?"

Bartz shrugged.

"What was he wearing?" Suzanne prompted.

"Jeans. T-shirt."

"Anything on the T-shirt?"

"It was plain. White."

"Tattoos?"

Bartz shrugged.

"Height? Weight? Fat? Thin? Did he have wings?" Joe was getting irritated.

"Um, he was taller than me."

"Everyone in New York is taller than you, Jimmy."

"Um, six feet? A little less? More? I was sitting down. I don't know!"

"And you bought the ring from him?"

"No, I thought it was hot."

"He was selling stolen jewelry."

"Yes. No! I didn't *know,* I just thought, you know?" Bartz was wringing his hands, the cuffs jangling. "I said I didn't have the money to buy it, and he said keep it. Said he couldn't look at it without thinking about his girlfriend."

"And you didn't find this suspicious?"

"You'd be surprised what people give me. It's the God's honest truth, ask Kramer; he knows when I'm bullshitting. I swear, he gave it to me." He paused. "Is there a reward? Because I found the ring and all?"

Joe and Suzanne stepped out without answering his question.

"What a ridiculous story," Suzanne said.

"He's telling the truth."

"Damn, I thought so, too. I just hoped that I was wrong."

Joe said, "The killer reads the article, worries that we're going to start looking at other motives and that he might be under the gun, but he's smart enough not to hock the ring himself. Gives it to a street vendor knowing there's a better than good chance the guy will pawn it."

"He's got to know we'll track the guy," Suzanne said.

"You heard Jimmy. He can't even ID the guy."

"You should get a sketch artist in here anyway."

Joe concurred. "I'm also going to check and see if there's a security camera that caught Bartz yesterday at that subway station. We might get lucky. And I know Kramer; I'll see what he says about this guy." Joe shook his head. "I don't see Bartz as the killer."

"And that's why his story has a ring of truth. Shit, we're back where we started."

"No, we have an advantage. Your friend Tony played the killer, and the killer did exactly what we wanted—pawned the ring. He just used a middleman."

Suzanne stared at Bartz through the window, but she was thinking about the guy in the cap. Smart, but he'd have to know Bartz's story would never hold water. "Do we pressure him or let him think he deceived us?"

Joe said, "Give the killer a little breathing room? Announce that we're interrogating a suspect?"

"Except that the killer would know Bartz's story is pathetic. He can't possibly know that Bartz won't be able to ID him."

"Let's see what we can learn from the sketch artist and security cameras. Maybe we'll get lucky."

Sean was driving toward Bridget Weber's house on the Upper East Side when Lucy's cell phone rang; she was surprised to hear Noah Armstrong on the other end.

"Hello, Noah."

"Lucy, there's been an accident."

Flashes of friends and family, bloody and dying, flew through her head. "Who?" Her voice cracked.

"Hans. He's in critical condition at Prince William Hospital. I can't talk on the phone, but I need you back at Quantico now."

"What happened?"

"I'll explain when you get here. Don't discuss this with anyone except Sean. Let me talk to Rogan."

Lucy handed the phone to Sean. He listened for a long minute. Lucy watched his face but couldn't read his expression. "Got it," Sean said, and hung up. He handed Lucy back her phone. "Noah wants me to put you on a plane ASAP."

"Put me on a plane?"

"Commercial. He's made a reservation for you; it leaves in an hour. He asked me and Patrick to stay here and follow through."

"What happened to Hans?"

"He didn't say—he was vague. He said, 'Follow up on the assignment Hans gave you.' My guess, it wasn't an accident."

First Tony, now Hans. "It's all connected to what happened to Rosemary Weber."

Sean maneuvered through New York traffic like a native and merged onto a freeway.

"It all connects here in New York," Sean said. "I'm going to call Suzanne and find out where she is, fill her in on the news about Hans, and have her or her cop friend pull the files on Theissen."

"Be careful," Lucy said.

Sean took her hand. "You, too, princess."

"What's going on?" Suzanne demanded when she met Sean in front of the Webers' narrow three-story town house on the Upper East Side. "You're thirty minutes late, and you tell me to *wait*? Sunday is usually the only day off I get, and yet I was up at the butt crack of dawn to interview a suspect, then ordered to rush over here, only to be kept *waiting* by a friggin' P.I.?"

Sean smiled and handed her coffee. "Black and sweet, right?"

She grabbed the coffee but didn't return his smile. "Where's Lucy?"

"Headed back to Quantico."

"Why?"

"It has to stay between you and me. Can't even tell your boyfriend."

"DeLucca isn't my boyfriend."

Sean coughed a laugh. "I was speaking metaphorically, but good to know."

She glared at him from under the brim of her Mets hat, all fire.

"Hans Vigo had an accident yesterday. He's in critical condition. Lucy was called back in, and my guess is that it wasn't really an accident."

"Why are you still here?"

"Hans asked me to find Peter McMahon. That's what I'm doing."

"Back up—is this the Peter McMahon whose sister was murdered when he was a kid? The case Tony was so curious about?"

"Four people involved in his sister's investigation are dead under mysterious circumstances."

Her brow furrowed. "Four people? Who?"

Sean ticked them off on his fingers. "Weber, Bob Stokes, Dominic Theissen, and Tony Presidio." He explained the suspicious circumstances of Stokes's and Theissen's deaths and how they might not have been accidents, or natural.

"McMahon has been completely off the grid for the last six years," Sean said. "No death certificate, no Social Security number in use, nothing. FBI is going through their channels; I'm going through mine. I traced him to college at SU; then he seemed to just vanish."

"There has to be something else."

"Agent Presidio's personal file on the McMahon investigation disappeared from his office the day he died. Something is going on, maybe it has nothing to do with Peter McMahon, but it's not easy to go completely off the grid."

"So you're thinking he's targeting cops who worked his sister's case because *why*?"

"I don't think anything at this point," Sean said. "I'm just going to find him."

"And you think Bridget Weber knows something she didn't tell me?" Suzanne sounded skeptical.

"I think Rosemary Weber has a lot of files and information on the McMahon investigation that may shed light on these deaths."

"So you don't think her murder has anything to do with the Cinderella Strangler case?"

"We're not going to know until the feds are done with their forensic investigation." Sean walked up the steps to the front door. "Hopefully, there'll be enough answers here to give us a clear direction."

Bridget Weber was five years younger than her sister, but judging by Rosemary's author photo on her book, they had looked very much alike—blond hair, blue eyes, and deep dimples.

"Thank you for agreeing to see us on such short notice," Suzanne said.

Bridget tried to smile but didn't quite make it. "Do you have information about Rosie's murder?"

"We're pursuing every possible lead," Suzanne said. "We just have a few questions. Did your sister discuss her books or what she was working on with you?"

"Sometimes. But I travel a lot for work, and when she's in the middle of a project she's very focused, doesn't talk to anyone but her research assistant, if that."

Sean said, "Did you talk about her current project?"

"The Cinderella Strangler? A little—she was excited about it. She said it had all the hallmarks of a bestseller." Bridget paused, then said, a bit sheepishly, "Rosie's first book was a big hit. None of her other books did as well as *Sex, Lies, and Family Secrets.* She was always looking for what she called a big, juicy story, and she thought this new one fit."

"Did she say why?" Sean asked.

"Not specifically, but anyone could see that the case was alluring. Underground sex parties, drugs, prostitution—the backdrop was more interesting than the crimes themselves."

Sean was grateful Lucy wasn't here. To Lucy, it was always the victims who mattered, not the trappings, and she would take issue with the sister's description.

Suzanne said, "When we were going over her calendar and notes, we noticed she had scheduled a meeting with a reporter, Rob Banker. Do you know him?"

"Yes, he was one of Rosie's closest friends."

"She canceled the meeting because she had a lead to follow. Did she tell you anything about it?"

Bridget shook her head. "I didn't see her before she left. I was out at dinner. I invited her to join me, but she thinks my friends are boring." She smiled sadly. "She did mention she had a meeting, but I didn't ask any details."

Sean said, "She dedicated her first book to a Newark police officer, Bob Stokes. Do you know him?"

Bridget straightened in surprise. "Actually, I do. He was one of the officers she'd known when she was a reporter in Jersey. They were friendly. But she hadn't talked to him in years until he came up here for the funeral of Dom Theissen. Dom was a friend of Rosie's. They talked a lot. I thought there might be something romantic between them, but she never said anything. I know his accident hit her really hard." Bridget began to look irritated. "I told all of this to the other FBI agent who came by."

"Who did you speak with?" Suzanne asked.

"Agent Presidio. You brought him with you earlier. Don't you remember?"

"Yes, I just didn't know he returned. What time did Agent Presidio visit you?"

"Thursday, late afternoon. Nearly five. He was on his way to the airport, he said. Is something wrong?"

"He died of a heart attack Thursday night," Suzanne said. "We never got his report."

Bridget put her hand to her mouth. "Dear Lord. I'm sorry. He just had a couple questions, then asked to see the files in the attic again."

"Did he take anything with him?"

"I don't think so. If he did, he didn't ask me."

"May we?" Suzanne gestured toward the stairs.

Sean followed Suzanne up. "What time were you and Tony here?"

"We left around three in the afternoon, went back to headquarters with Weber's notes from the original McMahon investigation. They were in shorthand."

"What time did he leave?"

"I don't know. I left him with the analyst and worked on reports. I didn't see him again." Suzanne pulled out her phone. "I'll find out."

Sean looked around the attic. Everything was well labeled. Suzanne walked over to a stack. "We only took the notepads that pertained to the missing files on the McMahon book. Tony had hoped an analyst could decipher Weber's shorthand and it would give us an idea of what was in the stolen files."

"Why did he come back?" Sean walked slowly around.

One of the boxes had a lid that was skewed. He looked at the label. It was from the year following the McMahon homicide, while Weber was still a reporter in Newark. "One of the notepads is missing," he said. He opened the box and noticed that Weber had meticulous labels. The front of every pad was dated. She went through at least one notepad a week.

"It's the anniversary of Rachel McMahon's murder that's gone," Sean said. "That's three months after Kreig's trial."

"Why didn't he tell me?"

"Maybe he planned to. We need to find out if he called anyone after he left here. And I'll call Noah and find out if he had the missing notepad on him."

They went back downstairs and Sean remembered that Tony had asked Bridget Weber more questions.

"Ms. Weber, when Agent Presidio returned, what did he ask you?"

"He wanted to know if she thought someone was following her. Specifically, he asked me if she was being stalked. And one more thing—how far back she kept her fan mail."

"We took all her mail," Suzanne said.

"Yes, and I told him that. He wanted to know about when she was a reporter, before she wrote the McMahon book. I didn't know, but I can't imagine that she'd keep anything that long."

Suzanne and Sean thanked the sister for her time and walked out.

Sean said, "Did you have any indication that Weber was being stalked?"

Suzanne shook her head. "No police reports, no restraining orders, nothing in her e-mails or notes, but I have an analyst going through them in greater detail. But

Tony said something earlier about her killer knowing everything about her. Her schedule, what she would do. He felt that her killer was confident she'd expose herself to him and not be scared."

"Did he say anything else to you when he left?"

"Nothing. I left him with an analyst to go over the notes we found here. She just sent me a message that he left headquarters at four thirty, plenty of time to get back here by five."

"I'm going to pull the newspaper archives from that missing week and see what Weber wrote. Tony thought it was important enough to take her steno pad."

"He should have called me." Suzanne was justifiably upset.

"He didn't know what he knew," Sean mumbled. "It was a hunch. Suzanne, I need a favor."

She rubbed her temples. "I'm not going to like this, am I?"

He grinned. "It'll be easy. Really. I need the accident report and autopsy for Dominic Theissen."

"You think it wasn't an accident."

"What I think and what I can prove are completely different, but yeah, I think it's highly suspicious."

CHAPTER TWENTY-NINE

Washington, D.C.

Lucy was surprised to find Noah waiting for her when she exited the gate at Reagan National. "I was going to take a taxi," she said.

"I want to fill you in, and the best place is on the road."

Lucy had first met Special Agent Noah Armstrong eight months ago during one of his investigations. Though she'd disliked him at the beginning—considering he had questioned her as a suspect in a murder investigation—they'd ended up becoming friends and he'd taken her under his wing during her ten weeks as an analyst in the D.C. regional office. Surviving a plane crash in May had solidified their friendship.

"How's Hans? He's going to be okay, right?"

Noah put his hand on her shoulder. "Lucy, it's serious. He's been unconscious since Security found him early this morning."

Lucy nodded, but her chin trembled. She swallowed and asked, "What happened?"

"We don't know exactly. Can we walk and talk?"

She nodded.

He squeezed her arm and then walked briskly toward short-term parking.

"Hans was working in Tony's office late last night. He made arrangements to stay in one of the bungalows Quantico has for VIPs and temporary instructors. He signed out of the building just after midnight and crossed a construction area on his way to the house. A scaffold fell on him."

"It really was an accident?"

"We're supposed to believe it was an accident, and that's what everyone will be told today. A scaffolding did collapse, but two things point to attempted murder. First, the structure of the scaffolding had been compromised. The lab is testing the metal, but it appears that an acid ate away at the base and all it would have taken was a light push to make the whole thing come down."

"And that's not a construction mistake?"

"It could have been, but the project manager has been working with Forensics all morning to account for the weakness, and he swears it wasn't his team. We don't know what the chemical is yet, but there are a lot of common products that could be mixed to eat through the metal. The second piece of evidence is that the security camera outside of the armory caught a shadow. No face, but there was definitely a person moving away from where Hans was attacked at approximately the same time. Where he was attacked is outside the camera's range."

They arrived at Noah's sedan and he opened the passenger door for Lucy, then closed it and walked around to the driver's side and started the car. Lucy blinked back tears and looked out the window as Noah drove out of airport parking.

"I'm sorry, Lucy. Hans is a good friend to both of us."

Lucy wished she hadn't gotten so angry with Hans

yesterday. He'd been such a loyal friend and mentor—his betrayal in pulling strings to get her in the Academy was done out of his belief in her. He did it for the right reasons; she should have forgiven him yesterday.

"Lucy?"

"I'm okay," she said quickly.

"I know this is hard on you."

"He has to wake up, Noah."

Noah glanced at her and Lucy thought he was going to say something, concern clouding his eyes. Then he didn't and looked at the road. A minute later he said, "Hans talked to Assistant Director Stockton yesterday about looking into the death of Tony Presidio. The lab came in yesterday and collected potential evidence, including Agent Presidio's bottle of Scotch."

"It had been on his desk when I found him. His BAC was elevated."

"There are some discrepancies in the autopsy and his body is being sent to our lab to be reautopsied, and an extensive toxicology panel has been ordered. There are some drug interactions that may have caused an elevated BAC. They're also specifically checking for legal and illegal drugs that may cause cardiac arrest."

"You think Tony was murdered." Lucy shifted in her seat and stared at Noah. "I told Hans on Friday that it seemed suspicious that Tony died and all the McMahon files were gone."

"Hans contacted the lab after he talked to you, then called Rick Stockton and opened a classified investigation into Tony's death. You, me, and Chief O'Neal are the only three people at Quantico who know about this investigation. And Kate—Hans told her last night, but she's not taking an active investigatory role. Everyone else will be told that Tony died of natural causes, case closed, and that Hans had an accident when he cut through a poorly marked construction site."

"Someone we know did this?"

"If Tony was killed at Quantico and not poisoned earlier, and since Hans was attacked on campus, the person responsible is either staff or someone from your class. Chief O'Neal is investigating the staff." He glanced at her. "You and I are investigating Class Twelve-Fourteen."

"My class? There are three new-agent classes here."

"Class Twelve-Thirteen spent the weekend with DEA trainees on joint border and jurisdictional situations, and Class Twelve-Twelve was on survival weekend."

"Survival weekend is still within Quantico boundaries."

"I have someone verifying that all class members were accounted for—it's possible, though unlikely, that someone could have slipped away. Everyone is paired up and between the survival grounds and campus is an active Marine training zone. Off-limits, well marked, and extremely dangerous to traverse. In addition, someone had to be following Hans to know when he left the building, or waiting in the construction area knowing that was the path he would take to his temporary housing."

Noah paused to merge onto the highway, then continued, "I have a list of everyone who was signed in, but as you know, there are ways to get on campus without signing in, or signing in later than you arrive. I pulled all records from the main gate. Those will be harder to fudge because they're maintained by the Marine base. But we need to consider everyone a suspect." He glanced at her. "Are you okay with this?"

She nodded, but she didn't feel okay.

"Lucy, talk to me. Once we get on campus we're not going to be having this conversation."

"Essentially, you're telling me that someone I know and trust killed Tony and attempted to kill Hans."

"It's not going to be easy, but I need you at the top of your game."

"I know." She took a deep breath. "I'll be okay." Would she? Could she look at her friends in the same way, knowing that one of them was a killer? One of them had manipulated her? Lucy always felt she was a good judge of character—and one reason she had so few friends was because she had a hard time trusting people. But here she had felt a bond instantly with her fellow new agents, a kinship because they were all in the same place—physically, professionally. And she liked them.

Noah said, "Fill me in on everything you know, and we'll go from there. Start with Dominic Theissen. Hans told Stockton last night that he wanted to look at his accident."

The comfort in reciting facts calmed Lucy and turned her mind from Hans to the job.

"Theissen got in the middle of a fight at a subway station in Queens and was pushed onto the tracks. The police ruled that it was involuntary manslaughter. Sean and Agent Suzanne Madeaux in the New York office are pulling the files on it."

"And Theissen was the media officer during the McMahon investigation."

"Correct. And he was friends with Rosemary Weber. Bob Stokes was a Newark cop when Rachel McMahon went missing, and Weber's main contact for her book, in addition to Theissen."

"While you were flying, Sean said Stokes came to talk to Weber after Theissen's funeral. He died of a heart attack the next day."

"Sean doesn't think it's a coincidence and neither do I. But to poison someone means that the victim trusted the killer, or the killer knew the victim's routine well enough to slip poison into their food or drink."

Lucy continued, "We also don't know whether Rosemary Weber's murder was linked—it's the odd crime. Theissen was ruled an accident, Stokes and Tony natural causes, why was Weber stabbed to death in an obvious homicide? In addition, poison is a predominantly female method of killing, while stabbing is male. There are exceptions, but few. Under any other circumstances I'd think they were unconnected, but the four individuals are linked by only one event."

"The Rachel McMahon homicide."

Lucy nodded. "It's why Sean is looking for Peter McMahon. Before Tony died, he said he wanted to find him. He led me to believe it was simply to make sure that he was doing okay in light of everything that has happened in his life. But now I wonder if he suspected something after Weber was killed."

"That McMahon grew into a killer."

Lucy didn't say anything. "It's suspicious that he's fallen off the grid."

"The FBI is looking for him, too."

Lucy glanced at Noah. "My money's on Sean."

"Mine, too. But don't tell him I said that."

Lucy smiled. She was relieved that Sean and Noah seemed to have developed a truce.

"The timing would make sense as well. When Rachel was killed, Peter McMahon was nine. Old enough to understand, but too young to feel he had any power over events. Everything was done for him, he was lied to; he was coddled, he was protected, but he was also old enough to know what was going on with his parents, and old enough to know what happened to Rachel. His grandmother took him away and shielded him from the worst, but when he was fourteen two pivotal events happened—at the worst psychological time. Weber's book came out, and his grandmother died. He was sent to live with his mother, but ran away a year later. When he returned, he went to live with his father, but that didn't last and he became an emancipated minor at sixteen. Went to college at SU, but Sean could find no record of him graduating. In fact, the last six years there is no record of Peter McMahon or Peter Gray—the two names he used."

"You're thinking the *now* is solved because he feels old enough to do something about it and he's mature enough to plan out meticulous crimes," Noah said. "Sean said that Tony made a stop on his way to the airport—he went back to Rosemary Weber's house and asked her sister if Weber had said anything to her about being stalked."

"What if Tony felt he was being followed?"

"Sean and Suzanne are trying to find out if Tony made any other stops on the way to the airport."

"If the three men were all poisoned," Lucy said, "and Hans was attacked by the same person, that means that the killer was in New York prior to coming to Quantico. We have to determine where they were murdered. Maybe Theissen and Stokes's deaths were exactly what they seemed to be."

"If we prove Agent Presidio was poisoned, we'll move to exhume Stokes's body."

"Did Kate tell you she also worked the McMahon case?" Lucy said. "It was one of her first, when she was still a rookie."

Noah didn't say anything for a moment. "Do you think she's in danger?"

"I don't know, but she needs to know there's a possible risk. If there is a killer at Quantico, they can get to her."

"If there's a killer at Quantico who's seeking revenge," Noah said, "that means they gamed the system. They got in, and we have no idea who they are."

"Noah—it's a lot of *ifs,* and I have one more. If Hans's accident and Rosemary Weber's murder are connected, that means there are at least two people involved." Lucy grew both excited and apprehensive with her new insight. "Unless my class is innocent and the killer is staff. Staff are the only people who can leave during the week."

Noah's expression turned dark. "And staff would know best how to get around holes in security."

CHAPTER THIRTY

New York City

Sean was antsy sitting around Detective DeLucca's Queens precinct waiting for Suzanne to work out logistics between the Bureau and NYPD. This was why Sean could never be a cop. Paperwork, jurisdictional arguments, rules. Mostly, rules.

He'd already pulled every article Rosemary Weber had written the week that Tony was interested in, and nothing popped. Sean then pulled the articles for the two weeks before and after. Again, other than an article about the anniversary of Rachel McMahon's murder, there was nothing that seemed suspicious.

He e-mailed the articles to Lucy and told her what he and Suzanne had discovered. She might see something he hadn't.

He called Patrick and asked, "Anything on Theissen's losing battle with the subway train?"

"I'm on my way to Rikers with one of Joe DeLucca's cop buddies to talk to the kid who pled on the involuntary manslaughter charge. From our read of the case, a disagreement between rival street gangs ended with fists flying. Theissen stepped in and tried to mediate, got pushed back as the train was approaching. Busy time of day, lots of trains. The conductor used the emergency brake when he saw the fight on the platform, but it was too late."

"And someone pled?"

"One year, in exchange for naming names. Official report is that there were three different gangs all using the same station. One kid made an off-color comment about another kid's girl, the boyfriend pushed him, a third party stepped in, and then mayhem. The kid in Rikers, nineteen-year-old Gregory Bascomb, was pushed into Theissen, then hit Theissen because he thought he was being attacked from both sides. Theissen then tripped over another gangbanger and fell on the tracks."

"No trial?"

"Nada. Plea deal was good enough for both parties, and they have several arrested for other charges."

"Why are you talking to this Bascomb?"

"If we're going off the theory that Theissen's death wasn't an accident, I want Bascomb to ID everyone on the platform who was involved in the brawl."

"You're thinking one of them might have planned this? That's a lot of assumptions."

"Maybe it was a crime of opportunity. You said Presidio wondered if Weber had been stalked. What if Theissen was being followed? The killer saw the gangbangers, understood the dynamics of how to manipulate the group."

"As a distraction. Possible." Sean wasn't sold on it because there were too many variables that couldn't be controlled. Sean didn't like leaving important things to chance. "I'm stuck in Queens waiting for Suzanne and DeLucca to figure out what to do with the guy who pawned Weber's ring."

"I'll let you know if I learn anything at Rikers."

Sean hung up and still Suzanne wasn't out of the inter-rogation room.

He flipped through the neat stack of files on DeLucca's desk. Nothing pertaining to this case. He stared at the computer. Why had Weber canceled her meeting with the reporter? Who was she meeting that night, and why hadn't she put it in her planner? Why meet at Citi Field?

According to the sister, Weber had been close friends with Theissen, who had worked at Citi Field in security up until his death.

Maybe Weber hadn't set up a meeting because of the Cinderella Strangler case—maybe it had something to do with Theissen's accident.

Or maybe that's what the killer wanted her to think.

Suzanne came down the hall. "So Rogan, we're letting Bartz go on a misdemeanor charge of selling stolen goods. NYPD will handle him. His alibi checks out the night Weber was killed."

"The killer gave him the ring?" Sean said.

"Most likely. But we don't have much to go on, Bartz is an idiot, the sketch artist is pulling her hair out, and secu-rity cams in the area aren't giving us anything except the guy's ass. He knew where the cameras were. Just like he knew where the cameras were in Citi Field and avoided them."

"I've been having a hard time figuring out why a re-porter with a long career and the gut instincts to match would meet *anyone* at Citi Field, even someone she trusted," Sean said. "If it was someone she knew, why meet there, in the middle of a baseball stadium? If it was someone she didn't know, why would she agree to it?"

"That's been bugging me all along."

"Her buddy Theissen worked there before he died.

What if she was meeting another employee? Or *thought* she was? "It would have to be legit; at least she *thought* it was legit. So there should be a record of the arrangement somewhere. An e-mail. A phone call."

"We have her cell phone records."

"When did she cancel her meeting with her reporter friend?"

Suzanne flipped through her notes. "I don't have a specific time," she said. "They were supposed to meet at a bar at nine thirty, but she called to cancel late that afternoon."

"Likely she set up the Citi Field meeting right before that."

"I'll have my analyst pull all the calls to and from Weber an hour before she cancelled on Banker. This just might be it, Rogan."

But the phone numbers didn't lead anywhere, and Sean was even more frustrated than earlier.

Rosemary Weber had called Banker at 4:45 Tuesday afternoon to cancel their meeting. She'd neither made nor received any phone calls on her cell phone or home phone in the hour before she canceled with Banker. Earlier in the day she'd made calls to the morgues in Brooklyn and Queens, to her assistant three times, and to the Starbucks where one of the Cinderella Strangler victims worked.

Suzanne was just as frustrated as Sean as they stared at the information. She picked up the phone without a word and called one of the numbers.

While he was waiting, Patrick called. "Thank God you're done; I want to go home," Sean said.

"Not so fast. I just spoke to Bascomb and we watched the security feed again. Several times in fact. He IDed every guy involved in the brawl except one."

Sean leaned forward. "Do we have a good image?"

"Unfortunately, no. The quality was piss-poor as it was and Bascomb IDed people because he knew them well or by what they were wearing. But I called my former brother-in-law, the D.A. in San Diego, and he called the D.A. in New York, and I'm on my way to pick up the original digital copy of the security feed. I have to return it before we leave New York, but—"

"If we have the original I can enhance it," Sean finished for him.

"We'll be in Queens in forty-five minutes; hold tight."

Sean hung up at the same time Suzanne got off her call. "We may have a lead on the guy who started the fight that knocked Theissen off the subway platform," he told her.

"And Weber wasn't only working on the Cinderella Strangler case. There was no reason for her to call Queens. I thought that was odd, because none of the victims were killed in Queens. She had called for a copy of Theissen's autopsy report." She pushed aside papers until she found the file. "We need to look at it again."

Sean said, "Maybe she knew something we don't."

"I'm getting a headache," Suzanne mumbled.

"No, seriously—if she pulled Theissen's report, she may have thought there was something more to his death than an accident. If she knew something personal, or maybe it was the timing, or something we wouldn't think to look at."

"We can't read her mind. We just need to do it all again. Talk to her assistant again. The professor. Rob Banker." Suzanne started taking notes.

Sean understood why Suzanne was getting a headache. If they were dealing with different crimes, different

cases, different suspects, until they knew what was connected and how, they'd be building scenarios that would
get them nowhere.

But he had one idea that might help.

He called Lucy.

"How are you?" he asked.

"We couldn't stop to see Hans," she said. "Not that it
would have helped. He's still unconscious."

"I'm really sorry."

"I'm hiding in my room because I don't want to face
anyone yet. No one knows the truth. Everyone thinks it's
an accident, and I have to hold up that myth."

"I'm planning on flying back tonight, though it might
be late. I have a theory I need to run by you. What if Weber was an anomaly? What if her murder was because she
was digging into Dominic Theissen's accident?"

"Okay, I can see that, but where do Tony and Hans
fit in?"

"I don't know yet."

"If connected, there's two people involved."

"I thought the same thing. But what if Weber was just a
quasi-innocent bystander? We just found out that she was
looking into Theissen's accident. Patrick interviewed one
of the gangbangers who pled to involuntary manslaughter
and he can't identify everyone involved in the brawl."

"You're thinking someone started it."

"And if that's the case, he was targeted. Is there any
way to find out if Hans, Tony, Theissen, and Stokes worked
any other cases together?"

"I don't know. I'd have to ask Noah if there's a way to
search the data with agent parameters."

"And more complex, I'd like a matrix of cases where
any three of the four were involved, and any two of the
four."

"What might be simpler is to look at Weber's articles and see what cases she wrote about, then compare that with the agent lists. If there is any—you're talking about four cops who can't talk anymore."

"But that's presupposing that she is a specific target, and I'm thinking she is a target because of something she learned. She was killed the same day she pulled all Theissen's files. I think that's the connection."

"I'll find out and call you tonight."

"Thanks. And I'll talk to Suzanne about it as well. Be careful, Lucy."

"You, too."

Sean hung up and frowned.

"What's going on?" Suzanne asked.

"Lucy is worried about Hans," he said. Then he ran his theory by Suzanne. "Can you think of a way to run it?"

"No, but our analysts might. Except I still have them working on the notes Tony and I found in Rosemary's attic."

"Maybe that's exactly where we should start—find out what stories she wrote that quoted Theissen, then dig up those cases and find out who else was involved."

"We're looking for a needle in a haystack."

"But we have one more thing coming our way—a suspect."

"Rewind. Why do we have a suspect?"

"The unidentified guy in the subway tape. Patrick will be here in"—he looked at his watch—"twenty-five minutes. With the original security disk. And maybe we can round up that Bartz guy again. Because we know that Rosemary was writing a book about the Cinderella Strangler, but she was also looking into her friend Theissen's death. She could have been killed for either reason."

"Or something completely different," Suzanne said.

* * *

"Watch the guy in the gray jacket and dark baseball cap," Patrick told Sean, Suzanne and DeLucca thirty minutes later.

Patrick had come through with the original digital security disk from Theissen's accident. "He's already there when Theissen comes down the stairs. There he is," Patrick said, pointing to a clean-cut man wearing slacks, a dark polo shirt, and baseball cap. He could be twenty or forty, the quality was poor and the images in black-and-white. The perspective was distorted because of the wide-angle camera.

The suspect was watching Theissen as he came down the stairs. A group of seven teenage boys walked behind him, a bit rowdy. This was the main station near Citi Field. According to the report, Theissen used the subway every day to commute to and from work, even though he left at different times. This was the end of his day.

"I watched the earlier footage," Patrick said, "and Mr. Ball Cap was there for twelve minutes, coming in on one train and just standing. But during that time, several trains, local and express, went through the station. He didn't get on any of them."

As they watched, a group of four—two girls, two boys—got off one train and crossed the platform. The two groups eyed each other. It was crowded, the end of rush hour. Ball Cap moved between the two groups and said something to one of them, then bumped him. The kid responded by pushing him, but as Sean watched he realized that though Ball Cap had been pushed, the reaction was aimed at the kid on the other side of him.

What had Ball Cap said? Had he passed the blame for the verbal assault off on another person?

Theissen turned and kept his eye on the groups, and

Ball Cap moved around the outside. There were two distinct situations—one was the pending brawl and the people drawn into it; everyone else moved to the perimeter, not wanting to get in the middle. Theissen stayed on the periphery, watching as a cop might to determine if the situation was getting out of control.

Ball Cap pushed Bascomb, the guy in prison for involuntary manslaughter, directly into Theissen. Theissen stumbled back. On the surface, Ball Cap appeared to be trying to get away from the fray.

"Did you see that?" Patrick said.

Everyone had missed it, so Patrick went back.

"Watch his foot," Patrick said.

As the scene replayed, Sean kept his eyes on Ball Cap's feet. After he pushed Bascomb into Theissen, Ball Cap moved to get away and in the process tripped Theissen as Theissen staggered back and tried to catch himself. The retired agent stumbled and Ball Cap used the crowd as a shield to slip away as Theissen fell onto the tracks.

"He kicked him," DeLucca said. "When Theissen stumbled, Ball Cap tripped him, then kicked him using the crowd's movement to hide his attack."

"Exactly. The fight was a diversion he caused. At first glance, he looks like he was defending himself, but when you see the whole thing and focus on his individual actions, it's deliberate," Patrick said. "Now here's the interesting thing—I talked to the transit cops and they said there was another incident very similar two days before. They don't keep the tapes this long unless there's an open investigation, but one of the officers said he remembered it because when he was called to the brawl he thought, *Not again*. Theissen was at the first brawl as well, and gave a witness report. What if Ball Cap attempted it once and failed, or he instigated the scuffle and figured out how to use the reactions to his advantage?"

"We can't use this to ID the guy. He looks like half the white guys in New York," Suzanne said.

"He's very aware of the camera location," Sean said.

"So we reopen the Theissen accident as a homicide," DeLucca said. "I'll talk to my chief."

"I'll talk to my boss as well," Suzanne said. "If he was attacked because of his status as a retired federal agent, or because of a case he worked, we have jurisdiction. He's one of ours."

"Joint investigation," DeLucca said. "This is the New York subway; we have a vested interest in security improvements."

"Bartz gave us shit for the sketch artist, but he might recognize the guy again," Suzanne said. "Sean, can you get me a clean image of Mr. Ball Cap that we can show to our street thief?"

"We already let him go," DeLucca said. "He has to report to court on the misdemeanor charges next week, but I'll ask Kramer where he hangs."

Sean sat down at the computer and worked up a digitally enhanced image, but he could do nothing better than a shadowed profile. But the profile was sharp enough that someone who knew the guy well might recognize him.

Suzanne stared at the photo. "Hmm. A little better."

Sean asked, "Do you know him?"

She shook her head. "I don't think so. But—there's a little tickle in my memory."

DeLucca said, "He could have popped up at Weber's crime scene. I'll have our photographer send us the photos of the crowd."

"That's probably it. It's recent. Damn, I wish we had a better shot."

Patrick said, "I made a copy and will go through it frame by frame to see if I can get another image of him. It'll take some time, but I'm all yours."

"We still don't know if Tony stopped anywhere else between when he left you and when he boarded the plane," Sean said.

"Would he have had time?" Suzanne asked. "He boarded his plane at six forty p.m. Do you know when he went through security?"

Sean had already pulled the flight information. "He printed his boarding pass from a kiosk at six oh four p.m. He was cutting it close, but he didn't check any bags."

"And Bridget Weber said he left her town house after five. In traffic, it's at least forty-five minutes to LaGuardia from the Upper East Side, and that's the peak of rush hour."

DeLucca said, "He would only have had time to stop if it was on the way and he kept the taxi waiting. It's a bitch to get a cab during rush hour."

Sean considered that maybe the only stop Tony made was at the Webers'. "I have a call in to Noah to ask if Tony had the notebook on him. Maybe no one has unpacked his overnight bag yet." He glanced at Patrick. "Then we'll head back to D.C. I have a lead on Peter McMahon aka Gray I need to follow up on in person."

CHAPTER THIRTY-ONE

FBI Academy

Lucy wasn't at all comfortable with the role of spy.

She went to the gym hoping to avoid running into any-one she knew. Since new agents preferred to work out in the mornings or evenings, she usually had the gym to herself mid-afternoon. Today, however, Harden was run-ning Carter and Eddie through intensive drills. Eddie looked angry and Carter looked ill.

She stretched, then worked with free weights, hoping the guys would be done soon and she could use the equip-ment unobserved.

"Take five," Harden told Carter and Eddie after fifteen minutes. He approached Lucy. "I'm going to send Nix and Acosta to the pool for laps, if you want to join us."

She didn't, but at the same time a hard swim sounded like exactly what she needed to relax.

"Are they being punished for something?"

"Breaking curfew. Marines," he added under his breath. "Ten minutes, meet you at the pool." He walked back to Carter and Eddie.

Lucy wasn't sure exactly what Harden meant, consid-ering that they had the weekend off. She grabbed her swimsuit from her bag and changed in the women's locker room.

Ten minutes later, Lucy was cutting through the water with sure, even strokes. This was exactly what she needed to leach the tension from her muscles and focus on something other than Hans, Tony, and her unwanted role as spy.

After the swim, Lucy was surprised to see Noah talking to Harden. She dried off and walked over to Carter and Eddie. She pulled off her swim cap. "What did you two do?"

Eddie said, "Broke curfew."

"You didn't sign out for the weekend?"

"Bingo. Carter was wasted, I was driving."

Harden called out, "Acosta, Nix, you're both mine for the week, but you're done for today."

"Sleep, then dinner," Carter said. "See you at the mess hall?" Carter asked Lucy.

"I'll be there." She started to walk out with them when Noah called, "Kincaid, a minute please?"

Carter gave her an odd look, and Lucy shrugged. Harden left Noah and Lucy alone in the pool room.

Noah said, "I e-mailed your private account with the whereabouts of every new agent on Saturday from midnight until two a.m. Half were on campus. I'm verifying their background information, but you also have access and you need to be on alert for any discrepancies."

She nodded, but looked at the door, hoping Carter, Eddie and the others would forgive her when this all came to light.

Noah eyed her. "What's troubling you?"

"Other than the obvious? My mentor is dead and Hans is in a coma?"

"Lucy, I know this is hard—"

"I can handle it," she snapped.

"You're angry."

She turned away and stared at the pool. The water was settling down from the laps. Watching it calmed her. Water always gave her peace.

"It's being a spy," she said quietly. "On my *friends*. I don't know if you've noticed, Noah, but I don't have a lot of friends."

"You have many friends." Noah sounded confused.

She shook her head and faced him. "I have lots of family, and I love them, but my friends are few and far between. I haven't kept in touch with anyone from high school or college. No one. I thought—" She shook her head. "Never mind."

"Lucy, you know you can trust me."

She shouldn't be talking to Noah about this, but she was tired and upset. "I thought I was forming lifelong relationships with some of the people here." She jerked her head toward the door. "Carter and Eddie, for example."

"You'll be happy to know they're in the clear. They went out with a bunch of their Marine buddies from the base, didn't come in until nearly three in the morning. Fortunately, Acosta doesn't drink and we don't have a DUI situation, but it was still a serious breach."

Lucy sighed in relief. "Two down, thirty-one to go," she mumbled.

"You still can't talk about this, even with them."

"I know. I don't have to like it." She took her hair band off her wrist and put her hair up.

"Chief O'Neal and I cleared Tom Harden first thing this morning and I just gave him a quick debrief. If you need to talk and I'm busy, you can go to him. But still, be discreet. You might want to touch bases with him now—he wants to talk to you."

"I wouldn't make a good CIA agent."

Noah cracked a grin. "I don't think you would. But you're going to make a great FBI agent."

If I stay.

But she didn't say that to Noah.

Lucy found Tom Harden in his small office off the gym. Harden wasn't a special agent; he was one of the few instructors who was a civilian. He'd been in the Army special forces and when he got out ran his own gym while getting his degree in physical training and nutrition. Five years ago Quantico brought him on to lead their revamped new-agent PT program.

"Noah said you wanted to see me," Lucy said.

"Sit down." He motioned to the only other chair in his office.

She did, antsy.

"Hans is a personal friend of mine."

"Have you been to the hospital? How is he?"

"I went by this morning. I have one of the nurses sending me updates. There's been no change."

She let out a long breath.

"I'll let you know if there's a change in his status," Harden said.

"Thank you." She looked at him, curious. "You're not a federal agent and Hans was never in the Army. How do you know him?"

"In 1999, a year before I left the Army, I was tasked with protective detail in Kosovo. The FBI agents and scientists were sent over to identify victims of genocide. There were several operations where small groups of agents went out to remote burial sites, we had a few close calls with insurgents, and Hans and I remained friends after it was over. He told me about the opening here five years ago. I never planned on working for the federal government—I liked having my own gym. But I was given a lot of leeway to develop this program, and I owe that to Hans. I'm proud of what we've accomplished here, and more confident that we're sending out agents who are both physically and mentally prepared for the tasks they face."

"No complaints from me." Harden worked them thoroughly, but Lucy saw the purpose in everything they did and had personally benefited from it.

He smiled. "Not you, but not everyone is as in shape or dedicated to staying that way. Other than your very bad habit of eating granola bars to replace meals."

That he knew this detail about her bothered her. "How do you know?"

"In light of what's going on—Noah briefed me—I need to tell you something. Hans asked me to test you. Off-the-books. I agreed because it's my job, but it was also before I knew you. The pull-ups the other day was a test. I know what you fear, and I needed to make sure you can handle it."

The truth sunk in. "You knew Hans got me in."

"No. Not until yesterday afternoon. After you left, he told me, which explained why he wanted to assess you differently. Harder than others. I put the pressure on you for the past four weeks to confirm you can handle it. That part's over—with the investigation right now, I need you to trust me. That's why I'm coming clean."

Lucy felt manipulated and upset but, to her surprise, not as angry as she thought she should be. "Who else?"

"Who else was testing you? No one."

"Are you certain?"

"Hans doesn't trust a lot of people, but he would have told me."

"He told you I quit."

"You're still here."

"My ID was at the desk. I guess he didn't accept it."

"For what it's worth, completely unbiased, I don't think you should quit. If I was going to pick two agents I'd want on my team, it would be you and Carter Nix."

"Why Carter over Eddie?"

"Carter thinks for himself and Eddie is a soldier at heart. We need both types in the Bureau, and I love military folks coming in for a second career. But if I were building a team, I'd want loyalty, dedication, intelligence, and physical stamina. And I'd want those who see more than what's on the surface. Instincts. Working as a team is important. But using your instincts to benefit the team is crucial. Because when you're in the foxhole with someone, you have to be able to trust them with your life. And sometimes, that means breaking the rules."

She smiled. Sean would like Harden.

"What Noah is having you do isn't easy, but it's necessary," he continued. "He wouldn't put you in this position if he didn't think you could handle it."

"Thank you."

"One more thing. Who told you about the hiring panel?"

"Are you ordering me to tell you?"

"No. But I will if that makes you more inclined to share."

"Why is that important?"

"Because the only people who knew, until you found out yesterday, were the three people on the hiring panel, Hans, and Rick Stockton. That means that one or more of those three agents who interviewed you told someone after they were debriefed and told never to discuss the situation. It's a security breach. Personnel issues may seem minor on the surface, but revealing confidential information leads to other breaches."

"It wasn't someone on the panel."

"If I guess will you tell me?"

Lucy was intrigued. "I'm not going to play twenty questions."

"It was Rich Laughlin."

Lucy was stunned. "How did you know?"

"I noticed him watching you and his body language told me he was angry. I couldn't imagine what you might have done, so I kept my eyes open. Then Friday I walked out with Kosako and he said your score plummeted from ninety-three to thirty-two. It surprised him, and me, so I asked if there was a weapons problem. He noticed Laughlin standing in your peripheral vision and how your eye kept moving toward him. He thought it was a problem because of tactical training issues—but I put two and two together."

"He doesn't like me, but I think it has something to do with Kate. I'll take care of it myself," Lucy said. "I appreciate your understanding, but just as I don't like being singled out in my training, I don't like being cut any slack. I'm going to have to deal with more agents like Rich Laughlin when I get out of here."

"You will. Hans asked me to find out for him, because he needs to know who on the panel can't be trusted."

She stood, uncertain what Harden expected from her, and simply said, "Thanks."

"I may not be a federal agent, Kincaid, but I have your back."

She smiled. "I'm glad."

To her surprise, talking with Harden helped Lucy put her assignment in perspective. Lies and deception weren't in her personality, but this was an assignment. She didn't have to like it, but she had to get it done—and do it right. The obvious reason was because someone here may have killed Tony and put Hans in ICU. That person needed to be exposed.

But the other reason, just as important as justice, was that this was her job. If she couldn't perform a basic undercover investigation, what kind of agent would she make when it counted?

It was why Laughlin's presence was the true test. If she couldn't handle the pressure he put her under, then how could she handle real pressure in the job? If she let his hatred affect her—to the extent that she quit—who won? Certainly not her.

Lucy made her way over to where Carter and Eddie were eating at the table their group usually spread out on. Carter had heaped comfort food on his plate—mashed potatoes, meat loaf, and green beans.

"No loud noises," he said. "My hangover is almost gone."

Eddie laughed and Carter hit him in the arm.

"I'm getting too old to go out with these young Marines."

"I thought they were your friends?" Lucy said.

"Two of the guys, Dorman and Renko, were in our unit. We met up with some of the new guys."

"You're thirty-four, buddy," Eddie said. "You shouldn't have even tried." He winked at Lucy.

"You were sober; you should have dragged my ass out of there."

"I don't need alcohol to have fun." He leaned over to Lucy and in a loud stage whisper said, "I'll show you the pictures later."

Reva rushed over and dropped her tray on the table next to Lucy. Carter groaned.

"Tell me *everything*," she demanded.

"Excuse me?" Lucy stared at the energetic Reva who plopped down on the seat next to her.

"About your weekend with your hot boyfriend. Where'd you go? What'd you do? Does he have a brother?"

Margo sat down across from Reva. "I'm sure Lucy doesn't want to share details here." She waved her hand toward the men at the table, then gave Lucy a half smile. "Reva and I will expect the scoop after dinner."

"There's nothing to talk about. I've been seeing Sean since January."

"How did you meet?" Reva asked.

Lucy didn't feel comfortable talking about her personal life. But wasn't that what friends did? Share details about their life and hobbies?

"He's my brother's partner. They're private investigators." Rogan-Caruso-Kincaid Protective Services did a lot more than cut-and-dried investigations, but Lucy didn't want to go into details. "I met Sean when he and Patrick opened the D.C. office of RCK. Sean's brother and my other brother run the California office."

"Keep it in the family," Oz said as he sat down with Jason. He grinned at Carter and Eddie. "I'm surprised you guys are still standing. I walked by the gym after my run and Hard-ass was working you both into the ground."

"It's worse when you have a hangover," Eddie teased.

"Thank God I was a Marine, or I would be dead now," Carter said.

"Hoo-rah!" Eddie said.

"Hoo-rah!" Carter repeated.

"Where's Alexis?" Oz asked. "Working with Gordon on her shooting?"

Reva leaned forward and in a conspiratorial tone said, "I think she and her husband got in a huge fight last night."

"Knock it off," Margo said.

"Just saying, she was yelling at him, then she went for a run late. I asked if she wanted company and she blew me off."

"Because you're a big gossip," Oz said.

Reva looked hurt. "I don't mean anything by it. I just think you should know, so when you see her you'll know why she's so upset."

Lucy understood where Reva was coming from. She *was* a gossip, but she wasn't malicious. However, this was the perfect opportunity to start filling in the time line.

"Next time," Lucy said, "maybe you should ask her. I think she's lonely and missing her family."

"It's not like I wanted to knock on her door at midnight," Reva said. "I was beat. But maybe next time."

"Hopefully they work it out," Lucy said. Midnight, that wasn't going to help. Most of the new agents would be in their dorm rooms by midnight. Alone. That wasn't going to make this easy.

Eddie changed the subject. "I didn't know you were a fish, Kincaid."

"College swim team," Lucy said, glad Eddie had taken the lead in diverting the conversation.

Reva snorted. "What she's not telling you is she had a chance to try for the Olympic team."

Lucy reddened and stared at her food. "It wasn't like that," she said. She didn't want to talk about her past, and even though it wasn't a secret that she'd been a championship swimmer in college, any discussion might bring up what happened at her high school graduation. She didn't even know how Reva found out. It wasn't a secret, but it wasn't like Lucy had announced it.

"You gave up that opportunity?" Margo said. "Wow."

"I swam in college because I enjoyed it. I didn't want to make a life out of it."

Carter bumped Lucy with his shoulder. She shot him a surprised look—then he winked. It was a reassuring look. Did he understand her need for privacy? "Aren't you search and rescue certified?" he asked, gradually changing the subject.

She said, "Water search and rescue. Mostly search, not as much rescue, when I was with the Arlington County Sheriff."

"I didn't know you were a deputy," Jason said.

"I wasn't—I was in the office developing first-responder plans, plus I worked on the search-and-rescue team."

"I thought you'd worked at a morgue," Reva said.

For all her effort not to be the subject of any conversation, Lucy found herself in the middle. She ended up lying just to get the attention off her. "I guess I really didn't know what I wanted to do with my life." She grinned. "And all of you are in second careers in the FBI as well, aren't you?"

"Don't know if I'd call my three-year tour a career," Margo said.

"Didn't you do something before you were a paramedic, Oz?" Carter asked.

Oz glared at him. "Thanks, Nix, buddy."

"What?" Reva asked. "What'd I miss?"

Carter laughed. "Before Oz was a paramedic, he was a stuntman."

"Seriously?" Reva asked, eyes wide. "In Hollywood?"

"How'd that happen?" Jason asked.

"By accident, really. I used to skateboard, surf, bungee jump—when I was a teenager, I did some *really* stupid things, trust me. I think I've broken half the bones in my body. But my true love was dirt bikes. A director saw some of my stunts when I was at a competition and hired me. It paid my way through college."

Carter had Oz talking about some of the movies he worked on, and Lucy was both interested and relieved that the conversation had turned away from her.

Oz, Jason, Margo, Reva—all on campus when Hans was attacked. And Lucy had to confirm where everyone was between midnight and 2:00 a.m. without them knowing.

CHAPTER THIRTY-TWO

Georgetown, Washington, D.C.

Little surprised Sean, but when he saw Assistant Director Rick Stockton waiting in front of his Georgetown town house when he and Patrick arrived back late Sunday he was surprised.

"You could have called first, Director," Sean said.

Stockton smiled with half his mouth. "You think I came out here without knowing you'd already landed?"

Score one for the director, Sean thought. Sean unlocked the door, disconnected the alarm, and gave Patrick a glance. Patrick nodded and said, "I'm beat. It's been a long two days. Director."

"Good to see you again, Patrick."

Patrick went upstairs and Sean led Stockton to the back of the town house. "Beer? Scotch?"

Stockton shook his head. Sean grabbed a beer from the refrigerator.

"Hans Vigo's condition hasn't improved," Stockton said.

"Noah told me what happened. It doesn't sound like it was an accident."

"I sent Armstrong to investigate. Only he; the Bureau

chief, Lynda O'Neal; another staff member inside; and Lucy know that it was attempted murder."

"Prognosis?"

"None yet. They know they need to do surgery, but can't until the swelling on his brain has gone down." Stockton sat at the bar. "I'll take that Scotch now."

Sean poured the best Scotch he had, an eighteen-year-old Laphroaig whiskey.

Stockton looked at the bottle with a grin. "JT."

JT Caruso, one of the founders of RCK, had served with Stockton and Sean's oldest brother Kane as a Navy SEAL. Sean had known him since he was a kid. "He sends me a bottle now and again, but I'm not much of a Scotch drinker."

Something was definitely up with Stockton. Sean leaned against the kitchen counter and let Stockton enjoy the drink. He avoided asking questions, though he had many.

Eventually it came.

"Why did you run a background check on Special Agent Richard Laughlin?"

"How do you know I did?"

"Cut the crap, Rogan."

Sean wasn't about to tell Stockton anything, not until he found out why it mattered. "I didn't break any laws or obtain any classified information, so why do you care?"

Stockton's expression was stern. "He's an FBI agent."

"Why would the assistant director care about a *legal* background check on an agent? I run backgrounds all the time, usually a lot deeper than what I did on Laughlin."

Stockton sipped his Scotch and didn't break eye contact. Sean had run the search quietly; there shouldn't have been any flags thrown up, unless the FBI was already watching Laughlin. Most of Sean's research was passive—except for the credit reports.

"You flagged his financials," Sean said. "That's the only way you would know that I ran his credit."

"Who hired you to investigate a sitting FBI agent?"

"No one."

"Stop bullshitting me."

"I did it because I wanted to."

Stockton stared at him, a tick in his jaw, and Sean realized there was something bigger here.

"What did he do?" Sean asked.

"I want the truth, Sean."

"So do I."

Stockton slammed his glass down. "Why the games? Why won't you just tell me?"

"I'm not playing games. You asked me who hired me. I told you no one. I'm not lying. Is he a suspect in Hans's accident?"

"No."

Sean believed him. "What do you want?"

"If no one hired you, why did you run a background?"

Sean decided to give him most of the truth. "He's harassing Lucy."

That response seemed to surprise Stockton. "Lucy asked you to do it?"

"No," Sean lied. "But when she told me he was making her nervous, I decided to dig around and find out why."

Stockton reached over and retrieved the Scotch, poured a finger, and sipped. "And did you find out why?"

"More or less. As much as I could find out legally."

"You have a theory."

"I do."

Stockton didn't say anything. Sean decided it didn't matter if Stockton knew or not. "Lucy wants to handle it herself. She doesn't want me, or you, or anyone butting in."

"But you ran a background check anyway."

"And again, I ask, why do you care?"

"Agent Laughlin has been undercover for the last year in a major drug and money-laundering sting in a joint operation with the DEA. We sent him to Quantico as a class mentor until the trial."

"As protection?"

"It was a dicey op, but we have the bad guys in custody. Just wanted to make sure one of them hadn't hired you."

Stockton wasn't being completely honest with him, but Sean let it slide for the moment. "I'm stunned you'd think I wouldn't check out my clients," he said.

"Point taken." He sipped. "Why does Lucy think Laughlin is harassing her?"

"I said, she wants to handle it."

"I'm not getting involved. Just curious."

Sean didn't believe that, but it couldn't hurt for Stockton to know that one of his agents held grudges. He told him what he knew about Laughlin's and Kate's shared work history.

Sean put his beer down. "Now my question to you is, how does Laughlin know Lucy didn't pass her FBI panel, and why would he tell her Hans got her into the Academy?"

Stockton kept a poker face, but his eyes told Sean the information came as a surprise.

"I'll answer that," Sean continued. "To demoralize her. To make her doubt herself. He doesn't know her; he doesn't have any connection to Lucy *except* through Kate. So I think Laughlin was buddies with Standler and he blames Kate for Standler's death."

"That's weak."

"Maybe it is, but unless you have other information, that's what I'm going with."

Stockton drained his Scotch and put the glass down. "Thank you for the Scotch, and the truth," Stockton said.

"Anytime. You're practically family." Sean trusted few people in law enforcement; Rick Stockton was an exception. In addition to being close to RCK, Stockton had proven to be both discreet and smart.

"Learn anything in New York?"

"Already gave the intel to Noah."

Stockton nodded. "You're still searching for Peter Mc-Mahon?"

Sean walked Stockton to the door. "That's the last thing Hans asked me to do, as I explained to Noah. He never legally changed his name to Peter Gray, but he was using it for years. Peter Gray disappeared six years ago. My guess is he either went completely off the grid or changed his name, this time legally. I'm working on a couple angles from his time at SU." Sean had a buddy in Syracuse who would be pulling files at the police station first thing in the morning.

"Kate's also working on tracking down McMahon. A little competition never hurt." Stockton smiled and left.

Sean ran up the stairs and logged in to his computer. Lucy was online. He called her.

"Rick Stockton just paid me a visit. I think he's looking at Laughlin for something completely different than we are." He told her about the case in Detroit and the "protection" by being put at Quantico. "There's something fishy about the whole thing."

"It's Stockton's job to protect his agents. It makes sense to me. Laughlin may be a great agent and a jerk at the same time."

"It was the way he asked, the way he assessed my answers."

"Did he have an update on Hans?"

"He's the same. How are you holding up?"

"I'm okay. Better now, anyway. All I have to think about is Hans lying unconscious after someone hit him over the head—if these people are really my friends, they'll understand."

"Did you get the photo I sent?"

"The guy in the subway station? I didn't recognize him, but it's not a lot to go on. I don't know if I saw him that I'd recognize him."

"And the articles?"

"I'm reading them now."

"I sent Noah a message about a notebook of Rosemary Weber's that Tony took before leaving New York."

"We went through his overnight bag—it was in his car—and the notebook wasn't there. Are you sure he took it?"

"He could have brought it into his office. Maybe it went the same way as his file."

"Meaning, someone stole it. What year was it?"

"The anniversary week of Rachel McMahon's disappearance. That's why I sent you the articles from that week. You read Tony's file—maybe you'll notice something."

"I'll try."

"It's all we have for now. Watch yourself, Lucy."

"I love you, Sean."

Sean hung up, wishing he could just pop in and see her. But he had his own tasks, and if they were going to get to the bottom of what was going on in New York and at Quantico finding Peter McMahon was one major step.

The guy might be innocent in all this and just trying to disappear from his past.

Or he could have a vendetta he was in the middle of enacting.

Sean sent Lucy an encouraging e-mail, then went back to his notes on McMahon. He itched to find the guy. Kate was good—one of the best—but Sean was better.

Especially since Stockton didn't say anything about Sean having to find McMahon legally.

CHAPTER THIRTY-THREE

Three Years Ago

I walked out of the courthouse expecting freedom, but only fear followed me.

How long until that crazy woman found me again? *Cami.* I had loved her, but I'd loved a lie.

I'd always thought whoever was harassing me was a bully. Some jock who liked to pick on the little kids who couldn't, or wouldn't, defend themselves. But I'm six foot two now, I work out at the gym every morning, and I can defend myself.

But only if I see them coming.

I changed my name for a second time. The first had been to protect me from the media, and I'd taken Grams's last name. But this time, I needed to do more than fill out a form. I needed to be a new person. Someone the woman who wanted me dead couldn't find.

I was getting in my new car, the one registered under "Gray Manning," and saw Detective Charlie Mead striding toward me. He'd made detective fast, but I wasn't surprised. He was a smart man and the only person on earth I trusted.

No bad news. I can't take any more bad news. "Gray Manning," he said.

It would take a bit of getting used to, I realized.

"Charlie."

He stopped just short of my car and scratched the back of his neck. I was going to miss him. He was like Rachel, only a big brother rather than a big sister. We'd become friends. I went to his wedding last year. I liked his wife, and she liked me. It was normal. The only normal I'd ever had.

"I'm sorry I couldn't find her."

"You tried."

Trying didn't satisfy him.

"I'll keep on it."

I shook my head. "No prints, no photos, no name. She found me when I transferred from SU. The sketch gave us nothing. This is the only way."

"I'm not giving up," he stated. "You deserve to have your life back."

"No. I don't want that life. I'm going to make a new one. But I'm going to miss you and Tina."

"We'll keep in touch—through that account I set up for you, okay?"

I nodded. "You're the only one who knows where I'm going."

"As far as I'm concerned, you're in witness protection, of sorts."

Some people might think that a twenty-one-year-old man going into hiding—legally changing his name, burying his past, teaching at a poor public elementary school in Brooklyn to avoid seeing anyone who might know him—was a weak man.

But I need peace. Anonymity that a big city can provide. I need to be someone else. I don't need to know why someone wants to hurt me just like I don't need to know why my parents are selfish or why my sister was murdered or why I'm here.

These things just *are*.

I said, "Thank you."

"Peter," Charlie said softly. "If anything feels strange to you, if you think she's found you, call me, okay? Anytime, day or night."

"I will."

But I knew I wouldn't. If she found me again, she'd kill me.

Because even now, after everything she'd done to me, I don't think I could kill her.

How can I kill someone I don't even know?

CHAPTER THIRTY-FOUR

FBI Academy

Sean had e-mailed Lucy nine articles that Rosemary Weber had written during the month that Tony seemed to have been interested in when he returned to the Weber house. Lucy read them multiple times, made a list of names, places, and facts, and nothing jumped out at her as being important. She put them aside in the wee hours of the morning to sleep for a couple hours, and she woke up tired.

"Great," she muttered. It was defensive driving time, and Lucy was exhausted.

"Up late?" Reva asked as they walked the half mile to the car track.

"Catching up."

"I'll bet. I wouldn't want to study if I had a boyfriend as hot as yours."

Lucy shook her head but smiled. Reva was predictable, which made her comfortable.

Carter caught up with them. "How you doing?" he asked Lucy.

"Fine." She eyed him suspiciously. "Shouldn't I be?"

"You've often said how much you were dreading the driving test."

"This isn't a test," Reva said.

"I don't like driving, but I got a pep talk from Sean." Lucy didn't feel apprehensive like she thought she would. In the whole scheme of things, driving didn't feel as weighty as it had in the past. Though her rape and near death seven years ago had been traumatic and terrifying, the thought of losing her family was in many ways worse. Talking to Sean about the car accident when she was five had helped her come to terms with her fears.

"He's a good guy," Carter said.

"Yes, he is," Lucy agreed.

Her fellow new agents gathered around the driving instructor, Agent Chris Robinson, and listened to his instructions. The course seemed easy enough. They'd be practicing defensive driving, driving through obstacles, and accident avoidance. No high-speed chases or high-end tactical.

Driving would take all morning, but Robinson had it down to a well-oiled system. Two separate tracks were set up to expedite the lesson.

She looked at the others waiting for their turns behind the wheel. Could one of them have killed Tony? Attempted to kill Hans? Lucy had already ruled out a small group of agents who'd been in the lounge watching a movie until 1:30. Gordon, the gun expert, had been there as well, and she'd learned through him that the group of five had walked back to the dorm together. It would have been extremely unlikely for any of them to have rushed off to the construction site and attacked Hans. Oz was part of the group, and Lucy was relieved. One more of her inner circle cleared.

A van drove up to the edge of the driving track and two people got out. One of them was Rich Laughlin. He looked right at Lucy. She didn't turn away. She'd been upset Saturday after he told her about the hiring panel; now she was simply angry.

He may have planned to try to upset her, but she wouldn't allow herself to be intimidated.

When it was Lucy's turn behind the wheel, she felt Laughlin's eyes on her. She had a hard time controlling her physical tension—her hands clenched the wheel and her jaw tightened.

Robinson said, "Relax, Kincaid."

"You should know that I was in a serious accident as a young child. I've been a nervous driver most of my life."

He smiled. "No pressure. All I want you to do right now is get to know your vehicle. Drive around the track twice, keeping your speed at a steady thirty miles an hour. Then we'll run through the drill. The obstacle course is simple; it's all about control."

"Okay."

"You keep looking at your classmates."

She hadn't been; she'd been glancing over to find out where Laughlin was. She didn't say anything.

"Don't worry about them—it's just you, me, and the vehicle. Good. Keep going, one more lap."

By the time she was done with the second lap she wasn't focused on Laughlin. She listened to everything Robinson told her to do—speed up, stop, avoid, do a one-eighty—and by the time her session was done she felt good about it.

"Not bad for a nervous driver," he told her. "You did very well on the obstacle course; you have a good eye. You're still hesitant to speed up quickly, and you need more confidence with higher speeds, but we have time to work on that. Would you object to two extra sessions over the next two weekends?"

"I'd like that."

"You won't be the only one. There's a half dozen of your class I'll be working with."

"Great." She let out a long breath and got out of the car smiling.

"Not bad, Kincaid," Carter said as he took her place in the driver's seat.

They had an hour break for lunch after the driving lessons, and Lucy needed to meet with Noah about the personnel files. She grabbed a sandwich to go and went into the main building.

"Looks like you need to go back to driver's education," a voice behind her said.

She turned and saw Laughlin.

She glared at him but didn't say anything. An anger she was unfamiliar with bubbled up, and she worked on containing it.

He stepped close to her, his body only inches away, and said in a low voice, "You may have cut corners to get here, but there's no way I'll let you graduate if you don't perform."

She clenched her jaw. He was deliberately goading her, just like he'd been silently doing since she'd arrived on campus.

"I don't know what your problem is with me, Agent Laughlin. I don't think it's fair that you're basing your opinion of me on your problems with my sister-in-law."

"And what exactly did Kate tell you?"

"Nothing. I can read between the lines."

He smiled, and that irritated Lucy more. "You think you know everything, don't you?"

She stared at him. "I know a lot more than you think."

"Watch yourself, Kincaid."

It was a threat, over and above what would be called for

in this situation, and Lucy's stomach clenched as she realized maybe she didn't know what was happening, maybe there was something bigger going on.

Laughlin turned to go and thought he had the upper hand. Lucy said, "There's a time and place for everything, Agent Laughlin. I will figure out exactly why you hate me."

Lucy thought he was going to continue walking away, but he stopped and faced her again. "Do you want to know why you shouldn't be here?" He stepped closer. "Because people like you, people who cut corners, who become martyrs, who think they are somehow owed something, get killed or get their partner killed. Don't ever forget it. You're the weak link."

He walked quickly away and Lucy stared after him. She should be upset, but she was more confused than angry.

Laughlin was projecting. She hadn't seen it before because she'd been certain he and Kate had an unpleasant past. And that may have contributed to it, but the reason why Laughlin had it out for Kate, and for her, was because he had lost someone he cared about—and blamed them.

This definitely wasn't about her or Kate, not exclusively. Sean hadn't found out everything she needed to know.

It was time to call in a favor.

Lucy tracked Noah down in Tony's office, shutting the door behind her.

"I set up my laptop in the corner for you to access the personnel records," Noah said without looking up. He had his own stack of paperwork.

She sat down and looked at the list of names in the folder. The new agents who were cleared were crossed off.

She crossed off Oz, Gordon, and the other three guys who'd been watching movies until late Saturday.

Noah said, "Sounds like you've been busy."

"Hit a lot of birds with one stone," she replied. She pulled up "Reva Penrose" and started reading. She was looking primarily for inconsistencies—things in her official record that didn't match what she'd said. Background checks were extensive but not perfect. The further back, the easier to hide potential problems.

She stopped for a minute and looked over at Noah. "Do you know Agent Laughlin well?"

"I don't know him at all, other than he's one of your field counselors. I met him briefly this morning at a staff meeting."

"I need to find out if he lost a partner on the job."

Now Noah looked up. "Why?"

"Something he said to me today."

"You have to give me something more."

"He has a problem with me, because Hans pulled strings. He's the one who told me about it. And he doesn't like Kate. I thought he had an issue because he knew Kate's former fiancé, who was killed in the line of duty. Some people blamed Kate and her partner for the ambush. But I think he's projecting his own pain and guilt, blaming us for whatever his partner did."

Noah leaned back in his chair. "If I find out, how are you going to use it?"

"I don't know. But his attitude is only going to get worse until he confronts why he has this animosity."

"What did he do to you?"

She looked back at Reva's file. "Nothing."

"Lucy."

Noah didn't have to ask. But Lucy didn't want to complain, especially now that she was beginning to understand the source of Laughlin's struggle.

"He's been watching me closely—closer than my peers. I think because I'm managing under the scrutiny, he's challenging me. That's why he told me that Hans got me in, for example."

"But that's not the only thing he's said."

She shook her head. "It's not important what; it's important why."

"I'll find out." He went back to his files. "Chief O'Neal hasn't been able to clear Laughlin. He has insomnia and walks around campus at all hours of the night. He used his card key to access the dorms at three oh five Sunday morning. But this isn't unusual for him."

"Motive?" Lucy pondered the situation. "I don't see Laughlin as sabotaging the scaffolding and then when Hans is down hitting him over the head with a rock."

"Until we know for certain, be careful with him."

Noah's phone rang. "It's Suzanne," he told Lucy. "Suzanne, I have you on speaker. Lucy's here."

"Hey, Luce, I gotta make this quick. I know what Agent Presidio did with the notebook he took from Weber's place. He mailed it from the airport to the analyst who is transcribing all of Weber's shorthand. With a note."

"Read it," Lucy said.

"'Ms. North'—that's the analyst," Suzanne explained. "'Please transcribe this notebook as soon as possible. Weber wrote about another missing girl, but I don't understand her shorthand. Call me when you get this.'"

"That's it?" Lucy asked.

"That's it. North is working on it right now. I'll e-mail you the file when she's done."

"Would Weber's assistant know about that case?" Noah asked.

"I'll ask. But why would Presidio care about a completely different case?"

"Maybe he saw a connection. Or," Lucy said, "he was in Newark at the time. He said something was lurking on the edge of his memory."

"I hate when that happens," Suzanne said. "Noah, did you get my report on Theissen's case being reopened as a homicide investigation?"

"I did. Thanks for copying me into it."

"It's part of the bigger picture here. I just wish I could see it, because nothing makes sense."

Lucy glanced at her watch. "Noah, if you don't leave now, you're going to be late for your first class."

He sighed. "This is the part I'm not looking forward to at all." He said to Suzanne, "I have to go. Keep me in the loop." He hung up and his phone immediately vibrated. With an odd expression, he answered, "Hello, Rogan."

Sean was calling Noah? Had he found Peter McMahon?

Noah did a lot of listening, then said, "Call me if you learn anything." He hung up. "Sean has a lead on Peter McMahon in Syracuse. He's already there."

CHAPTER THIRTY-FIVE

Syracuse, New York

"Thank you for agreeing to meet with me."

Syracuse police detective Charlie Mead had agreed to meet Sean at a Starbucks near the police station. Mead looked younger than Sean thought he'd be considering his distinguished record. He'd been a rookie six years ago when Peter Gray filed a police report for vandalism. Now, Mead was a detective on the sex crimes squad, two years younger than Sean but with a seasoned air that made Sean think more of Noah Armstrong.

"It's not everyone who's willing to fly a couple hours for a copy of a police report."

"Faster than mail, and no one would fax it to me. Apparently, you are the gatekeeper of all things about Peter Gray." He handed Mead his business card.

The cop looked at it critically, then put it on the table in front of him. He sipped his coffee. "Why is Peter Gray's file so important to you?"

Sean had a suspicion that Mead knew exactly why it was important, but decided being as honest as he could be would yield him the answers he needed. Mead was a cop, through and through, one of the guys who had an internal lie detector and uncanny instincts.

"Mr. Gray seems to have disappeared off the planet. I need to find him."

"Why?"

"You know that Peter Gray was born Peter McMahon, correct? That his sister was killed when they were kids?"

Mead nodded once.

"Two federal agents and one detective, all involved in the investigation into his sister's death, were killed within the last two months." That was a stretch. There was no proof that any of them were murdered, but Sean would bet his last dollar he was right.

Mead didn't respond, but his body tensed. He was definitely interested.

"Last week, Rosemary Weber, who wrote the book about the McMahon family, was stabbed to death in Queens. All her files related to her research into the Rachel McMahon murder and trial are missing."

"Why is a private investigator contacting me and not the feds? Or NYPD?"

"RCK consults for the federal government on many cases. If you need confirmation that I'm assisting the FBI in this matter, I can give you the name and number of my contact."

"You still haven't told me why you want to find McMahon."

"He's either a killer or a potential victim. We won't know which until we talk to him."

Mead seemed to assess what Sean said. He'd made a bold statement, but it was the truth.

Mead reached to the seat next to him and picked up a thin folder. He tossed it in front of Sean.

Sean opened it. Inside was a typed report, signed by

Mead. Detailed in the report was a disturbing list of vandalism and violence. McMahon had found a dead animal in his bed, notes threatening his life, and there had been at least one attempt to kill him—his brake lines had been cut. Had he not thought quickly and veered up a slope in the road, he would have been seriously injured or killed.

"Do you know who did this?"

Mead shook his head. "It was a difficult investigation. At first no one in my department believed him. They wrote up reports, but nothing came of it. They dismissed it as college pranks. He stopped coming in, but the stalking didn't stop."

"You believed him."

"He came in one last time, when a butchered pig had been left in his bed and his girlfriend found it. He was nineteen. He was concerned about her safety, so I took him to her house. Except that she'd lied to him. Forensics showed that someone had scrubbed Peter's apartment and removed all traces of the girl who called herself Cami Jones. He stayed with me for a while and changed colleges. When he graduated she came after him again, only this time I was there. She ran, and we agreed that the only way he would be safe was if he changed his name and became someone else."

"Where is he?"

"I'm not telling you until I talk to Peter and check you out."

"It's critical, Detective."

"You can keep that file. There's a police sketch of the girl. She'd told Peter she was a year older than him, but I have my doubts. She could have been anywhere between twenty and thirty. I only saw her that one time, and it was briefly, but she had a distinctly different appearance from the last time he'd seen her—she may have had some work done. Nothing major, but enough that the sketch might be a bit off. When Peter knew her, she had long, dark blond hair. She had medium-length streaked hair when I saw her.

"I tried to run her, but there was no record. No record *at all*. No Cami Jones. She sat in on classes at SU, but was never registered. She used an elderly woman's house for her drop spot, but told Peter her family issues were complicated. Turns out the woman didn't know her. Peter, even after all he's been through, was very trusting. He'd been on his own since he was sixteen."

Sean looked at the drawing of a young, pretty girl. Not exceptional, but sweet. Girl next door.

He also knew that the FBI could get a warrant for Peter's new identity and location, and he suspected Mead knew that as well, but Sean didn't want to threaten the cop. He suspected he'd get the information faster if Mead volunteered it.

Mead leaned forward. "Peter is my brother now. I will do anything for him. He's not a killer; I stake my life and reputation on that. Which means, if your theory is right, he's in trouble only if his identity is exposed. I'm not putting him in the line of fire. Understand?"

Sean tapped his card. "See the small print? Rogan-Caruso-Kincaid Protective Services. If you tell me where he is, I can guarantee his safely."

Mead didn't look like he believed him. He said, "Turn the page."

Sean went back to the file. The last page was a photocopy of a typed note. A threat.

I'LL FIND YOU AGAIN.

"Have you talked to Peter recently?"

Mead shook his head. "I don't know exactly where Peter is. I don't want to."

"How do you contact him?"

"He has a P.O. box, and I'm not going to tell you where. Give me twenty-four hours."

If he only needed a day, he had another way to get ahold of Peter.

"Why do you think he was targeted by this woman?" Sean looked at the sketch again.

"That's the million-dollar question. He has no idea, but it started his freshman year of high school. I looked through every yearbook from his high school and there was no one named Cami Jones, Cami, or anyone who looked like her. I tracked down several of the blond, Caucasian girls and they didn't even come close. After he ran away, the harassment stopped, until his third year at SU, after he met Cami."

"He didn't put two and two together?"

Mead shook his head. "The harassment didn't start until nearly a year after he met her."

Peter had been targeted since he was fourteen. Weber's book came out when he was fourteen. That couldn't be a coincidence.

"Did he show animosity toward Rosemary Weber?"

"The bitch who wrote that book about his family? He didn't like her. He only mentioned her once; he wasn't obsessed."

"I need to talk to him. If all this is true, he may be in danger."

"He *is* in danger; that's why he has a new identity. Anonymity is the only thing that protects him. He's not a fighter—he runs away. And maybe that's what keeps him safe and sane."

"Maybe, but he's still in danger."

Mead didn't want to share. But he said, "I'll contact him, ask him if he wants to talk to you."

"The mail takes too long."

Mead grinned humorlessly. "I didn't say his P.O. box was the only way I could communicate with him."

CHAPTER THIRTY-SIX

FBI Academy

After her afternoon classes, Lucy went back to Tony's office. Noah wasn't there, but she used the key he'd given her to enter.

She wanted to get through this as quickly as possible. Margo had already asked her if something was wrong, and Lucy dismissed her anxiety as concern for Hans. That was in part true, because there was still no change in his condition.

Because it was so easy to slip in and out of the buildings without using a passkey, Lucy couldn't assume that just because someone had clocked into the building at any one time they didn't leave and return using another passkey.

She had twelve new agents left to clear, who had all been in their rooms after midnight on Saturday, according to the passkey access report.

She'd looked at Reva's personnel files earlier and sent Noah points to reverify—such as her legal name, her hometown, her parents and sibling information. She was so chatty Lucy knew a lot about her, and nothing in her file contradicted anything that she'd said.

Margo was from New York City, which gave her a connection with the location. She was quiet, smart, wasn't friendly with most of the new agents. It didn't surprise Lucy that she and Margo had become friends, but that Margo and Reva had seemingly bonded was odd.

Jason Aragon was older and mature, a lawyer, and according to his personnel file he took on cases and causes that most would shy away from. He'd never been married, but according to his file he had been engaged once, right out of law school. His fiancée was killed in front of him during a gang-related shooting in Los Angeles—wrong place, wrong time. He'd become an anti-gang crusader, and his personal statement indicated he wanted to work the anti-gang task force as a special agent. He had extensive knowledge of gang activity and warfare, plus an acute understanding of the law. He'd made a name for himself as a prosecutor going after the most violent offenders, at great personal risk.

Lucy had known him four weeks and he'd never talked about his past. He wasn't chatty like Reva, but why hadn't any of this come up?

What was she thinking? She knew why—because he didn't want to talk about it. Just like she didn't want to talk about her past. Some things were better left unsaid.

Jason had no connection to the East Coast in any way, but an event like what had happened to his fiancée would change him.

She switched databases and using Noah's log-in checked to see if there was a case file on the nine-year-old shooting. Nothing federal.

She made a note to look into that case deeper, then went on to Alexis Sanchez.

She'd been recruited out of the Denver FBI office after

she applied for a special agent position. She was highly desirable because of her accounting background.

Marital status: Divorced, Carl Sanchez.

Lucy frowned and made a note. She thought Alexis was still married. Didn't she mention a husband? Or did she say "ex-husband"? Lucy couldn't remember the specific verbiage, but she definitely believed from their conversations that Alexis was married.

She had a four-year-old daughter, Melissa Camille Sanchez, born in Denver.

Lucy relaxed a bit. Husband or ex-husband, Alexis still had family issues to deal with, and it couldn't be easy being two thousand miles away from her daughter. She'd mentioned that her mother-in-law was watching the child and that she didn't like Alexis, which would make it doubly difficult.

But it was one small discrepancy between what Alexis had said and the truth.

Noah came in. "I thought I'd find you here," he said. "Have you found anything?"

"Nothing major, but I'm looking. I'm halfway done."

"Good." He sat down, not behind the desk but on the couch. "I talked to Stockton about Rich Laughlin."

"I wish you hadn't. I didn't intend to use our friendship."

"You're not. Your instincts were dead-on. Last year, in the middle of Laughlin's joint undercover operation with DEA to take down a major international drug operation centered in Detroit, he lost his partner. She was DEA, but what Laughlin didn't know at the time was that she had a personal vendetta. She'd grown up on the streets of

Detroit, lost friends and family to the drug war. She came back to fight it. From what Stockton said, she was extremely good at her job, extremely bold. In undercover work bold is good—but it can also make you reckless.

"Just before she was killed, Laughlin told her to back down or their cover would be blown. She pushed—sacrificing herself to save Laughlin. Her actions saved a lot of people, and ultimately gave the FBI and DEA the information we needed to take down the largest and most violent gang working drugs between Detroit and Canada."

All the pieces of the puzzle slipped into place. "She died and Laughlin believes it was because her past made her reckless."

"Maybe it did."

"And maybe it made her better at her job. She succeeded."

"She died. She bled out after multiple gunshot wounds."

"We all risk dying. The question is, was there any other way? If she hadn't pushed, would more people have died?" No one could know, especially since they hadn't been there.

Noah handed her a thick file. "Eyes only, Lucy. It doesn't leave this office."

"Thank you." She put it in the drawer of the desk she was using and looked back at her computer screen. Noah sat at Tony's desk. "I'm not reckless, Noah."

"I never said you were."

Lucy viewed Laughlin in a completely different way. His anger and rage, focused on Kate—who had been part of a clandestine operation that ended up with both her fiancé and partner dying and Kate going off the grid for revenge—and Lucy, who had suffered at the hands of a brutal rapist and killer before taking his life. She could see how Laughlin thought they were risky as agents.

But Kate had proved herself over and over, and Lucy

didn't have a death wish. She wanted to be an agent to affect change and make a difference in the lives of innocent people and victims, not simply to take out as many sexual predators as she could before she died in the process.

Her past definitely shaped her present, but it also made her smarter and sharper, not more violent or reckless.

She put Laughlin out of her mind and focused again on digging into the background of Alexis Sanchez.

She'd graduated from Penn State in Scranton with a major in accounting. She'd had jobs in Scranton and Syracuse before moving to Denver six years ago.

Syracuse.

Sean was following a lead on Peter McMahon in Syracuse.

Alexis was born in Trenton, New Jersey, and moved to Newark after her parents divorced, when she was twelve.

New Jersey.

Rosemary Weber had lived in Newark and was the crime reporter for the major paper.

It was a connection. Tenuous, but the only connection in all these files to McMahon or Weber. Alexis had worked in Syracuse during the year Peter McMahon had fallen off the grid. She'd lived in Newark when Rachel was killed. Had they been friends? Lucy checked birthdates. Doubtful—Alexis had been seventeen at the time.

Alexis's maiden name was Todd—that name sounded very familiar. Lucy looked over all the personnel notes and couldn't find a "Todd"—first name or last—anywhere. But she'd seen the name recently. In a newspaper article?

In Tony's notes.

The name Todd had been in Tony's original file, the one that had been stolen from his office.

Lucy carefully read Alexis's entire file, focusing on the background check from her childhood. And there it was:

Camille Todd.

When Alexis was seventeen, her twelve-year-old sister, Camille, was abducted—one week before Rachel McMahon. But Camille's body wasn't found for nearly a year.

There was nothing else in Alexis's file about her sister's murder. Alexis went to college, moved to Denver, and seemed to have no contact with New Jersey after. Her father remained in Trenton, retired career military, and her mother remained in Newark, where she'd died of breast cancer three years ago. Alexis had a brother, Kip, who lived in New York—

—Kip Todd. Weber's research assistant.

Suzanne had mentioned him when Lucy and Sean were in New York Saturday. He was a grad student at Columbia and would know how to make Weber's files disappear in archives.

"I got it, Noah," Lucy said. "Can you check if there's a federal case on the abduction and murder of Camille Todd? Same year as Rachel McMahon."

Noah typed. "We have a file. Give me a minute to access it. What did you think of the sketch Sean sent? Did you recognize her?"

"Sketch? I didn't get anything from Sean." She looked at her phone. No service.

On Tony's computer she logged in to her personal e-mail account. Sean had sent a picture he'd taken with his phone.

She stared at the image. If she'd seen it on its own, it might look familiar, but because she had just been reading Alexis's file she knew it was Alexis Todd Sanchez.

There were some differences—the nose in the picture was larger and the hair was completely different—but it was her eyes that gave her away.

"This is Alexis Sanchez. She's in my new-agent class."

Noah picked up his phone. "Chief? . . . We have a suspect. Alexis Sanchez. I'll meet you in your office."

He turned to Lucy. "You're certain."

"Yes. She lived in Newark, where Weber lived. Her sister was abducted and murdered at the same time as Rachel McMahon. Her brother was Weber's research assistant."

"There's no proof that she killed anyone. Where was she Saturday night?"

"In her room. But there are ways of getting around that." She thought of all the times her group had entered the building together. Only one person needed to use their passkey. "I think I can prove she left."

"Why would she?"

Lucy walked over behind Noah's desk and took the keyboard from him. She scrolled through Camille Todd's file and stopped on the autopsy report. "I have an idea. Camille Todd went missing before Rachel McMahon. Bob Stokes was the responding officer. Because it was a suspected abduction of a child under fourteen, the FBI was called. Tony Presidio was the case agent. One week later, Rachel McMahon goes missing and all resources move to her disappearance."

"That's a thin motive."

"It's in the autopsy report. Camille was alive for nearly a year after her abduction. When she was found, the coroner determined that she'd been dead for two weeks. Her killer was never found. Rachel died in less than twelve hours, yet the FBI and Newark police focused on finding her. It makes sense—most kidnapped children are killed within seventy-two hours. The more time that passes, the colder the trail gets."

Noah scanned the report. "They didn't think there was a connection."

"Two completely separate cases. But the McMahons had all the attention. The lies, the sex parties, the media—Rosemary Weber—was all over it, relegating Camille Todd to one sentence."

"I want you in the interrogation."

She nodded. She could do this.

"I'll call Suzanne Madeaux and tell her to pick up Kip Todd. Let's get them both in custody and then piece together the rest of the case. There are some holes."

"Not as many as you think."

Noah's phone rang. "Armstrong." He listened. "I'll go. I'm taking Kincaid with me." He hung up. "Alexis signed out at the gate. O'Neal went to her room and her personal effects are all gone."

Lucy's face fell in shock. They were so close to answers! "How did I tip her off?"

"I don't think you did."

CHAPTER THIRTY-SEVEN

Five Days Ago

I don't read the newspaper or watch the news, but some events are impossible to miss. For example, I pass by the newsstand on 94th twice every day on my way to and from the subway station. I can't avoid the over-sized headlines. Things like "President Visits Egypt," and "NYPD Officer Killed in Gang Shoot-out," and "Lindsay Lohan Back in Rehab."

Sometimes I'm amused by what people find important or interesting. But mostly I'm sad.

Wednesday evening a headline made me stop for the first time in the three years I'd been living in Brooklyn.

REPORTER AND AUTHOR ROSEMARY WEBER MURDERED

I stared for a long minute, long enough for the cashier to get antsy and tell me how much the paper cost.

I handed him the money and took the paper. I didn't read it on the subway—I wanted to read it in private.

I teach third grade at one of those schools people want to forget exist. Schools where kids don't have enough to eat, where parents forget they have responsibilities, where most of the kids only have one parent, or grandparent, to care. Schools where survival is as important as breathing. But the eight- and nine-year-olds I teach still had hope. And my job, as much as making sure they could read and had basic math skills, was to maintain their hope for one more year. Maybe I could do it so well because I remembered third grade better than any other year in school. While some kids forgot the time evil touched them, I lived with it every day. Vibrant and alive.

I knew when one of my students was being abused.

I knew when one of my students didn't have dinner or breakfast.

I knew when one of my students had seen darkness like I had.

And even amidst all that, I gave them hope. Like Grams saved me, I tried to save them.

In my three years, I've had ninety-eight students. I remember all their names, from Abraham to Zachary, Anne to Zoey. Nine of them are dead. Six dropped out of school before sixth grade. Twelve moved on to other schools, most because they were removed from violent homes and put in the system. And one is in juvenile hall for murder. He was eleven when he killed his neighbor for no reason he ever shared with me.

But I knew the reason. He'd lost all hope.

I took the *Times* home with me, to my small one-bedroom in a pre-war Bay Ridge building. I'd lived in the apartment since moving to New York, and I didn't plan on moving anytime soon. I was close to the water and even had a view of the bridge from one window. Bay Ridge was quiet and a good place to relax after spending the day teaching in East Brooklyn.

Somehow, bringing the paper across my threshold saddened me. As if I'd lost something or violated the sanctity of my home. My appetite was gone as well. I opened a can of diet soda and laid the paper on the table.

I stared at it for several minutes while sipping my drink until, resigned, I sat down and read the story.

I read the article, penned by a reporter named Robert Banker, twice. I might have memorized it, because some sentences kept repeating in my head.

Former Newark reporter and true crime author Rosemary Weber was stabbed to death Tuesday night at Citi Field while the Mets played to victory.

The police had no clues, no leads, and were investigating her murder with the FBI.

Ms. Weber is the author of three true crime books but is best known for her number one bestseller, *Sex, Lies, and Family Secrets,* which detailed the tragic rape, kidnapping, and murder of eleven-year-old Rachel McMahon and exposed her parents to charges of emotional abuse and neglect.

And because no newspaper could refrain from repeating the drama that had been my life for the first nine years, Banker brought up my parents' lifestyle:

Aaron and Pilar McMahon had been swingers, putting on elaborate sex parties for friends and neighbors while their two children played upstairs. It was one of their "friends" who killed their daughter, but their lies to police stymied the investigation for days.

I often wondered what would have happened differently had my parents told the truth that morning.

I often wondered if I could have saved Rachel if I'd called 911 at three in the morning when I found she wasn't in her bed. Intellectually, I knew she died early that morning and even if I had called and if my parents hadn't lied Rachel would have still died before Benjamin John Kreig was found.

I had to believe that, or I would have killed myself.

Grams told me, before she died, that Rachel had been killed shortly after her abduction and nothing I could have done would have changed that outcome. She knew I harbored deep guilt and anger over what had happened that night and the subsequent days. I believed Grams, because I had to or go insane.

But I still, sometimes, wonder.

Though I no longer answered to "Peter," I was glad my name wasn't in the article. I wasn't even mentioned.

The article ended with:

Rosemary Weber was researching her next book, about the Cinderella Strangler who suffocated young women at underground parties during a four-month stretch in New York City last winter. Police had no comment as to whether her murder had anything to do with her research.

I remembered the dead reporter. Not as a person, but as words. Her newspaper articles were talked about by everyone. Even though Grams had done her best to protect me, Weber's byline was everywhere. But it was the book that hurt the most. She told the world that I had been the one who exposed my parents as lying to police. I didn't care that people knew, but she made me out to be brave, when I felt smaller than a speck of dust. She printed a picture of me at Rachel's funeral—alone. Grams had been standing right next to me, but the angle of the picture had cut her out, giving Weber an iconic image that still haunted me.

Alone.

Suddenly I didn't want the newspaper in my house. As if just its presence would bring back despair and fear. As if the paper could somehow transmit my location to the woman I'd been hiding from for years.

I left my apartment, walked to the alley, and threw the newspaper into a garbage can.

I didn't feel any better.

Something had changed. Maybe I had. Reality invaded my home, reminding me that I didn't exist. That Gray Manning was a work of fiction.

I went back to my apartment and waited for the other shoe to drop.

CHAPTER THIRTY-EIGHT

New York City

Kip Todd lived in a small studio loft in SoHo. Suzanne met Joe DeLucca and two uniformed NYPD officers outside the building. "No doorman, manager gave me a key," Joe said. He ordered the uniforms to split and take front and rear entrances. "Second floor."

They took the stairs up. Joe knocked on the door. "NYPD, open up."

Nothing. No response, no sound of movement.

Joe glanced at Suzanne. "Ready?"

She nodded.

He put the key in. "It's nice working with you on a case." He grinned. "We should do it more often."

"Just watch my ass," she said, then moaned when he laughed. "You know what I meant.

"FBI and NYPD," Suzanne said. "Kip Todd, we're coming in."

They cautiously entered the one-room apartment, guns drawn. Joe checked the closet and bathroom while Suzanne looked in the cabinets in the small kitchen space. The bed was a futon. There weren't many places to hide, and Kip wasn't in any of them.

They holstered their weapons and looked around. The studio was L shaped, with two walls of windows. Small, but with new hardwood floors, a modern kitchen, and a bathroom not much bigger than an airport stall.

Kip Todd didn't have much stuff—a futon, end table, kitchen table with two chairs, and desk. The place was tidy, even the desk, though it was obvious someone had cleaned up and cleared out quickly. The printer was still there, with a cord that had connected to a missing computer. Phone cable for the Internet. A cell phone charger had been left behind.

Suzanne e-mailed her boss and asked for a warrant to track Kip Todd through his cell phone GPS. "It'll take a couple hours, but we'll get it," she told Joe.

Joe pulled on gloves and was going through Kip Todd's desk drawers. "He didn't grab everything," he said.

He pulled out a scrapbook. Every page was well designed, with care in picture placement. The first few pages were pictures of Kip Todd and his two older sisters, according to the labels.

"According to the information Noah Armstrong sent," Suzanne said, "Kip and Camille were eleven months apart."

After a half-dozen pages, newspaper articles and police reports replaced the photos. The headlines told the story.

**TWELVE-YEAR-OLD GIRL ABDUCTED
FROM PARK**

**SEARCH PARTIES STILL LOOKING FOR
TWELVE-YEAR-OLD GIRL MISSING SINCE
SUNDAY**

POLICE SAY THE RACHEL MCMAHON KIDNAPPING IS UNCONNECTED TO GIRL MISSING SINCE SUNDAY

The early newspaper articles were carefully clipped and preserved in the book. Passages had been underlined. Other than articles about Rachel McMahon that mentioned Camille Todd's disappearance, there were no other articles about McMahon or her family.

A year after Camille's disappearance, Todd had pasted in another article.

BODY FOUND IN WASHINGTON PARK RESERVE MAY BE MISSING GIRL

As the articles told the story of Camille Todd's body being found and identified, someone had blacked out paragraphs. Suzanne did a quick search on her smartphone for one of the articles and found out that all the paragraphs that had been blacked out related to comparisons between Camille Todd and Rachel McMahon. In fact, as the journalistic story continued, more and more dealt with rehashing Rachel's murder and less about Camille's disappearance.

According to the police reports, there was never a viable suspect in Camille's abduction and murder. However, the autopsy indicated that she'd been dead only two weeks before her body was discovered.

Joe was disgusted. "What guy keeps the autopsy report of his sister? There's pictures—wait, these are evidence photos."

"He could have stolen them." Suzanne turned the page. The last page in the scrapbook was really two pages, torn from a copy of Rosemary Weber's book *Sex, Lies, and Family Secrets*.

Suzanne's blood ran cold.

One week before Rachel was kidnapped from her bedroom while her parents swapped sex partners, another young girl was abducted. Camille Todd, twelve, was playing at a neighborhood park on a cold but sunny Sunday afternoon when she went to the public bathroom. No one saw her alive again.

Officer Robert Stokes of Newark was the first responder to both 911 calls. "We immediately ruled out any connection between Rachel and Camille. Camille was taken from a public park in broad daylight, and Rachel was taken in the middle of night from her bedroom." Stokes was proven correct in his analysis after Rachel's killer was identified as Benjamin John Kreig. Kreig had an airtight alibi for Camille's disappearance.

"The first seventy-two hours are the most critical in any stranger abduction," FBI Media Information Officer Dominic Theissen said. "Camille had been missing for a week when Rachel was abducted. We always hope that these victims are found alive, but after a week the chances are less than one percent. We focused our resources where we felt they would do the most good."

Unfortunately, both girls met tragic ends. Rachel's body was found six days after she was raped and murdered; Camille Todd was found nearly a year later.

"Theissen and Stokes were involved in both investigations," Suzanne said. "What are the chances that Tony Presidio was as well?"

"Look at this," Joe said. He pulled out a second scrapbook. This book was thicker and a complete mess.

"Shit," Suzanne mumbled when she opened it. "It's everything about Rachel McMahon and her family."

"There are pictures of her brother from what? Junior high? High school?"

"That's when it starts." She turned pages and watched as Peter McMahon grew up. There were handwritten notes about where he lived and his routine.

"Todd has been following him for a long time."

"It makes no fucking sense."

"I'm not a shrink, but maybe Todd felt a kinship with Peter because they both lost their sisters to violence."

"I don't think it's kinship. I think this guy is crazy."

"We met him. He's not crazy. Methodical and obsessed, maybe."

There were photos taken from afar of a kid they presumed was Peter McMahon from the time he was fourteen until he was about twenty. There were some labels to help identify the places, and it fit with what little Sean Rogan had found on the guy. Then nothing until a series of photos printed from a cell phone camera. The quality was poor and they were all taken from a distance.

"This is more recent," Joe said.

Suzanne assessed the photos. "That's the Saint Patrick's Day parade, but I can't tell what year."

"I think it was this year—I know this street; that closed storefront he's standing in front of shut down end of December."

"Here's another recent photo of McMahon at a cemetery." Suzanne frowned. "I don't recognize this place."

"Neither do I."

"McMahon may have been off the grid for a few years, but it looks like he's been found."

"Was Todd stalking him? What was his endgame?"

"Hell if I know, I can't see inside his head. Let's box this up and take it to the Bureau. Noah and Lucy are on their way and she's a criminal psychologist. She was instrumental in profiling the Cinderella Strangler, and without her that loony tune would have killed even more people."

While Joe bagged the two scrapbooks, Suzanne tried Noah. His phone was off—he was probably still on the plane. She then called Sean Rogan.

"Where are you?" she asked.

"Just landed at the Executive Airport."

"You're here in the city?"

"I know where Peter McMahon is."

"Tell me."

Sean hesitated. "I can't."

"This is a federal investigation, Rogan. Tell me where he is or you're obstructing justice."

"He's now my client. Detective Charlie Mead retained RCK and I'm his bodyguard. That was the condition on which I got his location. I'm not telling anyone where he is until I have him in my custody."

"Kip Todd has recent pictures of him. He probably knows where he lives. The FBI is perfectly capable of protecting him."

Sean hung up.

CHAPTER THIRTY-NINE

Charlie Mead had talked to Peter McMahon, aka Gray Manning, and arranged for Sean to meet him at a neutral spot in Brooklyn.

Sean felt exposed, especially in light of the information Suzanne had shared and what Noah had sent to him about Alexis Sanchez. If she and Todd knew where Peter was, why wait to go after him? What was their game? Already Sean was on alert. He'd been trained in personal security, but it wasn't his primary responsibility at RCK. He didn't like going on a job with virtually no intel on his client or the people out to get him.

Peter McMahon had disappeared and reinvented himself because he had to, and Sean didn't blame him. He deserved to be left alone. But if the Todds knew where to find him, he was in immediate danger, especially now that the Todds were on the run.

Sean had no idea *why*. It bothered him because it was illogical. If the Todds felt law enforcement had mishandled their sister's case, Sean could see the logic in targeting those involved. But Peter had been nine when the events that tore apart the two families had occurred. There was no connection between the crimes; the only big difference, as far as Sean could see, was that Rachel McMahon's murder got more attention in the media.

It was nearly eight and Lucy and Noah should be landing at LaGuardia any minute, if they weren't already on the ground. Lucy would have a theory about it, and hopefully it would help them figure out Kip and Alexis's next move.

Psychopaths, even if smart, didn't always think logically. Maybe logically to *them,* but not to an average person. That Lucy could understand these people sometimes unnerved Sean, but then again there was nothing average about Lucy.

Peter had never been safe. If Suzanne was right, Todd had located him several months ago. Now that the Todds were exposed and the FBI and NYPD were on their tails, they would go directly to their endgame.

Sean spotted Peter walking down 3rd Avenue toward Sean's rental. Peter was tall, an inch taller than Sean, and too thin. Though Peter was only twenty-four, his hair was dotted with gray.

Sean didn't like having a car in New York—he wasn't familiar with the streets, and traffic could be a problem. But he didn't want to be without transportation. His sole task was to get Peter to safety, then contact Suzanne and Noah. He hadn't been lying to Suzanne—he'd sworn to Charlie Mead that he could protect Peter, and he wasn't going to fail either of them.

Peter had picked the meeting spot, but it was only four blocks from his residence and Sean didn't like that. He had to assume that the Todd siblings knew where Peter lived. Sean had wanted to grab him at his apartment, but Peter was too nervous to give him the address. Sean had researched it while flying back to the city. Once he had

Peter's new name, it was easy to learn everything about him: his residence, his employer, where he liked to shop.

Peter glanced over his shoulder and Sean's instincts buzzed. He surveyed the area but didn't see anyone following Peter. Unfortunately, there were a lot of people on the street. This must be Brooklyn's version of restaurant row.

Sean got out of his car and crossed the street to meet up with Peter.

"Charlie sent me," he said.

Peter seemed both relieved and apprehensive.

Sean took his elbow and steered him toward his car. "Are you being followed?"

"I didn't see anyone."

"But?"

"I felt something."

Sean didn't dismiss Peter's concerns. Lucy had the same sixth sense about being watched, born of violence, and Peter may have developed the same instinct.

"I have a place; I just need to get you there. Do exactly what I say." Sean handed him a burner phone. "If we get separated for any reason, get to a safe place and call the last dialed number."

Peter pocketed the phone. He glanced at Sean and said, "Thank—" then stopped. He stared over Sean's shoulder. "Cami?"

Sean didn't look; he acted. His job was to protect Peter, not confront the Todds. He pushed Peter into the first storefront. It was a delicatessen and the patrons all stared at Sean when he walked straight through to the back ushering Peter in front of him.

He glanced once over his shoulder and saw a woman walk into the shop and glance around. He hadn't met Alexis Sanchez, aka Alexis Todd, when he'd visited Quantico the other day, but he had to assume that it was her—the same woman who'd passed herself off to Peter as Cami Jones for over a year.

The staff in the back yelled at Sean, "Get out! We'll call the police!"

Sean ignored them and continued maneuvering Peter through the kitchen, then the crammed supply room to the back door. He glanced through the security screen before opening it and slipping out with Peter.

"I should talk to her."

"No," Sean said.

"There has to be a reason."

She's a nut job. "Let's get you safe. Then I'll tell you everything."

Peter hesitated, and Sean grabbed his arm and pulled him along. It was like he was in a daze, unsure what was going on or who to trust.

"Do you trust Charlie?"

"He saved my life."

"Then trust me."

Sean didn't know if both of the Todds were trailing them or if they had spotted him when he got out of the rental car. He couldn't risk going back to 3rd Avenue, so he asked, "Where's the closest subway station?"

"Ninety-fifth. It's only two blocks away."

"Let's get moving."

Sean monitored their surroundings, assessing anyone who looked out of place. It was getting darker, which would help them disappear in the streets if necessary. But right now at dusk he felt too exposed.

He saw Alexis emerge from the shop and look both ways before she saw them. She picked up speed in the alley.

Sean waited until he and Peter turned the corner from the alley to the street, then said, "Faster."

Sean had pre-purchased two MetroCards when he and Lucy were in New York on Saturday. He hadn't thought they'd need them but didn't like to go unprepared. He was glad he had them now.

He rounded the corner and they rushed down the steps to the 95th Street subway station. Out of the corner of his eye he saw a church and considered detouring there but dismissed it—he didn't know the layout, and considering it was near dark, the church might be locked. Sean didn't see Alexis, but that didn't mean she wasn't there or that she might not assume they went to the subway.

"Is there another entrance to the subway?"

"Yes."

Either they could exit from the other side or Alexis could come down the other entrance and trap them. In fact, if both Alexis and Kip were trailing them, they could be boxed in. Damn, he shouldn't have come down here!

"Stay close."

Sean glanced at the subway map. They were at the end of the R Line.

He said, "We're taking the first train and getting off at the next stop."

"How did they find me?" Peter asked. "Did they follow you?" He didn't seem hostile, but there was an accusatory tone.

"They've been tracking you. Have been since March."

Peter shook his head, but his eyes told Sean he believed him. "Are you sure?"

"Yes." He moved Peter to behind a pillar. Sean could see one of the main staircases, and the other was partly in view.

"I think I knew," he said quietly.

Sean sent Lucy and Noah a quick text message.

At 95th St. Subway, Brook. Have PM. ATS pursuing.

"A couple of times I thought someone was watching me," Peter continued, "but I'd been hiding for so long I didn't trust my instincts anymore. Do they know where I live?"

"Assume they do. No one followed me."

"Charlie told you everything?"

"I needed to know what you faced in Syracuse, why you changed your name."

"I don't understand why these people are coming after me."

"You and me both." Sean heard a train coming far down the tunnel. He didn't see Alexis or Kip on the stairs. There were only two people waiting, together, for the train. It was a quiet Monday night.

"Get ready," he whispered. "Follow my orders."

The train was closer, ten seconds or less. Peter took a step toward the platform and Sean grabbed his arm. "Stay."

"FBI! Don't move!"

It was a female voice. Peter looked perplexed and turned to look toward the voice.

"No," Sean said, but it was too late.

Alexis was running down the stairs, gun drawn.

"FBI! Everyone down."

Shit.

The train was pulling fast into the station. Alexis glanced at it, and Sean pictured the attack against Theissen at the subway station in Queens. Was she planning on using the train as a diversion or a weapon?

Sean stayed behind the pillar, gun drawn.

"You said the FBI was helping," Peter said.

"She's not FBI," Sean told him.

Peter looked around the pillar. "Cami," he whispered.

"Peter," Alexis said. "Come to me. I'm here to help you."

"Don't," Sean said. He squeezed Peter's arm. "You can't trust her."

Alexis shouted out, "Peter! We have to hurry or it'll be too late. Please, trust me."

"Remember what Charlie found," Sean said. He didn't know what Alexis's game was, but she'd most likely killed Tony Presidio and put Hans in a coma. "She lied to you. She killed an FBI agent."

The train stopped at the platform. Several people got off. Alexis moved toward Sean and Peter. She didn't seem concerned about her own safety. Sean couldn't risk hitting an innocent bystander by firing in the station. He glanced toward the train. The warning to clear the doors alerted them that the train was about to depart.

Sean said, "Now!" He grabbed Peter and propelled him toward the open door.

"Peter!" Alexis shouted.

Sean heard gunfire and a searing bolt of pain shot up his calf. He rolled into the car; Peter stumbled and hit his head on the pole.

"Stay down!" Sean shouted.

Sean pushed back the pain and trained his gun toward the closing door. He saw Alexis's stunned expression. Then she raised the gun to fire again, aiming at Sean, not Peter. Two teenagers ran behind Alexis toward the exit, preventing Sean from having a clear shot.

Sean rolled away from the door as Alexis fired again. The bullet hit the side of the train as the doors closed.

No one else was in the car. Peter lay on the floor, unmoving.

"Are you hurt?" Sean asked.

Peter didn't say anything.

"Peter! Are you injured? Dammit, were you hit?" Sean crawled toward him.

"I'm okay," he said, voice cracking. Shock.

"Are you sure?" Sean looked for visible signs of injury. Peter had a bump on his forehead from hitting the pole. Other than that, he was fine.

Sean waited until they were in the tunnel before he examined his own wound.

"You're bleeding," Peter said.

Sean took out his pocketknife and cut off his jeans at the knee. The bullet had gone through the muscle in his calf, straight through. Not serious, but he needed to stop the bleeding.

He cut the jean scrap into strips and tied one as a tourniquet right below his knee. Then he took off his T-shirt and tied it tight around the open wound.

This wasn't the first time he'd been shot, nor would it be the worst, but damn, it hurt like hell. He pulled out his cell phone. No signal. He typed in a message to send as soon as he had one bar.

PM and I are on R train, will exit at Whitehall. Please meet there with first-aid kit.

"Peter, listen to me. Alexis Sanchez is not an FBI agent. She was at the FBI Academy for the past four weeks in training. Why, I have no idea. It may have been to collect information, or to target someone. She may have killed a federal agent, tried to kill another. Her sister was Camille Todd, who was kidnapped and murdered around the same time as your sister. I don't have all the answers, but if she has the chance, she will kill you."

CHAPTER FORTY

Noah had been on the phone for the last ten minutes while driving to the Whitehall subway station in lower Manhattan, talking with NYPD and the FBI to determine what went on at the 95th Street subway stop. Police were already on the scene and Alexis Sanchez was gone. Suzanne and Detective DeLucca were getting a copy of the security tapes and Lucy hoped they provided some answers. She had a lot of questions.

Sean didn't say who'd been shot, but Lucy knew it was Sean. If it was Peter, Sean would have told her to call an ambulance.

As soon as they arrived, Noah flashed his badge at the cashier and he and Lucy were let through the kiosk. They ran down the stairs while Lucy dialed Sean. "We're here," she said.

"I have Peter under the sign on the west side of the station."

"West side," Lucy said to Noah.

"I see him."

Sean was sitting bare-chested on a bench, his bloody

leg out in front of him. He had a hand on Peter, who looked like he wanted to bolt.

"It's not serious," Sean said by way of greeting. "Just grazed."

By the amount of blood, it wasn't just a graze.

"Lucy, escort Mr. McMahon to the car; I'll assist Rogan."

"I can walk," Sean said, standing. He hobbled toward the elevator.

"Manning," Peter said. "I legally changed my name to Gray Manning. But I guess you can call me Peter."

"We have a lot to discuss," Noah said. "But I don't like this exposure."

"I have a safe hotel," Sean said.

"We're going to the Bureau," Noah countered. He glanced at Peter, assessing, then looked at Lucy.

Lucy knew what Noah wanted. What kind of state of mind was Peter in?

"Peter," she said softly, "we need to talk about what's been happening. You may have information that's vital to finding Kip Todd and Alexis Sanchez. Are you up for it? We wouldn't ask if it wasn't crucial."

"Okay," he said, still in a daze.

She nodded at Noah, and Noah said, "Just for a debrief. Then you can secure him, Rogan." He looked at Sean's leg. "I can get a protective detail."

"I'm fine."

"Hardly," Lucy muttered.

"I heard that."

Noah drove and Lucy sat in the back with Sean. She turned on the lights and took off the shirt he had wrapped around his leg. "This isn't a graze," she said.

"Do we need a hospital?" Noah asked.

"Yes," Lucy said at the same time Sean said, "No."

Sean said, "I'm not going to the hospital. The bleeding has stopped. It was a twenty-two. The hole isn't much bigger than a bee sting, and that's what it feels like."

"You need stitches."

"Maybe one stitch. You can handle that, princess."

She glared at him. He smiled.

"Bureau," Sean said. Lucy decided to let it go. There'd been a lot of blood, but Sean was right—the damage was minimal.

She cleaned and taped the entry and exit wounds, then bandaged the leg. "You should still get checked out."

"Time enough when we catch the Todds," Sean said.

"Were you followed?" Noah asked.

"No. Sanchez was following Peter. Where were you coming from?" Sean asked Peter.

"I had a staff meeting this afternoon; stopped at a place I often eat dinner. I didn't want to go home after talking to Charlie."

"They could have followed him from school," Sean said.

"How did they know where I teach? How'd they know my name?"

"I don't think they did, not at first," Lucy said. "I haven't seen the evidence from Kip Todd's apartment, but going on what Suzanne said, he spotted you in the city back in March. He knew you were here."

"It's a big city," Noah said. "Peter was a needle."

"Not really. Alexis, when she was Cami, knew Peter was studying early childhood education. It was reasonable to think that Peter had become a teacher. If they troll the Internet for staff, they might get a hit, but seeing Peter in the city narrowed them to this region."

Sean said, "Never underestimate someone determined

to find you. It's extremely difficult to go completely off the grid, even with a name change and new Social Security number."

Noah added, "They may have hired someone to do it."

"She could have had anything on me," Peter said. "We were together for over year."

Sean said, "Peter, you said you thought you were being watched. When did it start?"

"It's been on and off. I always felt safe at home, but after I read about Rosemary Weber's murder I had a feeling my life was going to be turned upside down. Anytime there's another article in the paper, I wait for reporters to track me down. After I changed my name and moved to Brooklyn, I thought it would end."

"How did Sanchez get to New York so fast?" Sean asked.

Noah said, "She left Quantico at three in the afternoon and told the gate she was going to a drugstore. She never returned. Her car was found at Dulles long-term parking, and she boarded a four thirty-two flight to JFK, no luggage."

"Do you know what tipped her off?" Sean asked.

Lucy had worried she'd said or done something, but she couldn't think what. "No. She was gone before I pulled her personnel records and discovered the connection with New Jersey."

"If I had to bet," Sean said, "it came from that lowlife street thief who pawned the ring."

"How so?"

"NYPD released him; what if he went back to Todd and told him about the interview? Maybe Todd got antsy and called his sister."

"We're pulling her cell phone records and all Todd's records, but so far we've found nothing," Noah said.

"They could have burner phones," Sean said.

Noah turned into the federal building parking lot and showed his ID. "We're running down leads. The brother hasn't returned to his apartment or his office at the library. NYPD has staked out both places, and we have a patrol covering Weber's sister."

"They've had this plan in the works for years," Lucy said. "He has another place."

"How can you know that?" Peter asked.

"Alexis befriended you six years ago. They could have killed you then, if they wanted you dead. They had something else planned, but wanted to keep you in sight."

"Let's brief everyone together," Noah said. He parked and they got out. Sean had to surrender his gun at the security desk.

They went up to the Violent Crimes squad and Suzanne greeted them at the elevator. "So you're the famous Noah Armstrong," she said, shaking his hand. "Good to finally meet you."

"Suzanne, likewise," Noah said. "This is Peter McMahon. He had his name legally changed to Gray Manning and has been a teacher in East Brooklyn for the past three years."

"Dangerous schools," Suzanne said.

"I teach third grade," he said quietly.

"Shelley." Suzanne motioned to an analyst. "Would you please escort Mr. Manning to an interview room? Get him whatever he would like; keep him company. You're not under arrest, Peter. But we need to talk."

He glanced at Sean as if for permission.

"Go ahead, Peter. I'm not leaving without you."

Shelley walked off with Peter. Lucy, Noah, and Sean followed Suzanne to an interview room. She introduced Noah to Detective DeLucca, who was reviewing digital security tapes.

Noah asked, "Is that the footage from the subway?"

"Yep," Joe said. "We also checked out all survelliance cameras in the area and I've pieced it together."

He pressed a button. "McMahon—"

"Manning," Sean said.

"Manning, McMahon, whatever he's going by—"

"Let's call him Peter," Suzanne said. "For simplicity."

"*Peter*," Joe said, "was on the subway and got off at Fourth and Eighty-sixth at seven oh five pm."

"We were meeting at eight on Third and Ninety-third," Sean said. "Why wouldn't he take the subway down to Ninety-fifth? It's the closest."

"Because I caught him on a traffic cam going into a mom-and-pop restaurant at Third and Eighty-seventh. He stayed for thirty-nine minutes and left. No cameras until the subway."

Sean said, "I spotted him just before eight. I planned on waiting until he slipped into the bar we were meeting at, but I spotted Sanchez trailing him."

"Sanchez," Joe said. "I caught her, too, coming out of the subway behind Peter. He didn't see her. I don't know why she didn't confront him at the restaurant. She passed it and must have been waiting until he left."

"Maybe she hadn't found out where he lived yet, but they knew where he taught." Suzanne pressed a few keys. "Two weeks ago, this popped up on the school's Web site."

Lucy leaned over. It was a photo of Peter with his class. Suzanne said, "This was last year's third-grade class. They were recognized at the beginning of this year for achieving the greatest increase in test scores from beginning of school to end of school. The mayor presented the award."

The caption read: "Gray Manning says all children are capable of learning if given the right support and motivation."

"The article ran in the *Times*," Suzanne said. "We know Todd had been trying to find Peter, and with this article he now knew Peter's new name and where he worked."

"And that prompted him to put his plan in motion," Lucy said.

"And exactly what was his plan?" Joe said. "It looks like he's taking out everyone he's crossed paths with."

Lucy shook her head. "He's methodical. Extremely organized. And he's been planning this for a long time."

"I'm going to have to agree with that," Suzanne said. "Joe, consider what Cleveland said."

Joe nodded. "Professor Cleveland, Todd's faculty advisor, said that Todd wasn't Weber's first choice. Her first two choices backed out at the last minute, no explanation. We're trying to track them down now. By the time she went back to the applicant pool, several had found assignments. The post went to Todd."

"Did Cleveland know about his sister?" Noah asked.

"No. He said Todd was a competent but not outstanding student and never talked about his family."

Lucy said, "I need to see the scrapbooks you found."

Joe handed her two evidence bags, each with a scrapbook. She opened them up. The first was essentially a tribute to Camille Todd and media time line of her kidnapping, the investigation, and her subsequent murder. The second, ten times thicker and far less tidy, was a montage of clippings about everyone who had been on the Rachel McMahon investigation.

Except not everyone. Lucy began to take notes. Fast. Everything came together quickly in her head, pulling together what Sean had learned from Charlie Mead and what Suzanne had found in Kip Todd's apartment.

"Lucy?" Sean asked.

She glanced up. Everyone was looking at her. How long had she been focused on the scrapbooks?

She smiled sheepishly and said, "I don't have all the answers, and won't until I talk to Kip or Alexis, but I know why they targeted Peter."

Joe raised an eyebrow. "You got me. I can see that they were targeting him, but how can you tell motive?"

"Fifteen years ago, Kip Todd identified with Peter. If you look at the notations in the first scrapbook, he considers himself almost a brother to Peter. They both lost their beloved older sister. They both suffered. There was no hatred of Peter or the McMahons initially. In fact, I suspect that for a while the Todd family believed that whoever killed Rachel had killed Camille, only Camille's body hadn't been found.

"A year later, Camille's body is found. It's old news, not generating a lot of press. But the one-year anniversary of Rachel McMahon's murder is suddenly big news. A weeklong series of articles, rehashing the swingers' lifestyle, the investigation, the trial—where was the justice for Camille? It's like no one cared what happened to her."

"How old were Kip and Alexis?" Suzanne asked.

"Eleven and seventeen when she disappeared. There are some holes in the articles. For example, we don't really know the circumstances of her kidnapping other than that she went to a public restroom at a public park and didn't come back. Was she with her family? Her brother? Her sister? Guilt is a powerful and deadly motivator."

DeLucca said, "I read the police reports. Cops interviewed every sex offender in a twenty-mile radius, everyone at the park that day."

"And I have the FBI file. It's even thinner," Suzanne said. "No suspects. No substantive profile."

"Who wrote it? Tony or Hans? They were both profiling back then, and both worked on the Rachel McMahon case."

Suzanne looked. "Hans Vigo. But not until after her body was found. He wrote that the suspect was a pedophile who lived alone in a remote area. Manual labor, farming, or heavy machinery by trade. Worked alone, kept to himself, nondescript. Wouldn't arouse suspicion. He likely had a dog and used the animal to lure his victims into a place where they could easily be taken. He would be of small stature but deceptively strong."

Noah added, "He kept Camille until she started her menstrual cycle, then killed her."

"There was a note added to the file two years ago," Suzanne said.

"From Hans?"

"No, it's an administrative note. Five years ago in Pennsylvania, a forty-nine-year-old man was shot and killed by police after the failed abduction of a ten-year-old girl. The note said that profilers deemed the suspect had a sixty-five percent chance of being Camille Todd's killer. He'd been living in the neighboring town up until a year after Camille's body had been found."

"How many victims were attributed to him?"

"Confirmed two—bodies found on his property. Looking through unsolved cases, the BSU determined that five others were definitely his handiwork. Those families were notified. But there were seven victims who were likely but unconfirmed. Their families were not notified."

Lucy said, "So the Todds never had closure. The parents divorced before Camille was abducted. Then Camille goes missing and they have no idea what happened to her. They had hope when Rachel went missing that the police would find her because they had to be connected—same age, same general area—but Rachel's case turned into a media blitz, and when her case was solved everyone forgot about Camille."

Joe took issue with that. "No one forgot. I'm a cop; I've never forgotten a missing kid. I look at their pictures every damn day."

Lucy said, "I'm trying to get into how the Todds felt. How Kip and Alexis turned their confusion and grief into a conspiracy to murder."

"What you're saying," Sean interjected, "is that they felt Camille was forgotten because Rachel's case got all the attention."

Lucy nodded, then continued, "Look at this second scrapbook. It wasn't until *after* the autopsy that the record keeping became messy. When Kip originally started, he felt a kinship to Peter, until he found out that Camille had been alive the whole time. While Rachel was already dead, all the police and FBI were focused on finding her, not Camille. It doesn't matter that there was more evidence and more witnesses to Rachel McMahon's murder; they're looking at the investigation from the outside.

"Dominic Theissen was the public face of the FBI. He's the one who verbalized the seventy-two-hour window. The Todds think that the police gave up after seventy-two hours and presumed she was dead."

Joe said, "In the police reports, it looks like they felt she might have drowned. The creek was running high and kids playing close to the banks have slipped and fallen in the past, washing to shore miles downstream."

Lucy nodded. "With Rachel, everything appeared to have been done right, and with Camille, everything appeared to have been done wrong—from the Todds' perspective. Officer Stokes, who later became a detective, had been the responding officer to both crime scenes. Theissen spoke for the FBI. Tony Presidio was the FBI case agent—because initially, they believed the cases were connected. But Tony stayed with the McMahon case all the way through. Camille became a cold case, passed on to another agent when Tony moved to D.C."

"That doesn't explain Hans," Noah said.

"He wrote the profile."

"How would they get that report?" Joe asked.

Noah responded, "Not difficult. It's not a classified file. Alexis Sanchez may have accessed it from Quantico."

"You don't know?"

"It would have been in Tony's files," Lucy said. "I think that's why she wanted the McMahon file—for the newspaper articles that talked about Camille's kidnapping. She didn't want Tony or me to make a connection to either her or Kip, now that the FBI had interviewed him."

Suzanne said, "If Tony had connected Rosemary Weber's murder to McMahon, he may have seen the Todd name in the files, and traced Kip Todd back to Camille. Kip wasn't hiding."

"But Alexis was, using her married name, lying about her marital status."

"But why now?" Joe asked. "It's been fifteen years."

"It started ten years ago," Sean said. "Two things happened. Peter moved back to New Jersey, and Rosemary Weber published *Sex, Lies, and Family Secrets.* Peter was harassed in high school." He pulled out his laptop and showed the group files he'd downloaded. "Kip Todd was a junior when Peter was a freshman. Same high school. But Kip, who has a degree—not in literature like he told you but computer engineering—hacked into the school system and deleted all his files. When Patrick was in Newark he grabbed a physical copy of the yearbook. And there's Kip. It's the only record that he went to the school—if you call them and ask, there are no computerized files. And

Patrick followed up—all physical copies were destroyed after they were digitized."

"When did he do it?" Lucy asked.

"When Peter was in Syracuse," Sean said. "At least, that's my educated guess."

Lucy suspected that Sean knew for certain but that he hadn't found the information through legitimate channels. She worried that someday his hacking skills were going to get him in trouble, but she had to admit that they often came in handy.

Lucy said, "They lost track of him when he ran away. Kip graduated from high school. Peter got his GED, then he went to college a year early. Kip would have been in college at the same time, and since Peter hadn't legally changed his name or hid his identity, he was easy to find."

"And Alexis got close to him? To psychologically torture him?" Suzanne shook her head. "They're sick."

"They're methodical sociopaths."

"What I don't get is how Alexis beat the FBI background check," Joe said. "Don't you guys run your new agents through a vigorous system?"

"Yes," Noah said, "but she didn't lie about anything. Just because her sister was murdered doesn't disqualify her from being an agent. When she interviewed, she lived in Denver, she was married, she had a daughter. All that was true. When she and her husband split, she amended her file. It's all there, in her file, but unless you know what to look for, it's not going to raise any concerns."

"Why go through all that trouble to become an FBI agent if you're only going to leave in the middle of training?"

"My guess?" Sean said. "They wanted information they couldn't get without being an insider. Either on their sister's murder investigation, or maybe they believed after

Peter disappeared from Syracuse that the FBI knew where he was."

Noah concurred and added, "Also, I don't think Alexis planned on killing Tony so soon after killing Weber. But when Tony himself went to New York, she panicked and poisoned his Scotch."

"Do we have a confirmation from the lab that his Scotch was definitely poisoned?" Lucy asked.

Noah shook his head. "We're waiting on more tox reports. Right now, an ERT unit is combing through her dorm room looking for trace evidence. If she's guilty, we'll find it."

"Why kill Rosemary now?" Lucy mused out loud.

"Because," Joe said, "Rosemary was looking into the Theissen subway accident. The day before she was killed, she requested the autopsy report, the police report, and all security footage. Maybe Todd thought she'd see something that would nail him. Though we can't confirm from the security tapes that Todd was the person who tripped Theissen, he fits the general description."

"Theissen's death set the chain of events into motion," Suzanne said. "They'd quietly taken out Theissen. They may or may not have poisoned Bob Stokes. Kip Todd is keeping an eye on Rosemary—maybe he got the internship to see if she had information about Peter. Or maybe just to get close to her before he killed her, like Alexis got close to Peter."

Noah asked, "Did they conspire to kill Theissen? Or was that the brother acting alone?"

"They had to be working together," Sean said.

"Why?"

"The only way Alexis could have known Tony was working with Suzanne was if her brother tipped her off."

Suzanne said, "They're both looking very guilty."

Lucy considered the facts they knew and all the conjecture and speculation. "I'm having a hard time figuring out which one of the siblings is dominant. Traditionally, it's the male partner, but he was much younger when Camille was kidnapped. How his mother and his older sister responded to their grief would have a huge impact on him. He may have put himself into the protective role, that he needed to look out for them because he couldn't protect Camille. Yet, Alexis went into the lion's den—she was one of us. She ate with us, studied with us, lived with us. She kept up the act at all times. That shows an intense and controlled personality, capable of extreme emotional restraint."

"I've looked at this security footage a dozen times," Joe said, "and she wasn't trying to kill Peter. I think she wanted to disable Sean."

Sean concurred. "She wanted Peter to go with her. When I wouldn't let him, she shot at me."

"She could be fixated on him," Suzanne said.

"If Peter isn't a target, why was he stalked for so many years? In high school and college? Why did Alexis pretend to be someone else?" Lucy looked through the scrapbooks again. "Except . . ." She hesitated.

"What?" Noah prompted.

"There are two distinctly different targets. Those who elevated Rachel's murder and minimized Camille's—in the eyes of the Todds—would be Rosemary Weber and any law enforcement involved in either investigation. Then there is Peter. Peter had nothing to do with any of it. He didn't talk to Rosemary Weber; he didn't do anything to make himself the center of attention. If anything, he diminished himself and became inconsequential. He moved, changed his name, disappeared. And still, they sought him out."

"Or," Suzanne said, "one of them did."

"You're not thinking that Alexis isn't part of this whole thing," Joe said, "or being manipulated by her brother? She attacked a federal agent and shot a civilian."

Lucy considered Joe's comment. "I think Alexis is fully cognizant of her actions. I don't think she's being manipulated by her brother. They planned everything out, from Agent Theissen to Rosemary Weber to Tony Presidio to Hans. It's Peter who doesn't fit. Especially since Sean says she aimed to kill him, not Peter."

"Alexis and Kip could be in the middle of a falling-out," Noah said. "And we need to capitalize on it."

Suzanne and Lucy laid out their theory about Kip and Alexis Todd to Peter. He didn't say anything for several minutes. Lucy didn't blame him—it was an incredible story.

"Why do they hate me? What did I ever do to them?"

"Nothing," Lucy said. "You became the object of their sociopathy. When their sister was killed, they had no one to blame. They blamed the police, the media, your family, everyone, because they felt helpless."

Suzanne added, "You were a convenient target for them."

It was clear that Peter didn't believe them, not completely.

"There may be another factor we haven't uncovered," Lucy said. "There's a lot we don't know about their childhood. There's a lot we don't know about their relationship. Detective Mead gave Sean your file, which helps with the time line."

Suzanne slid a recent picture of Kip Todd in front of Peter. "Do you recognize this man?"

Peter stared at it. He shook his head.

Suzanne then slid a picture of Kip Todd from Peter's

yearbook ten years ago. Kip had changed a lot—his hair was darker and he was heavier in high school.

"What about him?"

Peter stared and frowned. "Maybe."

"Maybe?"

He shrugged. "I remember a short, pudgy kid when I was a freshman. We didn't have any classes together, but his locker was near mine. He talked to me a few times, but I didn't have friends and didn't want to make any friends." He looked at them. "My grandmother had just died. My mother was a slut. You'd think after everything that happened, how humiliated they were when their sex parties were exposed, that she'd clean up her act. Instead, my mom goes to one extreme and sleeps with every breathing male, and my dad goes to the other extreme and becomes a fire-and-brimstone-preaching dictator who says sex is evil. I missed my sister, but I missed her even more after Grams died." He paused, looked at his clasped hands. "Which seems weird after five years."

Lucy said, "It's not weird." She hesitated, then said, "When I was seven, my best friend—my nephew—was killed. He was practically my brother; we saw each other every day. Like Rachel, he was kidnapped from his bedroom. Senseless. I still miss him, and every once in a while, even now, I feel almost overwhelmed with loss. It comes and goes quickly. On the one hand, I want to hold on to that feeling because I want to remember him; on the other, it feels so real, so painful, I never want to feel it again."

Peter seemed to find peace in her understanding.

Suzanne showed him a recent picture of Alexis. "Do you recognize this woman?"

"It's Cami. But different."

"But you think it's the same woman."

"I know it is. I loved her. She had lighter hair back then—I knew she'd dyed it, but I never saw her with brown hair. And her features are a little different—maybe fuller? Rounder? But it's her."

"Her name is Alexis Todd Sanchez."

He frowned. "She's married?"

"Divorced."

Lucy considered something. She opened the file and looked at the birth records of Missy Sanchez. Alexis said she'd just turned four. That meant she could have been conceived in October, right before Alexis left Syracuse after allegedly putting the dead pig in Peter's bed—Lucy needed Alexis's medical records to know for certain.

Or they could call her ex-husband.

"Excuse me," Lucy said.

Suzanne looked at her oddly, but Lucy slipped out.

Noah and Joe were watching through the one-way mirror in a room next door.

"What are you thinking?" Noah asked Lucy.

"The time frame—what if Alexis wasn't the one who put the pig in Peter's bed?"

Noah was skeptical. "She scrubbed down the apartment, lied about where she lived, was never a student. She lied about everything."

"They were having sex. I think he's Missy's father."

"That's a big leap."

"The timing is right."

"She's involved, Lucy. Even if Tony was poisoned in New York, or if his death was truly a coincidence, she attacked Hans."

"I think she did both, no doubt in my mind. I think she's as much involved in all of it as her brother. Except for Peter. I think she truly wanted to warn him, to protect him."

"I trust your hunches," Noah said, "but that doesn't help us find her, or her brother."

"I have an idea to draw Alexis out," Lucy said. "But I need to confirm my theory."

"All right," he said. "What do you need?"

"To talk to her ex-husband."

CHAPTER FORTY-ONE

Peter had quietly agreed to the plan when they debriefed him, but Lucy wasn't at all sure that he was psychologically ready to confront Alexis. She'd been the first person he'd trusted after what happened with his sister, and Alexis had done more than destroy his trust—she'd killed his hope. He'd become a hermit, outside of teaching young kids. He had no friends, no social life, no future.

Because Alexis and possibly Kip had seen Sean, Sean would be Peter's visible bodyguard. Alexis also could have seen Sean at Quantico and know that he was involved with Lucy, but they would have to take that chance. Lucy was banking on her psychological analysis that Alexis would come to warn Peter or try to justify what she'd done.

Lucy had enough experience with psychopaths and sociopaths, plus a master's in criminal psychology, to make this call, but she'd always had backup. She'd always had Dillon or Hans to help talk things out. Now she had no choice but to go it alone.

Sean and Peter went up to Peter's apartment. Joe was coordinating NYPD on the street. Sean set up a camera so that Noah and Lucy, who were in a vacant apartment down the hall, could watch and listen. Suzanne would remain hidden in Peter's apartment.

Lucy's theory was that Alexis would act quickly, possibly tonight and no more than twenty-four hours from now.

Noah shook his head at the screen as he watched the living room of Peter's apartment through a phone that Sean had programmed to transmit to his laptop. "Sean has all the toys," Noah told Lucy.

"Private sector," Lucy said. "It pays better."

Sean was trying to get Peter to loosen up a bit, but Peter was wooden and worried. Finally, Sean turned on a baseball game that had been played earlier in the day, keeping the volume on low. It was late, after one in the morning, and Peter drifted off to sleep in his chair.

Lucy asked Noah, "Have you heard about Hans?"

"Same condition, but the swelling has gone down. If it continues, they'll perform surgery tomorrow morning."

"That's just as dangerous as the accident."

"It's the only thing that will save him."

"That's what they told us about Patrick, and he ended up in a coma for nearly two years."

"You never told me what happened."

"I assumed everyone knew. It's in my file." She didn't know where the bitterness came from. She was used to this.

Noah said quietly, "I only read what I had to know when I was investigating the vigilante murders. I knew about the coma, but not why."

Lucy stared at the screen.

"You don't need to talk about it, Lucy."

She shook her head. "Adam Scott had me on an island outside of Seattle. He falsified coordinates and sent them to Kate. Kate didn't believe the information, she thought there was something wrong, but the FBI verified them and the agent in charge of the investigation took a team down to Baja, California. It was a trap. Scott had used the cabin in the past; he rigged it to explode. He was watching through a video feed. My brothers Patrick and Connor went down with Jack's mercenary team, along with four agents. Scott watched through a video feed—I know, because he showed me—and when they breached the cabin, he blew it up." Lucy would never forget watching Patrick half-running, half-thrown from the cabin. It still haunted her.

"Patrick had a severe head injury that required surgery, but he was conscious and joking on the way to the hospital. He didn't regain consciousness after the surgery. The doctors didn't know for certain, but suspected it was a rare reaction to the anesthesia. When he was younger, he'd had his appendix out and slipped into a coma for several days."

"Did they operate again?"

"No. He just woke up one day. Out of the blue." She smiled. "The last couple years hasn't been easy for him. Not just the physical deterioration. San Diego PD replaced him in the cybercrimes unit. Patrick had taken it from next to nothing to state of the art. But as you know, cybercrime is constantly changing. Patrick could have had his job back, but working for someone else. He was a lot like Sean—had an intuitive understanding of computer security. He lost his edge.

"Connor, our other brother, is a P.I. and asked Patrick to join him, but Jack wanted Patrick at RCK, and Patrick needed to get out of the family nest." She paused. "I love my family, but it's hard to forge your own path when everyone tries to do it for you."

"He's a good man."

Lucy smiled. "Yeah. He and Sean became close. I don't think Patrick realized when he went to Sacramento to work for RCK that he was going from one overprotective family to another. Sean and Patrick opened up RCK East to get out from under the thumb of their big brothers." She glanced at Noah. "You and Sean are good now, right?"

"As good as we'll ever be," he said.

"Why does that sound ominous?"

Noah didn't say anything, and Lucy didn't push. She didn't want to make waves. She liked Noah and owed him a debt for training her, supporting her, helping her become a good agent. She considered him her closest friend, outside of her family.

But she loved Sean. He was her best friend. It was as simple as that. She didn't want to choose sides between career and Sean. She wanted both.

Everything mattered more—her career, her family, her life—because she had someone to share it with.

Noah's phone, set on intercom, beeped. It was De-Lucca. "Heads up, possible Sanchez entering building. She has a key."

"Roger that; hold your position."

Noah said to Suzanne, "Did you get that?"

"Roger."

They waited. It felt like forever but was only three minutes before Alexis used a key to get into Peter's apartment. On the screen, Lucy watched her quietly close the door. She walked down the short hall and looked at Peter, now pretending to sleep on the chair. She then turned toward Sean on the couch, also pretending to sleep.

"Suz," Lucy said, "she has a gun in her right hand."

She raised her gun toward Sean.

Suzanne came out of the bedroom and karate chopped her arm. She dropped the gun, turned to face Suzanne, but Suzanne kicked her legs out from under her and had her on the ground in seconds, her knee in Alexis's back.

Sean hobbled over and put his gun on Alexis while Suzanne cuffed and searched her. By the time Alexis was on her feet, Noah and Lucy were in the apartment.

Peter rose from his chair and stared at her. "Why?"

"He knows where you are. He'll find you."

"Let him come," Suzanne said, sitting Alexis down in a chair. "We're ready."

She shook her head. "He won't come now. He's the smartest person I know. And patient. He'll wait."

Lucy sat down across from her. "Alexis, tell Peter the truth. He deserves to know why you went to Syracuse."

Tears welled in her eyes. "You don't understand how hard it was for us after Cami disappeared. She was just . . . gone. We didn't know where, if she was dead or alive. Kip blamed himself because he was there, at the park with her. Mom told them, watch out for each other.

"But it wasn't until you came back that Kip changed. He wanted so desperately to be your friend. He wanted to talk about your sister, and his sister, and you wouldn't. He became fixated on you and everything about Rachel and the investigation."

Suzanne said, "You were part of it."

She looked down, but Lucy saw the anger in Alexis's face. When she looked back up, it was hatred. "Feds like you fucked up the investigation. Cami was alive for a year. And no one cared; no one was looking; no one believed she was alive. Do you know what she suffered at the hands of the man who took her? The pain? Repeated rapes? Torture? For *a year*. All because Rachel's family had this wild life. All the attention was paid to *her*. Her killer was caught and in prison while Cami continued to suffer."

Peter said, "None of that was my fault."

Alexis softened when she looked at him. "I know that, baby. I know. That's what I told Kip, but he didn't understand. When he found you in Syracuse, I convinced him to let me get close. I tried to protect you. And for a while, it worked. Kip was in college, and focused on finding out what really happened to Cami, on tracking the cops who screwed up the investigation. I fell in love."

"Is that why you put the dead pig in my bed?"

"That was Kip. I walked in and saw it and realized he was going to kill you. That's why I cleaned the apartment and disappeared."

Lucy said, "Why didn't you tell the police?"

Alexis looked at Lucy. "You of all people should understand how broken the system is! We had a plan, and it worked."

"You just didn't want Peter to be part of the plan."

"Kip agreed to stay away from Peter if I left him, so I did. I did it to protect you." She implored Peter, "I love you, Peter."

"When did the plan change?" Lucy asked.

"When Presidio went to New York. He was looking in all the right places; if he figured it out before we were done, it would blow everything."

Lucy said, "You stole the file after you poisoned him."

"I had to. I didn't want to do it like that, I wanted him to know why, but I had no choice."

"You killed him?" Peter said in disbelief. "You killed an FBI agent?"

"Three cops," Suzanne said. "Retired agent Theissen, Detective Bob Stokes, and SSA Presidio. Plus you put Assistant Director Vigo in the hospital."

"He was looking into Presidio's death. It was a heart attack, it should have been dismissed as natural, but he was suspicious. I had to do it."

"You can make amends, Alexis," Lucy said. "Help us stop your brother before he hurts anyone else."

She shook her head. "You'll kill him."

"He needs help."

"By locking him up? Like a criminal?"

"He killed at least two people—Rosemary Weber and Dominic Theissen."

Alexis stared at her defiantly. "So?"

"This is getting us nowhere," Noah said. "DeLucca and I are going to put her in Holding until I can get a transport to federal prison."

"Alexis," Lucy said. "You killed a federal agent. That's a death penalty charge. Help us stop your brother and I will help you."

"So I can go to prison for the rest of my life?" she snapped sarcastically.

"Do you want your daughter to suffer for the rest of *her* life? Don't you want to see her grow up?"

Alexis's eyes teared. "Peter. Take care of Missy."

Peter stared at her. "What?"

"She looks just like you," Alexis whispered.

"Alexis," Peter said quietly, squatting in front of her, "I don't understand why you and Kip blamed the police for what happened to your sister. But I know your pain more than anyone." He glanced at Lucy. "Lucy and I both understand. You can't let him finish whatever he's doing. It needs to end now."

Tears streamed down Alexis's cheeks. "I'm not going to turn on my brother."

Peter stood and gazed down at her. "I understand."

She sighed in relief. "Go, far away from New York."

He shook his head.

"No. I'm staying here. I love my job. Those kids mean everything to me. I've been running since Rachel died. I'm not running anymore."

"He will kill you," Alexis said emphatically. "Don't you understand? He'll kill you. That's all he wants now."

Noah motioned for Lucy. She walked over to the small kitchen and he said in a low voice, "She's stalling."

"I think she's torn. She honestly cares about Peter and doesn't want him hurt."

"She's loyal to her brother."

Lucy nodded.

"Something's wrong. She might have come here to warn Peter, but she knows her brother's near. Lucy, try to get the info out of her, but I'm calling in Tactical." Noah stepped into the hall to make his calls.

Lucy walked back over to Alexis. "Where is your brother now?"

"I don't know," she said, looking at Peter.

"You do. I think you came here to warn Peter, but you know Kip is already on his way."

She didn't say anything.

Sean said, "Peter, come with me."

Suzanne cut him off. "You're hardly in prime condition. I'll take you and Peter to the safe house, and you can babysit him."

Sean was going to argue—he hated being out of the center of an operation—but he looked at Lucy and she nodded. "You're not one hundred percent."

"My eighty percent is better than most hundreds." He winked. "But I'm with Peter. Be careful, Luce."

Noah came back in. "We have a problem. Alexis mirrored your computer at Quantico, Lucy. Every communication that's come in through your e-mail, she saw."

Lucy turned to her. She felt violated and angry. But it explained how Alexis knew when to leave. "You knew Sean had sent me the sketch Peter had made at Syracuse."

Alexis didn't say anything, but her eyes revealed the truth.

Sean took Lucy's phone. He opened it up, inspected it, then reset the system. "There's no bug, but I reset the codes so nothing you send on the phone will go through your computer."

"We can't use the safe house Sean set up on the chance the intel has been compromised," Noah said. "DeLucca has a place NYPD uses. He's calling in an unmarked car to transport Peter, Sean, and Suzanne there. NYPD will cover the exterior. Lucy and I will take Sanchez to Bureau headquarters."

Lucy turned back to Alexis. "You can stop this."

Alexis shook her head. "No, I can't." She looked at Peter. "I'm sorry, Peter. I tried to save you. But you sided with the wrong people. I wish it were different."

Peter was heartbroken and confused. Lucy took him aside. "Peter, don't let her get into your head. This isn't your fault. She's playing by her own set of rules. To her, it's Kip and Alexis against the world. She wanted you to join them. Because you didn't, you're the enemy. Don't forget that."

He didn't say anything, but the pain in his eyes hurt Lucy. "I don't want to run," he said.

"You won't have to. We'll find him."

CHAPTER FORTY-TWO

"The cars are here," Noah said.

It was after three in the morning, and the street had been quiet for thirty minutes. NYPD had searched the neighboring buildings and public areas and there was no sign of Kip Todd or any threat.

"We're taking Alexis out first through the front. Two agents will take her to headquarters. Once we're clear, I'll call up and Suzanne, you come down with Peter. Keep your com line open, no unnecessary chatter. This guy hates cops. He's not going to hold back if he has a shot."

Lucy turned to Alexis. "This is your last chance. What is Kip planning?"

The woman stared at Peter.

Then she turned to Lucy and Noah. "Promise me I can see my daughter one last time."

Noah nodded. "If you tell me the truth, I promise visitation rights for your daughter."

"Just once. To tell her I love her. And to tell her about her father." She glanced at Peter, then closed her eyes. "Kip was here earlier today. He wanted me to tell him when Peter got home, but I followed Peter from the subway station to warn him. When I saw Rogan, I panicked. I knew I had to steer Peter away from his apartment.

"I told Kip afterward that Rogan already made contact and I tried to take Peter out myself. He was angry because he wanted to do it. He told me to watch the apartment, and he was baiting the trap."

"What trap?" Noah demanded.

"I don't know. Just that he knew how to get Peter out of hiding."

They all looked at Peter.

He shook his head. "I don't know."

Sean swore. "Charlie." He pulled out his cell phone and dialed. "There's no answer."

Noah said, "I'll have the Bureau contact the Syracuse police."

"My plane is ten minutes away," Sean said.

"I'm going," Peter said.

"No," Lucy and Noah said simultaneously.

"I'm not a prisoner, am I? Charlie is my only friend. He's the only one who believed me. He's the only one I trust. And I put him in danger by having him keep my secret."

Lucy said, "Alexis put him in danger by mirroring my computer. That's the only way they found out about how he helped you."

Peter turned to Alexis and shook his head. "I forgive you, because if I don't, I'll be full of the same hate you are. But if anything happens to Charlie or his wife, I hope you get the death penalty, because you're no better, no more noble, than the men who killed Rachel and Cami." And he turned away.

They went down the stairs to the main floor, staying

inside the small lobby until Joe DeLucca opened the door. "We're clear, but keep moving."

He walked in front of them, looking both ways. The passenger door opened and an agent got out. He showed Noah his credentials and opened the back door. Another agent got out and assisted Alexis inside. The two agents got back in and the car left.

"One down," Joe said.

"Change of plans," Noah said. "We're going to Syracuse."

Before he could explain, Sean came limping down the stairs. "I have Charlie Mead on the phone," he said, and put the phone on speaker.

"Charlie, I have Agent Armstrong here."

"I walked right into it. I'm sorry, Rogan."

"Where are you?"

Another voice came on the phone. "I'll exchange the cop for my sister and Peter McMahon."

"I can't do that," Noah said. He mouthed to Sean, *Are you tracing this call?*

Sean nodded.

"Then the cop dies. And I'll kill another cop every day until my sister is free and Peter is dead."

"I have to talk to my boss," Noah said.

"You have thirty minutes."

"Where are you?"

"Exactly fourteen minutes away." He hung up.

"Trace it, Rogan." Noah handed him back the phone, then called for more backup.

DeLucca called to his men, "I need two men on each entrance, two men inside searching from the ground floor up. Call for all available units, but be on alert. We'll be moving."

"Are you calling back the team with Alexis?" Lucy asked.

"No. I can't risk it. Mead is a cop; he knows we're not going to trade a cop killer for him. We have to find the location."

They went back upstairs. "Fourteen minutes away," Noah said to Peter. "What's fourteen minutes?"

Lucy got on her phone and brought up a map of New York City. She showed it to Peter. "He has Charlie Mead. What's fourteen minutes from here?"

"I-I don't know. Depends on traffic. Could be lower Manhattan, or—" He frowned. "My subway ride in the morning is about that long. The school."

"That's it," Sean said. "I couldn't complete the trace, but I narrowed it to a five-mile area in Brooklyn. The school is in the circle." He typed rapidly. "I'm trying to get a lock on Charlie's cell phone."

"Wouldn't he have turned it off?"

"Possibly, except he wants us to find him. That's why he gave us the clue."

Lucy said, "We have to be extremely cautious. He's not just after Peter. He'll kill anyone. He has no remorse, no real plan anymore."

DeLucca said, "My guys are mobilized. I told them to keep a wide perimeter around the school, no lights or sirens."

"I'm going with you," Peter said. "Charlie is here because of me. I'm not abandoning him."

"Do exactly what I tell you," Noah said.

The corners of Peter's lips curved up, just a bit. "That's what Sean told me."

Noah and Sean exchanged glances. Sean smiled and Noah sighed. "Rogan, you stay on com, monitor all transmissions, understood?"

"Yes, boss," he said.

Noah gave him an odd glance. "I don't think I'll ever hear that again." He said to the others, "Everyone in vests, no exceptions. DeLucca, do you have something for Peter?"

"Yes."

"Let's get suited up; time isn't going any slower."

The school in East Brooklyn where Peter taught was five stories of pre-war brick and a fenced concrete yard. Only faint security lighting around the doors and windows lit the building. Wholly different from the sprawling, green San Diego school Lucy had attended.

"We're early," Noah said. "Let's see if we can keep the element of surprise. Sean, at exactly twenty-nine minutes after the initial call, contact him. Tell him you're me, that you're out front. He'll ask about his sister; tell him we couldn't get her out of jail and we need more time. That you came in good faith to negotiate, and we're trying to accommodate him. How much time do we have?"

"Six minutes."

"Suzanne, stay with Rogan. DeLucca, come with us." Noah said to Peter, "Stay back." Then he looked sternly at Lucy. "You keep him safe."

"Yes, sir," Lucy said.

Peter said, "He must have bypassed the alarm system. But the gate is still locked."

"Rogan would probably say it's easy to crack," Noah said. "We have to assume, if his sister was telling the truth, that he has above average computer skills. We know he was a computer engineering major. Do you have keys?"

Peter handed him his ring. "The blue-coded key is to the main door. The yellow key gets into any classroom on the second floor, plus common rooms."

"What room is yours?" Lucy asked.

"Two-oh-one. It's in the southwest corner."

"That's where he is," Lucy said.

They quietly entered the building on the opposite side from 201. All security monitors were green—off, confirmation that Kip had disabled the alarms.

They stayed up against the walls as they walked down the hall toward Peter's third-grade classroom. Two doors down, Noah motioned for them to stop. He unlocked room 205 and they slipped in. "We need eyes on Mead before we proceed," Noah said. "I'm going through the ducts." He pointed to the ceiling. The air ducts were easily accessible through worn ceiling tiles.

He stood on a desk and pushed open the tile. He looked inside. "Damn," he said. "I won't fit." He looked at Lucy. "You." He cupped his hands. "Stay put until we get the air-conditioning on to mask sound."

"I'm on it," DeLucca said. He called to his team who were in the basement control room.

A half minute later, the air-conditioning roared to life. The units were on the windows but controlled by a central switch so the school could turn them all on and off together. The ducts were for heating only, but the air-conditioning was loud enough to cloak Lucy's movements.

"Visual only," Noah told her. "Give me Mead's exact location."

Lucy moved through the filthy duct toward room 201. It was a tight fit, but she used her arms to balance and move along slowly. In her ear com, she heard Sean say, "One minute until I call."

Lucy went slower as she neared room 201. She couldn't hear anything over the air-conditioning units. She turned on her flashlight to check out where she was—she needed to find the main vent in order to get a visual.

The opening was ten feet ahead. She turned off her light and slithered toward it.

Mead's phone rang at the same time she saw Kip Todd. He stood by the door. She didn't see Charlie Mead.

Kip said, "You're here?"

She rolled and craned her neck. She spotted Mead tied to a chair in the center of the room. His face was swollen and he had a cut on his arm that was bleeding.

She scooted away from the vent as Kip shouted, "That's not good enough!"

She whispered in her com, "Mead is restrained on a chair in the center of the room. He's injured."

"Good. Come back."

"I need to monitor this. Kip is angry."

Kip paced back and forth along the front of the room. A chair braced the door to the hall. But there was a door to the adjoining classroom that wasn't propped closed.

Lucy said, "The door in room two-oh-three isn't blocked, but Mead will be in the direct line of fire."

"How many weapons?"

"He's holding a nine millimeter. A rifle is strapped over his shoulder. He has a knife on his belt."

"Do you have a shot?"

Lucy wasn't a sniper. Being a good shot at the target range was completely different from being a good shot at a moving target.

"If I miss—"

"We're moving to room two-oh-three. Stay alert."

Kip screamed at the phone, "I will bleed him dry! His blood will stain the floor. Unless you bring Peter here now, two minutes, I will kill him." He walked over to the window. "I see you." He fired out of the window with the rifle.

Lucy bit her tongue to keep from shouting out. Sean

wasn't in the southwest corner, but DeLucca's men were exposed.

"A-ha!" Kip shouted. "One down, more to go." He fired again.

Lucy pulled out her gun. She couldn't use this vent; the openings were too narrow. And if she shot through the ceiling, she risked injury, loss of bullet velocity, and a skewed trajectory. She had to move to the larger vent in the center of the room.

She crawled as quickly as she dared.

"Status," Noah demanded in her ear.

"Getting in position," Lucy whispered.

The air-conditioning rumbled off.

Kip stopped shooting out of the window.

Lucy stopped moving. She was still three inches from the vent. She needed one more good slide to get into position.

She risked the sound.

She looked out the vent. Kip was staring at the ceiling, his expression alert.

Then she noticed this vent was too small to get her barrel through.

"I've been spotted," she whispered.

Kip aimed his rifle toward the ceiling. Lucy punched out the vent with the barrel of her gun, aimed at him, and fired. The first bullet hit him in the shoulder. He fired his rifle three times into the ceiling. She fired again and hit his hand. He dropped the rifle and grabbed his nine millimeter. He didn't aim at Lucy but at Charlie Mead.

She fired again as the door below burst open and Noah and Joe entered. They fired simultaneously at Kip. His body jerked and he stumbled backwards and tripped over a desk.

Joe rushed to Kip and kicked away his weapons, then checked his pulse. "He's dead," Joe said.

"Lucy!" Noah called.

"I'm okay. I might need a Band-Aid." Or four or five. Her arm burned, but she didn't think she'd been hit.

Noah pulled a desk over to the vent and jumped on it. Lucy saw the top of his head. She handed him her gun. He put it in his waistband. Then grabbed her by the arms and pulled her out headfirst. He held on to her as he scrambled off of the desk. He put her in a chair. "Were you hit?"

"No. I think it's splinters from the ceiling tiles. Or maybe I cut my arm on the vent. Stupid. But he was going to shoot Charlie."

Joe had untied Mead and was calling out for both a report and an ambulance.

Peter came in and rushed over to Charlie Mead. "Charlie?"

Charlie smiled. "You're okay."

"What about you?"

"Nothing broken."

"Why are you here?" Peter asked.

"When Rogan left, I was worried and wanted to make sure you were safe. I took the first flight, went to your apartment and that guy grabbed me outside."

"I'm sorry." Peter hugged him.

"I'm glad you're safe."

"An ambulance is on its way," Joe said. "I have one man down."

Noah swore. "Status?"

"Doesn't appear life threatening. I'm waiting for confirmation."

Four cops rushed in. Joe ordered two to stand guard

over Kip's body, and two helped Mead out of the building. Noah picked up Lucy.

"I can walk," she said.

"You're bleeding."

She frowned, feeling light-headed. "I'm okay. Just woozy. I think from the dust."

"You're black with dust and soot."

Noah carried her down the hall, down the stairs, and out to where Sean and Suzanne were standing with another team of agents.

"What happened?" Sean demanded.

Noah put Lucy down on the small strip of grass separating the street from the sidewalk. "You did good, Kincaid," he said. He stared at her and Lucy wished she knew what he was thinking. There was something odd in his expression. Then Noah turned to Sean. "She's all yours. Make sure the paramedics check her out thoroughly."

"I will," Sean said.

Suzanne leaned against her car while Noah walked away to coordinate the Bureau and NYPD. Sean sat next to Lucy and sighed in relief.

"I'm *fine*," she said. "A bullet grazed me, that's all. Maybe some splinters."

"You're going to the hospital."

"I will on one condition."

"You will on no conditions."

"Bossy, aren't you?"

"Luce, I'm just glad you're okay."

"Me, too," Suzanne said. "Another case together. Maybe you'll get assigned to New York when you graduate."

"I'd like that," Lucy said, then glanced at Sean. She couldn't read his face. They hadn't talked about what they were going to do when she graduated. The only thing she was certain about was that she wouldn't be assigned to the Washington, D.C., office. Very few agents were assigned to the field office they were recruited from.

Joe DeLucca came over. "Good job, Lucy."

"Thanks. I'm glad it's over."

"Suzi, we need to talk."

"Not now."

"Yes. Now." Joe stared at her and Lucy was surprised that Suzanne gave in.

"All right. Just don't call me Suzi." But she smiled, and Lucy's suspicions were confirmed. Joe and Suzanne had a history. Lucy couldn't help but be happy. She liked them both. And their body language, though they weren't touching, told her they liked each other a lot.

"What are you looking at?" Sean asked.

"Nothing." She smiled and put her head on his shoulder. "While I'm getting this gash in my arm sewn up, you have to let the doctor look at your leg."

"All right."

"That was too easy."

"I'm too tired to argue." Then he smiled. "Maybe we can share a hospital room. We can play doctor."

She laughed. "Don't you have a hotel room reserved?"

"I do."

"I think I can get a day off. Maybe two."

He kissed her. "Princess, you've earned it."

CHAPTER FORTY-THREE

Lucy returned to Quantico Wednesday night. She was surprised by the warm greeting from her classmates. "The assistant director himself came to fill us in on what happened," Reva said. "Rick Stockton. Can you believe it?"

"I'm just glad I don't have to repeat the story a dozen times," Lucy said.

"Just once," Carter said. "We deserve the details."

"You do." She smiled. "I appreciate your support, but right now I have to meet with the Chief. More reports."

She breathed deeply as she walked across campus, alone, to Chief O'Neal's office. Noah Armstrong was already inside.

"I've been briefed," O'Neal said. "You can rejoin your class tomorrow if you can make up the work. I spoke with Tom Harden and he said you can have a PT pass until Monday if you need it. Or, if you need more time, the next new-agent class starts in ten days. You can take the time off, heal, and join with the new class."

Lucy shook her head. "I want to stay with my class. And I'm fine. Just sore."

The doctor had removed twenty-nine plastic splinters from the ceiling tiles and stitched up a gash in her left arm where one of Kip Todd's bullets had grazed her.

"I'm glad," O'Neal said. "You fit with your class. And after what happened with Sanchez, you'll be instrumental in rebuilding class unity."

"I have one favor," she said. "Would you call in my field counselor, Agent Laughlin, and give me a minute to talk to him in private?"

Both Noah and O'Neal looked surprised, but she agreed. She left the room, and Noah said to Lucy, "Are you sure about this?"

"Yes. I left the files you showed me in Tony's office. Your office." Noah was taking over Tony's teaching position until they found a replacement. "Hans?" she asked hopefully.

"He was in surgery all day, now resting in ICU. Kate's with him. I can drive you there, if you'd like."

"If you don't mind."

"Lucy—" Noah stopped. She didn't know what he'd planned on saying, but she didn't think it was what he ended up telling her. "I put a commendation in your file. 'Outstanding performance while under fire.'"

Lucy laughed while she also blushed with the praise. "Literally. I have a lot to learn, but I'm getting there."

Noah hugged her. "I'm glad you decided to stay. Hans will be pleased when he wakes up."

Lucy hoped she and Hans could regain the friendship they'd once had.

Rich Laughlin walked in. Noah nodded to the agent, then left.

Lucy didn't say anything at first. She kept her eyes on Laughlin. The anger and frustration on his face were obvious, but his eyes questioned her. He didn't know why she had asked for this meeting; he thought he'd won—that he'd found a way to kick her out of the Academy.

"You're delaying the inevitable," he said, breaking the silence.

"What's inevitable?" she asked.

"You're one of the ten percent."

Laughlin was referring to the 10 percent of new agents who didn't graduate from the Academy. Last week Lucy would have been angry with his comment, but today she understood.

Laughlin continued, "Just because you performed this time doesn't mean you'll do it next time."

"I'm going to assume you've read my file," Lucy said. "Not just this last case, but my personal file."

Laughlin didn't say anything, but it was clear he had.

"You think, because I had been a victim of violent crime, and because I am obsessive about my work, that I'm also as reckless as Grace Johnson."

His face hardened, but his eyes lit in surprise. "You don't know Grace."

"Though we've never met, I know Grace. Her baby brother was killed because of gang violence. Her mother was gunned down in retaliation for testifying against her son's killer. Her father is in prison for murder. She was the good daughter. Fighting drugs and violence. One of the good guys. You trusted her because she was one of the best. She knew everyone. She was willing to do anything to end the pain and suffering of other families facing what she survived.

"You thought she was reckless—"

"Don't talk about her. Grace is nothing like you. Of course I read your file. You killed a man in cold blood."

"I did."

"You'll do it again." Laughlin stared at her, hatred in

his eyes. At first Lucy was intimidated, but then she saw beyond the hate, and the pain deep inside.

Laughlin continued, "You're on a vendetta. If you continue down this path, you'll get yourself or your partner or innocent civilians killed. Can't you see it?"

"A vendetta against who?"

He was surprised by the question.

"You said I killed a man in cold blood. You read my file; you know the man I killed raped me, put one of my brothers in a coma, and detonated a bomb in my other brother's house. Maybe I did have a vendetta against him. But he's dead. Whom do I have a vendetta against?"

"What would you do to people like Adam Scott? What would you do to stop them?"

"What would you do?"

"I'm asking the questions!" Laughlin was on edge. It was clear he hadn't expected her to confront him, and the more angry and upset Laughlin became, the calmer Lucy was.

She said, "You think I want to be an FBI agent so I have some sort of authority to take down bad guys any way I can."

"Exactly."

She smiled sadly. "You don't know me, Rich." She leaned forward. "I want to be an FBI agent so I don't take out bad guys any way I can."

He stared at her, confused.

"To me," she said quietly, "the badge, the gun, the responsibility that goes with being a federal agent, is my deterrent to taking the law into my own hands.

"Eight months ago I worked for Women and Children First! which was run by a former FBI agent, Fran Buckley. I loved Fran. She was my mentor. Then I learned she was using me to set up paroled sex offenders to be murdered.

"These men didn't deserve freedom. They should have remained in prison, because they were going to reoffend. It was in their psychology, their actions, their thoughts. I knew it; Fran knew it. I wanted them back in prison. Fran wanted them dead.

"It would have been easy for me to join that cause. To be a vigilante for justice. Because sometimes, justice isn't served. Sometimes, innocent people feel they have no choice but to fight back any way they can."

"I think you were involved. I think you knew exactly what Buckley was doing."

"Hmm." Lucy wondered if he really believed what he said. "If you have any proof, you should turn it over."

"How can anyone trust you?" he asked.

"All trust has to be earned. And that's the crux of your problem."

"*My* problem?"

"You trusted Grace. She betrayed the trust. Then she died. She died saving the lives of three other undercover agents, which should count for something. But you can't yell at her; you can't tell her she screwed up; you can't ask why she didn't trust you to back her up, why she changed the meeting place at the last minute. Maybe she had a damn good reason for doing so. Maybe if she hadn't changed the meeting place, more people would have died. But you don't know—the investigation into her death was inconclusive, but because you learned she had a history with the people she was trying to take down, you assumed the worst—that she screwed up because she was reckless, on a jihad against the gang who destroyed her family."

He glared at her, his face red. "How do you know any of this?"

"I know people like Grace Johnson." Lucy knew he wasn't referring to her psychology, that he wanted to know how she knew about the case, but she wasn't going to tell him. "I think Grace died to save many people who will never know of her sacrifice. I can't tell you if she was needlessly reckless. I don't know if she could have contacted you. You've never given her the benefit of the doubt, and now everyone who you think might have a vendetta is somehow unfit to carry a badge."

"I don't trust you," Laughlin said.

"I hope someday I earn your trust." Lucy was going to walk out then, but she remembered something else. "You knew Evan Standler."

He glared at her.

"And that's why you have been pressuring Kate. You used her guilt over the ambush where he was killed to try and get her to convince me to quit." That was a guess, but Lucy suspected she was right. And by Laughlin's expression, she was close.

"You think Kate screwed up and got your friend killed. Remember, Standler was *her* fiancé. The ambush was just that—an unpredictable tragedy."

"And then Kate goes rogue and disappears for five years in Mexico? You think that isn't a problem?"

"Kate saved my life," Lucy said simply. "I trust her as much as I trust anyone. And what really hurts is that you intentionally tried to sabotage our relationship. You played mind games with Kate, trying to get her to doubt me. Then when that wasn't working fast enough for you, you pulled out the Hans Vigo card and effectively used it. If I were a lesser person, I would have quit. I was very close. But if I had quit, I might become the person you fear I could be."

She leaned forward and said softly, "There are many organizations who would hire me because of my skill set. That I've chosen to work within a fairly rigid structure

and within the law should tell you more about my character and trustworthiness than what you think I've done in
the past."

"How do any of us know what you're going to do in
the future?"

"How do you know what you're going to do?" She tilted
her head. "If you had the opportunity to kill the man
responsible for pulling the trigger that ended the life of
Grace Johnson, would you?"

He didn't answer the question but instead said, "I'm
testifying against the cartel."

"At great personal risk. I respect that, Rich." She stood.
"Neither you nor I know what we would do in every future scenario. It comes down to character."

Lucy left the office. Chief O'Neal and Paula Kean were
standing in the outer room. Kean didn't look happy with
the situation, but O'Neal said directly to Lucy, "SSA
Kean has been briefed on the situation. Agent Armstrong
said he'd be waiting for you in the lobby. You will be back
in the morning?"

"Yes, thank you."

Twenty minutes later, Noah and Lucy walked into Prince
William Hospital. Noah showed his ID and was directed
to ICU, where Hans was recuperating after his surgery.
"Go ahead," Noah told Lucy. "I'm going to track down his
doctor."

Kate sat slumped outside the room, her eyes closed.
Lucy thought she was sleeping until she opened one eye.
"Hello," she said.

Lucy sat next to her. "How is he?"

"They said the surgery was a success. But he hasn't re-
gained consciousness."

"I talked to Rich Laughlin."

Kate didn't say anything.

"You should have told me."

"He was right."

"No, he wasn't." Lucy looked into Hans's room. All the pain and guilt and vengeance that had brought that scaffolding down on him. The hatred that had ended with four people dead and a man stalked for half his life.

"Kate, you're my sister in every way except blood. What hurts is that you believed him when he told you I was volatile. That you didn't trust me."

Kate leaned forward and stared at Lucy. "Is that what you think?"

"Yes. You didn't talk to me; you treated me like I really was here on some kind of vendetta. You of all people should know my heart."

Kate shook her head. "I never thought that. I meant, I thought he was right about *me*." She closed her eyes. "I'm teaching at Quantico because I'm too scared to go back in the field. Scared of what I might do. Scared that I'll make the wrong decisions. Quantico is safe."

Lucy took her hand. "I didn't know you doubted yourself. I've always thought you were the most confident person in the world." She paused, then smiled. "Almost as arrogant as Sean."

Kate laughed, but tears came to her eyes. "I don't think that's possible." She sighed deeply. "I leaned heavily on Dillon after you killed Adam Scott, and I began to rely on him to keep me propped up. Quantico is safe. Dillon is safe. I'm doing okay."

"Then Rich Laughlin came in and shook you up."

"That he did."

"Trust me, Kate. We're friends; we're family. Trust me not only to do what's right, but trust me with your feelings. We're all scared. But we do it anyway because it's the right thing to do."

"I love you, Sis."

Lucy hugged her. "I love you, too."

"Stop; I don't want to cry," Kate said. "I've been here all day, but I heard the second autopsy on Tony was complete."

"Yes, and the tox screening came back. Tony was poisoned with a sodium chloride mixture. It didn't show up in the Scotch initially because it wasn't a standard compound. I don't quite know the details, but they found it in his stomach. Once they knew what specifically to test for, they confirmed that he was poisoned through his Scotch. It happened very quick."

"So it was Alexis Sanchez."

"Yes. They're going to exhume Bob Stokes's body and run the same test on his remains. Speaking of Stokes, Patrick found the e-mail Agent Theissen sent to him. It related to the Cinderella Strangler case, and that Theissen was helping Weber with some of the background. Later, he said that he thought he was being followed and it might relate to one of his old cases, but he couldn't be sure. Then when Theissen had his accident, Stokes went to New York."

"You think Kip Todd panicked and killed him?"

"He didn't know what Theissen had told Stokes. Maybe Stokes recognized Todd, or maybe Todd feared he would if he investigated Theissen's accident."

"Or maybe," Kate said, "he was on the target list all along and Todd took advantage of his proximity."

"We may never knew for certain. Alexis isn't talking at all. She says she'll only talk to Peter, but I advised him not to."

"Why? He might be able to get answers we need."

Lucy had thought about that. "Maybe, but Peter is vulnerable right now. She's a master manipulator. She might not have wanted Peter dead, but she still was party to all this. I told him to give it some time. He seemed to be okay with that."

Noah approached and cleared his throat. "Hans is awake. You can have one minute with him."

Lucy and Kate walked into ICU after putting on gloves and gowns. Hans was pale and gaunt, physically weak. But his eyes were open.

"You're back," Kate said, and took his hand.

"Um," he responded. He tried to focus on Lucy.

"It's Lucy, Hans. Everything is fine. We'll fill you in later, but we're all safe."

"Good," he whispered.

The nurse cleared her throat. "Time," she said.

Kate and Lucy walked out, both with tears in their eyes. Kate hugged her sister-in-law. "I didn't think he would make it," Kate admitted. "Hans is the closest thing I have to a father."

"He's strong and stubborn and healthy," Lucy said. "Are you going home?"

"I'm going to stay a while longer."

Noah asked Lucy, "Do you need a ride?"

"Sean's here," Lucy said. "I'm reporting back to Quantico tomorrow morning."

"I'll see you then." He sat next to Kate and Kate began telling the story about how she'd first met Hans.

Good, Lucy thought. They'd all been through an emotional wringer after losing Tony. With Hans on the mend, they could focus on the positive.

She left the hospital and spotted Sean's Mustang parked

near the main entrance. She slid into the passenger seat and kissed him. "I love you," she said.

"Where did that come from?" He smiled and kissed her back. "Keep it coming."

"Hans is in recovery. He's going to be okay."

"You're crying."

"No, I'm not."

He wiped away her tears. "Okay. You're not."

"I have to be back at Quantico tomorrow morning."

"But you're mine for tonight."

"I'm yours forever."

He glanced at her as he sped out of the parking lot. "I knew that the day I found you standing at my door in the pouring rain."

"You did?"

"Yes, I did." He took her hand and kissed it. Lucy closed her eyes and smiled, happy and content.

"Where are we going?"

"It's a surprise," he said, glancing at her with a devilish grin. "But I promise, you'll be pampered all day and all night."

"You spoil me."

"I have an ulterior motive. I'm the one doing the pampering."

CHAPTER FORTY-FOUR

Epilogue

I drove to the cemetery outside Newark to visit my sister one last time.

For fifteen years I had been in a state of perpetual grief, an emotional zombie. I hadn't realized it until the FBI agent Lucy Kincaid said that Kip had turned his grief into rage and I had turned my grief into a lifestyle.

You have done so much in a short time, Lucy said. *Emancipation, graduating from college early, teaching at an impoverished school. Think of what you could do for these kids you love if you were happy yourself.*

Rachel's ghost was with me every day. She never aged, and because she was always eleven I still felt like I was nine, trapped in a grown-up body. I still ate Trix for breakfast and grilled cheese for dinner. I still felt guilty staying up late watching movies and eating in front of the television. And I don't think I've ever seen a movie rated PG-13, let alone a movie rated R. Maybe I never will. But it won't be because I think I'm nine.

I love teaching, and I know I can be a better teacher if I go to school without the weight of grief and guilt on my heart.

And the first step was letting Rachel go.

I turned and saw a man I'd never met walking toward me with a little girl I feel like I've known forever. Carl Sanchez and I had spoken on the phone several times over the last two weeks. He'd prepared Missy for this meeting.

He'd known all along that Missy wasn't his daughter, but he loved her.

He loved her so much, he was willing to share her. With her biological father.

I turned my back on the headstone and walked across the green lawn. Missy looked like me. More, she looked like Rachel. With dark curls and big blue eyes.

Carl and I shook hands. "Thank you," I said and he smiled at me.

I squatted in front of Missy. "Hello, Missy. Do you remember me? We talked on the computer."

She nodded and smiled, her big eyes so round and inquisitive. "I remember you, Daddy."

Then she hugged me and all the pain I'd ever felt washed away in a river of pure, unconditional love.

Coming soon…

From *New York Times* bestselling author

ALLISON BRENNAN

STOLEN